IMPLACABLE
ALPHA

IMPLACABLE
ALPHA

W. MICHAEL GEAR

DAW BOOKS, INC.
DONALD A. WOLLHEIM FOUNDER

1745 Broadway, New York, NY 10019
ELIZABETH R. WOLLHEIM
SHEILA E. GILBERT
PUBLISHERS
www.dawbooks.com

DEDICATION
If you Believe
In Freedom of Speech
and the Unrestricted
Freedom of Expression
Freedom of the Press
and
Artistic License
This Novel
is
Dedicated to
You.

ACKNOWLEDGMENTS

Implacable Alpha would not have come to you were it not for the faith, dedication, and industry of our publishers at DAW Books. Since the publication of *The Warriors of Spider* back in August of 1988, Sheila Gilbert and Betsy Wollheim have been friends, mentors, and partners in our science fiction. To have had their support and collaboration has indeed been a privilege and honor.

My thanks to all the staff at DAW Books, and I hope to work with them in the years to come.

We want to offer our appreciation to Cody's Chamberlin Inn. Elizabeth Scaccia keeps alive the creative spirit that once nurtured Ernest Hemingway. It has become our local retreat where Kathleen and I dissect plot and character. Many of the intricacies of entanglement physics, as well as the plot twists in *Implacable Alpha*, were solved over a beer and a flatbread.

As always, special thanks go to Theresa Hulongbayan for her dedication to our work and to our readers on the Facebook Gear fan club. Theresa walks on water!

ET CUM VITIUM SUM

I am. A state of being. Beyond that fundamental assumption, nothing can be proved. The philosophers and physicists assure us of that.

Sum. The Latin verb for "I am."

"I am" is the only thing a person can know with any measure of certainty. Beyond that, all is perception. An electrochemical creation within the brain.

I, however, know something else.

Et cum vitii sum. Latin for "I am flawed."

Because I am flawed, I have reached the highest rank I can achieve. I will never be more than an Imperator. A high commander, second in authority to the rulers of Ti'ahaule. I remain their instrument to command. What they order, I accomplish. That should be my only purpose. My total commitment.

But I am flawed. I desire.

And more than anything, I desire the Domina, Nakeesh.

If the Ahau knew, they would terminate me. They are the Lords, the living and immortal gods. The few remarkable men and women who have transcended every definition of humanity. Physically, mentally, emotionally. They have no tolerance for a character flaw like my ravenous desire to have Nakeesh.

I entertain these thoughts as I stand on the shore of the Nile and stare out at the river. This is not my world. Not my timeline but one split long ago from my own. The waves that wash the sand are those of the dim and distant past. The silt-opaque waters flow to an ancient sea, on an earth that will never be mine.

The people I see lifting water to irrigate their crops of teff and wheat by means of ancient buckets hanging from poles are a doomed population from whom no civilization will descend.

They are condemned by their distant future.

I turn and watch as Sak Puh, my scribe recorder, or ah tz'ib, studies her cerebrum. She must be seeing the same data that are reflected from my navigator.

Sak Puh looks up from the glowing blue holo projected above her cerebrum. "The data are clear, Imperator. Your navigator detects nothing from Fluvium or Domina Nakeesh's devices. There is no evidence that this is the timeline to which they traveled."

"But you do detect entangled particles?"

"I do, Imperator. Somewhere, sometime, in the future, these people will develop the technology."

I turn my attention to the five warriors in the quinque. They stand in ranks, being Third Sword, or Tres Gladii. I can see the unease in their eyes. How their bodies have stiffened in anticipation of my next command.

"Sterilize this place."

They know the orders as well as I do. Entanglement physics technology cannot be allowed. Not in any timeline but our own.

I watch as Publius Atole advances to the edge of the water. He unslings his pack from his shoulder and carefully withdraws a sealed stainless-steel cylinder. He turns the cap a quarter turn and heaves it into the river.

We hear it pop open as it hits the surface. The virus is exploding into the water where it will be carried downstream to infect all of Egypt. And from there, it will spread, following trade routes, carried everywhere that humans travel.

Lifting my navigator, I meet Sak Puh's startled eyes. Together, we extend our fingers to the glowing orbs projected above our devices.

In an instant, we are falling, feeling that expan-

sive ecstasy as we are transported to yet another timeline.

Behind us, the virus is loose. Humanity, the great apes, and other primates will be extinct within a century.

A job well done.

I wonder if I will find Nakeesh and Fluvium in the next timeline as it begins to form around us.

1

Grazier

General Elijiah Grazier might have only had two stars on his shoulders, but—as he liked to say—he punched well above his rank. His elaborate master bathroom was proof of that. The walls gleamed with polished marble, had a full-length mirror bathed in lights and matching golden Kohler faucets on the sinks, deep tub, shower, and bidet. The two-story house in Georgetown—just minutes from downtown Washington, DC—didn't look that impressive from the outside, just red brick with white accents. As in all things, it was what lay within that mattered.

Eli padded across Venetian black-marble tiles and onto the thick carpeting in his walnut-paneled bedroom. Tugging back the blankets on his oversized king bed, he pulled his pajamas straight and checked to see that everything on his nightstand was in order: phone, light switch, flashlight, his glass of water, and the M92 Beretta. The intruder alert button was hidden from sight next to the bed and below the table's top.

Hell of a day. But that was Washington. For the time being he had Bill Stevens, the president's chief of staff, by the balls. And he was squeezing. To Eli's disgust, President Ben Masters was cautious enough to keep his pit bull in reserve. As much as Eli would have loved to have cut Stevens' throat and left him behind as roadkill, the president would have disapproved.

Stevens could be dealt with. That was just "Potomac politics."

Eli's pressing problem was Skientia, the cutting-edge research firm. A team in their New Mexico lab had developed a powerful technology that allowed them to project and analyze entangled particles from the past. Events out in the Los Alamos lab might have momentarily chopped the head off the serpent, but on this new battleground, Eli Grazier needed Skientia's science and engineering know-how more than ever. That meant he had to rely on Dr. Maxine Kaplan and her engineer, Virgil Wixom.

Eli trusted Kaplan as much as he'd have trusted a black mamba. Wixom remained an unknown.

"So, is Kaplan smart enough to take the reins?" he wondered as he slipped his feet beneath the covers and lay back to fluff his pillow.

But more to the point, could he control her?

He was reaching to turn off the light when the contralto voice said, "Please do not try anything foolish. And before you reach for your pistol, I can assure you that I took the liberty of unloading it. The intruder alert is disabled as well."

Eli froze as a green-eyed woman dressed in black tactical clothing stepped out of his walk-in closet. Her auburn hair had been pulled back in a ponytail. The bone structure in her tanned face was a perfect balance of cheeks, straight nose, and full lips over a strong chin. Were the faint patterns on her cheeks and forehead the ghosts of scars, or just a trick of the light? She stood about five-foot-six and moved with an athlete's toned grace. Call it predatory. She didn't need the slung M16 or the knife and pistol on her belt to look dangerous.

What convinced Eli to behave lay behind the woman's hard green gaze: something weary, eternal, and strained. He got the distinct impression that she wouldn't think twice about putting a bullet in his brain. That she'd been tested—a lot—and always survived. Wherever she'd been, she'd seen and lived through it all.

"How'd you get in here?"

"Let's just say I go where I want, when I want, to whenever I want."

And it hit him. He remembered where he'd seen those hard green eyes: in the Grantham Barracks camera footage. She had been crouched over a dying man's body in the mental hospital's underground garage. "You're the woman who tried to kill Alpha and Ryan that day."

"Alpha? That what you're calling her?" The distaste in her words couldn't be missed. "Her real name is Nakeesh, and her title in the Ti'ahaule is Domina, not that the term means anything to you."

"Sorry about your companion."

"He was a good man." A faint smile. "Rare. In any age."

"Who *are* you?"

"I've been called a lot of things over the centuries. Nakeesh calls me the *Ennoia*. Means the embodiment of God's first thought. It's a mystical concept from another age. She and Fluvium once considered it a cruel and sick joke. Most call me Helen, from the Greek *'Elena*. As to why I'm in your bedroom? Nakeesh and Fluvium have to be stopped. Here. In your timeline. Once and for all."

"Fluvium's already dead. As to Alpha—"

"Are you still so limited? Despite what you've seen?"

Fluvium's not dead? Eli had seen the guy's desiccated corpse after it had been removed from a three-thousand-year-old sarcophagus.

The woman calling herself Helen studied him with that flat green gaze, one hand on the rifle slung at her shoulder. "Good. You're starting to catch on to the whole 'time' thing. If Nakeesh contacts Imperator, finds a way to get her hands on Fluvium's cerebrum, your world and your timeline are dead."

"Who's Imperator?"

"Your worst nightmare. Not that I give a shit. They've taken out better worlds than yours. It's just that this is the first time they've screwed up enough that I've got a chance to end it." With her free hand, she slipped a device from one of the pockets in her cargo pants and tossed it.

Grazier snagged it out of the air as she said, "Decide if you're in or out. All you have to do is press the silver button."

Grazier glanced down. The thing looked like a pager. Maybe two by three inches, a couple of ounces in weight. A prominent silver button could be seen on the black surface.

"In or out? You're going to have to be a lot more specific than that." Ely looked up to emphasize his point.

Not a trace of her remained. Not even a swaying of clothes back in the depths of his closet. But for the device he held, she might have been nothing more than a figment of his imagination.

In . . . or out?

He was about to pull his blanket back when a tingling presaged a crackling in the air around him. His skin prickled like a thousand ants were crawling over his body, and the lights went out.

2

Ryan

My name's Colonel Timothy Ryan. Normally, I didn't run meetings where we discussed the safety and security of the world, let alone the future of our entire timeline. I'm still hazy about what a timeline is. Theoretical physics was never my strongpoint. But there I was, staring down the table in the conference room at a team of physicists, Mayan scholars, and engineers. Not to mention General Eli Grazier, my current superior. Wearing his uniform with all its campaign ribbons, the two stars prominent on his collar, he sat in a chair off to the side so as to be inobtrusive. Right. Eli was about as inobtrusive as a crouching tiger.

My team was in charge of saving the world. It remained surreal.

I'm a mental health professional with both an MD in psychiatry and a PhD in abnormal psych. I'd spent my life working with service personnel who put their lives on the line for this country. And too often ended up broken and wounded in ways that didn't leave visible scars. It was one thing to teach a crippled vet how to walk again when he or she had lost both legs. Something entirely different when that person—in an effort to stop the pain—just wanted to end it all.

Working with mental illness was my passion, both in the service and afterward. It had finally taken me to Grantham Barracks, a low-profile military psychiatric hospital in the pine-covered foothills outside of Colorado Springs, Colorado. My battlefield was in my patients' heads. Sometimes I won, other times I didn't.

Along the way, I'd given up a wife and son, any kind of social life, and my list of close friends could be counted on three fingers. Or was it two? Been a while since I took time to keep track.

Sometimes the lines between the services got a little blurred back in the day, but nothing like what I faced as I sat at the head of the polished teakwood table in that plush conference room. I was on the opulent second floor of the Skientia lab building in Los Alamos, New Mexico. General Grazier had me fly down special for the meeting. Eli figured that it was time to bring all the disparate parts of the team together. We were three months into the analysis of data following Prisoner Alpha's "escape."

I glanced down the mirror-polished length of the table, past the others, to where Dr. Maxine Kaplan sat taking notes on a legal pad. She was an attractive woman in her late fifties, her graying hair pinned up, face thin and intense. For the meeting, she wore an expensive gray wool suit finely tailored to her slender body. She had been in charge of Scientia's entangled particle physics experiments. She had been trying to attract entangled organic molecules from the past. Imagine her surprise when the woman we call "Alpha" suddenly appeared in her lab.

"Dr. Kaplan? Now that we have three months' worth of data from the monitors in Lab One, is there anything that hints that Alpha's return is imminent? Any rise in energy? Some clue?"

She raised her eyes, giving me that evaluative look a superior imparts to a menial. One she believes to be hopelessly incapable of understanding even the simplest of concepts. She'd made it clear that compared to her experiments in physics, psychiatry was little more than make-believe medicine practiced by masked dancers pounding drums.

"Maybe Virgil could field that," she suggested, dropping her gaze to the legal pad where she continued to scratch out notes with an expensive golden pen.

Virgil Wixom—also a PhD—was her second. But for having to gasp for oxygen down in the darkness cast by Kaplan's shadow, the guy would have been considered world-class brilliant. Where Kaplan's talent lay in spitting out the theoretical ideas, Wixom was the nuts-and-bolts guy. He was the one who designed and then built the machines that would produce, collect, and analyze the entangled particles. He'd been Alpha's go-to guy who'd helped to build the machine that had allowed her escape.

Wixom—also with an old-fashioned notepad—sat at Kaplan's left. He scratched at his ear and said, "Currently, we're not picking up any meaningful increases in photons or emitted particles. I guess you'd say the fields remain boringly consistent."

"Nothing's changed?" I asked.

Kaplan raised censuring eyes. "As we stated in the last report. Assuming anyone read it."

I wondered if she'd used the same flippant tone with her Skientia bosses. One of them, Peter McCoy, had been left on the lab floor, shot through the heart. The other, Tanner Jackson, was missing, caught in the field generated by Alpha's time machine and whisked away to the future. Neither had been known for having anything resembling the milk of human kindness running even by a milliliter in their veins.

In his chair, Eli shifted, his gaze taking Kaplan's measure. He didn't trust her. Not that Eli trusted anyone. Along with being a two-star, the general is a high-functioning psychopath. There's not an ounce of remorse in the man's body. Eli does what's best for Eli, which generally boils down to survival and power. All of which were at risk after Alpha's untimely arrival.

Maybe placing the survival of our timeline in the hands of a psychopath wasn't such a bad idea. Eli would, of necessity, have to save the world and the timeline in order to save himself. And he wouldn't hesitate to do whatever it took to make that happen.

I glanced next at the anthropologists. In charge was Yusif al Amari, the Egyptologist. Yusif was a broad-shouldered man, early forties, with a coal-black beard. Along with a PhD from Cambridge, he'd been excavating his entire life. He'd helped Reid Farmer open Fluvium's tomb. And now—with a death sentence awaiting him back in Egypt—he was key to unraveling Fluvium's hidden messages.

"Ah, Doctor Ryan," he gave me a smile that flashed white teeth behind his beard. "I hope you are not expecting miracles. We have made some progress. What you would call the basics. Some of the narrative can be followed. Simple things. Like, 'In the beginning.' Or, 'Consider the following.' And then it becomes gibberish. Words don't make sense. It hit me, in preparation for this meeting, that Fluvium is using code in places."

"No surprise there," I said. "He wouldn't have wanted just anyone figuring out how to build a cerebrum." I glanced at our Mayanist. "Skylar? What have you got?"

Skylar Haines was an expert at Mayan hieroglyphics, totally brilliant. He read Mayan writing better than he read English. We needed him because the scrolls and writing recovered from Fluvium's tomb were partially written in Mayan as well as Egyptian and Latin. The only downside to having Skylar working on them was, well, Skylar. In his case, brilliance came at a cost. Given his aversion to most forms of personal hygiene, his stained and rumpled week-old clothing, oily dread-locks, and yellow-fuzzed teeth, no one wanted to be in the same room. As it was, people had left the chairs on either side of him empty.

He glanced sidelong at me through smudged bottle-thick glasses. "Um, dude, this is some heavy lifting, like challenging, you know? Okay, so, it's like the roots are there. Then it gets crazy complex. The glyphs are nothing like I've never seen. Complex with distinct differ-ences in prefix, positionals, and suffixes. I've never seen a lot of these prevocalics. And it has chunks of Latin tossed in. Like, short phrases right in the middle of a series of glyphs."

I stared at him. He could have been talking Greek. Even if it was Mayan. "Skylar, what does that mean in simple terms I can understand?"

"Best way to put it? Confusing as hell, dude. Like, what would Shakespeare do if you handed him a modern book on string theory? Didn't matter that he's the brightest and most creative mind when it comes to the English language in the 1500s. He's gonna see words in that physics text that he knows. Articles. Nouns. Verbs. Common words in English, right? And then he's gonna see a lot of words that make no sense at all. What would Shakespeare make of the words, quantum wave theory? He'd know quantum as the Latin word for how much. A wave is water in motion. He might know theory as from the Greek, meaning to contemplate or view. See where I'm coming from? And the grammar's different. Endings and usage have changed. Idiom is different. Think: 'Dost thou bite thy thumb at me?' In modern English, it'd be, 'You flip-ping me off?'"

"Yeah, I follow."

"Good, 'cause, dude, I could use a little time outa here." Skylar glanced around. "Like, you know, maybe get to Santa Fe? Score some real food. It's tough being Shakespeare for you guys without a little time to smell the roses."

"Oh, God," Dan Murphy muttered as he rolled his eyes. "Not again."

Murphy was the Mayan mathematics expert. Like Yusif, Dan de-spised Skylar. But then, he'd lived in a tent with the guy once on an excavation in Belize. Might have soured him on Skylar's, um, shall we say unique personality and hygiene?

"Dan?" I asked. "Anything on the math?"

"Breakthrough." He pushed his notebook out on the table, and I could see the intricate bars, dots, and ovals that made up the Mayan base twenty mathematics. "In our math, we use symbols for add, subtract, multiply, and divide. For a long time, what I was seeing in Fluvium and Alpha's math didn't make sense. I mean, obviously an equation, right? But then it hit me. It's all in the positioning. If the bars are horizontal and the dots on top, it's add. Bars horizontal and dots below means subtract. Vertical with dots left means multiply. Vertical dots right, divide."

"Brilliant," Yusif said as he fingered his beard.

"But what do we know?" Eli asked from his chair. "How does this help us?"

Maxine Kaplan shot a knowing glance at Wixom, a slight shrug of her shoulders indicating her boredom.

Murphy answered, "Not much, General. I mean, the equations are elegant, but like Skylar, I'm hitting a wall. I can see the pattern, but I'm losing the details. Maybe it's because I'm not a physicist."

Wixom added, "Murphy has shown me some of the equations. Hoped I'd recognize something. Be able to fill in some of blanks where the math doesn't make sense. I've drawn a blank."

Yusif added, "Remember, it took twenty-three years to unlock the secrets of the Rosetta Stone. We've only had three months."

"Don't bring up time," Eli told him pointedly. "The difference between now and 1799 when the Rosetta Stone was found, is that we could be extinct in a couple of hours. Our entire timeline essentially ceasing to exist."

Glancing at him, I could see that Eli knew something. Whatever it was, it had him worried. Really worried.

3

Grazier

Eli Grazier had an uneasy tickle in his gut. It happened when he was out of his element—and he *hated* the feeling. He had traveled in person to New Mexico and now perched on the bottom step of Skientia's Los Alamos Lab One. The room was large, thirty-by-thirty–feet square, and had a high ceiling festooned with lights, conduit, and pipes. Thick bundles of electrical wiring snaked in every direction; elevated workstations were strategically placed along the walls, now-dark monitors and keyboards at each. Up the stairs—on a raised platform in the back—a row of comfortable seats for observers stretched to either side of the heavy security door.

Eli hadn't earned his rank by being an idiot; he'd read the professional literature and fully understood what it meant to be a clinically diagnosed psychopath. He'd had numerous conversations about his "disorder" with Colonel Timothy Ryan. Grazier knew where he would score on the Psychopathy Checklist-Revised, or PCL-R: Well above the twenty-seven points on the test that indicated a positive clinical diagnosis.

Fortunately, he was high functioning. In an instant, he could be convincingly attentive, charming, and persuasive, but behind the mask, he remained totally focused and unemotional. That he suffered from neither guilt nor empathy, Eli considered to be pluses—as was his aversion to taking responsibility for failures. Unlike his criminal brethren, he concentrated on long-term goals and maintained perfect self-discipline. And, yes, psychopath though he might be, Grazier was smart enough to question each and every one of his actions, and he did so with total dispassion. The test left no doubt about his narcissistic and borderline tendencies. He would do anything, sacrifice anyone, to come out on top.

Thankfully, fate had placed him in charge of this present situation.

Grazier rocked on his heels and stared at the hemispherical void left in the middle of the concrete floor. A perfect sixth of a sphere, it looked as if it had been milled to the micron by a precision cutting tool. Hard to believe the missing concrete—along with the woman known as Alpha and Skientia's Chief Operating Officer, Tanner Jackson—was somewhere in the future.

The future? Grazier's stomach twitched uncomfortably.

Around the missing sphere, the scientists had placed a variety of detectors. Mounted on tripods, they were something cobbled together by Maxine Kaplan's team to record variation in the quantum fields. No one had ever had the opportunity to study the spot where a time machine had vanished. The severed power cables and the surviving base of a steel workstation, however, remained as they had been the moment after Alpha—or more correctly, Domina Nakeesh—had poured the power to her improbable contraption.

So where was she? A couple of seconds ahead of now? Next week? Sometime in the coming months? Years? Decades?

Who knew?

And there lay the root of his conundrum. This wasn't a typical military or political problem. Not something where he could outmaneuver, destroy, or defeat an enemy. The rules had changed.

Grazier took a deep breath, swelling his immaculate uniform with its perfectly pressed trousers; the colorful campaign ribbons on his chest shone in the lab's bright lights. He ran a hand over his close-cropped hair, flecked as it was with gray at the temples. A grim expression left the flat angles of his face strained, his broad mouth reflecting the bitter thoughts that lay behind his dark eyes.

Having his thumb on the very pulse of research, he'd been immediately aware when the strange woman "appeared" in Skientia's Los Alamos lab. She had "popped in" during a test designed to detect and attract entangled particles from the past, spoke no recognizable language, had no knowledge of history, customs, or modern science. Instead, she spoke something related to, but decidedly different than Italian, wrote in little pictures, and doodled in dots, bars, and weird symbols.

An idiot savant?

Some form of extreme autism?

Or an incredibly cunning and competent spy?

In the end she'd been labeled as "Prisoner Alpha," a maximum-security risk, and placed in the military psychiatric hospital at Grantham Barracks for evaluation and diagnosis.

"Lot of good that did," Grazier growled to himself as he stuck his thumbs in his belt. Alpha had escaped. Not only from Grantham, but—given the circular divot in the concrete—from the very "here and now."

Eli reached into his pocket and let his fingers caress the curious pager that he'd been given. That was baffling as all hell. But to have it happen in his own bedroom was truly disconcerting.

In or out?

At the sound of the door opening behind him, and shoes on the stairs, he turned.

Dr. Timothy Ryan walked slowly down the steps. Ryan was in his fifties, but taller and leaner than Eli. Silver was cropping into the man's short hair. A pensive look creased Ryan's thin face as he gave Grazier a nod before turning his attention to the hollow in the floor.

"They still talking up there?" Grazier asked.

"For all the good it's doing. We're off the map, Eli. Maxine Kaplan, Wixom, a dozen of their engineers and physicists, Rogers and a couple of his associates—they've been able to put a lot of the pieces together, but they still don't have a clue as to how long we're going to have to wait until we catch up in time with Alpha."

Grazier lowered his voice so that the guards flanking the door at the top of the stairs couldn't hear. "Does either Kaplan or Wixom have any idea about Fluvium's cerebrum? Any clue about Harvey Rogers and his lab up at Grantham? Why we relocated him?"

"No. We've left Fluvium's sarcophagus and scrolls here because we took them from Skientia. And the hope is that some of the translations will help us to catch up with Alpha, or have some kind of intelligence about the timeline they came from. Something that will click with Kaplan. Give us an edge."

"What's the word on Falcon? I'd give my left nut to have his perspective on all of this."

He referred to Captain James Hancock Falcon, perhaps the most brilliant mind Grazier had ever known. And the most delicate. Falcon suffered from a combination of Dissociative Identity Disorder and schizophrenia. The twenty-nine-year-old had an uncanny ability to discern patterns in data. At that moment, Falcon was catatonic after a psychotic break; he was lying in a special bed in the psychiatric ward in Grantham Barracks. Word was he might never recover.

"No progress on that front. Eli, for all we know, when those goons arrested him, the trauma may have driven him so deeply into his psychosis . . . Well, we all have hope."

"One of these days, I'll make Bill Stevens pay for that." Grazier's dry chuckle held no humor. "And *I'm* supposed to be the self-serving psychopath? Stevens is the one who swallowed Alpha's story—hook, line, and sinker. Bet she seduced him with just a single look from those weird blue eyes of hers."

"She possesses a remarkable magnetism. Something the likes of which I've never seen. Exotic, sensual. A presence that sucks the air out of a room." Ryan's smile turned bitter. "Nor have I forgotten that you came to the conclusion that I was under her spell."

"What is it about her? What makes her so stunning and magnetic? That she's from another timeline? Another universe? Whatever it is, she plays men like a master."

"Alpha is an enigma. Unlike any woman I've ever known. A couple of times in the very beginning, she tried a sexual ploy. Something feral, maybe hormonal. If I wasn't such a stickler for never messing with a patient . . . Well, who knows?" Ryan let his gaze roam the lab, then settled on the spherical depression in the concrete.

"This room is monitored every nanosecond of every day." Grazier pointed up at the two guards standing to either side of the security door, then to the cameras and motion sensors. "She suddenly materializes with that time machine of hers, and my people will swarm this room. I've got one of the best security teams in the country to keep an eye on things. They follow the chain of command, take orders directly from me."

"Hope so. It's the not knowing." Ryan fingered his chin. "The uncertainty that comes with the realization that we're not alone. That's a creepy feeling. Downright unsettling. Knowing that people can just pop in from other timelines. From parallel worlds so different from ours. That, like in the case of Alpha, they think we're completely expendable."

Eli shot him a sidelong glance. "Creepier than you can guess."

Ryan—psychiatric clinician that he was—caught the nuance. "Eli? What do you know?"

"That Alpha isn't the only one."

Ryan's penetrating gaze tried to pierce his defenses.

Eli preempted him. "Not here. Not in front of the surveillance. Suffice it to say, if my source is correct, we're nowhere near out of the woods yet."

Absently, Eli fingered the square shape of what he called "the pager" where it rested in his pocket. To Ryan, he said, "I'll brief you when we get back to the barn. Assuming, that is, that Major Swink can spool that Blackhawk up and get us the hell out of here."

Ryan lifted his sleeve, speaking into the mic. "Winny? You on deck?" He listened to something in his earbud. "Five minutes?" He looked at Grazier. "Where to, Eli?"

"Your place." That meant Grantham Barracks—the military psychiatric hospital outside of Colorado Springs, Colorado, where Tim Ryan had once been in charge. Now it was the home for a most improbable special operations team. The kind not even Hollywood could have dreamed up.

Grazier took one last look at the now-silent lab. Lot of drama in this room. They'd cleaned the blood up where the time-containment field had cut Dr. Reid Farmer's body in two. The same with the spot where Peter McCoy had died of a gunshot to the heart.

And there—where that hollow now mocked—Dr. Farmer had taken a couple of shots at Alpha. Maybe even mortally wounded her. The field that propelled Alpha into the future had also swept up the potato-headed Tanner Jackson, Skientia's ruthless chief operating officer.

"I'd love the chance to get my hands on you," Grazier promised the man. Jackson's attempt to have Eli killed had come within a whisker of success.

And now Jackson was traveling through time with Alpha?

"Come on," Grazier told Ryan as he started up the stairs. "The sooner you and your people are up to speed, the more likely we'll be able to deal with what's coming."

"And what might that be?" Ryan asked.

"How does 'the end of the world as you know it' sound?"

At the top of the stairs, the two uniformed guards saluted. Grazier returned it, glanced back. He wondered about those detectors. The room, so bright, large, and spacious, seemed to reek of an evil promise.

4

Stevens

In the security monitor, White House Chief of Staff Bill Stevens watched the Blackhawk lift off from the Los Alamos helipad. The big helicopter swung out over the Rio Grande Valley, rising and curving away to the north. Sunlight flickered along the craft's aluminum skin before it seemed to vanish against the distant mountains.

In the beginning, Bill Stevens had begun his rise to power running Ben Masters' campaign for governor, and then for the senate. Along the way, he'd learned all the tricks, tactics, and sleights necessary to triumph in American politics. Using them, he'd been able to catapult Ben Masters into the Oval Office. Like a satiated spider, he'd been contented in his Washington web. Right up to the day that he learned about the magical appearance of a startled woman in a distant New Mexico lab. It had come across his desk as a mere security alert.

Circumstances, and a familiarity with Skientia's research, had provided him with the real implications of Domina Nakeesh's mysterious appearance in Skientia's lab that day. Screw Ben Masters! Compared to the power that Nakeesh represented, the presidency of the United States was small potatoes.

Stevens rubbed the back of his neck. Tricky this, being here at Skientia's Los Alamos lab at the same time as that bastard, Grazier. Grazier was the only man who stood between Bill Stevens and the control of, well, just about everything.

"Too bad we know each other so well," Stevens muttered under his breath as he turned his attention to the other monitor. It showed a high-end conference room with an oversized table of tropical wood surrounded by plush leather chairs, walnut wainscoting, full-wall monitors for AV, and thick carpet.

People were rising from the chairs, engaged in mixed chatter as they shuffled notes and clicked laptops closed. Scientists, all, including Maxine Kaplan, Skientia's Team Leader. Knocking on sixty and attractive for her age, the tall woman dressed professionally, her body toned and fit. Her competence in both physics and engineering had earned her the top job on Skientia's entangled particle program. She'd taken it from the study of entangled photons to the creation and detection of actual entangled molecules. Backed up by Virgil Wixom—another PhD in entanglement who specialized in something called decoherence—they'd built the machine that accidentally had summoned Domina Nakeesh across the centuries. Sure, tardigrades were one thing. But a human being? Talk about mind-blowing.

Stevens shook his head. He was in the middle of it. Didn't mean he understood how Nakeesh had appeared in the middle of Skientia's experiment. The monitors had fuzzed out with snow. Pop. And as the monitors came back online, there she was, holding her navigator, staring around in complete disbelief. She'd been wearing a simple gray tunic, her hair pinned back. Sandals had been on her feet. In stunned silence, she'd gaped, blinked, and immediately began fiddling with her navigator, pulling up holographic fields, running her fingers through them.

Hadn't made sense at the time. Neither Kaplan and Wixom, nor the other scientists had understood how she'd gotten into the room. Kaplan, upon seeing the stranger, had triggered a security alert. Two of the techs closest to the Domina had rushed up, demanding to know who she was, how she got into the room. And, of course, not knowing a word of English, Nakeesh had panicked, turned, and tried to run.

The techs had tackled her, ripped the navigator away, and then the security team burst in and dragged her away.

Stevens shifted to the monitor that showed Lab One and the ominous divot in the concrete where Nakeesh and her time machine had vanished.

"Where are you?"

He shot a glance over his shoulder as Maxine Kaplan stepped into the room and closed the door behind her. "Learn anything?" she asked, indicating the rows of security monitors.

"Grazier just left with Ryan. Flew off in that helo. He doesn't have a clue that I was within a thousand miles. Thanks for taking my call. Getting me in here."

Her flinty brown eyes might have been scalpels the way they tried to dissect him. "This thing is huge. You understand that, don't you? One of those watershed moments in human history. Like the atomic bomb, or fire. The moment that woman appeared was a phase shift for our existence. There was before, and now there is after. Frankly, it scares the shit out of me."

"Jackson and McCoy had faith in you. More so than just the fact that you were Tanner Jackson's lover." He smiled. "Yeah, I know about that. I know a lot of things. But let's not get distracted. My interest here is what this means for the country."

"Bullshit. Your interest is what it means for Bill Stevens." She raised a hand to forestall him. "To tell you the truth, I don't have a clue as to what it ultimately means. I'm still struggling. In a blink of an eye, everything we thought we knew about physics was sucked right down the drain. What we thought we knew was called the 'Copenhagen interpretation' after a meeting in the 1920s between some of the brightest founders of modern physics."

"That was Einstein, Bohr, Heisenberg, and that bunch, right?"

"That's them. And yeah, there were always problems with the way Copenhagen couldn't explain the foundations of quantum mechanics. For example, why a wave function collapses upon observation. When does a measurement occur? How macroscopic does an observation have to be? Why do quantum systems evolve in nature as predicted by the Schrödinger equation only to collapse when we observe them? And it certainly doesn't explain entanglement."

"So why didn't the 'great minds' figure it out?"

"Because the Copenhagen interpretation was pretty good when it came to answering questions about specific problems. Sort of like the calculator in your phone. Tap in the numbers, press divide, and you get an answer, but you don't have a clue as to how the machine came up with it. It just worked. Same with entanglement. Don't sweat the small shit."

"And that's a problem?"

"Only for a minority of physicists. The rest of us were happy to plug and play. Copenhagen gave us the rules to the game. Why tie yourself in knots about the twinky details that don't make sense? Until Nakeesh."

"And then?"

"Then, in an instant, a supposedly crackpot curiosity of a theory becomes reality. We call it the Many-Worlds hypothesis. Goes back to 1955 and a graduate student at Princeton. The guy was Hugh Everett the third, a student of Wheeler's. He was bothered by all those aforementioned twinky details, especially because he was interested in quantum gravity. At a late-night drinking party with a couple of physics buddies—and enough sherry to deaden his inhibitions against kicking the holy shrine that was the Copenhagen interpretation—it hit Everett that the universe had to be a single wave function, and it interacted with itself at a basic level. When it did, it split, like two waves running together, bouncing off each other and becoming four waves. Each wave begins as a mirror reflection that in turn interacts and changes, spawning more waves that interact, change, and spawn more waves."

"I don't get it. The universe is made of stuff, not reflections. That chair over there doesn't split in two."

"Mr. Stevens, seventy percent of Americans are scientifically illiterate, and you're no different. Your genius is politics. That said, have you ever seen a particle? A wave function? Maybe tossed a field theory from one hand to the other?"

"No."

"And you won't. That's because, like the Copenhagen boys and girls, you're not into the twinky shit. But when you flip that switch over on the wall, the lights will come on. Slam a couple of hemispheres of weapons-grade plutonium together, you will get a fission reaction that will destroy Beijing. At least it will if the missile that's carrying it happens to be at the right longitude and latitude. Everett's Many-Worlds hypothesis became gospel the moment Domina Nakeesh popped into my lab."

He crossed his arms, studied her. "All right, so we accept that there are other Earths, other timelines, other copies of you and me constantly splitting off. How many?"

"Speaking theoretically, it's infinite. Whatever the Hilbert space . . .

um, that's the number of possible dimensions that exist in the universe. Whatever that allows."

Stevens rubbed the back of his neck. "Do you know how weird that sounds? Like a million copies of the world? A million copies of me? All existing at the same time? Where are they? Why don't we see them? Sounds nuts."

"Really? So, tell me, Mr. Chief of Staff, how thick is a wave function? How much space does it take to hold a couple trillion reflections? Not that 'space' is a good analogy to use." She snorted derisively. "Forget it. Listen, you don't need to understand the physics, or anything about the Schrödinger equation, or decoherence, or entanglement. All I need you for is to flip the light switch."

"You? Need me?" He felt the old hackles rise. "You know who I am?"

"Let me rephrase. We need each other." She nodded toward the monitor displaying the conference room. "We're at the beginning of this. Trying to figure out what it means, what the threats and dimensions are. The facts—as we know them—are that Nakeesh and Fluvium appeared in Egypt sometime around 1380 BCE to conduct a bioweapons experiment. My experiment to attract entangled particles from the past triggered Nakeesh's navigator, brought her here, and left Fluvium stranded in the past. He had a second piece of equipment with him. What they call a cerebrum. He died in Egypt over three millennia ago. The hope was that his cerebrum would be found in his tomb. It wasn't. It's gone. Vanished somewhere in the past. Nakeesh needs a cerebrum to get back to her timeline."

She rubbed the backs of her arms. "Me? I don't like Grazier. One of his people shot Peter dead. That woman, Karla Raven, manhandled me. But on top of that, on Grazier's team, I'm nothing more than a pawn surrounded by fools like those idiot archaeologists. I'm relegated to being a mere technician tasked with fitting the pieces together."

"And you want more?"

"The same as you." Her lips pursed. "We're talking about the awesome power of jumping between worlds. Through time. What that means—not to mention the ramifications—is immense, and we can barely grasp the possibilities at this point. Huge doesn't cover it. You have the power of the presidency behind you. You can make things happen."

He reached out, took her hand, and shook. "Partners. And don't worry about Grazier. He only thinks he's in charge. Play your part for the moment." He pointed at the monitor where the hollow left by Na-keesh's time machine filled the screen. "When she comes back, my people will move in."

5

Ryan

Helicopters weren't in my comfort zone. Never had been.

The day I retired from the Corps, I figured I'd left the last of the beasts behind—and good riddance. Since Alpha had entered my life, it seemed like I was in one airplane or chopper after another. And half the time we were either bouncing through turbulence or being shot at.

So there I was, back in a damned helicopter, feeling those tickly fingers stroking my stomach. You know the sensation—the one that comes just before you hurl your lunch all over the chopper deck.

It got worse each time Winny piloted the Blackhawk over one of the rugged mountain ridges where the updrafts tossed the big helo up and down. This was my last trip in the Blackhawk. Grazier had just procured one of the new Sikorsky SB-1 Defiant dual-axial birds. Winny was off for training as soon as we landed.

Great! We were getting rid of a reliable and long-tested helicopter for a brand-new-just-off-the-assembly-line-sure-to-have-teething-problems, dual-axial, super-maneuverable, hyper-complicated stealth bird that was sure to fall out the sky at the most inopportune moment.

I kept my eyes closed. Didn't want to look down, see the world slipping this way and that, let alone contemplate what it would be like to plummet out of the sky onto those jagged rocks, peaks, and all that jutting timber.

"You all right?" Grazier asked, his voice absurdly calm through the headphones.

I gave Eli a slit-eyed and suffering glare. "I ever tell you how much I hate flying in these things?"

Eli grinned in return, shifting in his seat to stare out at the scenery as we crossed the Sangre de Christo Mountains and dropped down along the front of the Spanish Peaks.

"Hey, Skipper," Winny Swink's voice came from the cockpit. "Smooth ride this time. What are you complaining about?"

I craned my neck to see past the bulkhead. Winny was in the right-hand seat, her wiry five-foot-four body clad in wrinkled fatigues. A firecracker redhead, her real name was Winchester Wesson Swink. She'd attained the rank of major in the United States Air Force despite her Antisocial Personality Disorder, or APD. They'd kept her—endured might be a better word—because Winny was gifted with so much raw talent that she could fly anything. She was good enough that she'd tested experimental aircraft at the Skunk Works, taught aerial tactics, been a hot shot at Red Star, and aced it all. Well, all but for washing out at NASA. The space agency tends to have no tolerance for either a surly attitude or miscreant behavior, no matter how good a pilot might be at the stick.

Eventually, as it always does, her APD caught up with her. See, Winny has two tripwires: One is her cooking. Boiling water is the extent of her culinary abilities, and she's touchy about it. And worse, she gets especially prickly about women who wear pink. In Winny's case, the final straw came when she encountered a mouthy four-star general's wife—a woman who tripped Winny's trigger at a DC cocktail party. The wife—dressed in dripping pink—had dared to question Winny's femininity. The reaction was so explosive it took four people to pull Winny off the poor woman, an action that got her grounded pending a psychiatric evaluation. You can guess where that went. In retaliation, Winny stole an F-22 Raptor off the line at Andrews, took it on a joyride around DC, and landed it on I-95 before taxiing onto an off-ramp. They found her at the intersection convenience store, perched on the wing, swinging her feet and sipping from a screw-top bottle of wine.

The Air Force kept face by claiming that Major Swink had heroically landed a malfunctioning plane, saving countless lives in the process. The moment the cameras were done clicking, she was summarily arrested, committed, and shipped off to my care.

I considered that as we hit an updraft that sent my stomach down somewhere between my knees. I swallowed hard, made a face.

I will not throw up. I will not throw up. I will not . . .

"Ryan, what is it with you?" Grazier demanded. "You're the one who rides all those hot Italian motorcycles. Tough Marine like you, I figured a short flight like this would be a piece of cake."

"Eli, why aren't you on a plane back to DC?"

His expression hardened. "You know Bill Stevens, right? The president's chief of staff? The guy's been with President Masters for years. Ran his campaigns. Stevens was thick with Skientia; they were major donors to the president's election. Through Stevens' influence, Tanner Jackson and Peter McCoy both had anytime invites to the White House. The Lincoln bedroom was one of their favorite places to stay when they were in the city."

I hated politics.

Eli paid no attention to my turning green as he said, "Stevens was behind getting you and your people arrested back in Santa Fe after Alpha escaped from Ward Six. He was tight with Alpha, took her to the White House to meet the president. Stevens knows more about this whole time-jumping thing than we do. Understands the awesome power that it gives to whoever controls the technology. With McCoy dead and Tanner Jackson missing, Stevens is angling to get control of Skientia. Now, you can figure out why he'd want that, can't you?"

"Entanglement physics," I told him. "Skientia was working on retrieving entangled particles from the past. The past part is important because using entangled photons for communication in present time, no one can read the message. It's essentially an uncrackable technology. By the very act of reading the message, it's destroyed."

"Right."

"But if you can retrieve entangled particles from the past, you can read secret communications from seconds, to minutes, to days, to weeks ago. Essentially, with the right kind of quantum 3D computer, you can eavesdrop on anyone. Government, military, financial, intelligence—no one is safe. More than that, no one knows that their communications have been monitored. Campaign strategies, troop movements, special orders, confidential memos, eyes-only intelligence—everything is compromised."

"Thought we had it all. That we'd beaten the Chinese, the Europeans, and everyone else to the punch. And then Alpha pops into that lab." Eli shook his head. "In that moment, everything changed. To travel back into the past, cross from timeline to timeline, enter parallel worlds, that's power like no one has ever seen, let alone contemplated." He glanced at me. "And you wonder at the struggle that's about to be unleashed?"

"If you control information and time, you pretty much control everything."

Eli kept giving me one of his calculating looks. "Now, put yourself in the president's hot seat. He knows that in the blink of an eye, everything we thought we knew, every rule in the book, is gone. A woman from another timeline—hell, maybe another universe for all I know—has popped into a research lab in New Mexico. And, God knows, it was a matter of luck that she popped into one of our labs and not one in China. How do you deal with that? Who do you trust? How do you keep it secret?"

"And Stevens thinks he can take it all for himself?"

"He's been in at the ground-floor level since the beginning. Briefed by Jackson and McCoy. Hell, the son of a bitch knew they were trying to kill me. Thought he had me by the balls that day I briefed the president. Was going to have me committed as a nutcase. Only thing that saved my ass? Stevens hadn't briefed the president, which really pissed off the old man."

"So why didn't the president ax Stevens?"

Eli's gaze was fixed a thousand miles beyond eternity as he stared at the Rockies. "Stevens has his own power base. And the guy knows too much . . . like where all the bodies are buried. If it were left up to me, he'd have an unfortunate accident. Assuming he doesn't have a file on me hidden somewhere that would land on some reporter's desk at CNN or Fox the day after his funeral."

The queasiness in my stomach got worse. "So, what do you see as the solution?"

"We play it out, Ryan. When it comes to Bill Stevens, the president knows he's in bed with a scorpion. Stevens took Alpha to the White House, probably to prove that the Many-Worlds hypothesis was real. The president is perched on the horns of a dilemma. He's got a security nightmare on his hands." Eli fixed on me. "God, I wish Falcon would snap out of his damned catatonia. I need to know what the game is, who the players are, and what they want. We're the only thing standing between survival and disaster."

"Why's that?"

"Tell you when we get to Grantham."

"That bad, huh?"

"If only Falcon was conscious."

But he wasn't. The fact that Eli—the man without a remorseful bone in his body—could look that grim sent a tremor through me.

6

Karla

Chief Petty Officer Karla Raven pulled the last of her kit from the Chevy Tahoe's rear deck and slammed the hatch shut. She slapped the roof, her signal to the driver that he could go.

Through cool gray eyes, she watched the Tahoe accelerate across the smooth concrete in Grantham Barracks' underground parking lot. The tires hissed as the vehicle passed the Skipper's blue-and-white–striped Ducati Diavel. Karla hoisted her heavy pack and stared thoughtfully at the motorcycle. Looked like it hadn't been moved since she'd left for her insertion, exfiltration, and evasion training four days ago.

Karla's path to the military psychiatric hospital at Grantham Barracks traced its way back to her enlistment in the Navy and her iron determination to be the first female SEAL. Took her three rollbacks before she earned her trident. Despite the hazing, she'd made Green Team, aced SEAL sniper training, and been assigned to a team. Earned an E7 and command of her own platoon. Until an IED in Afghanistan blew most of it away.

She'd been cashiered by a pimple-faced lieutenant over her PTSD. Well, and for the impulse control disorder, i.e., kleptomania. All of which had landed her here, at Grantham Barracks. A most improbable place from which to save the world.

Skipper hadn't moved his Ducati? "Must be something cooking," she muttered, turning to the glass doors and the level-four security guard who stood there.

"Hey, Chief," the man told her. "How was the vacation?"

"What vacation? I was attending a mental health care conference in Santa Fe." At least, that was the cover story. Grantham these days was about as hush-hush, eyes only, if-we-tell-you-we-gotta-kill-you as security could get. As if a special operations command could ever be hidden in a more unlikely location than a military loony bin.

At the door, she pointed to the Ducati. "The colonel hasn't touched his bike since I left."

"Heard he's been away."

Away? Karla kept her expression blank as she stepped through the glass doors, barely noticed the divots where small arms fire had been patched. The story was that two assassins had tried to kill Prisoner Alpha the day she'd been delivered to Grantham.

Too bad they didn't succeed. Would have saved us a shitload of trouble.

Even then, the male assassin hadn't made it. One of the security team had taken him out with a heart shot. Then the female shooter had shucked a device from the dying man's belt and vanished. To this day, they both remained unidentified—a remarkable feat given the facial recognition software and surveillance available to the government.

Karla passed another guard at level three, rode the elevator up, and was hustled through the level-one security into Ward Six. As she stepped onto the Ward floor, Staff Sergeant Myca Simond met her, saying, "Good to have you back, Chief. Sorry to rush you, but Colonel Ryan wants you in the conference room five minutes ago."

She gave the freckle-faced redhead a nod. "Roger that."

As they walked down the waxed-and-polished hallways, he asked, "How was the recertification and training?"

She could tell Simond. He had the same clearance she did. "Boring. They dropped me out of a C-130 in the middle of the night. I parachuted into a deployment of Abrams on a training exercise out at Piñon Canyon and spent the next three days running, crawling through mud and cactus, eating grasshoppers, and hiding while half the training grounds hunted my ass."

"They catch you?"

"Hey, Myca. What I just told you? That was all bullshit. I was only on the ground for about six hours." She gave him a grin. "Here's how it really went down. They figured I was going to do fancy SEAL shit. You know, disguise myself as a cholla, slither down drainages, wiggle snake-like in the brush, and sneak through the rocks. Instead, I walked into a mobile command post, stole a captain's ACUs, changed clothes, and drove out in a Humvee."

"No shit?"

"Most of my time in debriefing was spent explaining the downside to their total lack of security."

As they walked down the hallway, she missed the old Ward Six with its familiar cadre of patients. These days, most of the mental patients had been moved to Grantham's other five wards that were now under Dr. Mary Pettigrew's administration. Karla had only met the woman once. Dr. Pettigrew might have looked like everyone's grandmother: gray-haired; round face with a dimple in the chin; slightly overweight; and wearing glasses. She wasn't. The brief time Karla had spent in her presence, she found the woman to be a no-nonsense clinician dedicated to helping her patients.

As they reached the conference room door, Simond told her, "I'll take your pack, Chief. Put it in your room for you."

She watched Simond do his best not to stagger or grunt as he took the eighty-pound pack. She hid her grin as she entered the conference room.

If you didn't know the room's history, the fluffy and cuddly-looking animals drawn on the walls, the flowers and soft pastel colors, thick carpeting, and collection of beanbag chairs in the corner would have thrown you off. While the décor had been designed to soothe, to make patients relax and feel safe, it had become the war room where life-or-death decisions regarding the future of the world were made.

At the head of the table, to Karla's surprise, sat General Elijiah Grazier. She hadn't seen the two-star since the man had appeared in Santa Fe and more or less rescued them from the clutches of the federal government. Turned out that shooting up mansions, stealing aircraft, aerial combat over the Chesapeake, and gunfights in Los Alamos focused the attention of lots of different kinds of law enforcement—not to mention the infamous Bill Stevens.

Grazier had given Team Psi an out: They could work for him as a specialized black-on-black unit dedicated to Alpha and the threat she posed to, well, just about everything. Or they could expect a long incarceration in the federal penal system.

Now, with the exception of Captain James Falcon—whose chair

remained ominously empty—the whole team was present. On the way to her seat, Karla slapped Winny Swink's raised hand in a high five.

"Have fun?" the redhead asked.

"All but the airplane ride. Without you at the stick, we didn't do a single barrel roll."

Karla seated herself across from Catalina Talavera. Not quite thirty, Cat had two PhDs from Stanford, one in biochemistry and another in genetics. She might remind Karla of a porcelain doll with her large almond eyes, petite nose, and delicate chin, but since the days when Cat had tried to commit suicide on the Capitol steps to protest the misuse of her research, the woman had shown remarkable courage. Cat had been committed to Grantham for psychiatric "observation" and her own "protection." Not to mention that the Department of Defense wanted her locked away where she couldn't email classified bioresearch to the *New York Times*. That she was also an illegal alien and could have been deported back to Acapulco added to her mystique.

To Cat's right sat beanpole-thin Private First Class Edwin Tyler Jones. Cat Talavera and ET—as Jones was called—enjoyed a budding romance. Talk about yin and yang, ET was one of eight kids born of a single mother in a run-down black neighborhood in Detroit. Early on, he'd been recruited by one of the Detroit street gangs—the brothers having a use for his incredible computer skills. ET's passion was cracking codes, security systems, breaching firewalls, and penetrating cybersecurity. Having no better way to avoid arrest as the law closed in, ET built a new identity for himself, enlisted in the army, and ultimately had himself committed to Grantham as a preferable alternative to a cell in Leavenworth.

"Hey, Chief," ET told her. "See you made it back. Steal anything fun on the outside?"

Karla dealt with more than just her PTSD; the trauma of losing most of her SEAL platoon to an IED had developed into what they called "an impulse control disorder." In the old days it had been known as kleptomania. She just couldn't help stealing things.

"Would have swiped you a Rolls-Royce, but whoever owned it had taken the keys with them."

"Since when you worry about keys?" ET asked. "You hot-wire boats, cars, all kinds of shit."

"Okay, so they took the distributor cap, too."

He reached across the table, slapping and backslapping her fingers. "Effin' A!"

She didn't tell him that she had a gold lighter, shaped like a duck, that she'd palmed from the debriefing colonel's desk.

At the other end of the table, watching this interaction, Major Samuel Savage had a dyspeptic look on his bronzed face. Savage looked exactly like what he was: the descendent of Creek and Choctaw warriors. The complexion, lines, and planes of his face would have been perfect for an Edward Curtis photo. Raised on the Creek reservation in Oklahoma by his traditional Uncle Buck, Savage liked to recall that he was probably the only kid alive who ever had to do calculus in his head at the same time he was gutting a deer. No one was laughing when he graduated first in his class at West Point, took a field commission, and never looked back. While assigned to Army Intelligence in DC, he'd finished his PhD in indigenous religious studies, gone on to serve in the CIA's Intelligence Support Activity, and stumbled headfirst into the "Alpha" situation on a mission in Egypt.

As the only "normal" member of the team, Savage served as second in command under Dr. Ryan. The major still had trouble dealing with the fact that the rest of his team consisted of "mental patients." Even after they'd managed to pull his ass out of the shit more than once.

"Good to have you back, Chief," Colonel Ryan called from where he sat at Grazier's right. "How was the recertification exercise?"

"By the book, sir." Karla didn't figure she needed to tell the Skipper about the stolen uniforms, or the Humvee, or the fact that she'd exceeded mission parameters. The Skipper was known to worry himself needlessly over trivia.

Then Karla turned her attention to General Eli Grazier sitting at the head of the table, stopped, and saluted.

"Good to see you, Chief," Grazier said as he lazily returned her salute.

"You, too, sir." What in hell was Grazier doing at Grantham? Coupled with the fact that Colonel Ryan's Ducati hadn't moved in days, the signs were that some kind of heavy shit was about to come down.

Karla had saved Grazier's life when an assassin's bullet would have blown out the general's back. Ryan had made it clear to her that Grazier, being a psychopath, would throw her to the wolves in a hot second. And he'd never lose a minute of sleep over it. But then, as the saying went: "If you don't have a sense of humor when it comes to this shit, you're obviously in the wrong profession."

"Let's get this over with," Grazier said as he looked up and down the table. "For the time being, this is the most secure location available to us. As far as the rest of the world is concerned, with the exception of Major Savage, you are all mental patients confined to Grantham Barracks. And as to Savage? He died last month in Afghanistan."

Karla glanced at Savage, saw the stiffening of his features. The guy *had* almost died, being shot through the left lung during the infiltration of the Skientia lab. But for that chance round taking Savage out, they might have gotten to Alpha before she threw the switch that sent her into the future.

"In short," Grazier said, "outside of this room, only the president of the United States knows you exist as an official entity. Chief of Staff Bill Stevens, a handful of investigators and their staff, think you were nothing more than a group of escaped mental patients that I used as a cover to decoy them away from the real operatives who took down Skientia. I've done everything in my power to convince them I used that classification as a means of saving face for the Department of Defense."

ET was grinning. Figured.

Grazier nodded as if to congratulate himself. "We want to keep it that way. Not only is the world ill prepared to hear that people from other timelines can pop into ours, but it's research we don't want the Russians, the Chinese, Iranians, or others to be tinkering with."

Ryan leaned back. "You didn't fly out to Los Alamos just to attend the latest session with the research team there. This is the post-COVID world; you could have done that through a video conference."

Grazier spread his hands meaningfully. "I wanted to see the security feeds myself. See the spot where Alpha disappeared. And I wanted to have this meeting."

He extracted his smart phone, pulled up an icon, and tapped.

Karla watched the screen on the far wall come to life. She recognized the security video, having just been in the Grantham parking garage. On the screen, Dr. Ryan and a couple of orderlies stood a couple of paces out from the glass doors. The Skipper had a clipboard in his hands.

"What you're seeing here," Grazier told them, "is Prisoner Alpha's arrival at Grantham."

Karla watched the three-car security detail drive up, a black Suburban in the blocking position, followed by a Lincoln, with a Tahoe chase vehicle close behind.

The detail pulled to a stop, the security team bailing out, weapons drawn, to form a perimeter. An officer—a captain in dress uniform—emerged from the Lincoln's passenger door, reached back, and opened the rear coach door. Alpha, wearing an orange jumpsuit, emerged. Even then she looked stately, her blue eyes casting about, her confining chains somehow made irrelevant by the sheer magnitude of her personality.

Ryan was talking to the captain, then to Alpha, and the image fuzzed out.

"This is the familiar static discharge that some of you have experienced just before someone teleports, or whatever you call it."

When the image reformed, it was in the middle of a gunfight; most of the security detail lay sprawled on the smooth concrete. A man and woman, standing, were firing on full auto. Ryan had pulled Alpha down onto the concrete as the captain capped off rounds from his duty pistol. He was laid over the Lincoln's roof.

Karla saw the male assassin, a blond man, drop as if center-punched. At the same time, the captain's head exploded in a haze of brains and blood, and he went down.

The woman assassin screamed, "Dear God, no!" as she knelt beside the blond man. Lifted a box that Karla knew was called a navigator from his belt. The woman fiddled with it. Pulled another, the device called a cerebrum, from behind her, and ran her fingers through a projected blue field. The image went fuzzy again and turned to static.

Grazier reversed the feed. Using fingers on his phone, he narrowed the image to the woman. Zoomed in to focus on her face. Auburn-haired, green-eyed, she looked tanned, young. Maybe in her late twenties. Desperation reflected in the set of her full lips, the angles of her cheeks and nose.

"My missing assassin," Ryan said. "For God's sake, tell me you've found her."

"Actually," Grazier said woodenly, "she found me."

7

Ryan

I sat in shocked silence. Pensive worry reflected in Eli's dark and somber eyes. Around the conference room, the tension among my people could be felt, heavy in the air. It made a mockery of the bunnies, fawns, and pastoral scenes painted on the walls.

Everyone in Grantham knew that an assassination attempt had been made on Alpha the day she arrived. That wasn't the sort of thing that we could have kept quiet even if we'd wanted to. Two people had died: the male shooter and Captain Stanwick.

The bullet holes had been patched, the shattered glass doors replaced, and the bullet-riddled Lincoln had been towed out of the garage.

I'd spent hours studying the auburn-haired woman's image. Wondered who she was. How she had escaped. This, however, was the first time my people had seen the footage.

"She found you?" I couldn't keep the incredulity out of my voice.

Eli raised his eyebrows. "I was going to bed. In my own bedroom in Georgetown." He glanced around the table to make sure my people understood. "My house? Given what I'm privy to? It's like Fort Knox, only more secure and better monitored. Two separate agencies have security systems in my place."

"And this woman appeared?" Sam Savage gestured at the image frozen on the far wall.

"Stepped out of my closet." Eli ran fingers down the line of his chin. "Told me not to reach for my pistol, that she'd unloaded it. And that she'd disabled my alarm button."

"How'd she get in?" Karla asked, a skeptical frown on her forehead as she studied the image.

Grazier gestured at the projection. "You know what happens when they use the navigator and cerebrum. Like on the surveillance video, it knocks out the lights, plays hell with cameras and electrical systems. From reports like yours, Chief Raven, it feels like a wave rolling through you. Cuts your strings, as you say. Couldn't have stated it better."

"So, she still has the same cerebrum and navigator that she used here," I noted, staring at the boxes the woman cradled. Each was about the size of a thick hardback book, and I could see the faint haze of the holographics they projected.

Cat wondered. "Anything like a roof access, some—"

"No." Eli left no doubt. "When I checked with my security, they had nothing. Just two periods of static separated by about an hour and a half."

"Why'd she want to see you?" ET flexed his long spiderlike fingers on the table.

"To give me this." Grazier reached into his pants pocket. He produced a small square device. Might have been a garage door opener. Maybe two-by-three inches and a half inch thick. On the surface, I could see a silver button.

"She tossed me this. Said that she was here to destroy Alpha and Fluvium. That if I wanted in, I should push this button." He paused. "'In or out.' Her words exactly."

"But Fluvium's dead," Cat said. "We've seen the body. The guy's a mummy. Been that way for over three thousand years."

Grazier met Cat's eyes, smiled a sort of rictus at her. "That was my reaction, Dr. Talavera. My intruder wasn't impressed. Reminded me that I wasn't thinking the whole 'time thing' through. The implication was that by now, we should be grasping on to the fact that time isn't a constant."

"Which means?" Savage asked.

"Which means if Alpha pops back into our world, appears again in that hollow in Lab One back at Los Alamos, and manages to escape, she might damned well get back and rescue Fluvium. Essentially pull him out of our timeline before he dies of old age in ancient Egypt. If that happens, you, me, and the rest of us will cease to exist."

Karla asked, "Do you know how hinky and weird this all sounds, sir?"

"Yeah." Eli licked his lips. "And, Chief, we'd better learn the rules in this new game pretty damn *ricky tick* quick, or we're going to lose it all."

This was the second time I'd seen Eli look scared. It sent a chill through my belly. "So, what does it mean? In or out?"

Grazier shrugged. "Tim, like I said, we don't know the rules. Put this in perspective: These people pop in and out of our universe. We know that Alpha and Fluvium popped in sometime during the Eighteenth Dynasty three thousand three hundred years ago in ancient Egypt. They laced the Nile with a bioengineered algae."

Eli singled out Cat. "Good work on your part figuring that out, Dr. Talavera."

Cat responded with a self-conscious smile.

"Turns out that the bio agent they used may have been recorded as one of the famous 'Plagues of Egypt' where the Nile ran with blood. The algae known as *Oscillatoria* turns water red. But Fluvium didn't use all of his samples. The other was found in his sarcophagus, an even more deadly strain."

"Good thing that stuff didn't end up in someone's water supply," Cat added. "No one should die that way."

"You were the people who figured out that Fluvium and Alpha were using our world, and perhaps others, as testing grounds for what we would call bioweapons." Eli arched an eyebrow. "Clever, actually. Pick a timeline after it diverged from their own, and they could experiment with an entire planet's population. Infect it, jump ahead in time, and evaluate the long-term results. See what their meddling wrought."

How cold could a couple of people be? I could ask that? Given my profession? Let alone our own history of Nazi, Bolshevik, and Khmer Rouge atrocity?

The thing was, I'd been treating Alpha, cudgeling my brain to find a way to reach her when we all thought she was suffering from an undiagnosed and catastrophic mental disorder. The notion that I'd sat across from a mass murderer who would callously experiment on entire worlds, that I had looked into her eyes and cared for her welfare, sent a queasy tremor through my soul.

Was I that bad a judge of character?

Karla's gray eyes slitted as she studied the projected image of the auburn-haired woman. "Looking back, it's too bad your assassin didn't shoot straighter."

"Maybe," Eli agreed. "But what's to say our assassin's any better than

Alpha? This could be like choosing between two warring drug gangs, or deciding if you're going to back Hitler or Stalin on the Russian Front. Until we know the rules, let alone the objectives of either combatant, we shouldn't be picking sides."

"Wish Falcon was here," ET muttered uneasily.

We all did.

Me most of all.

Falcon was my patient. And I couldn't do a thing to help him.

8

Falcon

Falcon's skull might have been a bell the way Aunt Celia's voice seemed to reverberate around the inside. *"James, I know I can never be a mother and a father to you . . ."*

The words were coherent, but indistinct, tonally fuzzy around the edges as they vibrated with increasing amplitude inside his head.

Images formed behind Falcon's eyelids: sine waves of the vibrations rushing from left to right, varying in amplification, and breaking apart around the edges.

Sound made visible, comprehensible, when Aunt Celia's words were not.

Of course, Aunt Celia couldn't be mother and father. Her real name was Cecelia Jean Falcon, and she'd been what James' father called, "the spinster aunt." Aunt Celia had owned a sprawling mansion on ten acres up in Westchester County where she entertained, rubbed elbows with the elite, and had accrued a rather scandalous reputation concerning married men.

Mother and father were dead.

"I was eight when they died," Falcon told himself.

"They're gone," Aunt Celia confirmed, that familiar acidic anger in her voice.

"I know that," he cried.

"I'm all that you and your sister have left."

His sister. He wondered whatever had happened to Julia. Why he hadn't kept up with his little sister's life. Julia would be twenty-seven. She'd been a doctoral candidate at Columbia. Probability suggested that they would have hooded her by now. Julia had always been smart.

"Smarter than you, you weak piece of shit," Rudy Noyes told him in a smarmy voice.

The sine waves fractured on the back of Falcon's eyelids.

Rudy? When had he come? Falcon opened his eyes, glancing across the small room to where Rudy leaned against the wall. Posture insolent, Rudy wore a scuffed brown bomber jacket, had his arms crossed. In his long fingers, a switchblade knife clicked and flashed every time Rudy flipped it open and closed. A glittering of amusement lay behind his derisive stare.

Rudy's not here. He's a hallucination. Not real. Just part of my dissociative psychosis.

"Go away."

"You'd like that, wouldn't you, you little pussy." Rudy artfully twirled his knife around his fingers as he lifted his other hand to push long black hair over his ears. "Somebody's gotta tell you what a spineless shit you are."

"I'm not!"

"Wussy pussy, wussy pussy," Rudy repeated in a singsongy voice. "Falcon is a wussy pussy."

"Am not."

Rudy gave him a devilish grin. "Then why are you still locked in this room? No wonder you can't get laid. You couldn't pay a whore enough to pop your cherry, you spineless little turd."

With that, Rudy flipped him the bird, turned, and swaggered off toward the bathroom.

Falcon clamped his eyes shut, aware of the fragments of Aunt Celia's voice as they echoed hollowly in the darkness around him.

Cecelia Falcon had tried. She'd ensured he received the best private education, finishing his high school years at the all-male Salisbury School in Connecticut. She'd bought him a Jaguar XK on his sixteenth birthday, figuring the sleek car would ensure he was popular. Not only did he remain a misfit, but it also backfired. The other boys considered him even more pathetic and spoiled. She would have paid for his university if MIT hadn't offered Falcon a full scholarship to study math, theoretical physics, game theory, and complicated systems theory.

Falcon had been at MIT when the major first walked into his life.

"And a damned good thing I did."

Falcon's eyes snapped open at the authoritative voice. Major Bradley Kevin Marks sat in Falcon's worn easy chair where it rested in the corner. Marks, as always, wore his dress uniform; the creases looked sharp enough to cut a finger. The colorful campaign ribbons on the jacket's right breast dazzled in the light. Falcon could see the room reflected from the mirrorlike polish on those black shoes.

"Noyes? What a two-footed maggot," Major Marks muttered, squinting with his steely gray eyes. "I'd flush him down a toilet, and then I'd apologize to the sewer for the offense."

Major Marks looked to be in his fifties, tall, his silver hair short-cropped. A career officer, Marks reminded Falcon of a bulldog—and it wasn't just the man's strong jaw. But then, the major had seen it all.

"He called me a wussy pussy." Falcon placed a hand over his eyes as he leaned his head back into his pillow. He didn't want to see the acoustical panels overhead, let alone think of the little tennis-ball–sized camera up in the ceiling that monitored his every move. Like a gleaming black orb—maybe an oversized spider's eye—the thing had an eerie presence. A constant reminder that no matter how inviolate his room, he was still linked to the outside world.

It waited . . . just beyond the door.

"And all you have to do—" Major Marks' voice inserted itself into Falcon's thoughts, "—is get up, walk over, and turn the knob."

"I . . . can't."

"I expect better of you, soldier."

"You didn't see those eyes. Black pupils like pinpricks, ringed in pale blue like some washed-out ocean, and the whites so wide and scary."

"He was just a cop, Falcon. He's gone."

"Can't hurt me. Not while I'm here. Safe. In my room."

"In your prison." Marks' voice had no give as he looked around the small room. "That's the crying shame. You realize, of course, that you are doing this to yourself. The washed-out looking white guy with the pale hair and those watery-blue eyes? That was Special Agent Hanson Childs, Army CID. Him and all those MPs, sure, they wanted you locked away." Marks raised his hands to emphasize the room. "And you did it for them."

"I'm not going out that door," Falcon insisted, experiencing the first tingles of fear. "Those eyes are out there. Black dots of pupils in washed-out blue. Pain is out there. People dying. Suffering . . . and I don't want to hurt. Not anymore."

"People out there are depending on you, and you damned well know it."

Falcon rubbed his throat, fought the tightening. Like it was getting hard to breathe. Panic. It started to build. He could feel the thoughts as if they were physical things as they started to loop in his head.

Aunt Celia was shouting in that piercing voice: *"Jimmy, you are such a disappointment. I require the bare minimum of you. I cannot be the mother and father you lost. I ask so little, yet even that seems to be beyond your most facile ability to perform!"*

Falcon swallowed. "I'm sorry. My fault."

"Yes. It is . . ." Aunt Celia leaned over the polished table. Behind her, the tall grandfather clock from Germany tick-tocked in its carved cabinet. The flowered wallpaper seemed to ebb and flow at the periphery of Falcon's vision. He could feel little Julia's wide-eyed gaze where she cowered in the dining room doorway behind him.

"Jimmy, you are such a disappointment," Aunt Celia's voice started over. *"I require the bare minimum of you. I cannot be the mother and father . . ."*

The loop started its endless repeat.

As Falcon fell into the well of self-disgust, a faint voice could be heard from beyond the locked door.

"Falcon? Can you hear me? We're trying something different. A new drug."

The sound of the voice reassured him. That was Cat Talavera. Just hearing her was a relief. Then Aunt Celia's voice drowned it, declaring, *"Jimmy, you are such a disappointment. I require . . ."*

Like falling into a black pit, Falcon wanted to weep.

9

Cat

The most thoroughly monitored patient in Grantham's Ward Six was Captain James Hancock Falcon. Cat Talavera considered that as she tapped the syringe, then squeezed out the little air bubble to get precisely 1.5 ccs of her latest antipsychotic cocktail.

Cat had grown up as a DACA kid, brought to the USA at the age of six by her parents when they'd fled Acapulco. She'd excelled at school, earned a full-ride scholarship to Stanford, completed her bachelor's in two-and-a-half years, and earned a PhD in biochemistry, followed by a *second* PhD in genetics by the grand old age of twenty-nine.

When she'd discovered that her research had been used as a clandestine biological weapon to wipe out an entire village in Afghanistan, she'd tried to expose the operation; she'd emailed her research to the *New York Times*. And, distraught, she'd attempted suicide on the Capitol steps. She hadn't anticipated that NSA would intercept the email, or that the Capitol steps were so closely monitored with an EMT only minutes away. All of which had landed her in the military psychiatric hospital at Grantham Barracks.

Cat stood beside Falcon's bed, aware of the monitors that recorded his heartrate, blood pressure, oxygen saturation, and the helmetlike sensors on his head that measured brain activity. Lit by fluorescent lights, the room couldn't have been mistaken for anything but a hospital. The presence of Nurse Virginia Seymore in her scrubs only added to the effect. Now the woman crossed her arms, asking, "Think that will do it?"

"Let's hope," Cat answered. "The last formula elevated Falcon's dopamine levels while slowing activity in the limbic system. If I can just dampen Falcon's peculiar ring of fire."

"What's that?" ET asked where he leaned in the doorway.

"The ring of fire," Seymore told him. "It's a term used by psychiatric professionals to describe the ring of mental activity when most of the brain is active. Usually associated with attention deficit disorders. Like the whole brain is turned on without any ability to organize itself, all the areas are screaming at once. But Falcon's is different, unique to his disorder. Not so much a ring, it's more like a fountain emitting from the amygdala."

"Falcon has a pattern of brain areas that keep repeating," Cat explained as she slipped the needle into Falcon's IV and injected it. "Falcon is special and rare. His brain is organized differently. That's why tailoring a pharmacology for him is so hard. This latest one? I'm trying to inhibit the D_2 receptors in specific parts of his brain. Target it at the base of the fountain, if you will. If I can shut off the looping at the source, maybe he'll be able to break the compulsive repeats."

"He's a schizophrenic," ET interjected.

"More than that," Cat told him as she dropped the needle into the sharps container. "He's dissociative *and* schizophrenic. He hallucinates people, like Rudy Noyes, that Major Marks of his, and Theresa Applegate. But they're his alter egos, creations by the dissociative part of his personality. They appear to him as real as you and I do."

"Yeah. I know." ET rubbed his long skinny arms. "But what make him so damn smart?"

"It's how the neurons and pathways are organized, how they make connections. At the cellular level, Falcon's brain is patterned in a way that the brains in normal people are not. He puts information together in a unique way. We see it as intuitive, but it's just a different cognitive process."

"Comes at a price," Seymore said as she reinserted Falcon's IV. "Falcon might be brilliant, but until those agents put him into a catatonic state, the poor man lived in constant insecurity and paranoia. Only place he ever felt safe was in his room."

Cat stared thoughtfully down at Falcon. Medium-brown hair, five-foot-six, bland features, common physique. On the street nothing would have set James Falcon apart from the crowd. From the looks of him, he was the middle of the bell-shape curve white male.

But he was the brain who came within a whisker of stopping Alpha.

Wasn't Falcon's fault that the woman had managed to start her time device and skip away to the future.

ET considered the monitor where it displayed Falcon's brain. "I don't get it. Why's he still locked away? Thought catatonia was easy to treat."

Cat crossed her arms. "Normally, it is. Usually, it responds to a benzodiazepine protocol. That's part of the psychotropic cocktail we're using. In addition to his usual mirtazapine, I started with an intramuscular two milligram lorazepam injection. Usually that works within hours."

"Hey, we been at this for weeks."

Cat squinted. Fingered her chin. "That's why I've been trying to tailor a different drug cocktail. We're missing something."

"Like what?" ET wondered.

"Anxiety plays a role in acute catatonia. In this case, it was when Agents Hanson Childs and that *cholo* Jaime Chenwith physically assaulted Falcon. That was the psychotic break that left Falcon catatonic." Cat walked over to the image of Falcon's brain. "We know that catatonia affects these areas. This is the orbitofrontal which plays a role. And here, the prefrontal region is also involved along with the parietal and motor cortical regions."

With a flick of her fingers, Cat pulled up a sagittal section of the brain. "But when it comes to Falcon, I think the key might lie here. This is the amygdala. It's the flight-or-fight part of the brain, and it's buffered and balanced by this structure over here that's called the hippocampus. That's what I'm going to try next."

"Why not just up his meds?" ET asked.

"Dangerous," Seymore told him. "Catatonia, especially long-term acute retarded, which is what Falcon presents with, can be exacerbated. Made what we call 'malignant,' which could throw Falcon into fits that would literally burn up his body. Kill him. We're walking a delicate balance with his meds as it is."

ET stepped over, took Falcon's free hand. "Hey, you hear me? Falcon, my man, it's ET. Need you back, bro. Ain't got no one to keep me talking good. You don't come back, I gonna quit readin' them Shakespeare plays. Den wachuu gonna do, huh?"

Cat lifted an eyebrow at the retreat to street slang. ET was doing it on purpose, of course, hoping it would get a rise out of Falcon. When she looked up, it was to see the love in ET's eyes. That was the thing about ET; he might have come up the hard way, a poor black kid from a broken home in a trashed Detroit neighborhood. He'd never known his father's name. Could have been any of a parade of men who passed through his mother's life. ET had muled drugs, stolen, run rackets and scams, but down in his heart he was one of the most caring people she'd ever known.

ET sighed, letting go of Falcon's hand. "Figured, if anything, that'd bring him back. Falcon always loved to give me shit about the way I talked. I can hear him now, 'Language, Edwin, language.'"

"He always wanted more for you," Seymore told him.

Cat pinched the bridge of her nose, as if it would make her think better. "The mirtazapine isn't working anymore. This new stuff I'm trying? Without clinical trials, it makes me nervous."

"Why's that?" ET asked.

"Brains are complicated. All the years of research, the studies, and we still don't know why antipsychotics have the effect they do. We're affecting brain chemistry, but it's with a blanket effect. Soak the bloodstream with a serotonin inhibitor, an antihistamine, or something to stimulate dopamine. Then stand back and watch and wait to see what happens."

"And your new stuff—that's supposed to shut off the fountain?"

"That's the plan." Cat took a deep breath. "In the meantime, we stand back, watch, and wait." She frowned her concern. "But, ET, there's also another factor to consider. Part of it is up to Falcon. He's in there. Hearing us. Feeling everything. We may be able to treat the symptoms. But it's still up to him. Down there, deep inside, he may decide that it's just too painful out here. Too confusing and frightening."

On his bed, Falcon's eyes flickered behind their lids, his expression slack.

10

Childs

CID Special Agent Hanson Childs had that feeling of complete and total panic as he finally stepped up to the bank teller's window and produced the printout of his online banking account. For once, he was totally and completely grateful for Susan's anal habit of printing out his balance at the end of the month.

"Hey, babe," she'd always told him, "like, what if the bank gets hacked? You know, all their accounts get voided? Sent to China or something."

He'd always laughed at that. Figured that Susan was just using it as an excuse to keep an eye on his finances to ensure he wasn't fooling around. And sure, it wasn't like his job didn't have him on the road, working weird hours. As a field agent for the United States Army Criminal Investigation Division, he went when, where, and for however long they sent him. Susan was just high maintenance that way. She'd been cheated on too many times in the past.

Okay, she was high maintenance in other ways, too. Maybe that was another reason she kept an eye on his bank account. She wanted to be sure that he was spending every spare cent on her. The staff in the CID office in DC liked to call her his "future trophy wife." And she was gorgeous, all five-foot four inches of her, with sun-kissed blonde hair that fell to her butt, and the kind of body that . . .

"Can I help you?" the teller asked.

Hanson reached into his jacket pocket to produce his last month's printout. "Yeah, I got a problem. This is my account number. And here's last month's balance. Something's wrong. I've got an automatic deduction for my rent, car payment, insurance, credit cards. You know, I just pull it up and click? The program deducts it automatically? First week of the month, right? So I get into town, figure I'm going to pay my bills, and I've got nothing. Zero. That just can't be. I get paid on the first. Automatic deposit from the Department of Defense. Not to mention that I should have had a couple thousand still in the account before the deposit."

She took his printed statement, turned to her terminal, and typed in his account. Checked the account number and frowned at the screen. "Mr. Childs, I'm sorry, but you transferred the entire balance of your account to a bank in the Cayman Islands three days ago."

"I . . . *what?*"

"According to our records, you—"

"I never! Hey, I'm telling you, I was in New Mexico, and I didn't make any such transfer."

She studied him, pursed her lips, and said, "Maybe you'd better go see Mr. Halverstem. If this is a security breach or a hack, he can explain it."

Twenty minutes later, sitting in a cushy chair in Halverstem's overly air-conditioned office, Childs was told, "I'm sorry, sir. But if you didn't make that transfer, it was done with your pin, your thumbprint, and each of the three security questions was answered correctly. We'll report this to law enforcement, of course, but the bank has no liability in this matter. I'm sorry."

"But I have bills! And you people—"

"I'm *sorry!*" Halverstem leaned forward. "You're a military cop, right?"

"Army CID."

"Then you *know* how these things work."

Hanson was fully aware of how he looked when he was enraged. His pale complexion—accented by light-blue eyes and white-blond hair—turned a beet red. Not to mention his habit of puffing out his cheeks. As he stepped out into the bank's parking garage, people were looking at him askance. All he wanted to do was break things.

Somebody's going to pay!

"If it's the last thing I do . . ." He stopped, the words draining away.

The space where he'd left his baby-blue, high-performance Mustang was empty.

Hanson looked around, double-checked. Yes. Level 2, Row A, third space. He'd left the Mustang right there. A hasty check of his pocket assured him that he hadn't left the fob in the console. He thumbed the alert button, straining to hear the car's alarm system. Nothing. Just the sound of a distant Harley with loud pipes.

"What the hell?" He sprinted down to Level 1, found no Mustang. Then charged up to the roof, trotting along the rows of parked cars. No baby-blue Mustang!

Pulling his cell phone, he dialed 911, got the operator. Explained that his car was stolen, that it was a baby-blue Ford Mustang, not even a year old. That it had custom wheels and the high-performance package. He gave her the tag number.

Took fifteen minutes for a patrol car to arrive. The cop—a sympathetic Latina in her early twenties named Lopez—listened to Hanson's story, checked his CID ID, and started to take his information. She had just input the Mustang's VIN from his insurance card when her tablet chimed.

"The bank has cameras," he told her, pointing. "They'll have whoever took my car recorded on the security feed. We can—"

"Sorry, Agent Childs," Officer Lopez told him as she studied the readout on her tablet. "The VIN just cleared the system." She glanced at him, something hidden in her dark gaze. "Your car wasn't stolen. It's been repossessed."

Hanson gaped. "That's nuts. Repossessed? By who?"

"Hey, you don't make your payments, they take the car back."

"But I *made* the damn payments! Deducted right out of my . . ." He swiveled his head, staring at the glass doors that led into the bank. The bank that told him his account had been drained.

"But that just happened," he whispered. "Takes months before they'd repossess the car."

Lopez slipped her tablet into her belt. "Sorry, sir. When it comes to your car, you gotta take that up with whoever gave you the loan."

She turned back to her cruiser. "Baby-blue Mustang, custom wheels. Sounds like a nice ride. That's gotta hurt."

"Hey! I'm being scammed here!"

As she opened her door, she gave him a knowing squint. "CID, huh? You're in law enforcement. Figure it out."

Hanson stood there, fuming, trying to understand what had happened. Who would have done this to him, and why?

And then he remembered the cluster fuck in Santa Fe, how he and Jaime Chenwith had made the bust of their careers—only to have their asses handed to them at the moment of their greatest triumph. That arrogant two-star general, the escaped lunatics, and the endless nondisclosure forms he and Jaime had had to sign.

That had bothered him right down to his bones. The whole thing. Swept under the rug in the name of national security. Trouble was, he'd signed the damned forms. Hell, he'd run down and arrested people who'd ignored the warnings on nondisclosures they'd signed regarding national security.

But why would the government turn on him? He had kept his mouth shut. Welded. Never even hinted what he'd been doing in Colorado, let alone that he'd had anything to do with the mess at Aspen, Grantham Barracks, or Santa Fe.

With a sigh, he lifted his cell phone. Punched in Susan's number. Went straight to voice mail. "Hey, babe. I'm at the bank. I need you to come pick me up. You wouldn't believe the day I'm having."

That's when he realized that somewhere in the middle of the call, his phone had gone dead.

11

ET

Edwin Tyler Jones wasn't sure he liked all the changes to Ward Six, but the fact that they now had metal silverware and hard-plastic plates in the cafeteria was a definite improvement. Back in the old days, when the ward was full of people like Bubbles Meyer and some of the really psycho nutcases, all they got were paper plates, soft squishy forks, and knives that wouldn't spread warm butter without bending double. Making the transition hadn't been easy. It had taken Chief Raven going to the Skipper with the argument that if Team Psi was entrusted with firearms, billion-dollar helicopters, and the rest of the tactical gear, surely they could manage real plates and stainless-steel eating utensils.

That was the thing about Grantham: Sometimes old habits died hard.

ET was contemplating this as he cheerfully chopped his green beans into mouth-sized lengths with the still-not-very-sharp-but-at-least-unbendable dinner knife from the serving line.

He gave Catalina Talavera a wink as she carried her tray toward him. Seating herself, she studied her plate, and said, "I really miss being on the outside. For those few weeks I got used to food with taste."

ET swallowed down a bite of green beans. "And this is the good cook. Remember the one we had before Chief Raven bitched to the Skipper?" He grinned at her. "But, yeah, I coulda got used to eating at the St. Regis up in Aspen. Never had food like that in my whole life. When I's a kid? What it tasted like didn't matter. Just hope they was enough to keep the belly pains away. And you can forget a full stomach. Never had one of those till I run off with the Brothers. And then it was McDonald's, which I thought was the finest food in all the world."

She gave him that dark-eyed look, the one that tried to see all the way down into the bottom of him. "That worries me sometimes. Like,

I don't know who you really are, ET. Sometimes I don't know if you do, either."

Once he'd have "played 'er with the shit" as the Brothers would have said. That was always the safe way, the accepted way. On the street, especially with the Brothers, it was all about "puttin' on the tough." Gotta be what's expected of you. Only time to act soft with a woman was as a scam to get something from her.

But his time in Grantham had changed him. As if living for two years as a patient in a mental hospital wouldn't. First, it was being surrounded by some of the cases who flat-out told the truth no matter how blunt and pain-causing it might be. Second, was the Skipper and the therapists who had forced him to deal with himself. Third, was Falcon, the dissociative schizophrenic who had seen past the tough to become ET's friend.

Explain that back on the mean streets? The Brothers would have thought it was a joke, and then they'd have broken his neck and tossed his skinny black ass into the nearest dumpster to be compacted with the rest of the garbage.

He smiled at that. Glanced at Cat. "I been a lot of things. Falcon said I was a lizard. Some kinda animal that changed colors depending on the background."

"A chameleon?"

"That's it. That's how a child stays alive where I grew up. Times I had to disappear, 'cause to be seen, that was a sure way to get jacked. Probably why I turned to that computer they give me. No one pays attention to a kid if he's over in the corner clicking keys on a computer. He gets noticed? He gets picked for sex, or beating, or doing other people's trash. Wasn't till they figured out I had talent that they paid me any mind. Meant I had to change my spots, take on a different me. So I became a computer whiz. Had to learn the talk, how to make the machine work. Get stuff done. And when I told them if I could go take classes, get better at it, they made sure I went."

"Yeah, for crime."

"Cat, you gotta understand, I could do what they wanted with a computer . . . or with a gun. Which one's safer for me and everyone else? What matters was getting so good that I was valuable. Being valuable meant I was guarded, got things I wanted, like a clean place to sleep, locks on my doors, no rats running around all night long." He paused. "Kids that don't have value? They get told, 'Be my bitch' 'Go rob that store' 'Beat that guy up' 'Steal that jewelry.' They got no choice. Just do it. And if they get caught, ain't no sweat for the Brothers when they go down. There's always another kid."

"Never thought of it that way."

"People don't. Taught me early on that the only way I was gonna stay alive was to be smarter than everybody else."

"But Edwin Tyler Jones isn't even your real name. You made it up."

"Had to if I was gonna enlist." He paused. Remembering. Turned his attention back to her. "I love you, Cat. Saying that, I'm never telling you who that kid in Detroit was. What his name was. He's gone. Vanished in the past. You ask who I am? I'm Edwin Tyler Jones, and I'm someone wholly different from that kid."

"You sure about that? People are the sum total of their experiences, and there are parts of personality and behavior that become hardwired. This chameleon you claim to be? How do I know that's not just now, and you'll change again?"

He lifted her hand where it lay on the table, pointed to the scars on her wrists. "You still the pissed-off outraged spoiled little brat who cut her wrists on the Capitol steps 'cause her research was used to wipe out a whole village?"

She glanced away, pursed her lips, and shook her head.

ET chased the last of his Salisbury steak across his plate with what remained of his bread and sopped up the juice. Swallowing it down, he told her, "Stuff we go through, it changes people. Can't undo what you done in the past. That just is. What you can do, assuming you're not crazy like some of these people in Grantham, is learn what you done wrong and make yourself do better."

Her level stare was back, as if firmed up by something inside. "Heard you were on the computers all morning. Simond said you were gleeful about 'sticking it to the bastard.'"

ET speared the last of the Salisbury steak, chewed, and swallowed. "How's Falcon today?"

"No change." She arched a delicate eyebrow. "So, who are you 'sticking it to'?"

"Remember what they did to Falcon that day? How he looked in the hallway in Santa Fe? How they manhandled him, kept shouting in his face? Anyone with a single ounce of pity in their souls woulda known he was in trouble. And it ain't like we all wasn't telling them. The skipper, the chief, all of us. Them agents, they took him in that room and terrified him. You heard the slap."

"I could have killed them."

"Now, that's my Cat." He gave her another wink. "That old horseshit stuff about revenge is a dish better served cold? Maybe those two agents, Childs and Chenwith? Maybe they figure they walked, what with the NDAs they signed and all. What they did to Falcon wasn't just uncalled for, it was cruel. They're the kind of guys who'd have laughed while they turned on the gas at Auschwitz."

"What did you do?" Cat's fork stopped halfway to her mouth.

"Best way to stop someone from tormenting other people? I make it so they're so busy trying to put their lives together, they can't get their happy high from making other folks suffer."

"Tell me you didn't order them killed."

"Nope. Just adjusted their finances. The nice thing about a person's credit history? Once you make it disappear, they can't never get it back again."

12

Childs

The Rusty Bucket Tavern and Stone Fired Pizza had been a tried-and-true retreat for the Washington district CID. The bar was well stocked, the taps carried local microbrews, the food was good and reasonably priced. The place was just loud enough that shop talk didn't carry, but agents could still hear each other over the din. The décor was dark barn wood, burnished copper, and polished brass with comfortable rustic-leather chairs.

Where they sat at a table in the rear, Hanson Childs leaned forward and asked his friend and superior, Captain LeRoy Holloman, "Am I being tested?"

"I'd say so," Holloman told him, an eye squinted over his beer. "It's like you've vanished from the face of the earth. Your bank accounts, your car, your phone, evicted from your apartment, all your credit cards don't exist, I've never seen or heard the like. If God was picking a new Job, I'd say you were it. That what you've done, Hands? Pissed off God?"

Hands. He'd gotten the nickname as a shortened version of Hanson back in his high school football days. As a wide receiver, he'd set school records for catching footballs.

"Cap, I mean am I being tested over Santa Fe? What happened there? That whole investigation? Because if I am, I've never spilled a word. Or is that what they're trying to find out? See if I'll start asking questions? Demanding answers."

"Hands, all I can tell you is that I don't know squat. Whatever happened out west, I got it from on high that you were never there and your record would be altered to reflect that fact. So, if I were you, I'd keep every bean in the pot locked down."

"As if I'd ever spill them." Hanson rubbed his face, peered into the mirror behind the bar to see his pale blond hair gleaming in the lights, his light-blue eyes looking haggard. Was that really him?

I've lost everything. Overnight. Vanished.

How the hell did that happen? And when he'd used Cap's phone to trace down the problem, no one could even find the records. Like they'd been erased. And it was impossible stuff, like the fact that according to his loan officer, no payments had been made for six months since he'd signed the papers for the Mustang, when, damn it, he'd deducted them right along. Same with his apartment. The computer had him listed as five months in delinquency. Sam, at the desk, said that he knew it had to be a mistake, but the corporation in Florida that owned the complex insisted they had no record of any rent payments. Hanson Childs had to go.

For three days now, all Hanson had done was try to piece his life together. He just knew it had to go back to Santa Fe.

He took a deep breath, feeling sick. If Cap hadn't offered him a couch, let him keep a few things, Hanson would have been on the street. Susan's leaving had been the worst part. She'd refused to believe that the account on his computer wasn't a fake that he'd put there as a means to keep her in the dark. That he'd been playing the stock market, paying blackmail, or up to his eyebrows in some other form of malfeasance.

"Is that all the better you know me?" he'd demanded.

"I only know you as a tough cop," she'd shot back. "And now I find out you're either an incompetent one. Or corrupt. Or both!" And then she'd stomped out the door. Was refusing to answer any call when she didn't recognize the number. He'd been reduced to the level of pleading on her voicemail.

"NSA could do this," Cap noted after sipping his beer. "I mean it's, like, across the board. Your bank, your car loan, phone account, the credit cards, rent, that's a lot of places. Not just some simple computer hack."

"And don't forget my credit rating score. It's gone. No record of me. Who has the power to do that?"

"Hands, tell me straight: You sure you're not into something? Drugs? Payoffs? Some security breach? That this isn't more than just some black-on-black operation you stumbled into out west?"

"I swear, Cap. I've been by the book."

"The old saying was, 'Once Hands gets a grip, he never lets go.' You didn't let your emotions override your good sense?"

"How'd I get picked for Colorado? Why'd you send me?"

Cap chewed his lips, glanced around, and lowered his voice. "They said they wanted someone who'd get results fast. That they had a situation that needed to be cleaned up, and they didn't care how it got done. Oh, and that the SA had to be able to work with a partner. You fit the bill."

"Wonder if Jaime Chenwith's having the same shit pulled on him?"

"You tried calling him?"

"Can't. I'm under orders not to. The words were 'under no circumstances.'"

"I don't know what to tell you."

"Cap, my fucking life's been stolen," he roared louder than he should have. Fought to keep his heart from hammering through his breastbone. Fist clenched, he fought tears. Nothing made sense. He was a sergeant/ E-7 in the CID. One of their best, and he couldn't come up with a single lead when it came to figuring out who'd erased his identity.

"At least your check will come to my place on the first. Just be glad they still mail."

Hanson had managed to get that cleared up. But it was most of the month away. He had thirty-four dollars and fifty-five cents to his name.

Cap had said he'd cover him, let him have the couch. But after that? Base housing, for sure. Thank God he was in the army.

He noticed when the two men, dressed in suits, entered the front. Knew they were agents. Wouldn't have paid them the slightest attention. It was that kind of bar, after all. But when another two stepped in from the back entrance where it opened out into the alley, that changed the equation.

As they approached the table, Hanson's heart felt more and more like a lump of lead. This couldn't be happening. But it was.

"Captain Holloman," the first agent—a tall guy in his forties—said. "My apologies, sir." To Hanson he said, "Special Agent Hanson Childs, would you please come with us? We have some issues we'd like to discuss with you."

"I didn't do anything," Hanson whispered, feeling defeated as he slipped off the stool and started for the door. The agents fell in around him in a diamond. Just like they'd do when escorting a prisoner out of a room and they didn't want a scene.

Chancing a last glance over his shoulder, it was to see Cap looking desolate and shaking his head in disappointment.

13

Childs

For Hanson Childs, the trip seemed instantaneous and at the same time interminable. He was wedged in the back seat of a nondescript government Chevrolet Tahoe as it wound through DC streets. An agent sat on either side, keeping him sandwiched. As he would have done in their position, neither spoke so much as a word. That was standard procedure. And Hanson knew enough not to ask questions. These guys—even if they knew—weren't going to tell him squat. It was all part of the game, designed to make him uncomfortable, insecure, afraid, and compliant.

It was working.

His anxiety pegged the needle when they crossed the I-495 bridge into Alexandria, took the Patrick Street exit, and then a right on Pendleton. Several blocks later, the Tahoe turned into an alley. As the Tahoe made its way past dumpsters, Hanson tried to swallow. Couldn't. The effect was like a knotted sock stuck in his throat.

The vehicle pulled to a stop; the rear of a commercial building was illuminated by a cone of security light. In a dirty, whitewashed brick wall, a brown steel door and barred windows faced the alley.

"We're here," the driver announced needlessly as he propped his hands on the wheel.

The guy to Hanson's right opened the door, stepped out, and gestured. "Please don't make this difficult. You know the drill."

Hanson considered his odds, figured he might be able to take them both before the driver could get out. Then it hit him that he didn't have a single clue about what was going on. And what the hell was he going to get by running? One thing was sure; he needed some kind of answers to find a way out of this mess.

"I'm offering no resistance," he told the man. "Let's get this over with."

The two agents escorted him to the door. It opened as they approached, the man inside having monitored their arrival.

Hanson was led down a dingy hallway, then right into a crummy little office. He might have stepped into a Raymond Chandler novel: The place looked like it was last used in the 1930s. A battered wooden desk stood in the middle, ancient metal file cabinets and shelves crammed with yellowed papers to the right. An electric fan with a frayed cord perched on a credenza. The walls were covered with cheap wood-veneer paneling beneath stained acoustical ceiling panels. A single incandescent light illuminated the room.

Behind the desk, in an oak swivel chair, sat a tall man in a very expensive suit. The guy had silvering hair, a patrician face, and confident gray eyes. A cup of coffee was cradled in the man's right hand.

Something about him . . . Hanson couldn't quite place the guy.

To the officers, the suit said, "That will be sufficient. Thank you, gentlemen. If you'll wait out back, I'll let you know when I need you."

The two agents nodded and left without a word. The third guy, the door man, took a position just outside in the hallway, hands held before him.

"Staff Sergeant and Special Agent Hanson Childs," the suit told him. "I hear that your life has taken a severe turn for the worse in the last week."

That prickle of unease ran down Hanson's back. "You know anything about that? You behind it? Got a reason for ruining my life? 'Cause if you do, you're gonna find yourself in a whole world of—"

"Whoa! Easy there." The suit held up a cautioning hand. "Down, Sergeant. It's not me. Just the opposite, I'm on your side. I'm your way out of this mess."

"Why do I think I know you?"

"Name's Bill Stevens. I work for the president."

Holy shit. That was it. Stevens. The president's chief of staff. Some called him the most powerful man on the planet. The chill running down Hanson's back turned a couple of degrees colder. He swallowed, voice wavering. "What the hell am I doing here, sir?"

Stevens waved to one of the rickety chairs along the wall. "Have a seat, Sergeant. Want a cup of coffee?" He glanced up. "Mack, could you bring the sergeant a cup?"

As the man at the door departed, Stevens added, "I'm afraid it's not Starbucks, but it's better than nothing." Then, "Seriously, sit."

Hanson lowered himself to the closest chair, wary eyes on Stevens. "The president's chief of staff doesn't set up meetings in old buildings with a down-and-out CID agent. My guess is that you're a look-alike? An actor? Is that what this is all about? Some kind of setup? A way to play me? 'Cause I don't buy this for a minute."

"You're not being played, Sergeant. You're caught in the middle of a power struggle that could remake the planet. Which is why I'm skulking around Alexandria when I ought to be riding herd on Ben Masters. Since he was elected president, he's become something of a handful."

Mack reentered, handing Hanson a Styrofoam cup of coffee and stating, "Second car's just pulled up. I'll go let him in."

"Thanks, Mack."

"Him?" Hanson asked as Mack vanished down the hall.

"Yeah, well, you're not the only one to suffer the slings and arrows of outrageous fortune."

Down the hall, the door could be heard as it slammed. Moments later, Jaime Chenwith strode in, the expression on his face one of anger, frustration, and incipient violence. He stopped short, taking in first Stevens, and then Hanson. Quick thoughts played behind his dark eyes, then a faint smile bent his lips. "Hey, amigo. This shit just gets better and better."

"Yeah, well, my life's not turning out so well."

"Mine, either," Jaime muttered. Turning to Stevens, he did a double take, gave a slight shake of the head. "This ain't happening, man. Uh, I mean, sir."

"Take a seat, Master Sergeant. And, yes, it's happening. First, I want you to know that neither I nor any of my people are behind your recent misfortunes. And before you ask who is . . . well, we're still working on that little problem. Our search for the hacker who cleaned out your accounts dead-ended in Belarus with a two-bit scammer who doesn't have the necessary skills. Our guess? He's just a cutout."

"What the hell is going on?" Jaime asked, stepping forward. "My bank accounts, my credit rating, my mortgage? It's, like, all fucked." He swallowed. "Apologies for the language, sir."

"Not a problem. Couldn't have said it better myself. Have a seat, Sergeant. Mack, another cup of coffee."

As Jaime seated himself uncertainly, Hanson asked, "You, too, huh? Everything I had went away. Funds, phone, apartment, even my beautiful blue Mustang. Susan beat feet. I'm sleeping on a friend's couch, for God's sake."

"'Bout the same with me." Jaime slitted an eye. "It's like a fucking apocalypse."

Mack appeared with coffee, stepped back out the door.

Stevens gestured at the room. "Sorry for the cloak and dagger, but this is about the safest place I could come up with on short notice. No chance that anyone could listen in, present or past. Mack got the key from a real estate agent this afternoon. Nothing electronic on any of us. We can talk."

The chill intensified in Hanson's spine. "You want to tell us what's going on, sir?"

"Yeah, and here's how it fits together: You two were chosen to go after the people who raided the Skientia mansion in Aspen. Discern who was behind that little charade. Bring them to justice, especially given that it involved stolen government aircraft, a rather messy shootout, a media circus, and lot of unwanted attention."

"Yes, sir. But the rest is a matter of national security." Jaime glanced at Hanson, wet his lips. "You'll have to go through channels for the details, sir."

"Gentlemen, I'm well aware of what Grazier did to you in New Mexico. It's no secret that I'm the president's right-hand man. I've got every security clearance on the books." Stevens reached down, handed them each an envelope. "Those are orders, signed by the Chairman of the Joint Chiefs of Staff reassigning you and authorizing you to cooperate with my investigation." A pause. "You may take a moment to read through and absolve yourselves of any reservations you may be feeling."

Hanson tightened his gut muscles against the runny feeling inside, scanned the lines, checked the signatures. Figured that—hell, yeah—they must be genuine. He glanced at Jaime, seeing the man's unease. They both shrugged in unison.

"What went down out there?" Stevens asked softly. "The short version, please."

"Yeah, well, the fingerprints in the stolen Forest Service chopper got us a hit on a Major Winchester Wesson Swink," Jaime told him. "Prints off a discarded MP-5 magazine at the Skientia mansion matched those of a Chief Petty Officer Karla Raven. Both were supposed to be institutionalized at Grantham Barracks, a military psychiatric hospital outside Colorado Springs. A bunch of local burglaries led us to a room at the St. Regis in Aspen where we picked up additional evidence implicating Dr. Timothy Ryan and more of his patients."

Hanson added, "Grantham Barracks was a bust. None of the patients implicated were on the premises. A tip took us to Los Alamos, where, unsurprisingly, Skientia had one of its labs. By the time we arrived, the action had already gone down. It was like a war zone. Six dead, four critically wounded. From there, we tracked the suspects to the Buffalo Thunder Resort, called for backup, and placed them all under arrest."

Jaime leaned forward, eyes glittering. "That's when General Grazier walked in and pulled the rug out from under us. Said everything that had happened was classified. Had us sign a slew of nondisclosure agreements. Told us to hit the road."

"And what did you do?" Stevens asked.

"We followed orders, sir." Hanson stiffened in defiance. "That's what we do. Down to the letter. I never, ever, so much as breathed a word of what went down out west. So, if wrecking my credit, confiscating my money, and fucking me over is some kind of punishment or test, I pass. Whatever this is about, I didn't deserve it."

"Me, either," Jaime muttered.

"Like I said, I don't know who's behind your recent misfortunes." Stevens studied them, seemed to like what he was seeing. "You really believe that a bunch of escaped lunatics pulled this off?"

"Do you, sir?"

"Not a chance in hell. The prints on that magazine? The Forest Service helicopter? It's to mislead us. Perfectly played, I might add. Of course, it was crazy. We're to believe escaped nuts from an insane asylum orchestrated the whole op? I call it a perfectly played diversion with Raven, Swink, and the rest nothing more than ready-made fall guys."

Stevens waved a chiding finger back and forth as if in negation. "My call? Grazier has a top spec ops team hidden away somewhere. But, damn it, try as I might, and even with the strings I've been pulling in the Defense Department, I can't figure out who the hell they are. They're not private sector. If they were foreign, Israeli, French, maybe Brits, we'd have some clue." He studied them. "You were there, face-to-face with Grazier's psychos. What did you think?"

Jaime grinned. "Batch of whackos, sir. Half of them were in tears."

"Like I thought. They were a diversion to keep the heat off the real operators." Stevens paused. "Very well, gentlemen. Want to find out what's going on? Get your lives back? If you're in, I can have you placed on special assignment. Classified. You would report only to me and my team leader."

Hanson Childs felt the hammer slamming down, crushing anything like a normal life. This was "deep state" Washington. Where the real power lurked. And Stevens was a major player. Childs could feel the jaws closing around him. "Become a pawn in the game?" he asked softly, heart thudding.

Jaime sucked down a draft of his coffee, worried eyes fixed on Stevens.

Stevens slipped two sets of papers across the battered desk. "These are documents outlining your duties, mission, and privileges, along with a presidential authorization. What they used to call a 'get out of jail free' card. In short, as long as you follow orders, you're untouchable. It's payback. All it takes is a signature."

Hanson finished off his coffee and set the cup to the side. Taking the papers, he read through the legalese, squinted at the president's notorious zigzag signature.

"What do you think?" Jaime asked him, voice husky.

Despite the little voice in the back of his mind that shouted *Don't do it!,* Hanson asked, "Sir? What's this really all about?"

Stevens nodded slightly, as if pleased that Hanson had hesitated. "What you were part of in Colorado and New Mexico? Those were the opening shots in a campaign that will decide the future. I don't mean what the future might bring. Oh, no. I mean that whoever prevails, he or she will actually control the future. That's what the research at Skientia was all about."

Still, Hanson hesitated, could see the disbelief in Jaime's expression and posture.

"Hey," Stevens added, "I know it sounds crazy, but in Santa Fe, Eli Grazier jerked your shorts up tight and past your ears. For the moment, he thinks he's got me by the balls. My bet is that he's behind your latest problems. Sign those papers, and you not only get an expense account with a suite at the Mayflower until you're activated, but you get your chance to hunt down Eli Grazier and the culprits that caused all that mayhem in the Rockies."

Hanson took the offered pen and signed.

14

Ryan

I considered the Capresso machine to be one of my greatest triumphs in the post–Santa Fe days. I'd placed the requisition in with all the other equipment that my team had requested. After Eli waved his magic funding wand, the American taxpayer—and who knew how many future generations—picked up the bill.

Karla's trick SEAL equipment, ET's computers, Cat's biochem lab, all totaled up to a wince-inducing sum, but the price tag for Winny's new helicopter, not to mention the aircraft she could co-opt on a moment's notice, left me speechless.

What the Capresso machine cost wasn't more than the equivalent of a subatomic particle in the universe of Ward Six's new budget.

I knew better than to ask Eli, who oversaw funding for all this. Plus, when you think about it, the notion that we were now the first line of defense against inter-dimensional raiders was sobering. The reality that Alpha and Fluvium had appeared in our past, were using our branch of the timeline to conduct bioweapons experiments on a global scale, went beyond anything Mengele could have contemplated during his most devious days at Auschwitz.

Imagine it if you will: You want to test a vaccine against a particularly vicious strain of smallpox that you've cooked up in a lab. Pick an alternate branch of the timeline, pop into their past, inoculate the population, and release your insidious plague. Pop back to the present in your branch and write up the notes. Pick a time a few hundred years in the study population's future and pop back in. Viola! An entire two-hundred-year epidemiological study has run its course. See who's alive and who's dead. Just record the data, take your samples, and pop back to your original branch. It's all there, an epidemiological record of evolution, morbidity, mortality, side effects, and vaccine efficacy covering two hundred years.

I had to admire the cold-blooded elegance of it. Even if it begged the question: So what if you inflicted misery, suffering, and slow and hideous death upon millions? After all, it wasn't your world, just an alternate branch somewhere in Hilbert space.

Did that make the suffering, death, and horror any less morally offensive?

Those thoughts were rolling through my head as I cradled my cup of fresh-brewed foam-topped Capresso coffee and walked through the gleaming halls to Harvey Rogers' lab. It was once a suite of rooms where we kept the worst of the OCD patients. After knocking out a couple of walls, pouring concrete into forms over an insane amount of rebar woven into lattice and adding a three-hundred–pound security door, we had a place to safeguard Fluvium's cerebrum, the brain that calculated the N-dimensional pathways that allowed the navigator to find its way between the infinite branches of timeline.

The navigator, of course, was still somewhere in the future with Alpha. Eli's plan was to grab it and Alpha the moment they popped back into the present. Eli considered keeping the two pieces of alien equipment in any kind of proximity to Alpha would be a security risk of the highest sort. So, while research proceeded at Los Alamos, Harvey ran his own analysis of the top-secret cerebrum here at Grantham.

The door was open, voices audible as I approached and called, "Anyone home?"

"Just us mice," Rogers called back.

I stepped in to find Harvey Rogers perched with his butt on the corner of his desk. In the swivel chair he reserved for visitors, Sam Savage reclined with his muscular legs crossed. Didn't matter that the guy was dressed in Dockers, a button-down shirt, and loafers, he still looked like he'd just stepped off the reservation. But meet those quick black eyes and any doubt vanished about the man's West Point education—he'd finished first in his class—or the PhD in indigenous religious studies from Georgetown. As a specialist in covert operations, first in the army and then the CIA's clandestine forces, Savage had excelled.

Rogers was just the opposite: a beanpole of a physicist, he—and his lab—had come to us from Aberdeen Proving Ground. The guy was a stereotypic geek with bottle-bottom glasses, wore a stained lab coat, and had one of those thin and pale faces covered with a week's scraggle of patchy beard. Rogers' specialty had been in the study and analysis of communications equipment, specifically that which was being developed by our geopolitical adversaries. Two generations ago, he would have been Alan Turing's alter ego at Bletchley Park, jazzing over an Enigma machine. The difference between then and now was that Enigma could be defeated by the technology of the time. Rogers hadn't a clue as to how the N-dimensional qubit matrix for the cerebrum had been manufactured, let alone how to program it.

It frightened him.

If Harvey Rogers was frightened by a piece of technology, I was smart enough to be terrified to my roots.

"Am I disturbing anything?" I asked, coming to a stop inside the door.

Harvey had his desk and chair in the back. One wall—covered with oversized shelves—sported all kinds of electrical gizmos; the other wall consisted of solid computer, its nodes all stacked and wired together. A separate dish on the roof connected it to the cloud somewhere. The intimidating vault door dominated the imposing concrete wall. Behind it lay the lab and cerebrum. The latter resided in yet another safe.

Savage was in the cushy chair, so Harvey rolled his desk chair out and shoved it in my direction, apparently happy to keep his perch on the desk corner.

"Not a thing. Join us," Harvey told me, blinking through his thick glasses.

"Trying to get my brain to accept this Many-Worlds hypothesis," Savage explained to me, a scowl on his face.

"Theory," Harvey corrected. "We're long past hypotheses. They've all been tested extensively since Hugh Everett published his *Relative State Formulation of Quantum Mechanics* paper in 1957. The idea that the universe was constantly branching into different timelines wasn't something people like Bohr could accept at the gut level."

"That makes two of us," Savage growled. "The way you explain this, I'm splitting into identical copies of myself thousands of times a second."

Rogers reached out one of his pens. I figured he was going to draw a diagram. Instead, he just clicked the button on the end. "You've flown in an airplane at low altitude?"

"Yeah."

"Fast?"

"Double yeah."

"Then up the game. So, let's say you're riding a hypersonic missile through the Utah Canyonlands. You know, all those deep, steep-walled winding canyons that branch in all directions. You're traveling at Mach Five. The walls are flashing past in a blur as you wind through the maze of sandstone rock. At each branching canyon, you can go one way or the other. Let's say you go left. Making that choice splits you. You don't feel it. All you can see is straight ahead. Tunnel vision. The canyon rushing toward you, past you. You aren't aware that other 'yous' are racing down their own canyons, splitting. For them—like you—there is only the canyon they're in, unwinding before them. The splitting happens so fast you can't see it."

"So, it's all about perception?" I asked, sipping my coffee.

Rogers fixed on me. "You're seeing the timeline you're following because this is how it looks, how it feels when you live in a Many-Worlds universe. People thought the sun moved around the Earth for millennia because it felt like they were standing still when they looked up at the sky. It wasn't until it was proved that the Earth was moving around the sun that people understood that this was how it felt to be standing on a rotating planet moving around a stationary star."

I gestured with my coffee. "So, Harvey, how many of these branches of timelines are there?"

"Depends on how many dimensions there are in our universe. They call that Hilbert space. The number's probably big enough that you could consider it endless." He tilted his head at the locked vault. "Like that cerebrum in there, if my understanding is correct, it can make more calculations than there are particles in the universe. Maybe by a factor of ten." He clicked a staccato on his pen. "And that, Dr. Ryan, is one of the things I lie awake fretting about."

Savage threw his arms up. "All right. How does Alpha find her way through the multitude, and once she does, what lets her and this Fluvium character flit between them?"

"I don't know. Not for sure. Somehow, the navigator finds the way and the cerebrum computes the course. The interaction between the two pieces of equipment allows the field generation that carries her between branches."

"But they're separate worlds, right? Like different. As I understand it, once the separation takes place, the copies don't touch."

"Goes back to Everett," Rogers told me. "His fundamental assumption was that the universe is a single wave function. That's the tie."

I said, "Being a psychologist, I'm a little hazy on this wave function thing."

Rogers twiddled with his pen. "Wave's kind of a misnomer for the lay person. Think of it more as a cloud. The cloud can be thought of as energy vibrating in all dimensions. Where the cloud is thickest is where—if you happen to measure it at the right time—you have the highest probability of observing a particle."

"So," Savage asked, "where's the particle that's the universe?"

"It's everywhere," Rogers said, exasperated. "Here's the thing: I was trained in the Copenhagen tradition. Observation created the reality. Many-Worlds was something we scoffed at. I can still give you a dozen reasons why it doesn't work: like the law of conservation of energy, for one. I'm supposed to believe that each time the universe branches, energy is halved? And it happens, for all intents and purposes, infinitely? That means that each version of you must, under the law, contain half the energy you did prior to the split."

"I don't feel like I'm wasting away," Savage replied.

"And there's entropy," I added, delighted to toss in what little physics I might have actually known about.

"Entropy isn't really a problem," Rogers told me. "It works the same in either interpretation. Look, if you want to know all about the details, Google Hugh Everett and the Many-Worlds interpretation. Google the physicists David Deutsch and David Wallace. You can knock yourself out learning the theory, all about decoherence and entanglement. Me, I got a problem. Behind that vault door I've got a box locked away that shouldn't exist. Some lady just vanished from Lab One in a time machine, and she's got another box that shouldn't exist. The Mayanists are studying a guy who's supposedly from another timeline. All of that points to the fact that Alpha and Fluvium really did come from an alternate branch in the timeline. My problem isn't proving Many-Worlds; it's figuring out what to do about it."

"Makes you wish all those physicists hadn't spent the last century shrugging off Many-Worlds, doesn't it?"

Rogers just gave me a humorless scowl.

KA'AAK

I stare at the fire. It burns brightly in the desert night. Crackling, popping, it sends sparks and smoke dancing and twisting up into the darkness. I like using the Yucatec term, ka'aak, rather than the Latin term, fuego. Yucatec is a more descriptive language. It sees fire as something alive, more of a force of nature with magical properties.

I can make these distinctions. Being of noble blood, I can trace my ancestry back six centuries to Claudius Varinus Brutus and his marriage to K'awil K'an Tun, sister to Ahau Wak Chan, or Lord Six Sky, the ruler of Tikal. My family's history is so tightly interwoven with Ti'ahaule as to be one. Some of my relatives even rose to the rank of Ahau in the days before the Lords became immortal.

Given my understanding of history, I am fully aware of the responsibility that now lies on my shoulders. The Ultima Ahau ordered me to find Fluvium and Nakeesh. To ensure the return of their navigator and cerebrum. And, if possible, I am to run down and kill or capture the Ennoia and recover her stolen devices. I am not to rest until that task is completed.

Across the fire, Sak Puh is watching me. She has removed her helmet, letting her dark hair drape down her back. She is Yucatec, commoner-born, from a lowly agricultural lineage consisting of farmers and cacao growers. Subservient menials. She remains cowed in my presence. Wary as a forest deer forced to walk at the side of a jaguar. By whatever freak matching of genetics, she was born with a remarkable mathematical and computational ability that earned her a placement in academy. Her proficiency there garnered her a position as a novice ah tz'ib, or scribe recorder.

Given the danger of jumping timelines, she was assigned to me. For this mission. I would have preferred a higher-ranking scribe recorder, one who understood what it meant to be noble, to share lordly blood and heritage. Instead, I got Sak Puh. A simple-minded peasant with the mud of the fields still stuck between her toes.

The turbulence in her soul is reflected from her doe-large eyes. I can see it in her set of her chin, the tension in her moon-round face.

"You have questions?" I ask.

At their fire, twenty paces away, I can see the quinque glance in our direction. In the distance, a jackal howls.

"Was it really necessary?" she asks. "You destroyed an entire world."

"The world is not destroyed," I reply. "It will be there if we ever need it."

"But all those people . . ." She frowns, which does nothing for her features. "An entire planet's population . . ."

"They were a threat." I point at the cerebrum where its outline is visible in her pack. "You understand the power contained in these devices? Why we are on this mission? Nor are we the only team searching for Nakeesh and Fluvium, or for the Ennoia."

She nods, clearly disturbed. Asks, "You have done this many times before, haven't you?"

"A few," I reply.

"Have you ever gone back to a timeline you've sterilized?"

"I have."

"What was it like?"

"Rather pleasant, actually. Walking among the ruins, all you hear is birdsong."

The look she gives me in return is even more troubled. I am of the growing opinion that if she survives this mission, I will have to dismiss her with prejudice.

But then, standards have to be maintained.

15

Kaplan

Maxine Kaplan was hunched at her desk, a cold cup of coffee having sat for long enough to leave a scummy ring inside the white ceramic. She pinched the bridge of her nose as if she could force understanding into her muzzy brain. On her large Apple monitor, lines of numbers flowed in vertical columns. The data—collected by the detectors monitoring the crater in Lab One—might have been nothing more than random noise. If there was a pattern, the statistical programs couldn't pick it out.

She blinked, saw what might be a pattern begin to form . . . only to have it fade into the endlessly random assortment of numbers. Or was she just imaging things? She blocked the numbers. Tagged them. The statistical program immediately analyzed the data, declared them a chance occurrence at the .05 level of confidence.

When Kaplan and Wixom had originally installed the detectors, they'd expected to find patterns of energy, like a wake left behind in the passage of Domina Nakeesh's time travel. That they hadn't was forcing her to think about time in a different way. Nakeesh hadn't "accelerated" through time, or at least hadn't left any trace of momentum in the classical sense. Instead, the transition appeared to be instantaneous. One moment she and Tanner Jackson were there; the next they—along with the machine, most of Nakeesh's workstation, and a chunk of the floor— were gone.

Wished to hell I'd had detectors focused on that sphere when they went.

She sighed, staring around her office, packed as it was with printouts, rolls of diagrams, spreadsheets, and drawings. A giant flowchart marked in red, blue, and green took up most of the whiteboard that covered one wall. Her old stereo with its stack of CDs perched on a file cabinet in the corner.

For whatever absurd reason, the lyrics of a 60s song about time being on her mind started to play in her head. The clock on the wall flipped over to 9:37. That was PM. She'd been at the lab for almost ten hours now. Time to pack up and go home. Try and sleep while she wrestled through whatever kind of nightmares were going to finger their unsavory way through her brain.

Since the night of Nakeesh's disappearance and the raid where Bill Minor and Pete McCoy had been killed, nightmares had become a constant. Especially the image of Reid Farmer's partial body. What remained had looked as if it had been sliced off and cauterized. Grisly as that was, she lived with the knowledge that the other half of it was somewhere ahead of her in time, and she'd probably have to stare at it, horrified all over again.

Kaplan twisted her Montblanc pen closed. Flipped over the pages of notes on the yellow legal pad where it rested on the desk. She was about to rise when a soft knock came at her door.

"Yeah?"

Virgil Wixom—faded jeans visible beneath his white lab coat—stepped into her office. The lines around his weary blue eyes accented the gleam where his balding head shone in the overhead lights. Exhaustion lurked in the set of his narrow mouth. Tonight, at least, he looked a lot older than his forty-two years.

"Surprised that you're still here," he said softly. "You as frustrated as I am?"

She flicked a hand at the data streaming down the monitor. "It's just air, Virg. And it's behaving like a room-temperature gas should." A pause. "We're going to have to think about time differently."

"What's to think? Given what we now know, we can pretty much prove that the Wheeler-DeWitt equation is correct: The quantum state of the universe doesn't evolve as a function of time. If it did, Nakeesh and Fluvium could not have traveled back from their branch of the timeline to our past. When we ran that fateful entanglement experiment, we created a beacon that Nakeesh's navigator fixed on. One that brought her from 1380 BCE to the present. She didn't age, and it was perceptively instantaneous. One moment she was on the banks of the Nile in ancient Egypt, the next she was standing in Lab One."

"Time," Kaplan whispered, staring at her digital clock. "Given what Nakeesh teaches us, it can't be fundamental to the initial conditions of the universe. It's emergent. A sort of construct to allow us to explain the evolution of the universe, its variability, and the interactions of the wave function. But we take it as fundamental. It's part of the Schrödinger equation, for God's sake. So that's the conundrum. How does Nakeesh violate one of the foundations of our understanding of reality?"

Virgil gave her a wooden stare. "Maxine, we need a whole new epistemology, a new way of looking at what we accept. Amplituhedrons, de Sitter space, Heisenberg, relativity, even the notion of space-time itself."

She stared aimlessly at her computer. "When we asked her, Alpha was insultingly vague about it all." She mocked the woman's accent: "'You do not have understanding. Telling is waste of my effort.' How many times did she say that?"

"Too many." Wixom raised his hands defensively. "Hey, I just built what she told me to. From that, we can extrapolate how her time machine functioned. The thing created oscillations of energy fields that somehow—programmed by her navigator—interacted across the diameter of the time machine. When the fields reached the perfect sine and cosine, they canceled each other. Essentially, the energy equaled zero, and she and Tanner vanished."

"The energy equaled zero," Kaplan repeated in a whisper, her brain imagining a series of self-canceling waves interacting within the circumference of that sphere in Lab One. "We're measuring the wrong thing." It hit her like a thrown brick. "Our detectors are looking for photons created by any trace of energy. I've thought of it like a wake behind a boat."

"So?"

"So we have that particle detector stored away somewhere up on the fourth floor, don't we?"

"We do. What are you thinking?"

"We know that photons pass through that space without being affected by what we'll call the 'Nakeesh' field. But what if we used particles? Shot them through a pair of Stern-Gerlach magnets, one vertical, the other horizonal, so that we knew they were uniformly spin up, spin right, and then passed them through the Nakeesh field?"

"The detector on the other side should still record the qubits as spin up, spin right," Wixom told her. "You think your Nakeesh field will change that?"

"What if it does?"

Wixom arched an eyebrow. "Then, at the minimum, we'll have a way to detect the Nakeesh field."

"And if we can detect it, we can figure out how to measure it. Measure it and we can describe it. Describe it and we can ultimately replicate it."

"And?"

"And we may not even need Nakeesh and her precious navigator."

Wixom's eyes narrowed as he studied her. "What are you playing at here? General Grazier was very specific in his orders. He didn't leave much room for leeway. He said, and I quote, 'You will monitor for Alpha's return. When she does, you will apprehend her, immediately render any medical aid she might require, retrieve the navigator, and separate it from her presence. Once she is stabilized and in custody and the navigator is secured, you will await further instructions.'"

"Yes, yes, and the same for Tanner." What the hell was she going to do with Tanner if he survived this? No wonder she was having nightmares.

Virgil crossed his arms. "I don't want to remind you, but Grazier's first impulse was to have us arrested, carted off, and locked away as national security risks. As far as he's concerned, we're the bad guys. We barely kept our butts out of the proverbial sling, not to mention our jobs. Essentially, we're on probation here. One screwup, and we can still go down."

She didn't dare mention Bill Stevens. Not that Virgil had ever been fully in the loop, but that would have to wait until after Bill made his move. She narrowed her eyes.

And then there was Tanner to consider.

Apparently, Wixom knew her well enough to interpret her expression.

"Maxine?" he asked softly. "I know you and Tanner had . . . well, a relationship. Back then, it wasn't any of our businesses, but now, with our changed status . . . ?"

"Are you trying to make a point?"

Wixom hesitated, was working over how he'd say it. She knew him well enough to almost read the thoughts rolling behind his tired blue eyes. Figured why make him suffer? and said first, "Yeah, it was mostly a matter of convenience. What? You think that banging on sixty, I'm the type to fall madly in love? Lose my head over a little sex and a bottle of champagne or two?"

Okay, "banging on sixty" might not have been the best way she could have phrased it.

Wixom didn't react the way she'd thought he would. Instead of some disarming platitude, he said, "I think you calculate the odds, Maxine. Figure what's ultimately in your best interest and act accordingly."

"Coldhearted bitch, huh?"

Wixom's only reaction was the tightening at the corners of his small mouth as he struggled to keep his expression blank.

Chuckling at her irritation, she added, "Guess I'm not as tired as I thought I was. Go find that particle gun. I'll adjust the detectors. Bet we'll have our first readings on the Nakeesh field by midnight."

She watched him go, thinking, *He's the weak link. Means I'd better keep a damn close eye on him.*

16

Ryan

It was a Diavel day. Yes, I had that immaculate Ducati 916 at home in the garage. The 916 was considered to be Massimo Tamburini's masterpiece of motorcycle design and engineering. Ask an average collection of Americans and all of them know Harley-Davidson. Maybe one out of six might recognize that Ducati is a motorcycle brand. But among motorcycle people, Ducati is a legend. Each model is a work of mechanical and visual art. People place Ducati motorcycles as centerpieces in living rooms and dens like they would statues by Rodin or James Earle Fraser. In the pantheon of Ducati motorcycles, Tamburini's 916 is to two wheels as Beethoven's Ninth Symphony is to music: absolutely sublime.

So, I rolled up the garage door, considered the gleaming red 916 where it rested on its side stand, and then I glanced out at the sunny Colorado morning. We were coming up on fall. Not that many riding days were left.

The 916 is like riding a scalpel; the slightest input to the machine provides a surgically precise and immediate response. Everything has to be exact, engine rpms matched to speed and the right gear. Riding the bike requires complete focus, a seamless melding of human being and motorcycle. When that happens, the effect is truly magic. You become one, the bike an extension of your body in a poetry of motion.

Fact was, I really didn't want to concentrate that hard.

Which left the Diavel. Mine is a Daytona blue with a white stripe down the tank and back fender. The only thing the Diavel and the 916 share is the Ducati name and the 90-degree layout of the twin cylinder engines. Where the 916 is a scalpel, the Diavel—that's Devil in Italian— is a hammer. Its soul is based on sheer horsepower overlaid by a veneer of gentility. The bike was well enough mannered that it could be ridden as a daily commuter—but keep twisting the wick, and you can incinerate that big honking rear tire and leave a smoking cloud of burning rubber behind when the light turns green.

Just straddling the bike, reaching across that long tank to the handlebars, you know you're taking hold of something visceral. And that's before thumbing the starter, feeling the power strokes, and hearing that big *testastretta* bark through its dual exhaust.

I tucked my gear into a saddle pack and strapped it on the back of the bike. Then I outfitted myself in my armored riding clothes. Armored? You bet. When we fall off, people my age don't bounce like we did when we were kids. We crunch. I'd crashed enough in my rowdy youth to learn my lesson. My helmet was the best in the business, but as I strapped it on, I purposely left the Bluetooth off.

This was my day to get away. Clear my head. The last thing I wanted was to field calls from the office.

I got out early enough to beat the traffic up US 24 to Woodland Park, let the Diavel idle its way past the coffee shops, boutiques, and microbreweries, then took the turnoff onto Colorado 67 headed for Cripple Creek. As the temperature dropped, I cranked up the electrics in my jacket and enjoyed the warm rush from the heaters in the handgrips.

The aspen had begun to turn on the high peaks. I could see a dusting of snow on the north slopes up above the timberline. God, I had needed this. Perfect therapy. The tension drained out of me like someone had pulled the proverbial plug.

I think better on a motorcycle. If you've never ridden, you don't get it. You can't. That sensation of motion and rushing air, of the road, and the passing of the world around you is unique. So is the relationship between you and the bike. Nothing with four wheels—not even the trickest sports car—can match the integration you have with a single-track vehicle. More than moving through space, it's becoming part of and interacting with the entire world. Sights, smells, temperature are all intense, unfiltered through window glass. The feedback from the road is immediate, personal.

In that clarity, I resettled my thoughts, shifted into third for a tight corner, and countersteered the Diavel into a tight lean. I'd picked the line perfectly, accelerated from the apex like a slingshot, and set myself up for the next corner.

Motorcycles were made for moments like this.

Cripple Creek used to be a mining camp. Now it's a tourist trap, and it was setting out to be a good day for business. Time for a break. I caught a cup of cappuccino at one of the sidewalk cafes, sitting at an outside table and staring at the Diavel where it was parked in the sunshine. Bike people do that. We can linger for hours just looking at our bikes, admiring the lines, the gleam of sunlight on the tank, bars, and pipes. Watch next time someone pulls into a parking lot on his or her motorcycle. As they walk away, seven out of ten will look back just to make sure the bike's all right.

How damn long had it been since I'd been able to just get away like this? My life had been like a whirlwind of jumbled events all the way back to the day when Alpha had vanished from her room in Ward Six.

Now, with time to finally think, how did I come to grips with all that had happened since that day? With the notion of Alpha herself? Essentially, she was an alien. Not a slimy green bug-eyed extraterrestrial, but a human from another Earth, and another time, separated from ours by . . . what? What the hell was a "branching" of the timeline? What kept those branches apart? I'd read Hugh Everett's paper as well as all those that followed from other physicists, and it still left me hazy on the details.

Like the fact that I was supposed to accept that, because of something called decoherence, the timelines were self-entangled to the point they couldn't interact with other timelines. A hypothetical state called recoherence would bring them back together, but if it ever happened, it would piss off a lot of physicists because time and space would have to run backward. Among physicists, time running backward is a big bad no no.

I stirred my little plastic swizzle stick through the cappuccino. The way Harvey Rogers had explained it, for the Many-Worlds universe to recohere would be the equivalence of the milk, coffee, and water in my drink spontaneously separating back into their three different components. So how did Alpha's navigator and cerebrum—being only really, really smart computers—allow her to skip from one milk molecule to another halfway across the cup? Let alone back into that molecule's past before it got poured into the milk?

Exactly how was I supposed to accept that the universe—or even this cup of cappuccino—was a wave function? Essentially a vibrating cloud of energy?

Compared to that, I'd rather tackle a catatonic violent schizophrenic in the middle of a psychotic break any day of the week.

"Tim," Grazier's voice echoed in my memory, *"Rather than worry about the theoretical physics, just accept that the rules have changed. Your job is to keep the people who have to deal with it sane, healthy, and prepared. You're our first line of defense."*

I'd been so busy supervising changes to Ward Six, monitoring contractors, reviewing architectural drawings, ensuring orders were delivered, and keeping track of supplies, I hadn't had time to figure out what that meant.

The first line of defense? As far as I could see, that was Grazier's security team down in Los Alamos. If Alpha popped back into Lab One, they were supposed to grab her, take away her navigator, and bring the device back to Grantham. I had no clue what happened to Alpha. Assuming she hadn't been mortally wounded when Reid Farmer had loosed a couple of rounds her way the instant she vanished.

At this stage of the game, it wasn't as if I or my people at Grantham could just hold up our hands, blow a whistle, and declare, "All you inter-time-branch travelers, cease and desist! Keep out. That's an order!"

I watched a Harley bagger with much-too-loud pipes roll past. I'd never quite caught the Harley bug. Whole different philosophy toward motorcycles. But then, you could say the same about Iron Butt riders—the men and women who rode eleven thousand miles or more in eleven days, crisscrossing the continent for a little trophy.

The takeaway was that the world was a more interesting place with all those different kinds of motorcycle riders—even with the "squids" popping wheelies on their sport bikes. They served as a microcosm for the whole planet. All seven-point-seven billion of us. People who wouldn't have existed if Skientia hadn't snatched Alpha out of the past, which stopped Fluvium from pouring out his bottle of weaponized *Oscillatoria* just so he could study plague on a planetary level.

Talk about unconscionably rude behavior.

Made me want to go back in time and kill him all over again.

I finished my cappuccino, hit the head, and walked out to the Diavel.

That's when I noticed her. She was across the street. Didn't matter that she was wearing a full helmet. Wasn't any way to miss that it was a woman in fitted black leather riding pants and jacket. I may be in my fifties, but I'm still a healthy guy who commits the unconscionable modern sin of "male gaze." The bike she stood next to was a gleaming black BMW RS: their sport version of the 1250cc boxer engine. A day pack was lashed to the passenger seat.

I gave her a two-fingered wave, strapped on my helmet, and straddled the Diavel. Pulling it up off the side stand, I thumbed the big twin to life, reveling in the cadence of idling exhaust pulses.

Leaving Cripple Creek, I caught the single headlight behind me. Sleek black bike, the two cylinders jutting out. Black-dressed rider, sunlight glinting off her midnight helmet. Had to be the BMW.

She stayed with me as I headed north on 67. Always hanging back no more than twenty yards behind.

Not that the Diavel was the finest machine for carving corners—the 916 would have been the preferred tool—but it wasn't any slouch, either. I'd learned my craft in younger years, having even aspired to a place on a factory racing team until college, and then the Marine Corps, intervened.

Set up and downshift, counter steer, trail brake into the apex, accelerate on the power curve, and catch the next gear. Poetry in motion, the Ducati's baritone blaring authority. I'm told by people who know that the only experience that excels that of leaning a motorcycle through tight corners is in the cockpit of a fighter aircraft.

With each set of corners, I'd glance at the mirrors, seeing the BMW right with me, leaned to the point the cylinder heads were almost skating on the asphalt.

The lady in black was good.

Hitting the straight at Tracy Hill, I had open road ahead of me. I'd like to say the Diavel made me do it. But it was probably macho shit hardwired deep in my brain. With no traffic for as far as I could see, I twisted the wick wide open and downshifted. As the Diavel hit its powerband, the front wheel lifted. With all hundred and sixty of the Ducati's horses unleashed, the BMW receded in the mirrors.

But damn!

At one hundred and fifty miles an hour, that two-lane road thinned into a mighty narrow ribbon. At the junction sign with US 24, I laid on the brakes. The Diavel—having the best Brembo discs and calipers in the business—tried to toss me headlong over the bars. Slowing, I made the stop, figured what the hell, and headed west. At Hartsel, I turned south on 9, missing the black BMW and its gutsy rider's company. When I reached the US 50 junction west of Canyon City, I rode out to Royal Gorge Bridge.

Seeing a parking spot with a bike taking up half the space, I pulled up, backed the Diavel in next to the black motorcycle, and cut the ignition.

Lifting off my helmet, I studied the black machine beside mine. No way.

The BMW RS gleamed in the sunlight, a faint tinking sound coming from the engine as it cooled.

Hey, there were a lot of black BMW RSs in the world. Well, okay, maybe not that many on the few roads west of Colorado Springs on that particular morning. Had to be coincidence.

Hanging my helmet on the Diavel, I unzipped my jacket and wadded it between the dip between the handlebars.

After I made the requisite pitstop in the men's room, I bought my ticket and walked out onto the bridge. The view really is stunning. Royal Gorge is a narrow crack in the earth, and the suspension bridge across it used to be the highest in the world. At the center, I stopped, staring at the distant Arkansas River below. It's nine hundred and fifty-six feet down those sheer rock walls. Less if the river's up.

I stood there, thinking of time, and space, and wondering how many worlds there are that have this same bridge, and how many "me's" were staring down like this. If I could believe the theory, there were thousands—and more splitting into their branches of the timeline each nanosecond.

The whole idea just comes across as baloney. You'd think, if you were splitting into clones, reflections, copies, or whatever you want to call them, you'd feel something. Catch a glimpse from the corner of your eye.

I tried. Shot a quick sidelong glance. And froze.

She wasn't more than five feet away, trim black leather riding pants conforming to muscular legs, her jacket unzipped, hanging open, as were the cooling vents in the sleeves of her Icon jacket.

Her gleaming black helmet rested on the walk beside her booted feet. The pack that had been strapped on the BMW's passenger seat now hung from one shoulder. Wind teased the auburn hair she'd tied into a pony-tail. In profile, her face was tanned, thoughtful. I'd have classified her features as Mediterranean.

So, last I'd seen, her RS was disappearing in the distance behind me when I whacked the Diavel's throttle wide open. And, believe me, I'd have known if she passed me. Other than that, she'd have had to fly the RS over mountains, or taken one of the Jeep roads to beat me here. Not only was the RS not suited to gnarly backcountry dirt roads, the bike would have been dusty.

Okay, I had to ask.

I stepped over. "Excuse me. Sorry to intrude. But you're on that RS, aren't you?"

Her attention still fixed on the stunning depths below, I could see the quiver of her lips as she smothered a smile. Her voice carried a curious accent as she said, "And you want to know how I beat you here, Doctor Ryan?"

"You know me?" I felt the first tingle of warning in my blood.

"The answer to that can take many forms. Here, I have something for you." She turned slightly away, unslinging her pack and reaching inside. I fixed on the box she withdrew, maybe the size of a thick hard-back novel. A series of lights gleamed on one side.

"Holy shit," I muttered. "That's Fluvium's cerebrum. It's supposed to be locked away in the vault in Ward Six. How the hell did you . . ." I looked up as she placed the device in my hands. Stopped short at the hardened green eyes that bored into mine. Realized—up close like I was—that she had a dusting of freckles across her nose. What might have been the faint ghosts of scars lined her cheeks, nose, and chin. She was thirty? Maybe younger. Somehow fresh and healthy. But for her eyes; I'd seen that look before in the faces of combat vets who'd spent too much time in the shit. It was the hardened gaze of a woman who had seen all of hell and lived.

"You want to know how it works?" she asked, her voice a baritone.

"Look closely at that blue button. If you place your finger over it, you'll feel the heat."

I stared down at the heavy box, hardly aware that she still had one hand in her pack. Feel the heat? A blue haze of figures—some sort of holographic display—appeared in the air above the top.

I carefully extended my index finger, expecting . . .

Everything went gray. The sensation was like my arms, legs, and head were being pulled from my body. And then there was . . . there was . . . vertigo spinning me into . . .

17

Kaplan

Maxine Kaplan stared at the readout. She should have been dead on her feet. Together with Wixom, she had been at it, catching catnaps only, for the last twelve hours. Didn't matter that she'd been up for thirty hours straight and should have been reeling. The data were too engrossing.

She sat on the steps in Lab One. The two guards up at the security door watched her with bored eyes. Before her, the hemispherical hollow in the concrete, the partial base of the research station, and the severed cables mocked her. The bright overhead lights left her squinting.

Wixom was working with the detector on the other side of the hemisphere, checking yet again to make sure that the machine was functioning correctly.

To her right—precisely positioned—the particle "gun" with its magnets rested atop a heavy frame. Positioning had taken hours.

Maxine had insisted that its beam pass through the exact center of the time-traveling sphere, figuring that if anything could be detected, it would be at the heart of the phenomenon. If they failed to measure anything of note, they could play with the margins of the hypothetical field at their leisure.

But they'd detected an anomaly from the beginning. Their spin-up, spin-right qubits—despite passing through atmosphere and across the twelve meters separating the gun from the detector—had registered without issue on the control test before placing the equipment in Lab One. They'd detected an estimated ninety-eight percent of the generated qubits.

Maxine ran anxious hands through her hair, blinked. Wished she had another cup of coffee. Her butt hurt from the concrete stair tread.

Wixom walked carefully around the hemisphere, veering wide where Pete McCoy's body had been. Maybe he thought that stepping on the spot where Pete had died would bring bad luck or affect the quantum future?

Seating himself on the step beside her, he said, "The detector's functioning well within parameters. It's not a mechanical error. Everything's set correctly." His weary blue eyes were fixed on the hemisphere, as if he were imagining the machine they'd built based upon Nakeesh's drawings and descriptions.

Maxine switched from fiddling with her hair to massaging the back of her neck, kneading the tired nuchal muscles. "Doesn't make sense. In the control experiment we were getting ninety-eight percent recovery. Shooting through the sphere, we're getting right at two percent spin-down, spin-left above background. We're not getting hits for any of the generated qubits."

"At least it's a reliable two percent. The measurement doesn't fluctuate while the gun's on. Turn it off, even the two percent of spin-down spin-left qubits vanish."

"So, where are our generated qubits going?"

Wixom, still staring dully at the emptiness between the gun and detector, said, "I want to try something."

Standing, he skirted the area of the sphere. Unlocking the wheels, he carefully pushed the detector around the hollow, picking a place roughly ninety degrees off the electron beam's axis. Clicking the wheels in place, he carefully leveled the detector. Flipping it on, he watched the monitor.

"Got anything?" Maxine fully figured he was going to say no. Hell, he was at right angles to the path traveled by the . . .

"Two percent spin-down spin-left," Wixom called. "Just wait."

He turned the detector off, unlocked the wheels, and rolled it to a point that might have been forty-five degrees from the beam's orientation. After he'd locked the wheels, leveled and aimed the detector, he flipped it on. Studied the monitor. "Two percent of our bad boys are still there."

Maxine stood, walked over, and switched the gun off.

At his monitor, Wixom dully said, "They're gone. Just reading random background now."

Maxine took a deep breath, did some quick figuring of the radius from the sphere's center compared to the surface area on the detector. "They're bouncing back from the center of the sphere, but they're changed. Mirror copies of the qubits we're generating."

Wixom rubbed his chin as he studied his monitor. "The photons didn't react because they have no mass. Good call to try the experiment with particles. Wonder what we'd get with straight neutrons?"

She studied the empty space above the crater. "Okay, so we didn't get a wake, as such. But something's definitely there. We can't detect the faintest lick of a magnetic field, but our reflected qubits come back as if they've been run through a Stern-Gerlach magnet. Doesn't make any damn sense."

"Maxine?" Wixom was frowning at his monitor. "Not only were the qubits changed, but they were accelerated. And, compared to the first of our readings, these last had a seventeen percent velocity increase."

"Almost makes you think something's coming, doesn't it? Like some sort of Doppler." She frowned. "Looks like we've hit the jackpot, Virgil. Now, all we have to do is figure out what it means."

"You going to tell the team?"

"No. And I don't want you to, either. Not until we understand what's causing the acceleration. And I don't think we're going to figure that out until we get a solid eight hours of rack time. So your orders are to go home. Knock yourself out with Ambien if you have to and come back Monday morning with your game face on and ready to do some hard math."

Wixom nodded, shut off the detector, and stared vacantly at the dark screen. She knew that look. The guy was uncomfortable, mulling data. But was he thinking of their mirror qubits, or what she was up to?

"Go, Virgil."

The guards straightened as she followed him up the stairs, paused at the top, and looked back at the quiet room with its smooth crater. Then, nodding at Grazier's two security guys, she stepped out.

Wixom was halfway down the hall, headed for the exit.

Good. She had a phone call to make. She could only think of one thing that would be accelerating those changed qubits.

18

Karla

Smacking sounds accompanied each impact as Karla Raven hammered the heavy bag. She leaped back, pivoted on the gym floor, and smashed kick after kick into the hundred-fifty-pound bag. Panting, she danced away, flicked the sweat from her eyes.

The heavy bag swung from its chains, casting shadows across the gym floor. The damn thing seemed to mock her.

The flashbacks had brought her awake that morning after a nightmare-filled sleep. She'd been back on that fucking road, headed out of Talach 3, her Humvee in the lead . . .

"Stop it." Karla forced herself to kill the image forming in her brain. Instead, she repeated the mantra that Dr. Ryan had taught her: "You didn't go to Jabac Junction. You took another road. You didn't drive down toward that shithole of a town. Didn't see that spilled basket of clothes . . ."

But she did. She was back . . . *bouncing and swaying in the canvas passenger seat as the Humvee hammered down the rutted excuse for a road.*

Behind her, Pud Pounder was standing, his upper body propped in the turret behind Ma Deuce, the Browning fifty-caliber machine gun.

The desert looked as flat as a lake bottom, but the terrain was illusory. Rains had carved patterns of narrow drainages across the flats. No more than ten to twenty inches deep, a person could still lie down and essentially vanish from as far away as thirty feet.

The late afternoon sun slanted toward the craggy and steep mountains in the distance. From up there, Haji would be watching her dust as Bravo Platoon raced out from T-3.

Karla was planning on that. She and her LPO, her light petty officer, had spent the last two days planning this op. They'd picked the series of rocky outcrops that stuck up from the flats just outside of the canyon mouth. The reason wasn't the outcrops themselves, but the deeply incised drainages that ran beneath them and met just east of the main highway.

A Marine convoy would pass over that road sometime around midday tomorrow. Not that it was any kind of secret, since an Afghan detail was accompanying the Marines. Given an Afghan's dedication to security, that meant every insurgent within a hundred klicks knew when and where that convoy would roll.

"We're on all their scopes now," Weaver said as he laid his right hand atop the steering wheel. He glanced at the driver-side mirror. "Socket's sniffing right up our ass. That reaming you gave him sure cured his lollygagging attitude, Chief."

"Just a reminder, boys," she said as she keyed her mic. "Sloppy means dead."

Golf's voice came through her earbud. "You sure they'll be able to figure out where we're going, Chief? Or should we send them a pajama-gram with a map?"

"They're not stupid." She allowed herself a grim smile. "Mostly. Their spotters are banging jaws as we speak. If we're unlucky, they'll figure out who we are and what we're up to. They do that, and they'll treat the whole operational area like a plague zone. We'll be bored stiff watching that convoy pass. But if we're lucky, they'll think we're a no-threat routine patrol, and they'll filter right down through those drainage channels. If they do, they'll pop up right under our noses. Air strikes will take out any we don't get to kill first."

"Jabac Junction ahead, Chief," Weaver said.

She could see the squat mud-and-stone huts. Flat-roofed and colorless as the hardpan her Humvees roared across. Hovels built out of the desert clays. Only a few families still lived there, tending a couple of gardens, a handful of goats.

Weaver was roaring down on the junction, the engine whining . . .

"No!" Karla screamed. She squeezed her eyes shut, pressed her hands to her ears.

Gasping for breath, she forced her eyes open.

Struggled for control.

She came to, crouched in a hunched ball, arms clamped over her head, on the polished vinyl floor in the Ward Six gym at Grantham. The heavy bag swung lazily on its chains.

Sweat ran down her skin, soaked the gray T-shirt she wore, trickled out of her hair and down her neck. Her hot breath kept coming in gasps.

Grantham. She was in Grantham. Not Afghanistan. Not Jabac Junction.

She hated flashbacks. They made her weak. Sucked away parts of her soul.

"Oh, fuck." With all the strength in her body, she staggered to her feet. Hammered the heavy bag, pain lancing up from her knuckles, through her arm and into her shoulder. She'd lived on pain. It had carried her through the brutal BUD/S selection, through S&T, through the hazing. Had allowed her to turn off everything that was Karla Raven so that she could be the first woman to make the Teams, to pass sniper school, to be promoted to command.

And she'd lost it all when her platoon was blown away at Jabac Junction. The roadside IED had been hidden in a basket of spilled clothes. Something she should have recognized as a threat.

"My . . . fucking . . . fault," she whispered.

Driven by rage, she attacked the heavy bag. Punched, kicked, body slammed it, until she sagged on the floor, sucking breath, her muscles trembling.

If only she could exhaust her memories the way she did her body.

She heard the door open, the sound of steps on the gym floor. Wearily, she forced herself up, turned, and shook her head as Sam Savage came striding her way.

"Taking a little rest?" he asked, curious stare absorbing her sweat-soaked wear, her flushed and wet face, the damp hair.

"Yeah, recharging myself so I can knock that superior-assed smirk right off of your face. What are you here for, Major?"

Savage's dark eyes flashed, then mellowed as he apparently thought better of it. "Sorry. Shouldn't have mouthed off. We've got a problem."

Karla wiped the sweat from her forehead. "What sort of problem?"

"Just got a call from the Fremont County Sheriff's Office. Two motorcycles were left in the Royal Gorge parking lot. The park called them in, was going to have them towed. The SO ran the VINs. One was stolen. The other, the Diavel, belongs to Dr. Ryan."

"I'm on it." She turned for the locker room, calling over her shoulder. "Fifteen minutes. I'll take the Tahoe."

"I'm going with you."

"Then get your shit wired, Major. This is the Skipper, so I'm rolling in fifteen."

She had to shower, dress, grab her gear, and clear her head. No way the Skipper was going to abandon that bike. Whatever this was, it was going to be bad.

19

Savage

Every bit of Sam Savage's concentration focused on the road as he flicked on the brights and sent the Tahoe rocketing up Highway 115. Didn't matter that he had the blue flashers going; they might cause traffic to pull over, out of his way, but the deer or an occasional elk wouldn't pay them the slightest heed. And he had to watch the corners, figuring that each of the yellow curve signs with a specified speed limit could be exceeded by maybe twenty miles an hour before the Tahoe's tires would break traction and pitch them off into the guardrail.

In the passenger seat, Karla Raven was checking the remaining equipment she kept in her third-line gear: radios, flashlights, rope, taser, various rolls of tape, zip ties, wire, and the like. He knew that she kept her kit in perfect order. Checking it again on the way, that was just ritual. Something spec ops people did. Double, triple, quadruple check, it didn't matter. Someone's life could hinge on it.

She repacked the last of her gear, sealed it, and dropped the pack to the floor between her feet. Shot him a sidelong look as he sent them careening around a corner and hit the accelerator on the straight. "How's the chest, Major?"

"Still a little sore. Good news is that I'm through the physical therapy." As he squinted at the road, the images played in his memory. Bill Minor had emerged from the Lab One door during Savage and Karla's infiltration of the Skientia lab. Karla had taken the brunt of Minor's attack, wrestling with him. She'd been trying to disarm Minor, to knock the nine-millimeter Sig out of the man's hand.

As Savage had rushed to help her, Minor had triggered the pistol. Funny thing that. Savage didn't remember the sound of the discharge. The effect was as if he'd been kicked in the chest by a horse. Then he'd been on the floor, blinking, trying to figure out what the hell had gone wrong. That only lasted for an instant before he realized he couldn't breathe. Looking back now, it might have been a dream, one in which Karla Raven appeared above him, her outline haloed against the fluorescent lights in the ceiling.

He didn't remember anything she'd said, didn't remember much except that a giant weight was crushing his chest. Could barely remember her rendering aid, ripping her "blowout kit" open and tearing at his shirt. Blowout kit: the small medical first aid pack used for combat injuries.

And then he'd awakened in the hospital with a tube in his throat. People had been rushing around. Having caught that brief glimpse, the world went away again until he awakened in the ICU with an armed guard at the foot of his bed.

Wasn't until the attending surgeon entered the room that Sam Savage learned he'd been shot through the left lung. In the wake of the carnage inside the Skientia lab, Karla had packed him out, and Winny had medevacked him to an Albuquerque hospital. But for their quick actions, he'd have died. Came pretty damn close to it as it was.

Now, here he was . . . he and Karla Raven. He chuckled as he braked hard, made the corner, and punched the accelerator.

"What?" Raven asked.

"I was thinking that the last time it was just you and me, I got shot. I'm worried that this time, Winny Swink isn't waiting with a helicopter to save my ass."

Raven turned her attention to the cone of light their headlights shone on the winding asphalt. "Don't think we're going to get shot at. Doesn't feel right. Doesn't make sense. Whatever went down is over. What matters is who'd take the Skipper? Stevens? We should be clear of his radar. Grazier assured us that Stevens bought the cover story. I heard he's still looking for a spec ops team . . . one off the books. That he didn't buy that Team Psi could have hit the Aspen mansion or the Los Alamos lab."

"Yeah, he's still looking. My sources inside the Activity as well as JSOC tell me that with his imprimatur, the NSC and NSA have had agents combing the records for any hint of an off-the-books team."

"Major, I don't want to push your button, but we're about as 'off the books' as you can get."

"They'll be trying to follow the money. We're not funded through DOD, DARPA, or any of the usual sources. Money's always the weak link, and so we should be covered in that regard. That, and the 'rumint' mill is completely quiet. SOF is a small community. Old friends get together over beer, people talk. If there was any clue that a bunch of crackpots who'd escaped from a psych ward had knocked over Aspen and Los Alamos, it'd be the talk of the town."

"A bunch of crackpots," she said softly. Then, "I get it that you're not happy with the assignment or the mission parameters. You really don't like us, huh?"

Savage ground his teeth, narrowed an eye as the Tahoe's suspension hammered over a bridge abutment. "Look, Chief, I ran special operations teams just about everywhere in the Middle East, Northern Africa, Afghanistan, and all the usual places. Maybe I'm just a simple guy, but I like working with professionals. I like having a cadre of talented people to pull from when I plan and tailor an op. Guys who've been in the shit, that I can trust. So step back and take a gander at it from my seat: Aspen, Los Alamos, they were all slapped together. Granted, we had to move when we did, but I ended up shot, Dr. Farmer's dead, and Alpha's escaped. Falcon's in a catatonic state. That little display of yours in the gym today? I caught you at the end of a flashback, didn't I?"

At her eloquent silence, he added, "My problem now is when will one or another of you guys wig out on me?" He shot her a glance. "Get where I'm coming from?"

Trees were flashing past in the headlight beams as he crested the pass and started down toward the Arkansas River.

Raven tightened her grip on the "Oh Shit" handle in the dashboard, as if bracing for impact. "What we did, we had to make up at the last second. So I'll cut you a break. You're from the head shed, that tidy little world of officers who flock around their tactical computers, bedazzled by the 'good idea fairy.' It's us enlisted folk who have to charge into the shit and make a direct action work so that you guys can pat yourselves on the back. You know, get one up on the competition as you check off boxes on your way up the ladder to retirement."

"Heard it all before, Chief. But here's a bit of flash traffic for you. I came up the hard way. Just like you. Made the cut for Rangers, gutted my way through to qualify for Special Forces Operational Detachment, and was selected for Task Force Green. I've humped my share of brothers out of the shit while their blood soaked through my second-line gear and down to my skin. So how about we stop swinging dicks and get down to the facts: This whole thing at Grantham's on the verge of being a cluster fuck."

"How's that?"

"Come on, Raven. You didn't get where you did by being an idiot. We're supposed to be the first line of defense against time warriors? It's as crackpot as it sounds. We don't know who they are, where they come from, or—outside of Alpha—what they want. We can't even detect when they come and go, let alone do anything about it. And, if we could, so what? How do we build a team? Transport? Handle the logistics? To do what? We can't define the mission, let alone how to complete it."

She sat silently, her gaze fixed on the mountain road they flew down. "Yeah, that bothers me. But Grazier's stuck. You heard how close he came to losing it all? Stevens told the president that Grazier had gone nuts, suffered a psychotic break. If the general hadn't known the president way back when, we'd all have been screwed, and Grazier would be locked in his own padded cell two doors down from the rest of us."

Savage nodded. Knew how close it had been, how the president had hedged his bets. Grazier himself had acknowledged that if Stevens hadn't already scheduled a White House visit for Alpha, that he'd have been arrested and quietly retired.

As Savage blasted past a slow-moving truck, he hit his brights and said, "Okay, Chief, I get it. Grazier's hands are tied. He's got a hidden black op that only the president knows about, one that he's funding from who-knows-where. It's made up of you guys, not because it's ideal, but because you had firsthand experience with Alpha, and, miracle of miracles, you almost managed to catch her before she skipped into the future. That still doesn't negate what we're up against: We're supposed to deal with a threat that no one would believe is real, with a team made up of . . . well, let's say 'mentally compromised individuals' working out of a psychiatric hospital, in an attempt to keep invaders—whom we can't even identify—from a parallel Earth from compromising our very existence."

"Ooraah, Major." She shot him a glance. "You CIA guys always this pessimistic?"

"Chief, there's pessimism, and there's reality. If I were a pessimist, I'd have never made it to West Point, let alone past PFC. I got to where I am at by looking at the problem as rationally as possible and figuring out how to solve it. Even if I had to do it on the fly. I was damned good at it until that asshole Tanner Jackson bitch-slapped me on Pennsylvania Avenue and took Farmer and France right out from under me."

Just thinking about that ambush in DC pissed him off all over again. And now Jackson, the son of a bitch, was somewhere in the future with Alpha?

He slowed as he hit traffic at Canyon City, people pulling over and letting him pass out of respect for his flashing blue lights. The city police—given a heads up from the Sheriff's Office—let them through town with nothing more than a flash of their headlights, and Savage punched the accelerator as they cleared the city limits.

"This whole thing stinks," Karla told him as they took the Royal Gorge exit off US 50. "The Skipper wouldn't leave that Diavel. That it was parked next to a stolen bike? That's no coincidence. Dr. Ryan's a bike guy, into the culture. He loves motorcycles and riding. It's his escape valve, his passion. If there was any way to get the Doc to lower his guard, that's how they'd do it."

"So you think this was planned? How? How would they know where he was going?"

"You gotta be kidding, Major. They could have tagged his bike with a tracker, employed a drone, shadowed him, satellite, you name it. And it's Saturday. Whoever's behind this, they know the Skipper's vulnerability."

At the park, Savage was waved through, found the sheriff's car in the parking lot next to the two bikes. They were gleaming in the halo cast by the security lights. A tow truck waited, the driver leaning against his fender, arms crossed. Some of the park personnel stood in a knot in the rear.

Savage parked, cut his lights and ignition. Karla was already out the door, swinging her pack onto her shoulders. He was hot on her heels, stopping before the sheriff.

"You're Major Savage? I'm Bill Meek. Glad to meet you." The guy was a typical Colorado county sheriff, right down to the cowboy hat, western boots, and gray hair.

"Sam Savage, sir. And this is Chief Petty Officer Karla Raven. Thanks for the call and the courtesy getting us here. Any information on Colonel Ryan's whereabouts?"

Karla had immediately gone for the bike, playing her Surefire E2D light over it as she searched for any clue. She went carefully over Ryan's coat where it was wedged between the bars, then his helmet hanging from the twist grip. Next, she crouched, studying the tires, the engine, looking for who knew what.

Sheriff Meek made a face, waved toward the park personnel. "No, sir. And this is where it gets a little strange. You see, the park here at Royal Gorge is like any other tourist-based attraction. They've got a huge liability worry, even more so with the bridge and canyon as well as the rides and zip line. As a CYA, and for insurance, they've got a comprehensive monitoring system. You want to come with me? Take a look at the tapes? Then you can make your own mind up about what happened here today."

Savage looked at Karla, a sinking feeling going sour in his gut.

20

Karla

The security office at the Royal Gorge Bridge & Park wasn't state of the art, but it certainly got the job done. Karla crowded in next to Savage and Sheriff Meek, the latter having figured the case was high profile enough for his personal involvement.

A kid named Mike was in charge of the computer and ran the security recordings from a cluttered desk; wires snaked from his PC to the three monitors on the wall. He was a *Game of Thrones* geek. Had posters of the dragons up on the walls. A little plastic Iron Throne toy sat by the side of his keyboard.

Mike said, "Yeah, we got a couple of cameras on the parking lot. So, like here, at 12:52, you can see the first bike pull in."

Karla watched a black BMW RS wheel into the frame, pull up at an open space next to the sidewalk. The rider backed the racy-looking bike slowly into place.

"It's a woman," Savage said as the rider stepped off, unstrapped a backpack from behind her on the passenger seat, and slipped it onto her shoulder. Only then did she undo a full-face helmet and—carrying it with her—walk off for the entry. The distance was too great to make out facial features.

"Nothing happens for almost five minutes," Mike said. "Then this guy rides in."

Karla recognized Ryan on his Diavel, saw him fix on the parking space, and paddle-walk his bike in next to the BMW. Ryan studied the RS thoughtfully, and Karla watched him lean his bike on its side stand and pull off his jacket and helmet before stuffing them onto the bike and heading for the gate.

"Okay," Mike said, tapping keys. "So, we go to the bridge feed. We keep a weather eye on this one. It's a long frickin' drop from the center of the bridge, right? Nine hundred and fifty feet to the river. We get all kinds of nuts. Suicides, base jumpers, idiots that want to toss rocks, bottles, and sometimes even people they don't like. Then we get the ones who just drop stuff to see it fall, and guys . . . it's always guys, who want to pee and watch it rain for nine hundred and fifty feet."

Karla watched as the woman, dressed in black leather jacket and riding pants, strolled out to the middle of the bridge. For long moments she stared around, taking in the view, her hands braced on the safety railing. Then she set her helmet down and swung the pack off of her back, checking something inside.

"Here comes your Colonel Ryan," Mike said, pointing to the Skipper as he walked into the picture. Even from the angle, it was apparent that he was oblivious to the woman as he stared down, stopping several times to take in the spectacular drop.

Stopping about midway, he braced his arms and looked over the side. After thirty seconds or so, Karla saw him nod to himself, straighten, and stop short at sight of the woman. She'd been studiously ignoring him.

Given the set of Ryan's shoulders and the tilt of his head, his body language reflected puzzlement as he walked over to the woman and said something. She finally turned, facing him. Then she handed him what looked like a large hardback book. Ryan studied it, ran his fingers through what looked like a faint blue haze . . .

The image on the monitor turned to fuzz, like the old-time "snow" on cathode-ray TVs.

"Son of a bitch," Karla muttered, recognition conjuring unhappy thoughts.

"This is the weird part," Mike told them. "The bridge cams are the only ones that went hazy like this. It's about fifteen, twenty seconds, and, well, see?"

The image firmed up again; the bridge reformed in the display, along with startled people in the background, some looking uneasy, as if unsure of their balance. Ryan and the woman had disappeared.

Karla ground her teeth, fists knotting. She glanced at Savage, saw the major's expression of dismay. Leaning forward to brace herself on the desk, she palmed the little toy Iron Throne. Couldn't help herself. Felt the rising panic.

"No sign of them after that," Sheriff Meek said. "They never walked off the bridge, or the security cameras on either end would have spotted them. We've got a lot of practice finding bodies in the rocks after all the jumpers we've had over the years. And the cams down in the canyon don't record anyone hitting the river. They didn't go over the side."

"They never showed up again," Mike added, flicking from screen to screen. "We monitor everyone who comes and goes. Wouldn't have thought anything of it if those two motorcycles hadn't been left behind. And then, when the one was found to be stolen, we called the sheriff immediately. That's, like, all we know."

"Can we get those recordings?" Karla asked as she slipped the stolen toy into her pocket. "And can they be enlarged, enhanced?"

"Sure," Mike told her. "Especially the bridge cams, they record in high resolution just for situations like this. It's in case something happens that might land us in court. You know, for jumpers, or if someone throws something off the bridge. All that liability shit."

"Back it up to just before static blanks the monitors," Savage said.

Karla watched as the recording firmed up. Stepped closer. Stared at the woman handing Ryan the curious box. Karla couldn't be sure, but that box thing was the same size as the cerebrum locked away back at Grantham. And the woman? She was too far away. Without ET's magic, Karla couldn't be positive of her facial features.

She asked, "Can you go back to the security camera at admissions? Get us a close-up of that woman as she entered?"

"Sure." Mike told her. "Just a sec."

He clicked keys, the images in one of the monitors flickering, fast-forwarding as Mike checked the time log. At the 12:56 marker, the camera caught the woman as she passed through the gates and paid admission. Mike froze it in mid-frame, catching the woman's features. Auburn hair, athletic-and-toned body in form-fitting black leather riding gear—and those green eyes couldn't be mistaken.

Karla and Savage both tensed.

"Anything you two want to tell me?" Sheriff Meek asked softly, his quick blue gaze shifting from Karla to Savage.

Karla could hear Savage's teeth grinding before he calmly replied, "Bet you know where we're going with this, Sheriff."

Meek chuckled under his breath, shook his head. "Yeah? Why am I betting we're suddenly on a National Security need-to-know basis?"

"Naw. You've been watching too many movies. This here? It's covered under a plain old-fashioned 'classified.' But if you could do us a favor? Keep an eye out for the unusual. And if anything—and I do mean *anything*—weird happens, let us know?"

"What about the stolen motorcycle out there?"

"You called that tow truck to pick up the bikes?"

"Yeah, that's Charlie Slade. He's our local guy. I can tell you, he's already bitching over how long this is taking. It's making me wince, 'cause I don't want the county to get stuck with the bill." Meek raised a suggestive eyebrow.

Savage rubbed his jaw, a hardness behind his dark eyes that Karla figured was mirrored by her own. Meek was reading it just as surely as young Mike was.

"If good old Charlie will load those bikes without getting so much as a scratch on them, and transport them to our facility, we'll cover his costs," Savage said evenly. "And you can let the BMW dealer know that their bike is all right. We'll get square with them."

"Anything else?" Meeks asked.

"For God's sake, just keep your mouths shut. None of this ever happened. A very nice lady by the name of Janeesha will dropping by tomorrow with a nondisclosure agreement that we'd really like you two, and anyone associated with this, to sign."

"No shit?" Mike asked. "Cool!"

Cool? Karla thought, *It wasn't anyone you care about who just got snatched off to who knows where or when.*

From the grim look, the major damned well knew what had happened on that bridge.

"You still feeling pissed off and lost?" Karla asked as soon as they were alone in the parking lot.

"Pissed off, yes. Lost, no. Suddenly, we're back in the game, Chief."

"Good, 'cause if that woman so much as musses a hair on the Skipper's head, I'm going to reach down her throat, grab hold, and rip her lungs out by the roots."

21

Ryan

I came to, as awake as if I had just closed my eyes. I blinked, surprised to find myself on my back and lying on a bed. The ceiling overhead was close, paneled in a peeled-wood veneer with textured strips over the paneling joints. That, along with the confining walls, led me to believe I was in a camp trailer. A fact that became apparent as I sat up.

The louvered windows—morning light spilling through on either side—couldn't be mistaken, nor could the built-in drawers, the narrow strip of carpet, or the sliding door that marked the extent of the cramped bedroom. Definitely a camp trailer.

The woman watched me from where she leaned in the doorway. The merest glance, and I knew she was what you'd call really healthy. The way her jeans fit, the musculature in her crossed arms, and that almost feline pose reminded me of Karla Raven. And then I really got a good look at her. Nope. This one was more like Alpha: that sense of the exotic coupled with a curious magnetism that defied any normal description. She just filled the room.

It wasn't until I fixed on her green eyes, the auburn hair, that I knew. "You."

"Sorry about the incident on the bridge. I needed to get you when you were by yourself. Fewer questions that way. Less commotion than if I'd snatched you out of your house, let alone Grantham Barracks."

"My people will be concerned."

"The American Indian and the woman have already recovered your motorcycle. It's safely back in the garage at Grantham by now. They'll be poring over the security tapes from the bridge."

Looking closely, I could see the faint freckles dusting her nose, the barest hints of scars. What the hell was it about her? She didn't look to be more than thirty given her complexion, the faint lines at the corners of her eyes, or the smooth skin at her throat. Her expression, however, the look she was giving me, reeked of eternity. As if those intense and too-green eyes had seen everything. I couldn't help but think that if you took an old, battered, and combat-hardened soul and transplanted it into an athletic woman, this was what you'd get.

I asked, "Who are you?"

"A long, long time ago in a world far, far away, I was named Maryam. After a much-too-short and misery-filled childhood, I took the professional name, *Helena*." She pronounced it with a harshly aspirated H and in an accent I couldn't identify. "If you transliterated the koine, it would be Helen. To Nakeesh and Fluvium, I'm the *Ennoia*. They consider it a derogatory term. Their own personal and sick joke."

"So, what do I call you?"

"Helen's good."

"Helen from where?" I asked. "Or, should I say, when?"

She smiled grimly. "To put this in a framework you might understand, in this amplitude of the timeline branches, I'm barely a footnote. That feces-licking dog Kepha . . . you'd know him as Peter, from the Greek word Petros, came out as the winner. His people wrote the histories in their favor. And either destroyed, erased, or perverted Simon's and mine. Made us look like craven fools, cheats, and charlatans."

She paused. "That's one of the reasons I really don't like being here. Leaves a bitter taste in my mouth."

"Then why are you?"

"Because Nakeesh is here. And, miracle of miracles, by accident you managed to separate her from Fluvium. While that stroke of luck stranded him and ultimately led to his current state of being dead, she's still alive. If Marvin hadn't been shot through the heart in your garage that day, we'd have finally taken care of Nakeesh, and you'd never have had a clue about any of this."

I rubbed my face, fitting it all together. Images from the bridge, about the flash of light, and my feeling of being pulled apart remained crystal clear. A stab of fear sent panic through my gut. "Where are we?"

"In a Forest Service campground." She gestured around at the camp trailer.

"In my timeline?"

"The intricacies of the physics aside, I relocated you about fifty linear miles to this trailer. I don't think you're up to jumping from branch to branch yet. It's considerably more involved than you might think. Well, it is if you want to do it with any kind of success."

"Like Alpha and Fluvium?"

She studied me, seemed to be reading my every thought. What was it about those bright-green eyes of hers? She might have been God observing a worm. Said, "Let's just say that their stay in Egypt was supposed to be in and out. But in the end, they do make my point: Transitioning from branch to branch isn't something one does lightly. The risks are real and the consequences deadly at best. Horrifying at worst."

"You seem to be doing quite well. Alpha came to us without a word of English. She couldn't understand the simplest of things. Came across as having savant syndrome."

"She arrived in your time from around the eleventh century in her branch of the timeline. A branch where Pompeius Magnus wasn't beheaded on an Egyptian beach, Marc Antony wasn't defeated by that psychotic *immanis,* Octavius. Vile shit of a human being that he was, he didn't become first emperor of Rome. In Nakeesh and Fluvium's timeline, no Jesus was crucified. Kepha didn't found a church in Rome. Rather, Nakeesh and Fluvium came from a branch where Lucas *Magna Nauta* sailed to what you call South America and up the coast where he encountered the Maya city states. Any of that ring a bell for you?"

At my blank look, she said, "Of course not. Different branch of the timeline, different history. In Nakeesh and Fluvium's timeline, Rome didn't fall. Angles, Saxons, and Jutes didn't settle Britannia, nor did the Normans invade. What you call England remained a Roman province speaking a Celtic and Latin language. And that, Doctor, is why Nakeesh didn't speak a word of what you call English. It never evolved."

"The tomb and sarcophagus," I said as the pieces began to fit. "Latin and Mayan. The languages Fluvium thought and spoke in. But why are you fluent in English, even the idiomatic uses of our speech?"

An eternal weariness lay behind her gaze. "If you were heading off to chase down a psychotic monster, say, someone hideous like Lavrenti Beria, who'd escaped into sixth-century Byzantium, would you just pack up and go tomorrow?"

"I, uh . . ."

"Not only would the language be incomprehensible, the culture would be beyond you. Nor would you have a clue about where in the city you might be, or how to solve the simplest of problems. You'd stand out like a blinking sign in your American clothes. The *collegia,* what you'd call the gangs, would pluck you naked for the novelty of it. Before morning, your lifeless body would be floating in the Bosporus. And that's assuming it was in *this* branch of the timeline where you share the history."

"You have texts on us? Ways to study us? Like, courses or something?"

The faintest irritation tightened the corners of Helen's lips. "It's a lot more involved than that. Done gradually, starting with a time close enough to the branching that a person can pass. Then you skip forward, moving through the centuries. Learning as you go." A beat. "Assuming you want to succeed. Otherwise you end up a corpse. Maybe burned as a witch . . . or, like Nakeesh, in a mental institution, should they happen to exist in that culture and period."

"Sounds like it takes a lot of time."

She gave me the kind of scathing glance she'd give an idiot. And maybe I was, given that my limbic system kept reacting to her presence in a way I hadn't felt since I was working with Alpha. What the hell was it with these women?

"Okay, so you've got a time machine. For some of us, this is still new. We're working our asses off trying to figure it all out. But more to the immediate point, Why the hell am I here? What do you want from me?"

"I want Nakeesh dead. I would have had that, but for a lucky shot from her guard that day."

"Yeah, well, you blew poor Captain Stanwick's brain out in return. I've played the recording of that day over and over. The rest of Alpha's security team was out because of the EMP, or whatever the displacement is that scrambles brains and electronics. Captain Stanwick was down. You could have walked over and shot Alpha without any other resistance."

Her gaze went distant for a moment. "I let myself get distracted over Marvin. Thought I was over that sort of attachment. And there are other considerations. I couldn't take the chance. No matter how it might have ended, if something had gone wrong, they'd have looked poorly on the loss of a navigator and cerebrum."

"They?"

I got a faint smile in return. "Want a cup of coffee?"

At my skeptical nod, she added, "You won't be any trouble, will you? Like they say in the movies, you won't try anything stupid?"

Given her unconcern, not to mention that sense of: "If you try anything, I may forget to leave you unmaimed afterward" dampened any ardor I might have had for an escape attempt.

She made way, and I stepped past a cramped bathroom and into a small kitchen.

Helen waved me into a bench-lined niche that surrounded a small table. The kind that folded down to become a bed. She pressed a button on the coffee machine while I caught myself admiring every curve, the symmetry . . .

You're not in high school. Think.

Male gaze be damned, I closed my eyes, forced myself to pay attention. I'd been teleported off the Royal Gorge Bridge. This was the woman who had appeared in the Grantham parking garage and tried to murder Alpha. She was from another branch of the timeline. Ten thousand questions began to percolate in my head.

"Marvin came from your world?"

"No. Different branch of the timeline but still in your amplitude. Which is why you can't identify his body. He was a scholar. Ancient languages. Wanted to know about a historical figure, a mystic named Simon Magus. I offered a trade. What I knew in exchange for tutoring in your culture and language. He had a wonderfully agile and adaptive mind to go with his remarkable charm." The wistful smile was back as the machine hummed and squirted coffee into a cup. "Cream and sugar?"

"Black's good."

She handed it over and started a second cup for herself.

"So, you're here. Why not use your cerebrum and navigator, zip ahead, and be there when Alpha comes out of her time warp?"

She slipped into the seat across from me. "You've been studying Fluvium's cerebrum, right?"

"We have. Care to help us with that?"

"No." She sounded definite about that. "Made any progress on figuring out how it works?"

"We don't have a clue. Something about fields, some kind of hand movements. Harvey's stymied. Just like Skientia was with the navigator until Alpha did her Houdini out of Ward Six and back into their lab."

"For a variety of reasons I won't go into, as well as for safety and security, the system requires two people to travel in time, let alone across the branches."

"You popped out of the garage when your friend Marvin was shot."

"A spatial shift. Like what you and I did from the bridge. That's one of the fail-safes. Allows us to flee a bad situation to a preprogrammed secure location, then we can recalibrate and ditch the branch altogether. That's Nakeesh's current problem. It takes two, and as long as Fluvium stays dead, she needs to train a new accomplice. As it is, she's got what you'd call a shitstorm on her hands."

"Oh, I don't know. Seems to me that as long as she stays in her time bubble somewhere in the future, she's pretty safe."

"That's not what I'm referring to. She answers to others, powerful people who don't like it when their minions fuck up, let alone lose their cerebrum and navigator to a bunch of clumsy primitives. But she does have an ally, a man who will cover for her."

"I take it he's not in our branch of the timeline?"

"He is not, and you had better hope he doesn't 'pop in,' as you call it."

"Bad dude, huh?"

"He's known as Imperator." She pronounced it EemperAhtor. "That's Latin for head leader. He's been obsessed with Nakeesh for almost a century now. If she can place her navigator in proximity to Fluvium's cerebrum, she can send out an SOS, contact Imperator. She's desperate enough to accept his terms. Become his prize possession and play toy."

"Play toy?"

"Totally. And in a lot of ways you don't want to think about." A pause. "Don't look so surprised, Doctor Ryan. Your current civilization's enlightened concern about personal liberty is not only an anomaly, it will turn out to be a passing fad. Always does. Human beings get the greatest power rush out of owning and controlling other humans as chattel. But what you really don't want is Imperator riding to Nakeesh's aid. You see, he will come. He will take her as his and cover for her mess by sterilizing your planet and your entire branch of the timeline on his way out."

"Sterilize?"

Her hard eyes showed no remorse as she said, "Down to bedrock. You get what I'm saying?"

22

Karla

This time they had a real clue. Karla had bagged the handgrips on the BMW RS before good ol' Charlie had winched it up on the bed of his tow truck and strapped it down next to the Skipper's Diavel. And yes, Karla had dogged the guy's every move to ensure he didn't so much as smudge either of the bikes with a greasy fingerprint.

It wasn't that she wanted to steal things, but damn it, with the Skipper kidnapped by the green-eyed woman, Karla's impulse disorder, and her distaste for Charlie and the way he leered at her, made her swipe one of his box end wrenches.

The motorcycles had been delivered to Grantham's underground garage a little after three that morning. Karla had Cat out of bed, dressed, and down to the garage with her lab gear within fifteen minutes.

News of the Skipper's abduction had shaken Cat down to her bones.

As the petite woman studied the BMW, she'd said, "It's a motorcycle, Chief. What do you expect me to find? You saw the video. Was the woman wearing gloves?"

"Yeah."

"Full riding suit?"

"Yeah."

"And the bike was stolen off a showroom?"

"Yeah. She took it for a test ride and never came back."

"So literally hundreds of people could have been sitting on this same motorcycle before she got on it. And then it was ridden around in the sun and the wind." Cat shook her head. "If there's anything organic on it, including the bug guts I see spattered all over, I will recover it. But don't hold your breath."

Cat had gone to work with her swabs, starting on the handlebars, then moving to the seat.

Needing something to do, Karla rechecked her third-line gear, stowed it, and figuring she wasn't going to sleep, went to the gym where she took out her frustrations on the weight machine, and then the heavy bag.

She was still at it at six when Major Savage leaned in, calling, "After action review in the cafeteria. Word is out. Everyone wants to know what's happening."

Karla reached for a towel, wiped the sweat away. "Yeah, Major. Be there in ten. Have coffee waiting."

In the shower, she wondered what was changing between her and Savage. She still didn't really like or trust the guy. But last night, some line had been crossed. Thinking back, she finally decided it had been the expression on Savage's face when he'd realized who had nabbed the Skipper. For Savage, it had been more than just an op, more than doing the job. He'd been alternately worried, pissed off, and concerned about the Skipper's health and welfare. That bought him points.

Karla dressed, made her way to the cafeteria. The nurses, the various staff, and the rest of her team were all there. All but Falcon. Savage sat at the head table, two cups of coffee steaming. At Karla's entrance, he gave her that slight tip of the head that indicated the spot next to his.

Karla took the chair, curious at the seating. It was the same that she'd used with her LPO back in the days before Jabac Junction.

"Yo, Major," ET called from where he sat beside Cat. "It's no. shit? That assassin bitch took the Skipper?"

Karla caught the signs as Savage tensed, noticed how he barely stifled the grimace. The man's demeanor indicated that he wanted to walk over and bitch-slap ET into next week. But then, that was ET versus regular army, let alone the SOF community.

Somehow maintaining control, Savage began in a monotone, relating the events as they transpired from the moment he received the phone call from the Fremont County sheriff, to the security video, the recovery of the motorcycles, and finally Cat's work on data recovery.

"We got any idea where the Skipper is?" Winny asked where she leaned her chair back on two legs, her feet braced on the edge of the table.

"Not a clue," Savage told her. "We're hoping Cat can come up with something."

"Nada," Cat said from where she sat beside ET. "If I recovered anything from the motorcycle handgrips, it will take a while to isolate, augment through the PCR, and catalog for haplotypes. Even then, if it is the assassin lady, I don't have a reference sample of her DNA to compare with."

"What do you have?" Winny asked.

"I've got rocks."

"You got what?" ET asked.

"Rocks. Sand and gravel. Little pieces thrown up by the tires that came to rest in nooks and crannies in the frame, engine, and suspension."

"I'll bite," Winny muttered. "What do little rocks tell you?"

"They tell me where the motorcycle has been. I can analyze the minerals and kinds of rocks. Then I can compare them with a geologic map of the Colorado Springs area. Roads are usually made of local materials. Sand and gravel generally come from pits close to the construction." She turned to the skinny computer whiz. "ET, can you get into the system? Colorado Department of Transportation will have records of where they obtained the road base and aggregate they used to build the roads. It should all be part of the permitting process."

"You got it, girl."

Winny raised a hand. "Okay, so the bike throws up sand and grit as it rolls down the road. We figure out where the bike has been. How does that help us find the Skipper? Remember? She used the navigator and cerebrum to pop him off the bridge. He could be anywhere, maybe not even on the planet anymore."

"That's baked in the cake," Savage agreed. "But if Cat's right, and she can work out the places that bike has been since it was stolen, at least it's something. Maybe we get lucky, and she's got Dr. Ryan locked away someplace close by."

Karla added, "It's got to be close by. The assassin lady, let's call her Green Eyes, stole the BMW on Friday, took her test ride in the afternoon. Then she used it on Saturday at noon to bait the Skipper. She planned the whole op, maybe right down to the minute. And that means the bike spent Friday night somewhere, probably within a hundred-mile radius. I'm guessing it wasn't a motel."

"Why?" Savage asked.

Karla gave him a knowing look. "Green Eyes would have known that the BMW dealership would report the bike stolen at closing time. You don't just ride off. They photocopy your driver's license and proof of insurance. And they figure they have whatever vehicle you rode in on as collateral. Colorado Springs PD would have immediately gone to the address on her driver's license. When they didn't find her or the bike, it would have gone out on the radio as a 'be on the lookout for' in Colorado Springs, the El Paso County SO, and all the surrounding towns."

"Which is how the Fremont County SO hit on it so fast," Savage replied.

"Right, but only dumb crooks steal a vehicle and check into a motel with it." Karla looked around at the others. "Cops on the night patrol get bored. SOP is to cruise through motel parking lots. They get a snapshot of who's passing through. Look for suspicious vehicles that match the profile for drugs, or maybe an Amber Alert. It's a way to pass the time, and they get hits often enough to keep it interesting."

"How do you know all this?" Winny asked.

"Part of our advance training. Classes are usually taught in conjunction with the FBI, NSA, and CIA on how to break into houses, steal cars, pick locks, get cameras into places they're not supposed to be. Then they send us out on the town to test our skills. Usually, local law enforcement is apprised of our activity. Still, it's our job not to get caught. Stealing cars is part of the gig. Never know when you might need a ride, right?"

"Can I take that class?" ET asked.

"So," Winny called, "Chances are it's a house? Maybe an apartment?"

"Or an expensive hotel," Karla countered. "Law enforcement assumes the high-end hotels have their own security. Petty thieves, child traffickers, and drug mules generally don't spring for a $400 a night single at the Antlers Hotel, let alone the Broadmoor."

"Right," Winny snorted. "They cater to a higher class of thieves, like politicians, federal bureaucrats, and high-society bitches wearing pink."

Cat interrupted, asking, "What about Dr. Ryan? What does this woman want with him?"

"Hostage, most likely," Karla said as she reached into her pocket to fiddle with the stolen Iron Throne. Somehow, that reassured her. "That, or it was a snatch for intelligence. Figures she can sweat the Skipper for everything he knows."

"Which is what?" ET demanded. "We still don't know how this shit's coming down. What's he gonna tell her? 'Yeah, soon as Alpha come out of her bubble down at Los Alamos, we gonna bust her ass.' Bet the bitch knows that."

"Maybe she's going to try and lever us," Savage speculated. "We've got a cerebrum, all of Fluvium's notes, not to mention control of the facility where Alpha will supposedly reappear."

"We're guessing out of our asses, people." Karla stared around the room. "Cat, you've got point on this. Figure out where that bike spent the night. Once you do that, the major and I will come up with a way to take it down. If we're quick and lucky, maybe the Skipper will still be there. That's it, people. Let's get to it."

She watched as they shuffled to their feet, filing off for their labs.

"I've been in touch with the police," Savage told her. "The driver's license the woman had was a fake. The address led them to the Walmart on Academy. And you'd never guess where she got the brand-new shiny Harley Street Glide she drove to the BMW dealership."

"Stolen?"

"Yeah, taken for a test ride."

23

Ryan

I sipped the coffee. Found it to be strong, full flavored. How Helen ran a steam espresso machine on the camp trailer's twelve-volt system amazed me. I assume she had a converter. Through the window, I could see pine and fir trees, a couple of campers, pickups, and some tents in other spaces. Early morning sun slanted through the conifers.

I kept forcing myself to keep from staring at Helen. It was still a battle to keep my brain and limbic system focused on anything but her. What the hell was it? Animal magnetism wasn't the right way to explain her. Whatever quality it was, just like with Alpha, I was drawn to her. Could feel the attraction. Reminded me of being a hormone-addled teenager in high school, and she was the lead cheerleader.

God, Ryan. Get it together.

Feeling really fine, almost dreamy, I asked, "How long was I out?"

Helen watched me like a hawk. "We left the bridge yesterday. I left you chemically immobilized while I saw to some things. I needed to make sure that there were no complications after your extraction. If it matters, your people were most prompt in their response. That level of concern for a superior is noteworthy; unless they are terrified of you, most commanders don't inspire that kind of loyalty."

"Maybe you don't travel in the right circles."

The hint of smile was the sort a tolerant mother would give an ignorant child. "The current qualities of your politics and military will be short-lived. Authoritative hierarchy is the ultimate state in evolution. The most egalitarian of societies rarely last more than a couple of centuries, and just a look at the news is proof that your republic is dying on the vine."

"There are those of us who don't see it that way."

"Doesn't matter what you think you see. In the end, it's always the masses who clamor for the dictator. The promise of predictability and security perpetually wins out over what you call 'freedom' and its uncertainties. While you have only your own history—which more than proves my thesis, by the way—when you study humanity across the branches . . . well, I'm afraid that, given your naive personal philosophy, you'd find the reality disheartening."

The way she said it sent a chill through me. What did so you say to someone who'd seen who-knew-how-many different worlds? How did you get your head around the notion that some Roman sailed to the Maya, that Jesus wasn't crucified, that they had a whole different history?

"Let's get back to the here and now. Why'd you kidnap me?"

"You'd call it intelligence work. Figuring out who the good guys are, what the strengths and values of various assets might be. I need to develop an understanding of the players. Who's dependable, who isn't."

"You already gave General Grazier that button, why come to me? I'm a low guy on the totem pole. You do know what a totem pole is, right?"

"Your personal chain of command runs from your president to General Grazier to you. Makes you pretty high on that pole, Doctor. Bill Stevens is firmly on Nakeesh's team, though I suspect she'd discard him if your president were subject to recruitment. Interviewing Grazier, as I'm doing here with you, would be considerably more difficult. He's constantly monitored. I am, however, interested in what you think of him. Tell me, Doctor, how would you describe the good general?"

"He's an admirable officer." Despite being dazzled by her, I applauded my wary caution with such an enchanting woman.

She chuckled. "I interpret that to mean you really don't like the man. He's just another commanding officer, and you're just the frustrated soldier, carrying out your duty to the best of your ability despite the failings of your—"

"Whatever you think of Eli Grazier, he's not 'just another commanding officer.' The man's as smart as they come, and maybe a little smarter. He's adept at politics, particularly focused, and not easily distracted from either the mission or advancing his career. Ultimately, he'll do whatever it takes, and after he's achieved the goal, he'll never look back."

"Not exactly warm and fuzzy." She narrowed an eye. "Narcissist?"

"With a dollop of borderline."

"Got it."

"You a psychiatrist on top of being a time jumper, assassin, and kidnapper?"

"Knowledge is power. When you and your people became part of the equation, I needed to know what you brought to the table. That, and when my attempt to kill Nakeesh left her stranded in your institution, anything I could learn about how you would analyze her increased my chances of destroying her."

"Why should I tell you?"

"Because we are both after Domina Nakeesh. And, well, you can't help it." She smiled. "Drink more of the coffee."

I did. Stared into the black liquid. Frowned. Thought of Alpha and Fluvium, and why they'd come to my timeline in the first place. "Granted, anyone who'd infect a world population with a genetically augmented pathogen, just to see what happened, doesn't exactly qualify for sainthood, but the way you talk sounds like vendetta."

"I have my reasons."

I considered my coffee. "So, let me guess. You took me because you're looking for allies. Given the current state of affairs, we're the only ones who might fit that bill. We know what Alpha's done and what she's capable of. We've acted against her. Came within a whisker of catching her. Like you said, Stevens is on the other side. And . . ."

I frowned. Something she'd said was nagging at me. I racked my brain. "This business of navigator and cerebrum. That it takes two. You said it's a security thing. So, if Alpha can't time travel or jump between branches without a partner, neither can you. And Marvin, your partner, is dead." I met her hard eyes. "Which means that until you find a new partner, you're as trapped here among us as Alpha is."

"Correct. Not that I'm worried about it."

I considered. Emotion aside, her best shot at getting out would be allying with Alpha. They both knew how the machines worked. Had the common goal of getting back to their timeline. Somehow, looking at this hard-eyed woman, hearing the steel under her voice when it came to Alpha, I didn't think that was a possibility. I had to ask, "How long have you been trying to get even with Fluvium and Alpha?"

"A while now," she said with dry irony.

"Chased her through a lot of branches of the timeline?"

"You might say that."

"This Imperator fellow that you mentioned, I take it that he'd react rather vigorously if you killed Alpha?"

"He most certainly will."

That she had changed to future tense wasn't lost on me.

"So you'll have to kill him, too?"

Nothing was humorous about her smile. "Oh, I'll try, Dr. Ryan. But, even if by some miracle I get him, it won't matter. At that point, the *Ultima Ahau* unleash *Inferni cum Xibalba*. When they do, I finally get to die."

"Finally?"

Again, the weary smile. "Let's just say that immortality isn't all that it's cracked up to be."

"Just how old are you?"

"My turn. Which of your people are the weakest? The most likely to defect to Stevens and possibly Nakeesh?"

"None of them."

The look she gave me, followed by her distrustful glance at my coffee cup, made me suspicious. "Did you drug my coffee?"

"Of course."

I should have been offended. Outraged. Instead, I smiled with amused euphoria, delighted by the chance to enjoy such a charming woman's company.

She archly said, "I find it hard to believe that *none* of your people would betray you to Stevens. He's the president's chief of staff. Your people are confined to a mental hospital. Stevens could offer them anything. Especially the pilot, Swink."

I considered that. "You're right, he could, with the exception of one very important intangible: Right now Winny has her choice of aircraft to fly. She's getting a new helicopter. Each time she's at the stick, it's a 'fuck you' to the Air Force. I don't think Stevens is savvy enough to understand that quirk in Winny's personality."

I lifted a finger. "And don't underestimate ET, either. Given his record, he's the most vulnerable of my people, but right now he's happily in love, not to mention safely anonymous to pursue what he enjoys more than anything, and that's being sneaky with computers.

"And since we're talking about ET, that leads to Cat Talavera. Stevens has two strikes against him before he even starts with Cat. He's establishment. The same kind of bureaucratic suit who used her research to murder an entire village in Afghanistan. Inherently, from the get-go, she wouldn't trust him or any of his representatives. Second, she was the one who figured out what Fluvium and Alpha were up to in Egypt, and it horrified her. The sun would come up in the west before she willingly joined Alpha's team."

"What about the major? Sam Savage seems a bit reluctant about his current assignment, not to mention having almost died from his wound."

How did she know that?

"He has his own trouble with Stevens, Skientia, and Alpha. My suggestion is that if you want to interrogate him, be my guest. You won't even have to kidnap him. He'll meet you over a cup of coffee at the Village Inn, and you can try and subvert him. That's what you're after, isn't it? Finding a new partner to get you home once you kill Alpha?"

Her stony gaze didn't waver. "Nice try, Dr. Ryan, but I'm sticking to the subject: Who can Stevens compromise? Raven?"

"Chief Raven is in many ways the simplest as well as the most complex of my people. The simple part is that every instinct she has is toward her team and her reputation within it. After having lost that once, she'll bend heaven and break Earth to ensure it never happens again."

"And this man Falcon?"

"It was Stevens' people who put him into a catatonic state. Assuming we can ever break him out of it, Stevens doesn't have the skills necessary to maintain Falcon's psychological equilibrium."

"If he's broken, why do you even include him? What good is he?"

I lifted an eyebrow. "Because when it comes to game theory, patterns, strategy, and analysis, he may be the most brilliant mind on the planet. For every day he lays in that bed, lost in whatever psychosis his dissociative and schizophrenic brain has conjured, I feel like I'm half blind and partially deaf." I paused, gave her a hard squint. "And, Helen, you may not understand this, but he's my patient as well as a good and decent human being, and it tortures me that I can't help him."

The look she gave me might have been bestowed on an idealistic child talking about dragons and fairies.

I tossed off the last of my coffee. "Must be a pretty tough world you come from."

"Oh . . ." She considered her words. "You might not be right about many things, Dr. Ryan, but you are about that." She stood. "You finished with your coffee?"

"Yeah."

"Then let's see about getting you back to your barracks."

"We using the cerebrum and navigator again? That hurts."

"No. We'll take the Ford F-150 that's parked outside."

"You have a pickup truck?"

"If I drove a Lamborghini Veneno, you might confuse me with Nakeesh."

24

Ryan

The F-150 pickup was a battered 2015 model, gray with the paint flaking off the hood. A durable-looking weatherproof duffle lay in the bed behind the cab. The irony of it couldn't be missed. I'd been snatched off the Royal Gorge Bridge by sophisticated alien technology that our best physicists couldn't comprehend, and now I was leaving a rather decrepit Teton camp trailer, riding in the worn seat of a battered pickup with a manual transmission.

Around us, the weekend campers had no idea that a woman from an alien timeline was in space 17 interrogating me about the relative strengths of my alien-hunting teammates. They wouldn't have believed it if it had been a *Star Trek* episode.

As Helen slipped into the driver's seat, I remained achingly aware of her. Fought that male urge to puff my chest, display my virility. Told myself I was an idiot, and then totally FUBARed it when I asked, "You have much experience driving? Want me to?"

She said nothing, punching the clutch and turning the key. The V–8 rumbled to life, and without a second's hesitation, she slipped it into reverse and backed out of the space. Shifting to first, she sent us forward seamlessly. Okay, so she had a lot more experience with a manual than I ever had.

"I have to say—" I forced my brain into gear, "—I'd have never thought to look for a camp trailer in a Forest Service campground. Not a bad idea. You can move wherever and whenever."

She turned onto the highway, again demonstrating her proficiency with a manual tranny as she shifted smoothly through the gears. I kept staring at her, muttered, "Get your head back in the game, Ryan."

"It's my extreme health," she told me.

"Excuse me?"

"You do better than most men. I wasn't expecting that. Especially drugged as you are. Humans are evolutionarily hardwired to respond to health along with the usual sexual stimuli. That's what your attraction is. Nothing more than your limbic system working the way sixty million years of mammalian evolution has programmed it to operate."

"We're supposed to overcome that in our supersensitive genderless new world."

"You might want to look at the rising rates of environmental phthalates, the estrogenizing molecules you put in things like detergents and shampoo, the xenoestrogens, um, those are the chemicals you're adding to your food. Not to mention the estrogenizing pollutants in your air, water, and soil. It's no wonder fertility, testes development, and sperm counts are dropping. You're chemically castrating and feminizing your males. Keep it up, and human reproduction in your timeline will be restricted to labs."

"So there's none of these pollutants where you come from? You just come by this healthy glow naturally?"

"Hardly. While it was anything but a pleasant experience, my immune system was altered and enhanced in a lab. Augmented. Necessary, of course. We're going to branches and times where all kinds of pathogens exist for which we have no immunity. Doesn't matter which branch you might be in—things like the Black Death, or smallpox, various strains of rubella—they all evolve separately in each branch, break out at various times depending on initiating conditions. And then there are all the different viruses with their infinite variations. Not to mention engineered gain-of-function viruses like your COVID in more advanced timelines."

"Knocked out the common cold, have you?"

"Diseases are as adaptive as humans. Our immune systems have to be able to identify and adjust to all the potential strains and genetic mutations. Same with allergens. Think of my modification as an intelligent immune system." She smiled. "The fact that we're attractive to people in the branches? That's just a byproduct, and it was my looks that got me into this mess from the start. Sure helps when you want to take a motorcycle for a test ride. That guy was on the verge of slobbering as he insisted that I take the key fob."

Was that her allure? That glow to her complexion? The sense of bursting health? Separating that from the equation, given her symmetrical face and poise, she was still a magnetic woman. Put the two together, and in another age, she'd have been called drop-dead gorgeous.

"What about these branches?" I asked to change the subject. "The way I understand the Everett Many-Worlds theory, there's billions of them. Each time a quantum event happens, the universe splits. How do you navigate between them?"

She shot me a sidelong glance as she slowed for Woodland Park, and I finally got my bearings. Now I knew exactly where we were.

The surrounding mountains, the businesses, and road markers were familiar. And I could feel the haze of euphoria starting to fade. What the hell had she put in that coffee? A string of traffic, headed the other way, was led by a group of Harley riders out for an afternoon ride.

"You don't have the language to define or comprehend the science. You'd need to speak ancient Yucatec for that. Probably the best way to describe it—in your terms—is the branch amplitude."

Her hand made a gesture where it was gripping the steering wheel. "Okay, so in your version of the physics, the entire universe is a wave function and it vibrates. The simplest way to think of it is to imagine the universe as an incredibly long string that was plucked by what you call the Big Bang. Just like on a piano, a harp, or a guitar, the string vibrates in the aftermath. The vibrations run to the ends of the string and reverberate like waves in a swimming pool. Each wave is a splitting of the branches as the waves run into each other, interfering, causing more vibrations. You with me?"

"Yes."

"Okay, so not every vibration has the same amplitude, um, the height and energy of the wave. Some are just tiny. Barely make a ripple. Others, where the waves converge, produce big waves with more amplitude. Those are the branches that carry the most energy. There aren't as many of them, and they last the longest. They spawn their own smaller amplitudes as they travel along. You are currently riding on a large-amplitude wave function. I come from another large-amplitude wave function that split from yours two thousand years ago."

"Okay, what about conservation of energy? That still work in your wave?"

She stopped for the traffic light, attention fixed on the pedestrians crossing the street. "Sure. In your physics, you give the universe an arbitrary energy value of 1. According to your theory, when the universe split the first time, it halved, each wave being 0.5, and when they in turn split, the four subsequent waves were 0.25, each branch dividing by two ad infinitum. What you call thinning."

"That's the biggest criticism of the Many-Worlds hypothesis," I told her as the light turned green and she accelerated. Woodland Park was doing a booming post-COVID Sunday business, all the stores, bars, and cafes crowded.

I made myself add, "If that's correct, we're so thin we're going to vanish. According to theory, the branches can never come together to reconstitute the energy because of decoherence. Uh, that means each branch entangles with itself. Like Velcro at the quantum level. Ultimately, the universe branches infinitely into nothingness no matter what the amplitude was when the branching started."

She gave me a dismissive, sidelong glance. "You get it wrong because you stumble over time. You people insist on including it in your most basic equations. You can't think of the universe without it."

"Hey, I'm not a physicist. All I know is that everything I've read says that time projects forward like a cone. You can't go back, and if you could, it would lead to paradox. You know, the old 'if you go back in time and kill your grandfather, you'll never be born to go back in time to kill your grandfather.'"

Even from the side, I could see Helen roll her eyes. "I will say this once: If the amplitude isn't strong enough to sustain what you call decoherence in the branching wave function, it will collapse. Those little branches? The faint vibrations? To put it in your terms, they are too thin. As a result, they recohere. With no amplitude to sustain them, time runs backward to the branch event. When it does, that little bit of energy merges back into the main branch. Essentially, the energy is reabsorbed. In your terms, conserved."

Frustrated, I cried, "But that's in the past. How can energy be reabsorbed way back when?"

"Because the notion of future or past is illusion depending on if the wave function is expanding or contracting. The branch is elastic. Get it? It shoots out, extending, stretching, but if it doesn't have the amplitude or energy, it reaches its limit and snaps back, recoheres. Like it never happened in the first place. Making you understand is not my problem. Nakeesh is."

I concentrated on that, trying to picture it in my head. Couldn't. But hey, I'm a psychologist. I'd been dragged kicking and screaming into theoretical physics. I still didn't have a clue about the mathematics, the tricky equations. I knew enough to consider things like time to be constants, that Many-Worlds theory bothered a lot of physicists, but that everyone agreed that what they called the "arrow of time" only ran one way.

Now a lady from another timeline was telling me it didn't. That the arrow, shot from a bow, reached its limit, only to fall back and re-stretch the bowstring.

Alpha and Fluvium somehow managed to go back in time from their Maya-Rome branch to our Eighteenth Dynasty Egypt. We had the physical proof of that in Fluvium's mummy, his cerebrum. Helen had the same kind of equipment, and nothing I knew about her even hinted that she wasn't as alien as Alpha. That kind of gave her instant credibility when it came to the whole time-isn't-real thing.

Okay, I told myself. *Visualize it, Ryan. A quantum event, with very low amplitude, branches the timeline. It zips out like it's on a bungee, with the entanglement that makes up decoherence holding it together.* "Then, because it doesn't have enough amplitude, it begins to recohere. Let me guess; it's the very entanglement that acts as the elastic to pull it back in time to the mainline."

"That's crude, but it illustrates the point," she agreed.

"So, there's thousands upon thousands of tiny amplitude branches constantly shooting off, snapping back into the past, and essentially vanishing," I said. "But some don't. So that means there must be a threshold. You got an equation for that?"

"Of course." She was now stuck in the Sunday traffic inching its way back down the canyon to Colorado Springs.

"I'd love to hear it."

She promptly started rattling off something that sounded like Martian. Lots of ks, ooses, sha sounds, and irregular consonants.

"What the hell was that?" I demanded.

"Yucatec," she replied woodenly.

"Mayan," I muttered, remembering that Fluvium and Alpha had been educated in a place called Dzibilchaltun—a center for science and technology in their branch of the timeline.

She added, "It helps to have a fundamental skill in base twenty mathematics. I told you that you wouldn't understand."

"How many of these large-amplitude branches of the timeline are there?"

"Sixteen that we know of in which modern *Homo sapiens* play a significant role."

"That's *all?* I thought there'd be millions. The theory . . ." I swallowed.

"Those are the ones that we've mapped with navigators. There are a lot more out there."

"Damn, just how big is that threshold?"

"Damn," she mimicked my tone. "Just how many branching wave functions has our almost-infinite universe experienced in the last fourteen-point-three billion years? And now, to use one of your quaint idioms, let me blow your mind again. What the hell makes you think that *any* of those known branches of the timeline exceed the amplitude threshold?"

"Because we're here, right? You, me, those other branches of the timeline."

"Or, to use your crude analogy, we're still stretching out, thinning the elastic of decoherence. At this point, decoherence hasn't reached its limit. The mathematicians who study this *think* they know the threshold, because, like you, they observe that we're still here. But what if this afternoon, tomorrow, a week from now, entanglement overcomes amplitude and this branch phase-shifts into recoherence? The elastic of recoherence pulls all of this back into the past, snaps it right back into the larger-amplitude timeline?"

I tried to synthesize that notion. "You guys ever seen that? I mean where you're traveling from branch to branch? Ever land on a recohering timeline by mistake?"

She turned off of US 24 and onto the cutoff to Grantham. We passed the McDonald's, the nail salon, and the State Farm Insurance office. Then the Gas-N-Go with the little bakery that made my favorite chocolate donuts.

She told me, "Maybe you weren't paying attention when I said that traveling between the branches could be horrifying. Landing in a reco-hering timeline? I'll leave it to your imagination."

"You've seen it? Experienced it?"

"If I had, I wouldn't be here. It's not something you survive. You understand terror, brain fugue, and the disintegration of reality better than I."

I contemplated that, hardly aware of the familiar sights rushing past the pickup's windows. How would the cognitive human brain react when everything around it was falling back in time? We laughed at the insanity of running a movie backward, but we did so while safely riding the arrow of time, sitting in seats, in a room, where only the image we watched was going backward.

I tried to comprehend it from Helen's perspective: she and her part-ner, leaving their timeline, headed for ours in the hunt for revenge. How did she prepare?

"Wait. Tell me something: You said that Marvin was from one of the other timelines, different from yours and ours. How many of these branches have you been to?"

She changed her grip on the steering wheel as we bounced over the potholes where last year's flash floods had almost washed out the road. A flock of Steller's jays flitted across from one batch of Ponderosa pine to the next.

After a too long pause, she asked, "Does it matter?"

"You haven't said a word about the world you come from. Well, other than it's a rather authoritarian branch. Is your timeline the same as Alpha and Fluvium's?"

She smiled as she pulled the pickup over to the side of the road. We weren't more than a half mile from Grantham. "Let's just say it's a long story and leave it at that."

"But you said that Alpha had superiors, that she was, 'in a world of shit' over losing the time equipment to a bunch of primitive barbarians. So, do you serve the same masters that she does?"

"This is your stop, Dr. Ryan." She indicated the door.

"We're still a half mile from Grantham. Why don't you come in, tell us more. Surely, we can work together, find a way to—"

"You really want to get out now. It'd damage that delightfully male ego of yours if I was to physically remove you from the truck."

"You're not listening. We need you. The things you can teach—"

"You have three seconds. One, two, three . . ."

I opened the door, unbuckled my seatbelt, and stepped out on the roadside as a line of Harleys roared by.

"How do I get in touch, Helen?"

"It's the same in every branch: 'Don't call us, we'll call you.'" As she said it, she reached over, grabbed my door, and slammed it shut.

With a curious wave of the hand, she accelerated onto the blacktop, caught a break in the traffic, cut a tight U-turn, and roared off back the way we'd come.

I stood there, smelling the vanilla odor of the pines, traffic whizzing past, feeling more confused than I'd felt in my entire life.

25

Falcon

"**H**ey, *Falcon, my man. Come to see you. Need you back, Gotta lotta shit coming down. That lady what tried to kill Alpha down in the garage? She 'napped the Skipper right off Royal Gorge Bridge. Used a navigator and cerebrum. Pop! And Colonel Ryan's gone.*"

Falcon, sitting on his bed, back to his wall, lowered his gaze to watch his hands where they twitched in unison, fingers fluttering and curling. He couldn't help it. His right foot kept bouncing, the action almost maniacal and beyond his control.

In the background, the faint strains of *La Traviata* could be heard rising and falling as Alfredo and Violetta sing "Sempre libera."

"You going to do anything about that?" Major Marks asked where he sat in Falcon's visitor's chair.

"Nothing that I need to do," Falcon replied, panic tingling and rising in his chest. The compulsive spasming of his hands got worse. Increased anxiety sent his pulse racing. He told the major, "Violetta's going to die. She always does."

"God, you're a pussy." Rudy Noyes almost spat the words. He slouched in the corner of the room, flicking his switchblade knife open and closed. His brown-leather bomber jacket hung open to expose a dirty T-shirt. "The fucking soldier here's talking about ET, you simpering little wuss."

"They don't need me!" Falcon cried. Pulling his knees up, he hunched into a ball. Kept his head down to avoid the major's eyes. Terrified of the disgust he'd see in Rudy's sneering face.

"Didn't you hear?" Theresa Applegate asked as she stepped out of Falcon's bathroom. She was wearing her ivory-colored cotton dress imprinted with red roses. The style was a 50's cut that fell below her knees.

Her too-thin calves came across as almost birdlike, slimming to rolled white socks at the ankles that contrasted with her black-strapped shoes. As she stepped out of the bathroom, she shot a worried gaze at the major and reached up to pull some of her unruly black curls back and fix them with a bobby pin.

"See," Major Marks muttered in irritation. "Even the skinny witch agrees. ET needs you. You have a command emergency, and you're going to sit there on that bed and short-stroke your paranoia. Soldier up, Falcon. You're better than this."

"Naw." Rudy uttered a nasal dismissal. "Know what would happen if I was to reach over and open that door? The little faggot would piss his pants."

"Would not!" Falcon mumbled under his breath.

"Soldier?" Major Marks asked. "I can't *hear* you."

"Would not!" Falcon repeated, rushing the words, his heart now hammering in his chest.

"Fucking little coward," Rudy said before he spit on the floor. "I'm gonna open the door."

Falcon glanced up in time to see Rudy push out from the corner of the room, his left hand reaching for the doorknob as his right snapped the switchblade closed and slipped it into the dirty pocket on his jeans.

"No!" Falcon cried, leaping from the bed, stumbling over to slap Rudy's hand from the knob.

In that moment, he could feel the eyes. Those horrible black pupils, like dots of soul-sucking and burning darkness as they floated in washed-out blue irises. They were there. Terrible and devouring. And if the door opened, there would be nothing between Falcon and . . . and . . .

"Yeah!" Rudy mocked. "Some hero. You're nothing more than shit on a sidewalk."

Falcon's pounding heart, the shiver that ran through his muscles, left him shamed. Empty.

He let his hesitant gaze rest on the door. Solid. Large. A heavy institutional hospital door. His only protection from those deadly blue eyes, from that gaze that would melt him into nothingness.

"Yeah, nothingness," Major Marks agreed sadly. "We had so much hope for you."

"Hey, Falcon? Whassup? You hear me, man? We need you." ET's voice came from somewhere above.

"They. Need. You." Major Marks said in a coaxing voice.

"No." Falcon swallowed hard, stepping back from the door, from the terrible eyes that he knew lurked just beyond that portal. "They need Chief Raven. Maybe Winny. The eyes are out there. Can't let them . . . Can't . . ."

"What?" Theresa asked, stepping hesitantly around Major Marks' crossed legs, the creases in his pants like knife edges, his shoes polished to a gleaming black luster.

"I'm not here!" Falcon cried, wheeling to face Theresa. "Don't you understand? The eyes looked at me. And they didn't *see anything!*" He sniffed, felt tears brimming. "I wasn't there. Just . . . empty."

"Yo, Falcon? Everybody here pullin' for you. Need you to make sense of what all's happening. Need your magic, dude."

"Need my magic?" Falcon clamped his eyes shut, aware that Noyes, Theresa, and the major were watching him, their gazes filled with . . . gazes . . . filled with . . .

Eyes had done this to him. Had burned through him. Turned him into a terrified blob of Jello. Left him cored out and hollow.

God, he hated to be empty.

"Gotta go now, bro. Big meeting. Gotta go figure out how to find the Skipper. Wish you was coming wi' me."

Falcon turned, caught his image in the mirror. His brown hair, the chin, medium nose. Average cheekbones. High forehead with brown eyebrows over . . . over . . .

There was nothing where the eyes should be. Only emptiness.

With a howling cry, Falcon knotted his fists. The burning rage came welling up from down deep. Those horrible blue eyes. They'd done this to him.

With a single blow, he smashed his mirror, splintering the image, destroying the reflection of those empty holes where his eyes had been.

26

Ryan

The Level Four security guard at the main gate just passed me in, greeting me with, "Good day, Dr. Ryan. Out for a walk?"

I gave the guy a smile and a wave, saying, "Yeah, needed the exercise."

Grantham Barracks—despite our special activity in Ward Six—was still a working military psychiatric hospital. The other five wards were run by Dr. Mary Pettigrew. She and her staff continued to treat a variety of patients and their specific disorders. Pick up a copy of the DSM-5, and you can get an idea of all the subjects we deal with. And yes, that includes the children of men and women in active service. They're housed in Ward Two. We also have Ward One, "The Walls," which houses the criminally insane. The other wards deal with the garden-variety disorders that any psychiatric hospital would handle.

That my abduction wasn't immediately commented on by the guard indicated that A, our Ward Six security was still functional, or B, that Helen had been blowing smoke when she said "the American Indian and the woman" had recovered my Diavel. In that case, no one knew I'd been whisked off the Royal Gorge Bridge.

Trust me, I've been lied to by the best. Wouldn't be the first time someone had tried to reassure me by telling me that all was well. "Yes, Dr. Ryan, I'm feeling much better now. No, Dr. Ryan, the voices are no longer telling me to set off a satchel charge at midnight in the officers' barracks."

Walking to the garage entrance, I followed the ramp down. There, by the door, on its side stand, the Diavel gleamed in the overhead lights. The black BMW was next to it.

Okay. It was A, then.

I walked up to the security officer posted at the entrance and saw his eyes widen. "Sir, you're supposed to be missing."

"Gone and back. Did Major Savage and Chief Raven recover the two bikes?"

"Yes, sir."

Looked like Helen had told the truth. That being the case, what was her source of information? Did she have someone inside Ward Six? An eavesdropping device? Could she be monitoring our communications? Or was it something even simpler, like a police scanner from Walmart that was set to the Fremont County SO's frequency?

For all that I knew—having been "chemically immobilized"—she might have gone to observe in person.

"I'll let them know that you're back, sir. They'll be relieved."

"No. I'll handle it. But if you could pass the word to the Level One checkpoint so they don't make a scene, I'd appreciate it."

"Yes, sir."

I took a second, glanced over at the spot where I'd first seen Helen firing an M4 on full automatic. What the hell did I make of that woman who'd been so desperate to kill Alpha? She'd have mowed down every one of us had Captain Stanwick not center-punched her partner, Marvin, with a lucky heart shot.

She'd truly cared for the guy. What had she said? Something about she should have been past such sentiment? That she wasn't, spoke to her innate humanity. Time and hard knocks hadn't beaten it all out of her. But then, Hitler had loved his dog, Blondi, and Stalin had doted over little kids.

Inside, I took the elevator, getting a nod and salute from the wide-eyed security officer who passed me into Ward Six.

"Where's the team?" I asked.

"Conference room, sir. They're in a meeting. Something Dr. Talavera found. That's all I know."

I thanked him and started down the hall. My stomach was rumbling. It appeared that chemical immobilization and a cup of black coffee just weren't cutting it, and breakfast in Cripple Creek had been long ago.

At the conference room, I pushed the door open, and stepped in.

Shoulders touching, my people were bent over a map of the mountains west of Colorado Springs: ET, Cat, Winny, Savage, and Raven. The map had been spread over the top of the conference table, the chairs all pushed back.

"Some of the gravel was easy," Cat was saying as she pointed to something on the map. "It's granite. Exfoliated from bedrock. The chemical composition of the minerals and size of the crystals mark it as having come from batholith, specifically the outcrops here on Highway 9 south of Hartsel. Given that we've got signals from the schist outside Canyon City, that means she traveled south."

"Okay," Savage said. "We've got sandstone from the Lyons formation on the outskirts of town that suggest US 24, and now Hartsel. What else are we missing?"

"A Forest Service campground north of Woodland Park," I told them, walking around to the head of the table.

"Skipper!" "Colonel!" "Holy shit! Where'd you come from?" "What the fuck?" all intermingled as they jerked bolt upright. I thought Raven was going to hug me. Being Raven, she of course restrained herself. Cat Talavera was under no such prohibitions. Winny watched with a certain distaste, as though she were loath to allow any display. ET was all wide grin, a sparkle of relief in his eyes.

"Take your seats, people," I said, as I peeled Cat loose. "I'll tell you the whole story."

"One thing, Tim," Savage declared. "You really get snatched off the Royal Gorge Bridge? Popped away by that woman?"

I waved them all down. "Page Myca Simond and send him off to the cafeteria for a sandwich, a burger, or whatever. I'm starved. And we need Janeesha in here to take notes. Contact both Yusif al Amari and Dan Murphy down at Los Alamos. Tell them to grab their research, beat feet out of Los Alamos, and get here as damn fast as they can."

"On it," ET said, dropping into his seat and tapping keys on his laptop.

I asked, "Does General Grazier know I've been snatched?"

"He does," Sam told me. "I called him on the red phone. Not only did he resort to colorful language, he demanded that we 'get off our sorry asses and get Ryan back.' Considering it was just you, sir, we went to Starbucks for pumpkin lattes instead."

"Yeah, and a good 'up yours,' too, Major." I gave the man a knowing smile. "I'll call Eli, tell him that Helen brought me back. That I'm fine. And we've got a shitload to figure out."

"Helen?" Winny asked.

"That's what she calls herself. Said it came from Greek. And Fluvium and Nakeesh called her *Ennoia*. Said it was a sick joke. Which is why I want Yusif and Murphy here. This is all tied to Egyptians, Romans, and Mayans."

"What's this woman's status, Skipper?" Karla asked. "Hostile? Shoot on sight? Snatch? Or what?"

"Not sure, Chief. But let's wait for the debrief, then we'll kick it around."

"She threaten you?" Winny demanded. "Hurt you?"

Karla stiffened in that way of hers, ready to kick ass.

"No. She made me coffee. Now, get me my sandwich, and let's get to work."

TIMOR

This is our sixth jump. An uncharted one. Dangerous lest we land in a reco-hering timeline. I can see the strain in the faces of the quinque. *If they survive this mission—are part of the rescue and recovery of Fluvium and Nakeesh along with their equipment—they will be promoted to Second Sword with all of its benefits and privileges. Nothing comes without risk, but I can see that each jump is taking its toll.*

I have overheard them talking, wishing that they'd worn combat armor. Car-ried heavy weapons. Instead, we're traveling lightly. They wear only cloaks and light mail which will stop arrows, swords, and knives. Our mission is not to fight. Only to find Nakeesh and Fluvium and recover their devices. If we get really lucky, we'll get a crack at the Ennoia.

Though, if that happens, I'm not sure but it would be better to call in a mille. *Let an entire legion take her down. Maybe they'll rape her to death in the process.*

We are working on the boundaries of plotted jumps. Which is where Fluvium and Nakeesh would have chosen a population for their red plague experiments. Somewhere along a historically parallel timeline.

Now, checking our instruments, neither I nor Sak Puh can find any reading or trace of our elusive quarry. Had they been in this timeline, popped into this version of Egypt, we would detect scattered entangled particles left by Nakeesh's navigator. Instead, we stand on the banks of yet another Nile—still silt-choked—and find nothing but an abysmal poverty. In this Egypt, there are only scattered farms, the floodplain mostly still grasslands grazed by goats and sheep.

These are truly "monkey people." Worthless. Dispensable.

Not the timeline Fluvium would have chosen for his red plague studies. He would need a thriving civilization for his epidemiological experiment to work.

Fluvium and Nakeesh have been under my supervision for several decades now. Both are remarkably talented, gifted in fact. I have alternately admired, hated, and loved them. To be more precise, I've hated Fluvium and loved Na-keesh. Been obsessed with her for years.

She is the woman who lies just beyond my reach. The one who has spurned my advances, dismissed my offers, and continuously turned me down cold. I dream of her at night. Imagine her writhing beneath me as I copulate with women that I choose for their similar looks. So much for fantasy. I want the real thing.

The quality of the work she and Fluvium do for the Ultima Ahau *makes her off limits. Where she not so valuable to the Lords, I would have taken her for my own years ago.*

Remember that I told you in the beginning that I have a flaw? I will do anything to possess Domina Nakeesh. Even travel from timeline to timeline, no matter what threat the monkey people who inhabit them might pose.

27

Childs

The instructions were that Hanson Childs and Jaime Chenwith were not to make contact before, during, or after the flight. They'd even taken separate cabs to different DC hotels for the night. Fortunately, the Hilton Garden Inn had a bar, and Childs had been able to nurse Grey Goose on the rocks while he contemplated his situation. At the desk, the next morning, Childs had picked up a FedEx package that contained his itinerary, ticket information, a new iPhone, credit cards, three grand in cash, and instructions.

Childs had followed the directions to the letter, traveled under an alias, and had no trouble with his documents at the TSA checkpoints along the way. The flight to Albuquerque had been routine. They had booked him in economy plus—which got him the extra leg room, and it was an aisle seat to boot. He'd seen Jaime Chenwith at the gate; his alter ego having been in Group 3. Jaime had been allowed to board before Childs' Group 4.

So, he was back in New Mexico, drinking vodka at another Hilton Garden Inn while the Astros played Atlanta on TV behind the bar. Two sales reps from Cleveland talked about sell-through and market share, and what an asshole Benito was. The middle-aged woman in the tailored gray suit at the end studied the screen of her laptop and flipped through what looked like legal documents. She could have had "successful lawyer" tattooed across her forehead.

New Mexico. He was all for it. Grazier had taken him and Jaime down just up the road on the other side of Santa Fe. Whatever that had been about, it had stemmed from the mess at Los Alamos. Now, he was back and aching for a rematch.

Not that either he or Jaime Chenwith had a clue about what was really at the root of all the trouble. Even in their initial investigation, that had been unclear. Something about a sarcophagus, archaeologists, and a shadowy female at the heart of it all. He and Chenwith had been concerned with who stole an airplane and then a helicopter, which had led to a small war zone at the Aspen Skientia labs. That had put them on the trail to Grantham and a deepening mystery.

Solid, old-fashioned police work had led them to Los Alamos and an ever-increasing body count. The trail had ended at the Buffalo Thunder Resort. That should have been it. Arrests made, offenders charged, and trial dates set. Military justice could take its course.

And here I am, the butt of some prick's bad joke. God, he wanted the son of a bitch who'd destroyed his life.

Problem was, he didn't have a fricking clue as to who had been behind it. Neither did Jaime. He just wanted to kill the miserable fucker.

That might have been the point. He couldn't help but wonder if Bill Stevens wasn't the wizard behind the curtain. Playing him and Jaime. Stevens, with his connections, could have orchestrated the whole thing. Waited until Hanson and Jaime were at just the right fever-pitch of desperation, and then stepped in like the freakin' white knight.

That was the thing about kingmakers like Stevens. They didn't worry themselves about the lives of their pawns. They just sent them out on the chessboard, used them as bait to trap the opponent's queen, and flicked them off the board.

Odd that he'd immediately segue to a queen, given that the mysterious Domina was a key player. He wondered who she was, why he and Jaime had only heard her name uttered a couple of times, and even then in nothing but the most reverent tones.

The next morning, feeling more than a little rocky, he choked down breakfast, packed, and was waiting at the curb when a white Dodge van pulled up at precisely 7:23. Rio Grande Shuttle Service had been printed in bright red letters on the side. The driver hopped out, asking, "Anyone going to Chimayo?"

"Yeah. Me."

Childs tossed his one bag into the luggage rack and wasn't surprised to see Jaime Chenwith, already in the back seat.

Within minutes, the driver had them out on I-25, headed north. He called over his shoulder, "It's okay. You can talk if you want. The van's been swept. We're past the cloak and dagger. ETA in Española in about an hour, give or take."

"Just the two of us?" Jaime asked, picking his way forward to a seat opposite Childs.

"Rest of the team's already checked in."

The rest of the team? He met Jaime's gaze, saw the slight shrug.

"Who do you work for?" Jaime asked casually. "DOD? Justice?"

"Same as you. All I can tell you is national security. The first rule is to keep your mouth shut. Follow orders. Do that, and a really nice paycheck is deposited in your bank account," the driver said laconically. "Josh Mack will give you the details when we get to the residence. For the time being, we're in a hurry up and wait mode. And right now, we're waiting on you two."

Jaime arched a questioning eyebrow.

"What do you think, bro?" Childs asked.

"Like you, someone seriously fucked me over. I want a little payback." He grinned, sitting back in the seat. "Besides, we signed the papers. It's official with me. Air Force has detailed me to something called 'Special National Security Operations.' So, I guess Stevens owns my little Latino ass."

The destination proved to be a La Quinta on Española's south end just past the turnoff for Los Alamos.

At the entrance, the driver pulled up and opened the side door. Childs grabbed his bag, stepped out, and glanced around. The New Mexico sun baked the parking lot where a line of white Ford vans had been backed into spaces.

Inside the air-conditioned lobby, a woman behind the desk smiled a greeting and handed over little envelopes with room keys, simply saying, "Welcome to La Quinta. Those are your rooms. Registration is already taken care of. If I can be of any assistance, please let me know. I'm supposed to tell you that you have fifteen minutes if you need to freshen up. Your colleagues will meet you in the Jemez Room at 10:00."

She pointed to the hall on the left that led to the meeting rooms.

"Thanks." Chenwith told her.

Their rooms on the second floor were adjoining, close to the stairs. After tossing his bag on the bed, Childs hit the bathroom, washed his hands, and checked himself in the mirror. He looked tired, eyes puffy.

Too much vodka last night. Splashing water onto his face, he called it good, toweled off, and headed for the stairs.

The Jemez Room was set up with an optimistic four rows of black plastic chairs facing a table with a single chair behind it. The laptop in the center was hooked to a projector pointed at the white screen to one side. A knot of guys were crowded around a side table. They were in the process of demolishing two big boxes of donuts and emptying a large cafeteria-sized pot of coffee. At a glance, Childs knew the type: fit, standing easily in their cargo pants, a low-level banter powering the conversation as they sipped their drinks and chowed down on donuts. Definitely security guys, the kind who were trained to knock down doors, take names, and kick ass. Their ages ranged from the early twenties to mid-thirties. Most had sleeve tattoos that ran up to disappear into their T-shirts.

One—an older guy who looked to be knocking on forty—caught sight of Childs as he walked in. Childs remembered him from the night of the meeting with Stevens. The man waved, calling, "Come on over here, Special Agent Childs. Get a cup and grab a bite."

Childs did, meeting the eyes of the others as they gave him the once-over. Yep, a cocky bunch of bastards.

"Special Agent Childs, I'm Josh Mack," the leader told him. "We didn't really get a formal introduction back in DC."

The man's grip was like iron, the thick muscles in his arms bulging. And he wasn't even trying to crack Childs' bones. That glint behind Mack's eyes left no doubt but that he had been in the shit and seen the worst.

Chenwith walked in with a slant of smile on his thin lips.

"Hey, gang," Mack called out, "Say hello to Special Agent Jaime Chenwith, late of the Air Force's Office of Special Investigations. Hanson Childs, here, was with Army CID. So, make your introductions, and welcome them to the team. As soon as the agents have their coffee and chow, let's get this show on the road."

What followed was a flurry of hand shaking, measuring gazes, and a slew of names to match with faces: Teddy Meyer, "Dirty Harry" Logan, Ken Sala, Lonnie Hughes, Steth Calloway, Billy Stump, Cal Spicer, Al Allison, and Eugene Chalmers.

"You two," Mack indicated Childs and Chenwith, "take these seats up front. The rest of you apes, plant your asses and let's get to work."

Mack took the seat behind the table and opened the laptop. The projector immediately displayed an aerial view of the Los Alamos compound. Mack used a laser pointer, saying, "This is the area of our operations." The beam focused. "This is our primary objective."

"Holy shit," Chenwith muttered from the side of his mouth. "That's the Skientia lab."

"Right," Mack told him. "Which is one of the reasons the two of you are here. You've been inside. You were there the night the shit went down."

Mack fixed on the rest of the room. "Gentlemen, we're here for one purpose. It's an extraction mission. We're going to go in and bring a woman out."

"Excuse me," Childs said, "but our understanding is that General Grazier put that building off limits. Aren't his people in charge there?"

"Yeah, they are." Mack raised an eyebrow. "Given that Grazier was the one who tossed you and Agent Chenwith into the grinder, is that a problem for you?"

"Not in the slightest," Childs replied. "This woman is the one they called Domina?"

"That's on a need-to-know basis."

"Which means, yeah, it's her," Jaime muttered again. "Look, we didn't get the whole story. What we did hear, though, was crazy. Just some weird shit about how she'd escaped in a time machine. That she'd got away into the future."

Mack nodded. "Yeah, that's my understanding. Our job is to get her back."

Steth Calloway, a tall dark black man asked, "The future? C'mon man."

"Don't worry about it, Steth," Mack told him. "All you have to do is get in, retrieve the woman and a machine she's carrying, and get her out."

Teddy Meyer, half laughing, asked, "So, like, if she's in the future, how do we know when to take that lab down?"

Mack told him, "We've got a source. Somehow, the source is under the impression that our future lady is coming back, and it's going to be real soon."

"Hey, I don't have to believe any science fiction bullshit," Lonnie

Hughes called from the end of his row. "We go in hot, get control of the building, and pull the woman out, right?"

"Right," Mack agreed and pulled up a view of the Skientia lab. "This is the building. Team One, you'll enter through this side door. The security cams will be off, so they won't know we're inside until it's too late."

"And if there's resistance?" Cal Spicer asked.

"Take it down any way you have to. Tranks are preferred, but the use of deadly force is authorized. We do this right, it won't come to that."

After a moment to let it soak in, Mack flipped to the next powerpoint slide. "So, let's get familiar with the internal layout of the building."

The planning took the entire afternoon.

28

Kaplan

Maxine Kaplan checked her watch. The time was 19:52 hours. She rubbed the back of her neck, stared up at the bright lights glaring down from among the cables and pipes that obscured the ceiling of Lab One. Before her, the hemispherical crater left vacant by Domina's time machine mocked her. So did the hum of the generator where it shot an endless beam of charged particles at the exact center of the sphere.

Around the periphery of the crater, the three detectors they'd placed at one hundred-and-twenty–degree intervals stood on their tripods, the screens registering each of the reflected particles. From the detectors, cables ran to Kaplan's laptop in its shielded case.

Maxine had taken the day shift. Left the nights to Wixom. Each of them monitored the detectors during their shifts. She'd run the math, had charted the linear acceleration as energy increased with each deflected particle. According to the detectors, the reflected particles were now moving at close to two hundred and seventy million meters per second. If the rate of acceleration remained the same, they would reach the speed of light, or C, within the next four hours.

The door opened. Virgil Wixom stepped in, nodded to the guards at the door, and carefully descended the stairs. He had a cup of coffee in his right hand, his notebook tucked under his left arm. A tortured frown lined his forehead, but then, that was pretty much his normal expression these days. Through his thinning hair, she could see his scalp gleaming in the lights.

"What are we up to?" he asked by way of greeting.

"Decelerating," she lied. "Down to two hundred fifty million. I've sent the data to your computer. Whatever we thought we were measuring, it's reversing." She gave him a weary smile. "I'm sorry, Virg. Go take a look at the data, then when you've seen what I've seen, go home. We've been at this for days without a full eight hours of sleep. I'm going to hang for another hour myself, and call it."

"What if we have a change?" He indicated the particle beam generator where it hummed on its mount. "Just because you've got a decrease . . ."

She gave him a disarming smile. "It's all right, Virg. I'm leaving the unit on. Got it programmed into my iPhone. If the energy with which the particles are deflected changes, increases, it will set off my phone alarm. I'll give you a call."

"Doesn't make sense that it would decrease," he said absently. "That flies in the face of our hypothesis that the closer we get to Domina's return, the nearer the reflected particle speed will be to C."

"Virg, I've been wrestling with that very thing for the last couple of hours. Doesn't mean we're wrong. Just that we're not taking some variable into account. Hell, maybe, for all we know, the field fluctuates. My crazy thought was that now that we're playing in Domina's backyard, we don't know the rules, let alone where the swing set is located. Maybe all we're getting is the bounce off the teeter-totter going up and down."

The stare he gave her was emotionless, almost blank. As if he'd turned his expression off. "Most everybody's checked out. Weird thing. The archaeologists got a mysterious phone call. Packed up a pile of Fluvium's documents, and drove off. You know anything about that?"

"No." She wondered if she should be concerned. No. Who cared? The fewer people in the building, the better. And besides, Skylar Haines and Yusef al Amari always made her nervous. Skylar because he was a leering filthy lech. Amari, well, she'd been an accomplice to the man's torture. And she suspected that he knew.

"Virg," she used her most persuasive voice. "Go home. Get a good night's rest. You've earned it. Trust me, I've got the lab covered."

"Whatever," he muttered, turned around, and trudged his way back up the stairs. The soles of his shoes slapped on the cement steps.

The fact that he didn't look back when he reached the door surprised her. She figured he'd at least shoot her one last look, maybe call "Good night."

With quick fingers, she called up the data she'd sent to his office computer. She'd been working on the program for a couple of days. Used some of her precious sleep time to make the plotted data points graph in a predictable manner.

As the door slammed shut, she sighed. "Sorry, Virg. But I'm doing you a favor."

Happy with what Virgil would see if he even bothered to go to his office and access the data, she cleared the display and returned it to the real deflector data. She watched the acceleration rising on her screen. Just in the time she talked with Virgil, acceleration had risen another three hundred thousand meters per second. Checked her watch. She had a little less than four hours now.

On her iPhone, she touched the texting icon. Watched the little green text bubble form, and entered, "Countdown: 3 hours, forty-five minutes."

A text came moments later. "Roger. We're rolling."

She glanced up at the two guards, both of the men looking bored. The rest of Grazier's security, six of them on duty, would be patrolling the lab in teams of two. Just as bored as these. Well, there were worse things than being bored.

She had things to do. Shouldn't be too hard.

Idly, she wondered what she'd say to Tanner Jackson if he stepped out of the bubble.

29

Ryan

What did it all mean? I pondered that, as I considered the car-
toonish bunnies, fawns, bobbing sunflowers, and waving grass
painted in soothing pastel colors on the walls. The beanbag chairs were
all stuffed into a colorful pile in the far corner where ET sprawled lazily
atop them, his computer propped as his long fingers tapped the keys. We
really needed a much more professional-looking war room if we were
the last line of defense for the planet and all of mankind in our branch
of the timeline.

I sat in the plastic chair at the head of the table, sipping coffee that
Janeesha had thoughtfully run to my office to brew. Sam Savage sat at
the far end, head down as he flipped his fingers around on his tablet.
He'd been irritated ever since we discovered that the Teton trailer Helen
had held me in was stolen from a backyard in a Denver suburb. Cat was
currently scouring it for any clue as to my abductor's identity. From Cat's
preliminary report, she had a couple of long, auburn hairs complete with
follicles that would yield DNA.

Once that analysis was complete, we'd have a whole new insight
into Helen.

I reviewed my notes one last time, trying to think of anything I
might have missed in my recounting of my captivity. It would have been
so much better if I had been able to record Helen instead of relying on
my memory. Especially the stuff about the branching timelines. Harvey
Rogers was already going over the notes down in his office.

Rereading that section again, I couldn't think of anything more to
add. It was as word-for-word as I could recall.

And then there was that business about Helen, Simon, and Kepha or
"Petros" as she'd called him. She said that in this branch, Petros had

triumphed over Simon. But what did that mean? Pompeius Magnus hadn't died on a beach in Egypt, and Octavius hadn't killed Antony and Cleopatra to become Augustus. In her branch, some guy named Lucas Magna Nauta had sailed to the Americas.

Helen wouldn't have brought it up if it weren't important.

I flipped back to those pages, then turned to my laptop. Janeesha watched me with worried dark eyes. Like the rest of the team, she was still here long after her mandated quitting time. She, too, could sense that we'd crossed some line we didn't understand. That the game had been elevated to a new level.

I input Pompeius Magnus and promptly learned that he's known today as Pompey the Great. That he waged a desperate battle for the control of Rome before Julius Caesar defeated him at a place called Pharsalus in Greece. And yes, he was murdered by Cleopatra's brother, Ptolemy Philopater, pharaoh of Egypt, on September 28, 48 BCE.

Okay, so he was one of the three men—called a triumvirate—who were fighting over control of Rome. How did the assassination of a Roman general who'd already lost the war lead us to Helen and Alpha battling in our branch of the timeline over two thousand years later?

I was glaring at the computer, reading the Wikipedia entry when the Egyptian archaeologist, Yusif al Amari, PhD, and soon-to-be-doctor Dan Murphy came charging into the conference room. Both had satchels over their shoulders, and each looked remarkably eager. Maybe I should get kidnapped by alien women more often. Everyone seemed suddenly so energized.

I checked the time, said, "Didn't figure I'd see you for another couple of hours. You get speeding tickets getting here?"

Yusif grinned, white teeth visible behind his thick black beard. "Let us say we were motivated. The less time we have to spend in a vehicle with Skylar, the better. And, of course, my police scanner picks up the New Mexico State Police. They radio in their mile marker when they make a stop."

Yusif's in his forties, black hair and beard, and an expert on Egyptian archaeology. Known as an excavator, Yusif was hired originally by Skientia to help Reid Farmer open Fluvium's tomb in Egypt. Things hadn't gone well for him after that all fell apart; he'd been grabbed out of an Egyptian prison, spirited off to Los Alamos, tortured, and rescued by

Karla Raven. Recruited to my team, he insisted that life as an exile in New Mexico had a lot more going for it than being a prisoner in the "new" Egypt.

Dan Murphy—tall and bean-pole skinny—used a thin finger to push his wire-rimmed glasses up on his nose. Murphy looked like what he was: a graduate student in archaeology from Harvard. His all-but-finished PhD dissertation was on Mayan mathematics, and Dan was the world's leading expert. He tended toward T-shirts, worn-out jeans, and grungy running shoes. The man's blond hair looked like it hadn't seen a comb in a couple of centuries.

Murphy jerked a thumb at Yusif. "He makes me nervous. The guy spends more time surveilling cops than Google spends watching everybody else. You'd think he was paranoid."

"I am." Yusif gave Murphy a dull-eyed look. "You have not had the enlightened pleasure of living in the new Egypt. Our relationship with the police is now one of trust. We trust them to impose their will at any and all cost to the people."

"So, Dr. Ryan? You really got kidnapped?" Murphy asked, slinging his satchel onto the conference table and pulling out a seat. Yusif was more professional as he lowered himself into a chair and opened his bag to start digging out papers.

I told him, "Abducted off the Royal Gorge Bridge in broad daylight. Got to tap my finger on a working navigator."

"What's that like?" Murphy asked.

"Sort of like having your arms and legs pulled out of their sockets. Your head feels like your skull is exploding from the inside, and there's a sense that you're falling through a black hole."

Deadpan, Yusif blinked at me. "Perhaps the Egyptian government should get such a device. It would fit right into the State Security Investigation Services . . . whoops, I forget; they are now the Homeland Security. Totally reformed. The kind of people who would love to employ such a device. Especially since, from what I can see, it doesn't leave bruises or contusions."

I took a sip of my coffee. "You got the emailed notes?"

"Been going over them on the drive up here," Murphy said, diving into his bag. "Yusif read while I drove. So, as I understand it, in Alpha's branch, this guy Lucas sails to the New World in what we'd know as the fifth century?"

"That's what she said. Lucas Magna Nauta. As close as I can remember the pronunciation."

Yusif said, "That is Latin, means Lucas the great mariner."

"She say anything about the Maya? Name of a king or city state?" Murphy had pulled out his laptop and was tapping the keys.

"Not that I could recognize. She was more specific about the Romans. Something about Pompeius Magnus wasn't murdered in Egypt in her timeline. My understanding is that because of that, Augustus didn't become emperor of Rome. Jesus wasn't crucified, and somebody named Simon triumphed over Kepha, or Petros in Latin."

"Petros is Greek." Murphy's forehead had lined as he sifted through notes.

Yusif had his own computer out, was tapping keys as he said, "I know the event where Pompey the Great is assassinated. After Julius Caesar defeated him at Pharsalus, Pompey discarded his clothes. Dressed as a commoner, the man fled with this family. He caught a boat to Egypt, figuring that he could find an ally in Ptolemy the Thirteenth, also called Theos Philopater. Philopater double-crossed Pompey. Had him murdered as soon as he set foot on shore."

"Nice guy," I muttered. "He play any other particular role in our timeline?"

"You would know Philopater as Cleopatra VII's brother and husband. Yes, *that* Cleopatra. Philopater figured to win Julius Caesar's gratitude by doing in an old rival. But when Caesar lands in Egypt, it has exactly the opposite effect. Caesar flies into a rage. He needed Pompey alive. Wanted to pardon him as a grand PR move to win the hearts and minds of all the Romans who'd sided with Pompey."

"So, what happened?" I asked.

"Cleopatra leveraged the event to form an alliance with Julius Caesar in order to take control of Egypt for herself. Philopater supposedly drowns in the Nile after Caesar and Cleopatra's combined forces shatter his army. The rest is history."

"Our history," I added. "In our branch of the timeline." I turned my coffee cup in my hand. "According to Helen, in Fluvium and Alpha's history, Pompey apparently survives. Something happens that keeps Octavian from becoming the first emperor of Rome. That, in turn, changes everything else leading to this Lucas Nauta Magna."

"Hey," Murphy said, "history is always a series of unintended consequences. What we call the official version of the myth. Sometimes, great events hinge on really small things. Couple that with what we now know about these timelines . . ." The guy shook his head. "Nothing's the same, kids."

"So, what have you guys got on a Kepha, or Petros, who triumphs over Simon? And why are they even important to the story?" I glanced skeptically between the two.

Again, it was Yusif who said, "The only reference I can find to both Kepha and Petros refers back to Shimon bar Yona."

"Oh, of course," ET muttered from his flopped perch in the beanbag chairs. "How'd we miss that? So, 'scuse me? Say what?"

Yusif arched a thick black brow, finding nothing humorous in ET's sarcasm. "Shimon bar Yona is the Aramaic name for the apostle Jesus named *Kepha*. That's Aramaic for 'the Rock.' In Greek, *kepha* translates as *Petros*. You know him as Saint Peter. The founder of the Roman Catholic Church."

I squinted, scratched my jaw. "According to Helen there was no Jesus in Fluvium and Nakeesh's timeline. But if Jesus exists in Helen's timeline, she can't be from the same timeline as Nakeesh. Helen, however, said that in her branch, Simon Magus triumphed over Peter. If he did, Simon Magus has to be a different guy than this Shimon, right?"

Murphy asked, "Does Shimon bar Yona come from Fluvium and Alpha's timeline? Or a different one?"

"I'm not really sure. Call it a hunch, but the way she talks about Fluvium and Alpha's timeline, it's like it's alien." I straightened. "So, we know that Fluvium and Nakeesh use alternate branches of the timeline for their experiments. Maybe they did something to Helen's branch? Something horrible? Maybe that's why she hates them so much?"

"Who hates who?" Karla Raven asked as she entered the room. She wore sweatpants and a baggy shirt. Had her damp black hair tied back in a ponytail. Looked like she'd come straight from the shower after her workout.

I took a moment to fill her in on the conversation so far.

From where he tapped at his computer, ET called, "Simon Magus! Got him. Called Simon the Magician. From Samaria." ET made a face. "Where the hell is that?"

"You never heard of the 'Good Samaritan?'" Yusif asked. "It was a region in ancient Israel." Yusif was tapping away at his own computer. "Ah, yes. The alleged heretic and a magician of great renown in the ancient world. Supposedly, he was an early follower of Jesus, got cross-wise with Peter. Ah, and most fascinating of all, Simon Magus' female consort was called Helen. Also known as the 'First Thought' of God. Conceived in purity. The 'Eternal One' is ultimately dragged down into prostitution, and then saved by Simon. Redeemed."

Where he sat with his tablet, Savage called. "Holy shit. Says here that Helen was called the 'First *Ennoia*,' that as God's first thought she conceived and gave birth to the angels and archangels. That despite having created them, she is finally imprisoned by them. They do that by trapping her in a human body. Condemned to be reborn in one female body after another, including, get this: Helen of Troy. Anyway, she finally ends up reincarnated as a whore in a brothel in Tyre. Simon Magus finds her there, buys her, and reveals her true identity."

Ennoia. I'd first heard the word when I was crouched over Alpha's body during Helen's assassination attempt. Was this true, or just an elaborate diversion on Helen's part?

"You have got to be making this up," Karla declared, pulling out a chair, reversing it, and sitting in it backward, her muscular forearms crossed on the back.

Yusif told her, "He is not. Simon Magus and Helen were what you would call competitors of Peter and his early Christians in the city of Rome. The early Christian scholars, people like Justin Martyr and Irenaeus, considered him the ultimate heretic and the biggest threat to early Christianity. Hated him with a passion. After Simon's death, they did everything in their power to convince people that Simon Magus was the incarnation of evil."

"Fake news? Even back then?" ET wondered.

"Religion and politics have always been a dirty business," Savage muttered. "Still, you've got to admire Helen's story. Conceived in the purity of God's first thought, she gives birth to the angels. Like all offspring, they turn on her, confine her existence to an endless cycle of mortal female bodies. Ultimately, Simon, who's God's agent, rescues her from the depths of degradation."

I said, "Helen told me that in her branch of the timeline, Peter didn't win. She and Simon did." I shook my head. "This is nuts. We're supposed to believe she's really the Helen in the Simon Magus story?" I paused, remembering her saying, *"immortality isn't all it's cracked up to be."*

"If so," Yusif mused, "she was one of the founders of Gnosticism. But for that vile monster, Constantine, that would be what the majority of Christianity practiced today. In Egypt, our Coptic church is still more Gnostic than Orthodox or Roman."

"The Eternal One," I mused, feeling nervous. "She said that Nakeesh calling her *Ennoia* was like a sick joke."

But what did that mean? More to the point, whose side was she on?

3Ø

Childs

The operation went like clockwork. Josh Mack had stepped into the conference room, eyes on his watch, and called, "Our source just called. If the math is correct, our target should be on deck at twenty-two hours forty-two minutes." He'd glanced around, amusement in his piercing black eyes. "Nothing like precision, is there, gentlemen?"

Mack's team had leaped into action.

Hanson Childs, Jaime Chenwith, and the rest had tossed their gear into the white vans, climbed in, and driven west on New Mexico 502 from Española, then up the long grade to Los Alamos. At the gate, the drivers had produced cards that allowed them to pass security. As soon as they accelerated down the drive, the ballistic nylon bags were unzipped. Weapons, lights, and kit bags were handed out, the trained operatives donning helmets and armor with an uncanny conservation of movement considering the restricted room.

For Childs and Chenwith, it was like watching a well-oiled machine working at high efficiency. They'd heard of Talon Agency. Word was that they weren't exactly scrupulous when it came to the morality of a job.

When Childs had asked Josh Mack about it, the detail leader had told him, "Hanson, there's times when having a bad rep can be an asset in this business. Especially when it comes to taking the bad guys down. Makes it easy to gain their trust when they think you're playing on the same level they are."

Given that they'd never trained with the team, he and Chenwith were relegated to the simple task of guides, additional eyeballs, and support. If the intelligence was correct, and Domina was located, he and Chenwith were assigned the responsibility of taking her into custody, securing the small computer that Mack had called a navigator, and en-suring her compliance during the rapid evacuation.

That was it. A simple snatch and grab.

As the vans pulled up against the curb at the big white Skientia lab building's rear door, Chenwith gave Hanson a knowing glance. "Last time we went in the front door."

"That was when we were high-rolling elite law enforcement with badges and a warrant. Now we're just lowly secretive special operatives."

Cal Spicer laughed from the seat ahead of them as he slapped a mag-azine into a curious looking automatic. The thing was based on an AR pistol action, but with a too-short, suppressed barrel and weirdly fluted magazine.

"Nonlethal," Spicer told them over the back of the seat. "We don't want to leave a cluster fuck of bodies lying all over the place like that bunch did last time."

"How does it work?" Jaime asked.

"Like a regular cartridge. Powder charge drives the dart down the barrel and cycles the action. The projectile is a fast-acting nerve agent contained in a dissolving pellet. The shape defeats fabric, fractures the protein capsule as it penetrates skin, and releases the sleepy-time juice inside."

Chenwith said, "I want one."

"Just get the woman out," Spicer reminded. "We'll cover the rest."

"Heads up!" Josh Mack called from the van's passenger seat. "This is it! Go!"

Childs saw the thick white security door open; a woman in a lab coat leaned out. Took him a second to realize where he'd seen her before: Maxine Kaplan. Skientia's head researcher at the labs. And in that mo-ment, it all made sense. She had been tight-lipped and angry when he'd questioned her at the Buffalo Thunder Resort. Disdainful of Grazier's team of lunatics. No wonder she'd taken the first opportunity to side with Stevens and betray Grazier.

The van doors burst open, Josh Mack's team sprinting across the narrow strip of lawn toward the door. Childs bailed out hot on Chen-with's heels, making the door just as Kaplan was telling Mack, "Cameras are off. Two security guards will be coming down the steps to check this door in less than three minutes. Two more are just inside the Lab One security door. If I'm right, we have ten minutes before Nakeesh is due back."

"Got it!" Mack was giving signals to his team as they trotted down the short cinder-block-walled corridor, through a fire door, and into the main hallway. The only sound was the slapping of rubber soles on the polished vinyl floor. The team was hustling down past the closed offices. Eugene Chalmers and Al Allison split off to cover the double doors at the stairway leading to the upper floors. Spicer and Stump stepped into the elevator, disabling it with a flip of the stop switch.

Up front, Teddy Meyer and "Dirty Harry" Logan slipped up on either side of the door leading into Lab One. With a nod, Meyer reached out, grabbed the latch, and pulled the door open. Logan took a half step into the gap, his weapon making two quick *fsst* sounds. And then they were in.

While the rest of the team split up to take control of the building, Childs and Chenwith followed Meyer, Logan, and Mack into Lab One. For Childs, as he stopped short by the seats next to the head of the stairs, the room echoed from his memory. He couldn't forget the first night when he'd stepped in, seen Peter McCoy's body sprawled, the man's chest dark-red with dried blood from a heart shot. Or the gruesome remains of the archaeologist, Reid Farmer, where his partial body had been pulled away from the smooth crater in the concrete at the bottom of the stairs.

Now the drugged guards—their limp bodies being settled into the seats by Meyer and Logan—gave the place a familiar chill.

"You having the same spooky thoughts I am?" Chenwith asked as he looked around the big square room with its cables, pipes, and dark monitors. The eerie crater in the concrete floor at the foot of the stairs was like a lurking threat.

"Yeah. Let's grab this bitch and be the hell out of here," Childs told him, wondering what to do next.

Maxine Kaplan strode in, jerked a nod at Josh Mack, and told them. "You want to stay back from the event center. According to my watch, we've got less than eight minutes. We'll want to be outside the Lab One doors. Anyone inside here is going to be laid out like a lump of meat."

"How do we know when she's here?" Mack asked, staring around uneasily.

"Oh, you won't have any doubt," she told him. "The lights, computers, monitors, everything goes down. You'll feel it run through you like a—"

"What the hell?" Chenwith pointed.

Childs followed his finger to what had to be the center of the missing sphere. He blinked, squinted, trying to make sense of the liquid and shifting pearlescent haze that was floating over the crater.

"She's early," Kaplan declared. "Come on. Outside. Now."

The last in line, Childs threw a glance over his shoulder as he stepped through the open door. The sphere had grown, a spooky nacre ball that seemed to eat the light. He stopped, gaping at the eternity welling and roiling inside that growing ball of . . .

The prickle, like a thousand ant feet swarming across his skin, sent a shiver through him. He was still staring, transfixed as the ball expanded. Then, just as he was on the verge of losing it, Chenwith's strong hand pulled him through the door to collapse in the hallway. There, he lay panting, hands on the cold vinyl floor. Around him, the others were staggering. Josh Mack had his hands on his knees, head down, feet braced, looking like a runner recovering from a marathon. Jaime had backed against the wall, fists pressed against the side of his head. Eyes closed, Kaplan had her head tucked, arms clasped around it as if for protection.

The lights went out.

The words whispered in his brain: *Got to save Kilgore. Got to save the world.* They were accompanied by a desperation that sent a pulse of energy down Hanson Childs' spine. The urge that drove him to his feet wasn't his. Almost as if another power had taken hold and propelled him back through the door.

The tingle began to fade as he staggered forward, almost toppling down the stairs as his balance faded in and out. Then came the lights, flickering, glowing in the overhead fluorescence.

Where the crater had been, an unusual contraption consisting of arcs of aluminum, mirrors, thick cable, and myriads of wiring now stood. A woman perched at a raised console, blonde hair in a ponytail. She wore a lab coat. Her gaze was fixed on the blue hologram that rose from the workstation top and the glowing monitor and console to one side. The woman was hunched, as if ducking something.

In an instant, the monitors and various lights at her station died, as did the hum from the big piece of equipment that rose from an intact concrete floor.

"Got to save Kilgore. Got to save the world." Childs kept repeating the words. Clueless of what they might mean. Didn't need to know. Only that they were important.

As he hit the bottom step, it was to see a section of a human body flop slowly onto the concrete, intestines and organs sliding out of a partial rib cage and gut cavity. Most of the head was attached to the partial torso, including the outflung arm. The thing looked as if a sword had cleaved a body in two and dropped a half onto the concrete.

An HK pistol lay on the floor just beyond the still quivering fingers. The partial corpse was nightmarish, as if it had just been sliced away with a laser. The eyes were still glazing in the man's head. Even as Childs stared, the chest contracted and went still. Blood continued to drain from every vessel. Fresh. Hot.

Childs swallowed hard, steadied himself on the stair railing. His brain kept stumbling, struggling to match up with his body.

He took a moment, fighting the urge to throw up.

As he tried to regain control of himself, the woman at the workstation shivered. He watched her straighten, place fingers to her hair where strands had been torn loose, and chuckle. Then she stood, turning to look around the room.

When she fixed her eyes on Childs, he'd never seen such a blue. As if they were powered by a light that burned into his soul. He had the mental image of a goddess, something conjured from the depths of imagination. A crazy sort of impulse like he should bow or something. Offer some sort of recognition of royalty.

Where in hell had that come from?

"Who are you?" she asked in an accented contralto. For a woman who had just emerged from a pearlescent gray ball, she seemed remarkably in control of herself. Even as she spoke, she was powering down the hazy blue holograph on the book-sized device on the desk before her.

"Hanson Childs," he gulped, fixing on her as she tucked the device close with one hand, stepped down. With her other hand, she was still fingering her mussed hair, trying to tuck it in.

"Hanson Childs." The way she pronounced it gave the words an exotic sound.

Another voice cried, "For Gods' sake! Don't shoot again!"

From behind one of the arcs of metal and cable, a man in a suit climbed up from the floor. His face looked bloodless, pale white with fear, the eyes frantic and afraid. Lights gleamed on a sweaty bald head, the shape of it odd, sort of thick at both ends like a potato. Hanson calculated the guy's silk suit to be worth about six months' rent.

Then the man fixed on the severed remains of the dead man's body. "Holy fuck," the suit whispered. He tripped over his feet in his scramble to get back. Having retreated to the rear arch of curving metal, he braced himself with one hand. Then he bent double and threw up all over one of the concave mirrors.

The blonde woman, watching disdainfully, muttered, *"Debilis vermiculous."*

Childs' brain had begun to work. He heard the door above open, mutters of "Holy shit!" "Damn!" And "I don't believe it!" as the rest of the team poured in.

Stepping down from the last step, he carefully kept his eyes from the severed portion of Dr. Farmer's corpse as he walked over to the woman. "Domina? We don't have a lot of time. We have to get you out of here."

The clatter of feet on the stairs behind him announced the arrival of the others.

She stood, imperious, looking around. Taking in the partial corpse on the floor, she said, "Too bad, *Agricola*. You miss last shot." Again she fingered the mussed hair that Childs realized had been torn by a bullet.

If the sight of the mangled human made any impression, she gave no sign of it. For a woman who'd just ridden a time machine, she came across as being rock-solid. She stepped down from the elevated workstation, avoided the spreading gore leaking from Farmer's body, and with her free hand, picked up the HK pistol.

Childs wondered if he should try and take it away. But then, that hadn't been in the briefing. And, supposedly, she was on their side.

Problem was, he still wasn't thinking well.

"Come on, people!" Josh Mack called. "We're on the clock. Let's shake it! I want us in the vans and moving in five minutes! Move your shit!"

Maxine Kaplan had pushed past the rest. Avoiding Farmer's pooling gore, she took the trembling man in the suit by the arm. "Tanner? Come on. We have to be out of here. Grazier will have alarms blaring across half the country by now."

So that was Tanner Jackson? Childs watched as the man ran a sleeve across his wet lips and chin. Wondered if the guy would puke again. He shook like a traumatized kitten as Kaplan—looking on the verge of throwing up herself—guided him around the body and up the stairs.

Jackson was whimpering, asking, "But who are these people? That man with a gun. Doctor Farmer. How did he get out of the interrogation room? Where's Bill Minor? He was just here. And Pete! He's shot!"

"Come on, Tanner." Kaplan was pulling him up stair by stair. "You've got a lot of catching up to do."

But as Childs escorted Domina Nakeesh up the stairs, he noticed she remained cool as frost. As if she'd expected nothing less. She kept the navigator clutched close with her right hand, the HK USP pistol, safety off, in her left. And, damn it, the mocking smile on her perfect lips made him wonder if she wasn't a couple of steps ahead of them all.

31

Grazier

Eli's bedside clock displayed 1:05 when the call came. Though used to being awakened in the middle of the night, this time his private line pulled him out of nightmares where winged black beasts— monstrous things like a chimeric cross between giant flying pterodactyls and leviathan-like vultures—soared across hideous firelit skis that flickered in blood-red and orange-streaked flashes. He'd seen the like when strobes of lightning illuminated smoke-blotted cityscapes.

The terrible creatures kept diving down out of the sulfurous air, reaching out with curving claws that glistened with a translucence as if they were made of black glass.

At the ring tone, he leaped up from his pillow, heart pounding, the lights coming up. Wiping his brow, Eli caught his breath. Shifted and lifted the receiver. "Grazier."

"This is Brewster, sir. In New Mexico. The Skientia labs were just raided, sir. Team from outside. Twelve MAM. Equipped with some sort of tranquilizer guns. Entered through the side door. They took down our security. And, General, there's no easy way to say this, but Prisoner Alpha . . ."

Grazier's heart continued to thud in his chest, muscles tightening for the blow. "Go ahead, Brew. Give it to me."

"Well, sir, the time machine's back. You know where that divot was in the concrete?"

"Yeah, I know."

"Sir, I have to report that the machine is back. Like it never left. We, uh, found the other half of Dr. Reid Farmer's body. Just lying there, sir. Bleeding and fresh. Like it had just happened."

"And Alpha?" Eli's heart leapt, hope beyond hope stirring in his chest.

"No sign of her, sir. Cameras and all were down. Gone fuzzy, you know? I guess that's what happens when—"

"Yes! Damn it, it does. You're sure. Absolutely sure that Alpha's not in the building."

"Yes, General. As my detail came to, we immediately locked down. Found the side door open. Secured it. If Prisoner Alpha came back with the machine, she's no longer in the building. Sir, the most likely assumption is that she was extracted by the raiders. The same with Tanner Jackson, sir."

"Shit." That meant that Stevens—the son of a bitch—had Alpha.

"One more thing, sir."

That dull feeling of impending disaster was running in Eli Grazier's blood. "Go ahead, Brew."

"Dr. Kaplan is unaccounted for, sir. She was in the building, working in Lab One, just before the raid. We have to assume that she was abducted along with Prisoner Alpha, sir."

"Was the lock on the side door compromised?"

"That's a negative, sir."

Eli grunted his irritation and anger. "Your assumptions are in error, Brew. She was in on it the entire time. Now, lock that place down. Anyone tries breaking in again, shoot 'em."

"Yes, sir. I'll call back when I know more."

Eli's other line, what he called the red phone, was ringing. The sick feeling in his stomach just kept getting worse. "Oh, and Brew, you be goddamn sure that no one fools with those detectors around the time machine. No one!"

"Yes, sir."

Eli canceled the call, opened the red line. "Grazier here."

"Hold for the president. One moment, please."

As Eli waited, he put it all together. Kaplan. That slimy bitch had been in Stevens' camp all along. Somehow, she'd known when Alpha was going to pop back in. When Eli got his hands on her, he was going to . . .

"Eli? Ben Masters here. I just had a call from Bill Stevens. It seems you've got a little problem out in New Mexico."

Grazier closed his eyes, controlling his breathing. "Yes, sir. It seems I do."

"Now, General," Masters began, *"I know there's bad blood between the two of you. So here's the bottom line: Stevens has Domina Nakeesh in his custody. He's bringing her to a secure location outside DC. We'll wring her dry of any information she has that will be of value to our scientific and defense programs. In the meantime, I want you and your people to stand down."*

By the time the call was over, Eli Grazier was wondering what, if anything, he could do to save the situation.

"Stevens," Grazier muttered. "He doesn't have the first fucking clue about who Alpha is, or what kind of threat she represents. Dumb son of a bitch is going to get us all killed."

But President Masters had tied his hands.

The sick feeling in his stomach was getting worse.

Eli ground his teeth. Took a deep breath. With a sense of inevitability, he opened the drawer on his bedside table and withdrew the pager Helen had given him.

"It's my world," he whispered. "My timeline."

Are you in, or are you out?

He pushed the button.

God, what he'd have given to be chased through a ruined and burning city by giant black vulture pterodactyl things.

32

Ryan

I barely beat a thunderstorm home as I idled the Diavel down my dark residential street in Colorado Springs and pulled up at my house. The lot sits at the end of a cul-de-sac. It's a brown split-level ranch. Half-bricked and topped with brown siding. The asphalt-shingle roof, lighter tan in color, matches the house; it's about as average suburban middle-America as you can get. Even the lawn looks spotty because the automatic sprinkler system never works the way it's supposed to.

I could have cared less. It was knocking on midnight, and I was exhausted. Too many hours at Grantham. I'd been blinking and owl-eyed on the ride home as it was.

I pulled up on the driveway, killed the *testastretta,* and toed the side stand down. Digging around in my riding pants, I found the fob and opened the garage door. It groaned and moaned its way up as I pushed the Diavel inside, backed it around, and left it on its stand next to the 916. In the second stall, my Jeep Wrangler waited patiently for inclement weather.

Peeling out of my armored riding coat, helmet, and chaps, I tossed them on the Diavel's seat. I hit the garage door button as I stepped through into the kitchen. The first drops of rain were spattering on the window behind the sink, leaving long, leaden streaks down the glass.

Reaching for the fridge handle, I had just pulled it open when my phone rang. Fishing it from a pocket, I placed it against my ear. "Yeah."

Outside of ketchup, mustard, a couple of cans of beer, and wilted lettuce, the shelves were looking pretty bare. Might be a can of beans for supper.

"Tim?" The voice in the phone was Grazier's. I made a face.

"Here, Eli. What's up?"

"Alpha popped back in about an hour and a half back. And, son of a bitch if Steven's men didn't time it so they were there waiting for her. She's gone. All that's left in Lab One is half of Reid Farmer's body, a broken time machine, and a bunch of my drugged and pissed-off security guys."

Everything seemed to stop except for my beating heart, the open refrigerator mocking me with its mostly bare shelves.

"Ryan? You there?"

"You said Bill Stevens' men were there to meet her? How'd they know when she'd pop back in?"

Grazier almost spat the words. *"Kaplan and Wixom had been tinkering with some sort of particle detectors. According to Kaplan's reports, it was looking ever more like a dead end. I had my people check the logs. She told Wixom to take the night off. My call? She and Stevens have been playing us the whole time."*

"Son of a bitch!" I tried to get my head around this latest setback. "What does it mean?"

"I'm not sure. I've got a team locking down the Skientia lab as I speak. Don't know if the time machine is functional, but there's no way it will work without a huge part of the power grid to run it. Even if Stevens had control of it, we'd know the moment he contacted the power companies to provide the juice necessary for a time jump."

"What about Kaplan?"

"No clue. I just got a flag from one of my people telling me that Wixom's home. I've got people rounding him up as we speak."

I made a face at the rain streaking down my kitchen window. In the glow of the overhead fluorescent light, and against the dark night, the smeared streaks looked depressing.

"Tim? You still there?"

"Thinking, Eli. So, Stevens has Alpha and her navigator. She can't use the time machine in Lab One to go anyplace but into the future. Even if she did, we'd have ample warning when she requested the power from the utilities. Last time she used the machine, the drain blacked out all of northwest New Mexico and the Four Corners."

"Fried a bunch of equipment, too," Eli agreed. *"Blew out switchgear, circuit breakers, transformers, and substations in three states. They weren't any too happy about the cost of repairs."* A pause. *"The good news is that Stevens and Skientia are on the hook for that."*

I mused. "Given what we know so far, without the cerebrum she can't go anywhere."

"If Kaplan's gone over to Stevens' side, they're going to suspect that we've got the cerebrum. Not that we made a big thing of it, but even Kaplan has to be able to figure out that Harvey Rogers wasn't transferred to Colorado just to change the light bulbs."

"Think Kaplan will tie it to Grantham? Tell Stevens?"

"I don't know. My inclination is to drop some breadcrumbs that lead him toward the Cheyenne Mountain Complex. Being locked in a vault buried two thousand feet under a million tons of granite would be a lot more logical place to put the cerebrum than in a mental institution. Not to mention that General Breyer and his folks take their security seriously."

"That might buy us some time. Meanwhile, I'll put Sam Savage and the Psi Team on alert. That way—"

"Already done. Texted him first thing. But, Tim, this changes the entire equation. I've been cudgeling my brain trying to figure out what Alpha could do to hurt us. Everything I can think of leads right back to the cerebrum. Without it, she's powerless to escape this timeline. Or to call this mysterious Imperator. It will take time for her to build another machine, and Stevens will have to buy off on it. Which means I'll hear about in time to stop it."

"What about Tanner Jackson? Did he make it out of the machine alive?"

"I haven't heard. But that's a whole 'nuther kettle of fish,' as my grand ma'am used to say. Skientia has resources Tanner can tap into. We've got the Los Alamos lab, but he's still got his laboratories at JPL, Houston, and smaller facilities spread around the country. Not to mention that the president owes him."

"And which way do you see your old buddy, President Masters, going? He going to back Stevens, or you?"

"For the moment, the president says to keep our hands off Stevens and Alpha. Says we're to stand down. The reason he gives is that Alpha might be more forthcoming and cooperative if she's in Stevens' company. I'd say he's playing us against each other. He's going to do what he thinks is good for Ben Masters. The man is a master politician. Ultimately, he wants to come out looking like a hero, be re-elected in a landslide, and go on to have the two-term limit upended by popular acclaim so that he can stay in office until he dies. He's waiting to see who comes out on top."

God, I *hated* politics.

"I've got my ear to the ground. If I get any kind of a line on where Alpha is, I want you and Sam Savage to figure out how to snatch her back on an instant's notice. Should be the sort of thing that would be right up your Team Psi's alley. Chief Raven will love it."

"Right, Eli. Thought the president ordered you to stand down. Did I ever tell you that you were a . . ." The phone went dead.

I lowered it, watching the rain streak my kitchen window. Damn it, this wasn't a game. Just snatch her back?

I muttered, "Eli, the last time we'd tried snatching Alpha, people died. A lot of them."

And this time, if there were casualties, they would be my people. Eli—psychopath that he was—wouldn't feel so much as a moment's worth of regret.

That notion was crawling around in my gut like fire ants when a voice from the dining room said, "Dr. Ryan? I think you have a lot bigger problem than Eli Grazier."

I half jumped out of my skin. Turned, and saw Helen, wearing black tactical gear, and she was holding a pistol pointed at my already jumpy stomach.

IUDICUM

As the new timeline forms around us, I struggle to put a name to the place. And then it comes to me: The great temple in which we stand is Ipet-Isut. I recognize the looming colonnade. Later, after the Eighteenth Dynasty, it will be called Karnak—the famous temple complex adjacent to the Egyptian city of Thebes. Even so, the great temple to Amun Ra impresses me as I glance around. Everything is painted with vibrant color. We tend to think of ancient Egypt as dusty, sandstone-colored stones standing against an empty sky. Instead, my team and I find ourselves in a magnificent building, high-roofed and open to the sides. Even the giant columns are painted in red, black, and blue. The floor beneath our feet is tiled in intricate patterns. Incense floats on the air.

We appear to have popped in during some sort of ceremonial event. The temple is crowded, and the corona effect of our arrival has knocked out a hundred or so; Egyptians are sprawled for half a stadia in every direction, and those at the margins are looking stupefied. The sight could be a holo-vid come to life. Brown people, their black hair in wigs, white tunics, golden armbands, and jewelry. Even the hairstyles look exactly as if they've been copied from Egyptian tomb walls.

Bringing up my navigator, I study the holo. And, yes, my heart leaps. It's detecting entangled particles. A lot of them. Is this it? Have we found Fluvium's elusive timeline?

"Ah Tz'ib?" I ask. "What does your cerebrum indicate? Do these particles have the same signature as Nakeesh's navigator? Or perhaps those of the Ennoia?"

Sak Puh's brow furrows in that now familiar frown. When she does that, it makes her commoner face look even more simple and bucolic. "Neither, Imperator."

Then her expression scrunches up even more, that look of alarm behind her dark and liquid doe eyes. "Does this mean . . . ?" She blinks, glances to the side to hide her weakness.

"Publius," I order. "The sterilizing agent, please."

I extend my hand as the legionarii reaches into his pack and extracts a stainless-steel canister. He slaps it into my hand, the metal oddly cold in the temple's muggy heat.

"Last one," Publius tells me. "After this, we have no more."

Is that true? Have we sanitized five timelines already in our quest?

"Imperator?" Sak Puh tries one last time. She is staring at the recovering Egyptians around us. There are men, women, and children. I can see the desperation in her eyes. "Should we not save that one? Perhaps for the Ennoia's timeline if we happen across it?"

As the Egyptians totter uncertainly to their feet, they begin staring, pointing, whispering, and weeping as they take in our dress, our reflective helmets, and feather splays of rank. They think they are seeing gods. Divine beings who have appeared out of nothingness. Some have already dropped to their knees, heads bent, arms uplifted. Wavering voices begin offering up prayers. My helmet translates the ancient Egyptian. "Lords of Light, gods of the sky, protect us," are the fervent pleadings.

"Protect you, I will," I call back, my voice automatically translated to Egyptian by the helmet speakers. And, so saying, I twist the cap on the canister and pitch it out among the crowd.

"Iudicum!" I cry, muting the translator. "Judgment! For the threat your children will never be!"

They are staring in amazement at the hissing cylinder that has landed among them. Their eyes are wide with awe, mouths open as the virus is dispersed. They look reverently at the container, and then back at us. One, a little girl, naked but for a wrap at her waist, actually picks it up. Giggles as she listens to it venting virus.

"Now," I tell the rest. "Let us be gone."

I glance at the shaken Sak Puh, see the tears in her eyes as she presses her finger into the glowing orb on her cerebrum.

When we finally return to Ti'ahaule, I will terminate her. A woman that weak should not be allowed to procreate lest she pass deleterious genetics to yet another generation.

33

Ryan

My second kidnapping turned out to be rather anticlimactic. No popping across half the country in the blink of an eye. No sudden explosion of my body. No fancy alien technology, or flashing lights, or marvel. Helen simply asked that I drive the Jeep. While she sat in the passenger seat and gave directions, I chugged Red Bull and black coffee in an attempt to stay awake. Jeep Wranglers aren't the smoothest of cross-country traveling vehicles. We buzzed and bumped our way down I-25 to Raton. Then, on Helen's orders, took US 64 west into the Sangre de Christo Mountains. Following her instructions, we ended up at a rather imposing log home on a forested lot just outside the resort at Angel Fire.

When I pulled into the drive and shut off the ignition, the time was 5:46. I kept yawning despite the stimulants I'd sucked down when we stopped for fuel in Raton. I was getting too old for all-nighters.

And, to make matters worse, Helen had talked little, her hard gaze fixed on the road ahead.

About all I'd gotten out of her was, "Alpha's out. Escaped."

"Good or bad?" I'd asked.

"The only good thing I can see so far is that Imperator hasn't showed up. Unless he's waiting for us at the house. He'll come for me first thing. Just as soon as Nakeesh tells him I'm here." A half smile. "He and I? We have unfinished business."

So, now we were apparently "at the house." In the silence that followed my turning off the lights, the only sound was the Jeep making tinking noises as it cooled. Helen might have been made of wood, her gaze on the dark house. Finally, she drew a deep breath, slipped the pistol from her waistband, and said, "Let's go see."

"What am I looking for?" I asked.

"If we're attacked, Ryan. I promise, I'll shoot you first."

"Wait a minute! None of my people, or Grazier's for that matter, even know this place exists. Let alone would attack. Shooting me—"

"Would be an act of kindness," she blurted, as she recovered her bag from the back seat.

Walking around the front of the Jeep, she added, "I could give a fig about Grazier. It's Imperator who worries me. Trust me. You don't want him taking you back to *Ti'ahaule* alive."

Okay, I trusted her. Complete with a cold shiver running down my back.

As we walked up to the door, I said, "You're really going to have to fill me in on all of this. Imperator, the *Ahau*, which timeline is which. I need a scorecard."

She used a key to open the door, checked the security system keypad, pressed a code, and locked the door behind us. She told me, "Stay here," while—pistol in hand—she cleared the rest of the house.

I waited in the stone-floored foyer, staring around at the great room with its awesome river-rock fireplace, the huge glass windows, and elk-antler chandelier. The furniture was Western themed: leather and plush. I could see a fancy kitchen opening in the back. A log staircase led to an upper level with a peeled-log balcony. The size of the place was evident in the time it took for Helen to clear it.

When she finally came trotting down the stairs, she called, "Looks like Nakeesh hasn't managed to contact Imperator. We might actually have a chance. Maybe your Mr. Stevens isn't as much of a fool as I think he is."

"Oh, I suspect he's a fool, all right." I walked wearily into the living room and plopped onto the overstuffed couch. Damn. I was right. The thing was comfortable as hell.

"Coffee?" she called from the kitchen as she placed her bag with what I supposed were the navigator and cerebrum on the granite counter.

"Sure," I told her, leaning back and closing my eyes. "Not that you're all that bad a captor when it comes to kidnapping, but seriously you really need to pick better hours."

I heard her laugh.

And it was the last thing I heard.

I wasn't supposed to drift off. I was a prisoner, after all. Maybe a hostage. And, with time travelers popping in and out, the fate of my world hung in the balance. Yet I fell into a sound sleep and dreamed of my son, Eric. We were playing baseball. While I pitched, he kept swinging and missing. All the time, yelling, "Dad, you really don't get it, do you?"

The worst part was that each time I looked over my shoulder, my ex-wife was standing behind the backstop, arms crossed, giving me that "I'm really mad at you" look.

As bad as a wife's "I'm really mad at you look" can be, it doesn't hold a candle to an ex-wife's soul-searing glare.

The clink of a ceramic cup on stone brought me awake. I blinked. Tried to figure out where I was. Through the wall of windows, I could see from the angle of the sun that we were well into the morning. How long had I slept? I glanced at my watch and winced. Almost nine thirty.

The house had a marvelous view of an alpine vista: tall gray-rock peaks, jagged and patched with a faint dusting of snow where they soared above the thickly forested slopes of pine, fir, and spruce. Patches of aspen, having lost their leaves, made a gray mosaic on the lower slopes.

"What the hell?" I yawned.

"Back with us, Dr. Ryan?" Helen asked.

She was sitting across from me, reclined in the giant leather chair, feet tucked under her. Nothing had changed; she still had that aura of health and magnetism. I thought she looked like an auburn-haired panther. She reached forward, pouring a cup of coffee from a carafe. The coffee table between us was made of sandstone, polished, and with petroglyph designs sandblasted into its surface. Both the navigator and cerebrum sat to one side, blue holographic fields shimmering above them.

She pushed the full cup of coffee across the table in my direction. "Who's Jenn? You kept talking to her in your sleep."

"Ex-wife. You don't want to know."

"Human beings are in a constant state of attraction, repulsion, and fission. It's part of who we are."

"You say that with a certain dull acceptance."

She reached for her own cup of coffee. "Dr. Ryan, the one thing that's changed over the years is that I am a great deal better at evaluating men."

"Like Marvin?" I asked. "Did you love him?"

That seemed to amuse her. "After a fashion. He was a good man.

Curious about so many things. Still surprised and intrigued by life, but in a mature way. Being with him allowed me to recapture a lot of the magic of discovery that I'd forgotten over the years. He continually surprised me, which took some doing. Much like you. You're a good man. Solid. Your Jenn made a mistake when she let you go."

"No, she didn't." I sipped my coffee. Good stuff. Must have come with the house. "I wasn't there for her. She complained that my patients meant more to me than she did. She was right, of course. You see, she was a strong and capable woman. Quite able to take care of herself, thank you."

"And your patients needed you more," she finished.

"I went where I could make a difference. Jenn, true to her nature, found the love of her life. My son got a much more responsive and responsible father figure, and I dedicated myself to making my patients' lives better. Wins all the way around."

"I rest my case." She leaned back with her coffee, sinking into the chair. She reminded me of a green-eyed tigress. I tried not to stare.

To distract myself, I told her, "My people think they know who you are. There was a Helen associated with a Simon Magus back in ancient Rome. She was also called *Ennoia*. You said it was a joke. But in our history, she existed two thousand years ago."

"That's me. At least the version that existed in this timeline. Mine split just before those events. Your Helen came to a rather bitter end after Kepha murdered Simon that day. Happened in the Forum. They were standing atop a raised portico. Having a debate about the true meaning of Yeshua's teachings. You'd know Yeshua as Jesus."

"Simon knew Jesus?" I asked in amazement.

"Of course. And believe me, he was a very different man than your timeline's Christian mythology portrays him. That day, Simon humiliated Kepha not only with his knowledge of the resurrection, but with several magical tricks. The same tricks Yeshua used in his sermons, by the way. All those miracles reported in your Bible? You have to understand that Yeshua was a master magician. He learned his craft from the Theraputae in Egypt. A fact that your Christians have erased from the record to make his legacy more acceptable to the Romans."

"Jesus was a magician?"

"References have survived. Even in your timeline if you're willing to look hard enough in the literature. He was even tattooed as magicians were at the time. Bet your modern conservatives would find that disconcerting."

Maybe telling a two-thousand-year-old woman that she was apeshit wasn't the brightest idea.

Helen continued, "Simon's mastery of Yeshua's magic tricks made it even more humiliating for Kepha. Not only was the crowd swayed by Simon's preaching, but awed by sleight of hand that Kepha, himself, could not master." She paused. "The man was always a dolt. Unimaginative. Bitter. Resentful. There was a reason he was called Kepha, 'the stone.' And it had nothing to do with that fable about being the rock upon which Yeshua built his church. It's taken two thousand years of historical revision and unfettered editorial imagination to turn idiot Kepha into the most remarkable of the alleged 'disciples.'"

"According to our historical records, Simon Magus said he could fly. St. Peter challenged him, and Simon fell to the ground and was killed or broke a lot of bones. But you say he was murdered?"

"I was there," Helen told me in a sharp tone. "Standing on that same ledge overlooking the Forum. Simon told the crowd that, with faith in the soul's salvation, they would have wings of glory when they reached the Kingdom of Heaven. And that they would fly, possessed of the divine spark. Simon stepped to the edge of the ledge and spread his arms wide. Kepha, slightly behind him, gave Simon a shove with his walking stick. And down my beloved Simon went to smack face-first on the paving stones in the Via Sacra." A beat. "It was murder, plain and simple."

Helen's lips curled. "All the rest? The stories about Simon and me bewitching people? What they call 'simony' in the Church? That's one of the reasons I *hate* this timeline. My wonderful Simon was expunged, trashed, and villainized. All because that worm, Kepha, lived to write the histories. Then came the defamations of that cullion, Ireneaus, then Origen's lies. And it just got worse after your Constantine."

"Those same records say that you were a prostitute that Simon rescued from a brothel in Tyre. That Simon recognized the eternal female spirit in you, what he called the *Ennoia*."

Her green eyes went distant with memory. "I was ten when the man my mother lived with sold me to the Golden Glory. It was the finest brothel in Tyre. The cunning bastard palmed extra gold by claiming I was a virgin." She snorted her disgust. "But by that time, he'd climbed into my bed enough times that I was well-worn for the trade."

I straightened, "You talk about it as though—"

"Enough, Doctor." She gave me a reassuring look. "I've had millennia to experience every humiliation, degradation, and use to which a woman can be subjected. Not even the *Ahau* can imagine a new take on debauchery. I've also had the opportunity to be loved, cherished, protected, shown great kindness, and adored in every fashion. Immortality gives a person a deep appreciation of reality. The ugly, the bad, and the good. And as I told you, I've become a pretty good judge of character over the centuries."

"What's your verdict?" I asked, fascinated. "About people, I mean."

"In your vernacular, Dr. Ryan, for the most part, people suck." She shared a frosty green-eyed stare with me. "But they do have moments of true benevolence, courage, and moral transcendence." She paused, her gaze intense. "If you understand that human beings are nothing more than herd animals and think of them as being exactly like domestic cattle, sheep, or camels, you'll never be disappointed."

"That sounds harsh."

"You asked for my judgment. People want what all the other farm animals want: food; shelter; to find a mate; copulate; raise their offspring; social status and respect; and to have a sense of security about it in the process. They are livestock, but with a sophisticated twist: They also have the desperate need to believe their state, church, or leaders will provide those things. That's the greatest difference between humans and the other herd animals. Goats don't pray for God or an *Ahau* to make their lives better."

"I think having hope gives people a will to go on. Especially my wounded veterans."

Helen's lips quivered. "Right."

"You don't believe that?"

"Maybe—at the individual level—hope helps your wounded vets. But for the general population, it becomes a scythe by which the rulers can maintain control of their masses. Hope can be forged into unbreakable chains that both keep the masses shackled to the turnstile and at the same time allow them to endure the misery."

"That's depressing."

"I've known too many tyrants, and the *Ahau* are the worst of them all."

"I guess we're lucky we don't have *Ahau*."

Her laughter reeked of bitterness. "You have *the people*, Ryan. Your vaunted republic is running on borrowed time. Your two political parties are tearing your country in two. Your population continues to divide itself into mutually exclusive camps of special interests. Your people are separating themselves into a new sectionalism. Your beloved Americans hate other Americans more than they fear their global adversaries. Where once you prided yourselves on democratic principles, your masses now fawn over demagogues. You are but a moment's breath away from either civil war, the election of a dictator, or the establishment of a military government based on the premise of 'keeping order.' And as you careen toward self-immolation, the Chinese, Russians, Iranians, and other enemies savor your collapse."

"You make it sound like we don't have much time."

She stared vacantly out the great windows toward the high mountains on the other side of the valley. "I've lived it too many times. People are flocking to the 'hope' provided by an autocrat. Someone who will promise to fix the things that are broken. Make their lives better. Promise the 'herd' anything they want to hear."

"I'd like to think we were smarter than that." I stared glumly down into my coffee.

Her voice softened. "I'll bet you would. I'm sorry, Ryan. In the end, the people always destroy themselves."

I was desperate to change the subject. "What about in your timeline? Didn't you say that Augustus didn't become emperor? What happened there?"

"In my part of the world, the Roman Republic would have flourished for another hundred and fifty years. A syncretic mixture of Simonianism and Mithraism were becoming the major religion. In China, the Han Xin dynasties would have merged, conquered most of Asia, including northern India all the way to Persia where they ran headlong into the Eastern Roman Empire. What you would call Black Death would have broken out and been particularly virulent along the trade routes. It would have sent the world reeling into a dark age that began in the early seven hundreds. Felix Magnus would have begun the

Renovation, which led to . . ." She smiled. "Never mind. The rest wouldn't make sense to you."

"Would have?"

"That timeline was sterilized by the *Ultima Ahau*." She took a deep breath. "So, in the end, what might have been doesn't matter, does it?"

I tried to get my head around that. "How do these *Ahau* justify the extermination of entire timelines?"

"Timelines are ephemeral, a wave function of variable duration. As the *Ahau* see it, those timelines are infinite in number and finite in existence. Expendable."

"I don't feel expendable."

The smile she gave me had a forced quality. "Neither do the *Ahau*. And given that they created the technology to travel between timelines first, they don't want anyone else to achieve or obtain it for obvious reasons."

I frowned. "I guess I'm dumb. I don't get the obvious reason."

Her brow arched. "Think, Ryan. If you had the technology, you could jump back into their past. Assassinate Pompeius Magnus on that beach in Egypt, thus ensuring that Augustus became Emperor of Rome, which would mean Lucas Magna Nauta would never sail to the Maya, and the science would never flourish in the cultural cross-pollination that led to entanglement being manipulated." She lifted her shoulders in a shrug. "Or you might take a more drastic action. Say release a sigma variant COVID virus, or a genetically augmented rubella or Ebola in the Forum. Let alone something even more lethal that neuters their entire past."

I rubbed my face, trying, yet again, to get a grasp on just what all this meant. The implications of "time" warfare were more complicated than 3D chess. The battlefield didn't just exist in the present and future, but included whether an adversary could access and change the past.

I said, "So, you're telling me we could jump into the *Ahau*'s past, change their timeline, but we can't jump back into our own?"

"Right. You can't send energy back in time where it already exists. It's like trying to pump water back into a running garden hose. What you can do is transfer energy to another timeline where it doesn't exist. So, if you were to use my navigator and cerebrum to go back in the *Ahau*'s timeline, they couldn't send agents from their timeline back to stop you. Just like you could not send, say, Karla Raven, back to that riverbank on the Nile to kill Fluvium and Nakeesh before they dumped their genetically engineered *Oscillatoria* into the water."

"But you could go. You're not from our timeline. You could go back, assassinate Pompeius Magnus on that beach. You could stop the *Ahau*. You're from a different timeline than *Ti'ahaule's*."

She stood. Walked over to stare at the autumn-clad mountains through the tall windows. "I've been 'neutralized.' Part of that constant physical attraction you're always fighting? Part of that energy that gives me what you call an aura? My bioengineering? That's from the *Ti'ahaule* timeline. Enough that I can't go back and sabotage their timeline or act to save my own."

I considered that as I sipped my coffee. The effect, in my mind, was like a thousand petals opening out of a flower. Or the fan blades spinning out of a jet engine, but branching at the same time. The complexity of it, layers upon layers of moves and countermoves. Send an agent to stop an agent who'd been sent to stop an agent who had been sent to stop an agent, and on and on and on.

"It could drive you mad trying to figure out which agent to send back to which point in time to stop an attack on a timeline," I told her.

"Now you're catching on." That flat look was back in her cool green gaze. "That's why the *Ahau* choose to sterilize a timeline. It's so much easier if they just scorch it down to bedrock. After all, the timeline will recohere eventually. Doesn't matter whether there's life on planet Earth when that happens. That wave function will still collapse."

"And you think that can happen here?"

"It will. If Nakeesh wins." She reached up, tracing a finger along the smooth glass. "If I can't stop her."

"What do you need from me?"

"Who's your best warrior?"

I began to tell her about Karla Raven.

34

Childs

Just after dawn, Hanson Childs sat in the plush suite atop the Loretto Hotel in Santa Fe, legs out and crossed at the ankles; he couldn't keep his eyes off Domina Nakeesh. He hadn't felt this way about a female since he was seventeen. The physical attraction had every nerve in his body tingling. Tried to figure out what it was that made the woman so enchanting.

And so threatening.

Nakeesh had a presence, an energy, that he'd never experienced before. He couldn't shake the crawly feeling that he was in the presence of an immortal, or some supernatural being. The sort who might have descended from Olympus into the demeaning company of mere mortals. It wasn't just that she'd appeared out of that roiling nacre ball of energy, but something about the way she looked and moved: magnetic and almost radiating exotic power.

Childs had never been a shrinking violet when it came to women. He'd always possessed a self-assured confidence that he was up to any situation. Been the ultimate alpha male. That character had carried him through high school, made him a football legend, and landed him scholarships. He'd graduated at the top of his class with a BA in criminal justice. Had fast-tracked up the ladder to make sergeant/E-5, then taken over investigations and training that led to special agent assignments. He'd taken down generals, Green Berets, and mass murderers.

Being "that" guy, he'd had had his pick of the popular girls in high school, dated sorority beauties in college, and adorned himself with attractive arm candy right up to the voluptuous white-blonde, Susan, with her *Sports Illustrated* bikini body and lustrous blue eyes.

Now, alone with this woman, he couldn't look her in the eyes. She had him on the verge of stammering. He could feel the blush rising at the very thought of it.

What was it about her? Tall, ash blonde, athletic looking, and almost too healthy, she wasn't a raving beauty, but her aura of superiority radiated like infrared. Made him feel like a tongue-tied adolescent in the presence of a ruling monarch.

She sat on the bed, legs out and pillows piled behind her. Still dressed in her lab coat, she wore tactical black clothing beneath. A strange combination for a woman who'd been running a science experiment.

For the moment, her attention was fixed on the navigator she'd cradled on her lap. The thing projected a blue holographic field that Childs couldn't decipher; the symbols and icons were unlike anything he'd seen. As he watched, Domina Nakeesh ran her slim fingers through the image, fixing on an icon and blinking, sometimes uttering a soft command. Each time she did, the holographic projection changed.

The slight lines in her brow deepened as she proceeded, hinting of continued disappointment and growing frustration.

"Trouble?" he forced himself to ask.

She might not have heard. Or he was such a low beast in her estimation, his existence was without consequence.

Childs sighed, crossed his arms, and spent his time studying the room to keep from ogling her. He'd never stayed in the like: this master suite of rooms atop one of the swankiest hotels in downtown Santa Fe.

He got to his feet, walked over to the windows. To the north he could see the high-dollar rooms in La Fonda, and beyond the twin towers of the cathedral, the adobe-style buildings that dotted the piñon-juniper ridges before giving way to the higher slopes. North and east, the mountains were pine-clad and seemed to waver in the stolid afternoon sun.

For something to do, he opened the door and stepped out onto the balcony with its chairs, potted plants, and remarkable views of Santa Fe Mountain. Leaning on the faux-adobe wall, he admired the pueblo-design roofs below. The hotel had been built like a pile of blocks. Very Santa Fe, very expensive, and despite being at the top of the hotel, the suite was a security nightmare. Anyone with even mediocre skills and a rope could scale the outside and access the room.

He'd have preferred a more modern hotel like the Hyatt in Albuquerque. Much better for Nakeesh's security. Better access control.

But no one had asked him. This was Josh Mack's call—and given that both Childs and Chenwith had protective service training, they'd been given the assignment of bodyguard. He had the room watch, while Jaime was in a chair in the small hall outside the door.

Childs took one last look at the view, thinking this would be a place to come back to if time and opportunity permitted.

Stepping in, he locked the door behind him. Checked his watch.

He might not have existed as far as the woman on the bed was concerned. The frown lines had chiseled deeper into her high forehead. Her broad mouth had pursed.

Childs made his way to the wet bar and stared at the single remaining packet for the little coffee machine: Decaf.

He glanced at his principal. The woman continued to give her navigator's holographic projection a wilting glare.

Hell, if she asked for a cup, he'd send one of Mack's team to run it down.

He poured the machine full of water, stuck the little plastic cup in the press, and snapped it closed. Then he pushed the button.

"*In inritum cadere.*" She said it softly. Made a small flick of the fingers, and the faint blue holo vanished. For a moment, she stared vacantly to one side, the corners of her mouth moving as though she were talking to herself.

"Trouble?" he asked again.

Her hot blue eyes met his. "How long am I here?"

God, she had a sexy accent.

"Josh Mack is securing transportation through Stevens' office in DC. We'll have you out of New Mexico within a couple of hours. They're routing a jet to the local airport. If it all goes like planned, they'll have you back in Washington by sometime—"

"What I need is here. In that lab." She rose, walking over to stare into his eyes.

She was taller than he.

The effect of those too-blue eyes mesmerized. Pinned him. Left him stunned, unable to fix on anything but that cerulean gaze that seemed to see right into his skull.

He broke away, shook his head. "God! What is it with you?"

She laughed, the sound of it musical and amused. "Have you killed, Sergeant Childs? Taken a life?"

He squirmed under her intense scrutiny. Knew he was being judged. But for what?

"Yes, ma'am."

"When? Where?"

"Afghanistan. Back when we were pulling out."

"Your life was in danger?"

"Hey, a lot of people were trying to make money off American equipment. Stealing stuff. It was a bust . . . Um, an arrest gone bad. One of the Afghans started shooting. It all went south. You do what you have to."

He forced himself to meet her evaluative gaze. Summoned some deep-seated resolve, much as he'd done with the high school principal years ago, and later with his DI at Fort Benning.

She seemed to make a decision, the sort he figured a rancher made when deciding on whether to keep a bull or send him to slaughter.

"Do you know what is at stake here?" she asked softly, her stare seeming to read his very thoughts.

"Some sort of time machine, ma'am. Weird stuff. That you're from some other timeline. That you built that machine back at the lab in Los Alamos. I mean, until I saw you just appear out of nothing, I thought it was all—"

"What do you want, Special Agent Childs?"

"Excuse me?" He was losing himself in her gaze, as if his soul had come loose and was floating. It was all he could do to keep from reaching out, crushing her body against his.

She stepped close, took his hand. The effect electric. As his heartbeat stepped up a notch, her voice dropped to a soothing whisper. "What do you want?"

I want you. But he made himself say, "I don't know. I guess I want to make a difference. I . . . I want to win."

What the hell? His heart continued to pound and his pulse to race. The room had grown too warm for comfort. Seemed like he was out of breath. He couldn't break her gaze as he asked, "What are you doing to me?"

"Making you an offer," she told him. "You want to win? Make a difference? What if I told you that if this, as you say, 'goes south,' it won't just be shooting. Your country, your world, it will all die."

"I don't understand." His thoughts kept coming unanchored, his whole body in emotional turmoil.

She smiled, exposing perfect white teeth. Sparkles of amusement danced in the depths of her marvelous eyes. The smooth white lines of her throat, the contour of her cheeks, even the gleam of the room lights in her ash-blonde hair sent tingles through him.

"Chemicals, *cari amator*. Just one of the many surprises I am capable of. A taste, if you will, of what I can offer. But I need a companion. Someone to help me save your world so that I can get back to mine."

He almost trembled as he clamped his eyes shut, broke that magical stare. Then he shook free of her hand and staggered back against the wet bar where his coffee had finally filled. God, he hadn't had an aching hard-on like this for years. Hoped she wouldn't look down, see his straining pants.

"Chemicals?" he asked unsteadily. Taking the coffee, he gulped. Didn't care that it burned his tongue and palate. Damn it, anything to resettle his spinning thoughts.

She took his free hand, her touch again sending a thrill along his palm and up his arm. The tones in her voice carried the same effect as a physical caress. "Pheromones, I think you call them. A way to communicate by scent. Stimulating, yes? Hanson, you need to know what I'm capable of. The dangers involved. That I'm being honest with you."

"Honest? About what?" He felt himself coloring, felt his blood rush.

"Your Stevens, the same as General Grazier before him, is going to lock me away. The last time, they put me in a psychiatric hospital. They made mistakes. I got away. They won't allow that to happen again." She inclined her head toward the bed. "What I was doing with the navigator? I was trying to summon help. Someone who will allow me to escape this timeline. To get away before the *Ennoia* destroys it. I *need* to go back to where I came from. Your people, your world, is not ready for the kind of technology I possess."

He stepped away, tried to focus on the vista of distant mountains visible through the window. Christ, if he could only think. "Why me?"

She chuckled, stepping close again. God, yes. He wanted her close. Even knowing that she was using him.

What would I do to possess a woman like this one? Be worthy of her?

That soothing voice of hers told him, "That you are here? Given the responsibility of guarding me? Bill Stevens would not have placed a *stultus*, a fool, in such a position. That tells me that you are resourceful, capable, talented, and skilled."

"Yeah? So?"

The way she fixed on him, he might have been the most important person in the world. "I told you. I need a partner. Someone to help me stay alive long enough to go home to my people. Someone to keep your world from getting caught in the crossfire."

"Who'd kill you?"

"The *Ennoia*. The *Ahau*. People you can't even conceive of. Did I not hear that you were following my path to Los Alamos? Did you not see the bodies? In Aspen? At the Skientia labs? Did you not know that Dr. Farmer tried to shoot me?" She fingered the spot where a bullet had clipped her hair.

He remembered how she'd taken the HK the first thing. The way she'd kicked Farmer's body.

"Tell me," she asked softly, stepping close again. "Given what I know, what I represent to them, do you think I should trust your Chief of Staff Stevens? Even your president?"

"No." He said it before he could think it through.

She laid her hand on his shoulder, and his heart began to race again as she stared into his eyes and set fire to his soul. "Will you help me?"

"I . . . I . . ." He seemed to be falling, weightless, into a depth of the most remarkable blue.

35

Karla

Karla sat, empty breakfast plate before her, and twirled the little plastic Iron Throne on the cafeteria table. She wondered if stealing the thing, that racing impulse she'd felt that night at Royal Gorge, had been prophetic. At the tables surrounding hers, the rest of her team was talking quietly. They were all wondering what the hell Alpha's escape meant.

The clock on the wall told her it was 7:24. The Skipper would be in by eight. The man was never late. He'd probably call a briefing, update them on whatever the news was.

She glanced up as Sam Savage pulled out a chair opposite hers and sat. A frown marring his forehead. "Just double-checked. I've got security as frosty as they can be. The lab is sealed. The cerebrum is locked away in its safe. Harvey Rogers has a trigger-rigged gizmo that's tied to the alarm. Something magical that he's cooked up. Anyone moving near the safe will set off one of Cat's nonlethal gases. So, if Alpha was to transport into the safe room, it will go off automatically."

"As if we would miss feeling the effects of that transporter field," Karla reminded. "You don't forget that."

"Hell, I felt it. Even with a bullet in my lung. I'll pass."

"How'd Stevens know, Major? If it was Kaplan, how could she have guessed when Alpha was going to pop back in?"

Savage stroked his chin thoughtfully. "I'd say those detectors were working better than we were led to believe." His smile was the kind that promised mayhem. "I'd say she played Grazier for a fool."

"I never liked that woman," Karla told him. "Thought she needed her ass kicked. You ask me, she resented the hell out of us for taking Skientia down."

Savage grunted in assent. "I think we're going to be on deck sooner than later, Chief. Alpha's been evacked by Stevens' people. The mysterious *Ennoia* pulled that snatch off the bridge with the Skipper, made a courtesy call on Grazier. Why do I think the shit's about to get deep?"

Karla rotated the little plastic toy throne on one leg, frowning. "How do we spin up for this? Damn it. We're clueless. We've got Winny ready to fly. She's been checked out on that new helo. Cat's lab is up and running. ET's reading everyone's mail, but he missed the Alpha snatch. Hell, I'm ready to sparkle bad guys and frag out Stevens' entire operation, but where? Who?"

She shook her head. "Why do I get the feeling the only person on earth who could make sense of this is Falcon. And he's happily locked away in la-la land."

"Glad you have faith in Captain Falcon, Chief. Me? I'm not sure you could make sense of this with a Ouija board."

She studied the man, taking in the fine lines around the corners of his eyes, his tanned skin and dark eyes. "I'm just afraid we're going to get hit with our pants down, Major. SEALs are trained to take the offensive. Own the initiative. Defense makes us nervous."

"Yeah," Savage agreed, "Me, too."

ET came stalking out of the serving line, his breakfast tray in hand. He crossed the room in his long-limbed and loose-jointed walk, pulled out a chair, and dropped into it.

"You look half shot," Savage noted.

"Yeah, well, I been up all night." ET yawned, exposing white teeth and a pink tongue. He turned haggard eyes on Savage. "Been trying to slip my way through Stevens' security. Figure it be up to me. Somewhere, Stevens has to have a way of communicating with whoever got Alpha. You know, hot traffic. Where they got her, what they gonna do with her. Grazier said it was a team that took her, right? They gonna have to report to Stevens. Tell him what's happening. I crack that, we know where Alpha is. We know where she is, we go snatch her back."

"Got that right," Karla agreed. She glanced at Savage. "That's something we can handle. ET keeps their security down. We deploy Cat's sleepy-time gas. You and me, on the point, grab the bitch. Then we fly out on Winny's helicopter."

Janeesha burst into the cafeteria, hurrying across the room just short of a run. Karla read the woman's concern, the hard set of her jaw, the way she fixed on her and Savage. Karla was already on her feet, asking, "What's wrong?"

"Got a phone call," Janeesha told her, voice clipped. "Claims to be that woman, Helen. Says she's got the Skipper. That if we want to get him back, you better be on the phone with her in the next five minutes. I asked, 'What if she can't make it?' and that woman, she just says, 'Then you might be in need of finding a new CO for the Psi Team.'"

Karla tossed the little throne up, caught it, and stuffed it into a pocket. Whipped her chair out of the way, vaulted a table where Myca Simond and Julian Hatcher were picking at their breakfasts.

She straight-armed the double doors, almost bowling Nurse Seymore over, and was in Janeesha's office in less than thirty seconds.

The phone was lying on the desk, and Karla scooped it up, saying, "This is Karla Raven. Now, talk."

After a couple of seconds of silence, a brassy woman's voice said, *"How do I know you're Chief Raven?"*

"Guess you'll just have to take that on faith. So, you're Helen, huh? How do I know you've got Colonel Ryan?"

"Oh, you don't have to take that on faith. Fifteen minutes from now, when he's supposed to arrive for work, he won't. Something tells me that the Colonel Ryan I've come to know isn't late. You could send someone to his house. Check to see that he's not there, but I suspect, Chief Raven, that you don't want to waste the time."

At that point, Sam Savage, ET, and Cat burst into the room, staring with worried eyes as they gathered around the desk. Janeesha, looking winded, made it last.

"So, how'd you take him this time? Seems to me Colonel Ryan wouldn't be dumb enough to stick his finger on your cerebrum's button again."

"Did it the old-fashioned way. I was waiting for him when he got home last night. Had him drive us to a safe location before I drugged and interrogated him. Did you know that he loves you?"

"Excuse me?"

"Oh, not that sad old man's sexual obsession to possess a young female, but a sort of elder's heartfelt devotion to a woman he knows is beyond his means. That sense of if only. He has a real weakness when it comes to you."

"Yeah? Well, bitch, that goes both ways. Now, why don't you stop the psychobabble shit and get to the point."

"I'm sure that you know Domina Nakeesh has made her escape. I'm thinking you might be the person I need to help run her down. From what I can glean from Dr. Ryan's analysis of your team, you're the most capable. And, if not you, maybe Savage. You can let him know that he's second choice if you fail."

Karla felt her gut winding into the old familiar cramp. "So, how do I help you track down Alpha?"

"It will mean some skipping around. First couple of times are a bitch. Feels like your body is being pulled apart. But you get used to it."

Karla felt that sudden rush. Cursed herself for the adrenaline junky she was. "All right. Turn Colonel Ryan loose, and we'll talk."

"We'll talk first. And then maybe I'll turn Colonel Ryan loose later."

"See, here's the deal: You obviously need me. You wouldn't be calling if you didn't. Let the Skipper go, and we'll see if we can come to an agreement. Now, why don't you just let him—"

"You people have a cute saying, 'Not my first rodeo.' Interesting idiom. Only two of the timelines use it, and Nakeesh and Fluvium have already destroyed the other one. So, no, Chief Raven. The kubos are mine to throw. Um, kubos, that's Latin for dice. That's an idiom you don't use. But enough of linguistics. You take that BMW motorcycle you brought back from the bridge and ride it out to Garden of the Gods. Leave it in the parking lot. Take the Siamese Twins Trail. Needless to say, you will come alone. If you don't, you'll never see me." A pause. *"You've got forty-five minutes."*

The phone went dead.

"What's up, Chief?" Savage asked, stepping around Janeesha's desk.

Karla hung the receiver in its cradle. "She says I've got forty-five minutes to get to the Garden of the Gods."

"You think she's really got the Skipper?" Cat asked, worry in her dark eyes.

"Yeah, Cat. I do."

"Options?" Savage asked.

Karla crossed her arms and settled a haunch on Janeesha's desk. "Play it for what it is, Major. The enemy just invited me into her company. So, I go. Consider it an SSE. Once I can place Helen on the friend-or-foe list, I either help her, or break her neck. Either way, we get the Skipper back."

"What's a SSE?" ET asked from where he'd been hanging in the background.

"Sensitive Site Exploration," Savage told him. "Consider it a reconnaissance." To Karla, he said, "I don't like it, Chief. We're back to making things up at the last instant."

Karla swung to her feet, started for the door. "Yeah, well, Major, you come up with a viable concept of an operation plan, and we'll discuss it over tea. Me, I'm grabbing my third–line gear and squirting out to see if I can rescue the Skipper."

"Hope you don't get your butt shot off," ET mumbled.

Yeah, Karla thought. *That makes two of us.*

36

Childs

Hanson Childs blinked awake to thin streamers of morning light shining past slits in the shades. He lay naked, his head on an oversized pillow. A soft powder-blue six-hundred-thread–count sheet was tangled around his waist. The viga ceiling overhead looked really cool with the plaster cupping around the dark-stained logs. It was a really nice bedroom where remarkable things had happened that, in retrospect, left him dazzled. Like fantasy come true.

What the hell did I do?

Hanson shot a quick glance to see the woman sleeping beside him. She, too, was naked down to the wrap of sheet covering her hips; a long left leg, however, protruded like erotic art.

Shit. It hadn't been a dream.

He'd found the house on Zillow, checked the photos showing lots of furniture, and called the realtor to discover it was still occupied, though the owners were in Mexico for a month. And, yes, if he wanted to make an appointment for a showing, she could accommodate him the following afternoon. And, no, she didn't have any other showings scheduled before then. Which meant a low likelihood of unanticipated visitors to the house.

Hanson had told the realtor he was looking at other properties, and he'd get back to her about a showing later in the week. Score one for his team.

At the public parking lot south of the Plaza, he'd offered twenty bucks to two college kids to take him and Nakeesh to Pojoaque and drop them at an address a block away. After the short walk to the sprawling adobe, it had taken Childs a couple of minutes to disable the security, break a window, and voila! A perfect safe house. A 1.6 million dollar one with a stocked wine bar, plush bedroom, and all the comforts of a home the likes of which he'd never had.

Ah, Santa Fe!

He turned his head to better study the woman sleeping beside him. Tried to make sense of every improbable action he'd taken the day before. A man like him didn't throw away his career over some woman—even one as magnificent as Nakeesh.

But he had.

That wasn't me.

Then who was it? What the hell had possessed him?

Hanson Childs played for the team. He was a loyal officer of the law. Followed the chain of command. Damn it, he did his duty. Was responsible. He didn't do stupid shit. Didn't lose his head like an idiot. Didn't run off with a prisoner. Didn't commit thefts and *didn't* have sex with a fugitive.

But he had.

Was it because he'd lost his identity, bank account, Mustang, and Suzy? Or the impossibility of Nakeesh? He'd *seen* her appear out of nothingness. Like frigging magic.

And now, in the faint light slipping past the shades, he could see the opulent bedroom with its Spanish-style furniture and Saltillo-tile floors covered with Navajo rugs. He was lying in the super-king bed where they'd fallen asleep after the kind of sex that had turned him every which way but loose. He'd always considered himself to be good in bed. But she'd done things to him that had left him sweat-drenched and quivering.

Reaching up, he scrubbed his eyes.

Had he really gone over the faux-adobe wall on the outside patio? Climbed down the blocklike exterior of the Loretto? Dropped from one floor to the next? He'd been amazed by Nakeesh's athletic ability. That look of delighted excitement in her eyes had kindled an anticipatory joy. As if, for the first time in his life, he'd found a woman who shared his daring and passion.

They'd broken in from a second-story balcony. Found the room unoccupied with its king bed rumpled, but a suitcase open on the luggage stand. He'd handed a colorful scarf to Nakeesh to wrap around her head. Swiped the fedora hanging on the desk chair, and donned a suit coat he found in the closet. Together, they'd slipped down a hallway, taken the stairs to the first floor, and exited to the parking lot. Careful of the security cameras, he'd taken her hand and vanished into the crowds of tourists headed for the Plaza.

Josh Mack's team, watching the lobby, the elevators—and most of all, Jaime Chenwith sitting in his chair outside the suite door—never had a clue.

So, what was Jaime thinking?

Lying in bed that morning, Hanson Childs felt a guilt like he'd never known. Jaime—despite the short time they'd worked together—had been a friend. A competent officer whose skill and devotion Childs had respected.

Chenwith had deserved better than to open the door, walk in, and find an empty suite.

Childs clamped his eyes shut. Squeezed the bridge of his nose.

What possessed me?

He'd deserted. No, worse, he'd defected. Abandoned and betrayed his team.

Or had he?

With the fate of the world at stake, where did his loyalty lie?

Bill Stevens? The man was the president's chief of staff. Where did he fit in the chain of command? He was an unelected civilian, for God's sake. Not military.

My loyalty is to my country. If he could believe Nakeesh, helping her get back to her timeline with the navigator was the only way to save it. And, lord knew, he'd seen the fear in her eyes when she mentioned the *Ahau.* Some kind of badasses from her timeline.

Most of all, where was the moral certainty in all of this? Nakeesh insisted that the entire world was in danger. In the crosshairs, as she put it.

Did he believe her?

Not for a second. Except he'd seen her materialize from that silver-gray ball of energy. Seen the time machine appear where there'd been a divot in the concrete floor of Lab One, and with it, Tanner Jackson, and Reid Farmer's body, still so freshly dead that it leaked fluids and twitched.

How did you tell a woman you'd just witnessed traveling through time that she was batshit nuts? That she was making this up and needed to be locked back in that mental institution she'd escaped from? Worse, what if she was right? That this timeline, *his* world, was in danger.

Good God, how do I determine who's right and who's wrong?

"Trouble?" Nakeesh asked. Like everything else about her, that accent remained enchanting as hell.

He opened his eyes, happy that her stare couldn't hypnotize him in the dim light. "Trying to make sense of it all."

"I know." She wadded her pillow under her cheek and turned on her side, gaze fixed on his. "The things you've seen and experienced and now know to be fact would humble and paralyze most. But you're a smart man. I wouldn't have chosen a fool for a partner."

"Partner?" he wondered. "Do you sleep with all of your partners?"

"If I am exhausted, of course. Sleep is—"

"I mean sex, Nakeesh."

Her expression hinted of confusion, then cleared. "Ah, *copulativus*." A soft chuckle. "Among my people it is for more than just making babies, *Si*? *Coitus* is an art. Like I showed you last night." Again the devious smile. "We made a good start. I think we have promise for much better. When we have time. When I am not hunted."

An art? Call that an understatement.

He checked his watch: 6:43. "We need to be moving."

She stretched, muscles rippling down the length of her body. Then she tossed her hair back, rose with a dancer's grace, and made her way to the bathroom.

Seated on the stool, she called, "Hanson, I must get back into the lab. There is a machine there. One they took from me."

"Your missing cerebrum?"

"No. This I made while in Grantham. Skientia has it. Locked away. In a closet. With it, I can find Fluvium's cerebrum. The machine, the doohickey, will point the way. Perhaps we must go to Egypt, *non*?"

He padded into the colorful bathroom with its Talavera tiles and gold faucets. Scowled at the toothbrushes belonging to the absent homeowners; wished he had his own. His kit, however, was left behind.

He wondered what Josh Mack, Jaime, and the rest were thinking. Hoped they had come to the conclusion that he and Nakeesh had just up and vanished. Popped out of this universe and timeline through some magical computation made by Nakeesh's navigator. It wasn't like the woman didn't have a history of doing just that.

"How are we going to get to Egypt? I've only got a couple thousand in my wallet." He scratched his chin, feeling the stubble. Wished he'd had his razor, too.

"With navigator and doohickey, I can take us both to Egypt. Anywhere I have signal, *si*? *Crudis est*. Painful. Disorienting. But it will function."

"Pop both of us in and out?" The knowledge was beginning to settle that he might be allowed to accompany her. To experience what no one in his world had. Not only instantaneous travel, but perhaps to another timeline.

Which begged the question: Did he want to?

That moment's hesitation evaporated in an instant. Damn right. If the opportunity presented itself, he'd darn sure take it.

But how to get back into the lab? That was the tough call. He started running scenarios through his head as he dressed and made his way to the kitchen.

The counters were granite; an eight-burner Wolf stove, and polished chrome Sub-Zero refrigerator gleamed in the recessed lights. The fridge had been cleaned out before the owners split for Mexico, so Childs whipped up a concoction made from items he found in the freezer: sausage, bacon, and fish sticks. Not exactly gourmet, but still food.

"You have a plan?" Nakeesh asked thoughtfully as she sat at the copper-clad breakfast bar and demolished the meal.

"There's a brand-new Cadillac Escalade in the garage." He held up the key fob. "And, best of all, these were in the drawer beside the door."

But it wasn't until he was seated behind the wheel, and Nakeesh had settled in the passenger seat, that he hit his first snag. The entire dash came to life in display. It might have been the bridge on the *Enterprise*. Hanson figured out that he could still turn the thing on by pushing the start button.

"What the hell," he wondered. "Is this a car, or an F-35?"

"I do not know this term," Nakeesh told him.

"Yeah, well, Scotty, beam me up."

It took him another five minutes of futile searching for the garage door icon before he gave up in despair, stepped out to the musical bonging of warning alarms. He hit the manual garage door opener and sprinted for the driver's seat.

Praying, he stepped on the brake and pulled the shifter back into reverse. As the entire dash illuminated to display the rear cameras, he let off the brake. The tricked-out Escalade moved. Victory!

Next problem?

How do I get Nakeesh into the Skientia labs?

37

Karla

Karla decided that she liked the BMW RS with its liquid-cooled boxer twin. The bike had a thoroughbred feel. Not like the Skipper's 916. Riding the Ducati focused every bit of her attention. Uncomfortable as hell, the seat felt like a board, and the rider was constantly bent into a racing crouch. The Ducati's race-quality suspension hammered over every bump. Each gear had to be chosen and RPM matched to speed, and the thing was as quick handling as it was temperamental and fast.

In contrast, the BMW was smooth-fast. Easy to flick through corners with a torque curve that allowed her to use the entire engine. Not to mention that it was a hell of a lot more comfortable. She could tuck in behind the fairing to avoid wind blast. The seat didn't have her butt going numb, and she came away with the impression that she could ride the RS all day and into next week.

Too bad the morning jaunt had to be marred by worry about the Skipper.

She let the bike purr as she coasted into the Garden of the Gods parking lot. This early, the lot was empty. Morning sun cast long shadows across the pavement and burned red against the sandstone spiers. The smell of juniper and pine mixed with blooming rabbitbrush. The currants had started to turn, the first shades of red in their leaves. Fluffy puffs of cloud rolled down from Pikes Peak to sail eastward across the blue sky.

Karla figured she was being watched, killed the ignition, and settled the bike onto its side stand. Swinging off, she unfastened her pack and slung it over her shoulder as her trained gaze searched the trees, rocks, and paths. Helen was good. Karla couldn't see any trace of her.

Into her com, Karla said, "I'm here. Not a sign of the Skipper or Helen. How's the tracker reading?"

It wasn't global, but Grantham could locate her anywhere in a four-hundred-mile radius.

"You're good to go. Signal's clear. Watch yourself," Savage said through her earbud. "I'm not more than five minutes behind you. I'll hold just short of the parking lot. Be there in five if you need back up."

"Yeah, roger that."

She took a last glance around, the tickle of premonition playing down her spine. "I'm taking the trail now."

And with that, Karla trotted off down the Twin Spires Trail. It was a nice walking path. Paved and wide. Moving warily, she kept scanning as the trail wove through junipers and pines, passing the occasional bench for sitting and enjoying the remarkable scenery. Knowing she was being watched tripped all of her triggers. Conjured images. That prickling sense of impending . . .

The Humvee lurches and rocks as Weaver follows the faint two-track out of the village called Tallach 3. Karla bounced and swayed on the passenger seat. Behind her, Pud Pounder was standing with his upper body propped in the turret behind Ma Deuce, the fifty-caliber machine gun.

"Jabac Junction ahead, Chief," Weaver said.

She turned her attention to the collection of mud-and-stone huts—flat-roofed, colorless . . .

Saw the basket of slipped laundry at the side of the . . .

"No!" Her entire body shook, stomach heaving. "God damn it!"

She came to. Found herself huddled into a ball, head down, waiting for the concussion that would blast her world away into pain and despair.

Karla sucked a ragged breath, adrenaline pumping with the frantic pounding of her heart. Sweat dampened her hot skin. Jabac Junction had been tan and dusty. The sky sere. Karla stared frantically at the surrounding pines and juniper. At the soaring red rocks that rose against a startlingly blue sky. Tried to make sense of the pale soil studded with autumn-pale bunch grasses, the scattered rocks and boulders.

Panting, feeling a sweat sheen, she braced a hand on the concrete path. Wondered where she was.

"Fucking flashback." She straightened. Climbed to her feet and tilted her head back.

"Chief?" Savage's voice asked in the earbud.

"I'm okay," she told herself more than him.

Swallowing, the effect was like a knotted sock stuck halfway down her throat.

Garden of the Gods. She was supposed to find Helen. The woman had the Skipper.

God fucking damn, concentrate!

Grinding her teeth, she started up the path again, battling to get her heart and breathing under control. Sweat cooled on her skin, helping to focus her staggering brain.

This is not Afghanistan. That war's over. I'm in Colorado.

The afterimages continued to filter through her, fading slowly as she forced herself to focus on the trail, on possible places where Helen might lie in ambush.

"Come on," she told herself. "Situational awareness."

"Chief?" Savage asked, his voice laced with concern.

"Shut up. I got this," she growled under her breath.

Do I? The episode left her shaken, fear and shivers dangling at the edge of her control.

The flashback had hit her while she was on an op. That scared her, unnerved her more than the flashback.

Worse, Savage had heard.

Bitch, you'd better damn well keep your shit wired from here on out.

Lose it at the wrong time? People could die. The Skipper could die.

And it would be her fault.

Jabac Junction all over again.

"Come on, Karla. No heroes, just hard work."

She had her pulse under control now, anger adding to her determination.

Even then, Helen surprised her, announcing from behind, "Easy, Chief Raven. I'm right behind you."

Karla whirled, dropping into a fighting stance, reaching for the pistol that usually rode in a tactical holster. Grasping empty air, she remembered why she'd left it behind. The job here was to get close to Helen. Once the Skipper was free, she knew a dozen ways to take the woman out.

Helen wore a tan blouse, slacks, and hiking boots. She, too, carried a pack. What looked like a cerebrum was held tucked close to her left side like an oversized book, her right arm propped on her hip. She gave Karla a thorough inspection, eyes greener in the morning light than in the video. The effect was almost unsettling. Her face looked tanned, and the auburn hair was pulled back into a ponytail. Something about her left no doubt that she was athletic and fit. Very fit.

"Helen?" Karla was delighted that Savage was smart enough not to make comments.

"Back on the trail there . . . you all right?"

"Nothing you need to concern yourself with. Where's Colonel Ryan?"

"Somewhere safe." Helen stepped closer, head cocked, gaze now questioning. "Flashback?"

"I said—"

"Get 'em myself." A slight smile. "Occupational hazard for people like us."

Karla let her pack swing free to dangle from her left hand as she walked toward the woman. If need be, she could drop it, instantly freed for action. As she closed the distance, she could see the faint freckles, and yes, even the pale traces of old scars. Looked like Helen had earned her nightmares the hard way. Any doubt she had vanished when Karla met that hard green gaze. Yeah, the woman had been used hard.

Karla asked, "Those flashbacks? That Alpha's work?"

Helen's full lips twitched. "Among others. But we're not here to discuss ancient history." She extended the cerebrum with her left hand, waved her right across the top, which caused the machine to project a hazy blue holograph. "Put your finger on the blue button."

"And just like that, you whisk me away? What if I say no?"

"Fine with me. I'll find someone else. Whatever happens to Dr. Ryan . . . well, it won't make any difference. If Nakeesh wins, your world is gone anyway."

"So you say. You could tell us anything. How would we know?"

"You wouldn't." Helen shrugged, glanced up at the closest of the sandstone spires. "Lot of energy went into lifting that bedrock from flat to vertical. Really a spectacular place. Nice park. Shame to know it's all going to be torched."

"How's that?" Karla resettled herself, keeping her balance forward on the balls of her feet.

If Helen noticed, she ignored it. "I take it Ryan told you what happens if Nakeesh sends a message to Imperator? On top of being depraved and cruel, he's a really sick piece of work. Once Nakeesh surrenders herself to him, he and his *quinque*—that's his team of five *sterilitati*—they hunt down and recover the missing navigator and cerebrum. After Imperator has taken possession of Nakeesh and gone back for Fluvium, the *sterilitati* ensure that nothing is left alive on their way out."

"Do you know how insane that sounds?"

"Wake up. Listen." Helen stepped close, her eyes lined into a hard squint. "These machines, the ability to slip between timelines, are the most closely protected and fiercely guarded technology ever invented. But then, telling you why is like trying to explain electricity to an Australopithecine."

The wind was whispering through the pines and junipers as Karla asked, "So, how'd you come by that cerebrum and navigator you've got?"

"Stole them." Helen's smile went grim, her eyes straying to the spectacular geology surrounding them. "And you don't want to know what kind of price I paid to do that."

Karla shifted, every nerve tingling. "If Imperator is so hot to get Alpha's machines, why isn't he here chasing down yours?"

"Oh, he would be. Faster than a photon, if he knew I was here. And he wouldn't bring his picked *quinque,* but a full *mille.* That's a thousand. They'd scour every inch of this pretty little planet of yours and leave nothing but tumbling rock in their wake after they captured me and Nakeesh."

"So, you'd better hope Alpha doesn't let it out that you're here."

Something in Helen's expression turned to flint. "Makes us all pretty much in agreement, doesn't it?" The flicker of humorless smile returned to her lips as she said, "Now, you want to save everything you hold dear? Put your finger on the button."

"Sure. Just as soon as you turn Dr. Ryan loose."

"You and I need to get something straight: I could give a shit. I don't care about your pathetic little world, backward as it is. Or your timeline.

Or much of anything, for that matter. My purpose here, and my only purpose, is to kill Nakeesh before she can make her escape. You help me do that? I'll do what I can to make sure your timeline stays intact so that you can finally destroy it yourselves."

"I'm not hearing a lot of commitment in your voice."

Helen pursed her lips, considered. "Maybe not. Optimism is for people who just don't know any better." She extended the cerebrum. "You can place your finger on that glowing blue button and help me take down Nakeesh. Or you can walk away."

"Your call, Chief," Savage said through the earbud, having listened to the entire conversation. *"You're the one looking her in the eyes."*

"If Dr. Ryan doesn't come out of this alive and unharmed," Karla promised, "I'm going to make you hurt like you've never hurt before."

"When it comes to pain? Chief, you don't have a clue."

Karla reached out, hesitated as she extended her finger. Then she laid it on the glowing light that projected from the hologram.

Her body contorted. Felt like it was being pulled apart. She fell, weightless, into a spiraling haze.

38

Cat

With a slim forefinger, Catalina Talavera tapped the syringe to seat the bubble, then pushed the plunger until it, along with a clear drop, was expelled from the needle's tip. She turned, staring down at Falcon. He lay on the hospital bed, his gown tucked neatly around him, while a blanket covered him to the stomach. But for all the tubes, the IV, and the contacts with their wires running to the various medical monitors, he might have just been asleep. What looked like a partial white-plastic helmet, or headband, ran from parietal to parietal. Rather than protective, it was the functioning neural imaging system that monitored Falcon's brain. The image it sent to the large monitor allowed her to watch Falcon's brain function in real time.

She gave him a benevolent smile and bent down. Pulling her long black hair back with one hand, she inserted the needle into Falcon's IV and slowly injected her latest attempt at tailoring a psychotropic therapy specifically to the man's genetics.

Cat disposed of the syringe in the "sharps" bin. Then she seated herself, taking his hand in hers. At the same time, she watched the monitor where the first of her isotope-tagged molecules were visible as Falcon's circulatory system carried them into his brain.

"Very well, Falcon. You've got me working at the cutting edge of pharmacological theory. This latest recipe is tailored to the specific proteins in your limbic system. I guess the shorthand is that I'm increasing the chemical activity in your hippocampus so that you can access memories of safety and using a different tailored molecule to block the constant release of corticotrophin releasing factor and adrenocorticotrophic hormone to keep your overactive amygdala from flooding your system with adrenaline and cortisol. That should dampen your constant fear. If we can just reestablish some balance between the two, maybe you'll come back to us."

She turned, watching the state-of-the-art brain imaging technology as it followed the isotope-tagged drug. And yes, even this quickly she could see an increased glow in both the amygdala and hippocampus. She'd done it! At least, the protein-specific targeting was working on the right basal ganglia. Now, would her carefully constructed molecules actually do what they were supposed to?

"What I'm seeing on the screen, Falcon, is that my chemical blockers are fixing on specific cellular neural proteins in the amygdala. Any moment now, you should feel your constant state of paranoia begin to fade. And when you do, I want you to remember that we're here waiting for you. That you're safe with us."

She patted his hand, stood, and hesitated as she started to leave. Walking back, she told him, "Falcon, I know it was terrifying when that man, Hanson Childs, sent you into, well, wherever it is that you've gone. But he's been taken care of. ET got back at him."

Falcon's face remained expressionless.

Cat pulled the chair over, seating herself. "While my magical concoction works on your GABA-A binding sites, how about I give you an update?"

She pulled up a knee, lacing her fingers around it, and began, saying, "So, Alpha, as you know, has come back to our timeline. And no sooner did she do so than President Masters' chief of staff, Bill Stevens, raided the Skientia lab and abducted her. Took out Grazier's team with tranquilizing darts.

"As soon as Grazier heard, he called the Skipper, who was immediately abducted, in turn, by Helen. Um, we've told you about Helen, right?"

And all the while Cat talked, she kept glancing anxiously at the monitor, hoping to see something, anything, that would indicate that her latest drugs were working.

But Falcon just lay there, only the faintest flickers of movement behind his closed eyes.

39

Savage

Sam Savage strode into the conference room, tossing his pack and gear into one of the beanbag chairs. "What have we got, ET?" he called as he rounded the table and bent over ET's shoulder to stare at the computer.

"Don't got squat, Major." ET scowled at his computer monitor. "Chief Raven's tracker should have given me a solid blip on the map. Thought this was Gen'ral Grazier's top-of-the-line shit. I get nothing in a thousand miles any direction."

Savage continued staring at the screen. The image covered most of the Rocky Mountains and Southern Plains. "She should be reading."

"Unless two things," ET told him. "Maybe that electrical field killed it like it scrambles the monitors and fuzzes things out. That, or maybe Helen ran a scan, found it, and smacked it with a hammer."

"That or Karla wigged out on us again. Something triggered a flashback out there on the trail. Sent her back to Afghanistan. And worse, Helen saw it." Savage clenched a fist. "Last thing you want is for the enemy to know where you're vulnerable."

"Chief Raven, she'll come through. You'll see. She gonna spring the Skipper." ET said it with such simple faith.

"Damn it!" Savage straightened, paced back and forth across the small room. "We're losing it, ET. It's like having a grasp on the reins, just to have them slipping through your fingers. How are we supposed to get on top of this when the other side is popping back and forth through time? Snatching people and teleporting hither and yon? Now Helen's got Ryan and Chief Raven. Alpha's vanished. Stevens has her, and he's running his own show."

ET leaned back, stroking his chin as he studied the monitor with its maddeningly blank screen. "Don't know, Major."

"I've never felt this impotent in my entire life."

"Well, this high tech sure ain't working." ET leaned forward, clearing the screen. "What we got, Major, is Stevens. He's using encrypted communications, sure. But it's our technology, nothing alien. Him, I can crack."

"ET, you may be our only hope." Savage spun around, wishing he could break something. "What I need is a miracle."

"I'm with you on that, my man." ET cracked his knuckles before diving in and tapping on the keyboard. "You got a miracle. Problem is, he's all gone catatonic. What you need is Falcon, and then this thing get all straightened out."

Savage gave the man a squinty look. "And just how, ET, do you expect a DID schizophrenic to sit up from catatonia and tell us exactly what to do to save the earth?"

ET muttered. "Hell, we be in a nuthouse. How's I supposed to know?"

40

Childs

The plan Hanson Childs had finally settled on was audacious, but he needed the right equipment. His suspicion was that if he was to obtain it, the window would be closing—and fast.

As he drove up Paseo de Peralta, he shot a sidelong glance at Nakeesh. Dressed in her tactical black, her ash-blonde hair back in a ponytail, she looked ready for whatever fate might dish out. Her eyes were forward, one hand on the grab rail on the pillar. She remained as enigmatic as ever, still exuding that aura of power and competence. How did she do that?

Childs tried to concentrate as they approached the Canyon Road light and stopped behind a line of tourist traffic. Memories of the sex they'd had kept replaying. He couldn't keep them out of his head. Especially now that the rush of incredulity and golden afterglow had passed. Could he finally think about it rationally? When she'd initiated the foreplay, he'd just gone with the flow. Let her take command. And that was the key word. Now it struck him that she'd been more like a dominatrix, but on a psychological rather than physical level. And there had been a mechanical quality to her movements. He assumed her orgasms had been real, but looking back, he wasn't sure she'd actually enjoyed the sex.

So, what was that all about?

Like, it was more than just two people making love, and it sure hadn't been about intimacy. More of a performance. One meant to dazzle and distract?

Okay, she'd succeeded. Left him with his loins ringing. And it hadn't just been her mastery of technique. More of her chemicals? Those alleged pheromones?

Looking back now, he wondered if the sex had been a move on a gameboard. Some kind of manipulation? Perhaps her way of reassuring him that he'd made the right move? A reward for correct behavior? A demonstration of her superiority? Like a gift bestowed by the queen on a poor hick from the hinterlands in the benighted timeline? Or did she really think it would bind him to her, that sex like that, intense as it was, would make him hers forever?

"Your thoughts?" She gave him a sidelong inspection as the light changed.

"I don't think Josh Mack would have pulled his team. Not yet. If it were my operation, I'd keep some of my assets in place at the Loretto. Just on the chance that you and I might pop back in. Unless they caught a glimpse of us climbing down the walls on the surveillance video, that's the most likely explanation of our escape, right? They'll think your navigator beamed us someplace."

"They know little about navigators."

"That's what I'm banking on." Not that he knew anything about the slim box Nakeesh kept so close.

"Banking? I don't know this term."

He'd noticed that. She seemed to have a good concept of the language, but acted like a fish out of water over the simplest of things. All of which reinforced the notion that without him to squire her around, she'd be helpless.

Another explanation for the sex? She was using it as a way to keep him hooked?

He turned onto Alameda Drive. The south side was bordered by the green space along the Santa Fe River with its walking path, trees, and picnic tables. Reaching the Loretto, they cruised past the adobe-walled parking lot. As they passed the hotel entrance on Old Santa Fe Trail, he was reassured to see "Dirty Harry" Logan lounging, his back to the adobe perimeter wall, a cell phone to his ear.

"Bingo. They're still here."

"Which means what?" Nakeesh asked as they motored past.

Logan didn't give them a second look. He was too busy watching two blonde tourists, both women in their twenties, wearing shorts, as they strolled toward the Plaza.

"Which means I can get what I need to get us into the Skientia lab."

He pulled into the public parking and backed into a space. Slipping the Escalade into park, he left the engine running. Leaning in her direction, he said, "I don't think you should come."

"Why not?"

"Doubles our chances of being spotted. Listen. The gear we need is in duffle bags in the back of the team vans. They're parked side-by-side against the far wall of the parking lot. Josh keeps one of the team posted with the vans at all times to ensure the gear is safe and that the trucks are ready to roll in an instant. I'm taking the nature path beside the river to slip past Logan. Once I'm opposite the vans, I'll go over the wall. Hope I can get the drop on whoever's got the watch on the trucks. Once I get a bag, I'll vault the wall, slip back into the park, and hotfoot it back here."

"Hotfoot?" She arched a blonde eyebrow.

"Means hurry."

The blue intensified in her gaze. "What if they catch you?"

He shrugged. Pointed at the clock in the dash. "It's 7:48. When the numbers hit 8:48, if I'm not back, you're on your own."

For the first time, he saw what might have been fear behind her concentrated stare.

"To drive, I pull lever." She pointed at the shifter. "Turn wheel. How does it know to go forward? Eye control? Mind interface?"

"Accelerator and brake," he pointed at the pedals. "But you don't have a clue about traffic laws or the rules of the road. You won't make it past Cerrillos before you're in a wreck." With a tingle of delight and arrogance, he told her, "Ditch the car. Walk away. My call? You'll find a sugar daddy in one of the hotels. Put the moves on him. Maybe he'll fly you off to Cancun or Peoria or wherever."

"I don't understand."

"Nope." He opened the door to a dinging and donging of chimes while warning messages flashed across the full-display dash warning him the door was open. "See you in half an hour or so."

Then he closed the Escalade's door behind him, glancing this way and that, searching for any sign of Mack's security team. If he could spot them before they caught sight of him, he still had a chance.

Crossing Alameda, he kept as close to the river as he could. River? All he saw at the bottom of the stone-lined drainage was a trickle of water that wouldn't have qualified as a brook back in Maryland. Luck was with him when he reached the crossing at Cathedral Place. A group of German tourists were waiting at the light. Given his pale-blond hair, Childs fit right in as he tagged along behind them.

With nothing but the adobe Loretto parking lot wall between him and the vans, he took his time, letting tourists pass until the sidewalk was empty. He leaped, swung a leg, and got a foot up. Then he levered himself up and over, scraping his elbows and forearms on the rough texture of the adobe.

Slipping over the wall, he dropped as silently as he could between two of the white Ford vans. Crouching, he waited, heart pumping, but no one came running. On hands and knees, he bent low and peeked under the vans.

There. Feet. At the front, by the first of the three vans. Had to be the guard. Easing to the front bumper of his van, he scanned the parking lot for observers, seeing no one but a family of tourists cramming luggage into a Chevy Equinox. They seemed totally preoccupied with fitting their huge suitcases into the back so as to allow the hatch to close.

Childs crept back, around the rear, and darted behind the first van. Surreptitiously, he peered around the side.

The person detailed to keep an eye on the vehicles turned out to be Lonnie Hughes. From the thigh pocket of his cargo pants, Childs took a zip tie. Slipping a hand into his shirt, he drew the 380 Sig from his appendix rig. As carefully as he could, wincing at the minute crunching where gravel ground on asphalt, he ghosted up behind Hughes. Caught him by complete surprise when he lunged, slipped a forearm across the man's throat, and pulled him back against the Sig's hard muzzle.

"Don't fight it, Lonnie," he whispered as the man tensed to throw him off. "Before you backheel me, headbutt, and twist, I'll blow your spine in two." Childs shifted his hold to rip the mic and earbud out of Hughes' ear. Dropping them, he used a foot to kick the communications gear under the van and out of reach.

"Who?" Lonnie rasped past the choking forearm.

"Just reach your hands back, easily, and you'll come out of this alive and with a story to tell."

"Childs?" He swallowed hard against the forearm. "What the hell?"

"Saving the world, amigo. Here's the thing. I'm not sure that Stevens is on the right side. You get that? Now, stop fucking around. I'm in this so deep, shooting you doesn't dig me any deeper. Ease those hands back."

Childs pulled the zip ties tight with one hand, then said, "Drop to your knees, Lonnie, and cross your ankles. That means, as you go down, a bullet will just take you higher in the body if I pull this trigger."

When Childs had Lonnie's ankles bound, he ripped a section from the back of the man's cotton shirt, wadded it, and stuffed it into Hughes' mouth for a gag.

Surveying his work, Childs holstered his little Sig Saur P238 and told the man, "Now, you just stay down. Don't wiggle around. I figure that once I'm gone, you'll figure a way to free yourself within, oh, five to ten minutes. So, dude, give me the time I need, and then you can howl and holler all you want."

Childs opened the cab door, hit the unlock button, and hurried to the rear. Opening the double doors, he reached for one of the black ballistic nylon bags. The one he got was stenciled with the name "Mack." Pulling it back, Childs zipped it open to ensure that it had the kit he thought it did.

He turned, hefted the bag to the top of the adobe wall. Had just laid his hands on the adobe when a voice behind him said, "Sorry, old friend. Got to stop you there."

Childs whirled on his heel, dropping to a crouch, only to see Jaime Chenwith step around the front of the van, his duty pistol held in the ready position. The man's eyes almost looked pained, his lips pursed into a hard scowl. "What the fuck are you doing? What's she gone and done? Grabbed you by the balls? Winked and wiggled her ass and made an idiot out of you?"

"Hey, easy."

"Hands up, bro," Chenwith told him. "And don't reach for that little belly gun."

"Where were you? I looked."

"Sitting in the third van, bro." Childs eased forward. "Rest of the team is tracking down flights, bus tickets, stolen cars, traffic cams, that sort of thing. Me and Hughes, being the bottom of the feeding order, got truck duty. Never thought you'd come back to hit the trucks. What are you doing, man?"

"Listen to me." Childs forced all the conviction he could into his words. "Stevens is the bad guy. If he gets his hands on Nakeesh, he's going to squeeze and suck her brain dry. And he's doing it for his own gain. Not the country's. If that happens, some guy named Imperator is coming from Nakeesh's timeline to get the navigator. When he does, bro, we lose. Get it? The only way . . ."

The crack of a pistol shot carried on the sunny morning air. Close enough that Childs jumped—that momentary seizure, the expectation that Chenwith's pistol had discharged coincided with his friend's jerk, the stunned expression. Those brown eyes went wide, Jaime's mouth gaping open.

And then the agent staggered sideways to brace himself on the van. The pistol clattered to the pavement. The expression on Chenwith's face had gone slack, disbelieving.

"Hey, easy," Childs soothed, stepping forward. He took Chenwith, pulled him to the side as he eased the van's driver door open. Settled Chenwith on the sill.

Where he still sat gagged on the ground, Hughes was bellowing muffled cries. The man's eyes had gone wild, panicked.

Childs stared at the blood on his hands. Then met his friend's dark, wet eyes, saw the terror and confusion.

Who the hell shot?

A second shot. Loud. Caused him to jump again.

At his feet, Hughes spasmed, then slumped sideways onto the pavement. Where the shirt had been torn away for the gag, blood began to spurt from a hole between the man's shoulder blades.

Childs whirled, blinked.

Atop the adobe wall, Nakeesh perched beside the tactical bag; the black HK she'd snagged from beside Farmer's dead body back in Lab One was held in combat grip. The woman's hard blue eyes might have been molten lapis.

"Come," she said. "We go."

Childs couldn't think. Brain reeling. Jaime was shot. So was Hughes. And he was in the middle of it. He half staggered his way back to the wall. Took her hand as she reached down. And, to his amazement, she pulled him to the top.

The extent of her strength didn't come as that much of a surprise after their sexual gymnastics the night before, but he hadn't expected her to have that kind of upper body muscle.

Dropping to the sidewalk on Cathedral Place, he pulled down the tactical bag and slung it over his shoulder. The echo of the gunshots kept replaying in his rattled brain. He saw it over and over again, the pistol's report. The look in Jaime Chenwith's eyes.

"Thought I told you to stay in the truck." It was all his reeling brain could come up with.

"What is the term? Gone to shit? That's what it looked like to me." Her words were dispassionate, no change of expression on her face. She walked beside him with a leonine grace. Seemed as unconcerned as if she were discussing the weather.

"You *shot* Jaime! And Hughes!"

"They would have complicated things, *si*? Instead of a complication, they are now a distraction to buy us time. You have equipment you need? All of it?"

It took him two tries to utter the word "yes."

They moved fast, crossing Alameda, slipping down the river trail, and crossing back to the parking lot. Miracle of miracles, the Escalade was still there. When Childs pulled the door open and slung the tactical bag into the back seat, the Escalade informed him that he'd taken the key fob out of range.

Fucking modern technology.

"You all right?" Nakeesh asked, something hard and implacable in her cerulean eyes.

"Yeah." He swallowed hard.

Took him five minutes for the shakes to subside enough that he could drive. The sirens could be heard racing for the Plaza as he turned them onto St. Francis and headed for the highway.

41

Karla

Blinking her eyes, Karla stared up at a drywall ceiling. There had been enough times in her past that she'd come to, not knowing where she was, that she sat up, did a fast three-sixty of the room, and vaulted off the bed. Looked like an average guest bedroom in an average house. Maybe ten by fifteen, small closet with a white door, dresser, doorway leading out to the hall. The one window with lacy curtains looked out at forest just past a chain-link fence. She was dressed, but the pockets on her utility pants had been cleaned out. Her earbud and com gear were also missing.

Last she remembered was being pulled apart, falling.

As horrible as that had been, she really shouldn't be feeling this good.

Easing to the door, she listened, faintly heard voices. Carefully, she turned the latch and stepped out into a carpeted hallway that sported pictures of Pikes Peak, a couple of dried-sage floral displays on a narrow marble-top table, and additional doors. These, Karla carefully checked, finding an upscale bathroom with toilet, marble tub/shower, and sink, and two additional bedrooms.

The hall ended at a custom-designed kitchen with a fancy island stove, oversized refrigerator, stacked ovens, wine fridge, and lots of gleaming granite countertops. The cabinets looked handmade. Expensive.

Karla hesitated before stepping out. She crossed to where the kitchen opened to the spacious great room with its vista. Windows looked out on tree-clad slopes that surrendered to distant mountain tundra and stone. There, the high peaks, snow-capped, met the sky. Backlit by the rising sun, they cast bars of light that angled toward the valley.

"I see you're up." Helen was seated, cross-legged, in a plush leather couch facing the windows. Colonel Ryan sat, leaned forward, elbows on knees, in a matching overstuffed chair. A cup of coffee rested before him on a table made out a single slab of sandstone. The cerebrum and navigator sat side-by-side on the table next to Helen. They cast a hazy blue glow that radiated above them.

Karla—still on alert—stepped out onto the slate floor, taking in the fitted-log beams, the giant rock fireplace with its bear rug, and the Navajo blankets hanging from the walls. "Nice place. I guess you're moving up from stealing travel trailers."

"Airbnb. It's a rental," Helen told her, uncrossing her legs before she stood and walked into the kitchen. "Something to drink? Coffee? Tea? Soda? Something stiffer?"

"No thanks."

Helen stopped, eyebrow arched. "Rehydrate, Chief. We're on the clock. Generally, you don't feel hunger after a jump, but I suggest that you eat. Otherwise, when the high plummets, you're going to think you're at starvation's door."

"It's all right, Chief," Ryan called. "Do as she says."

"How are you doing, Skipper? Been treated all right? What's your number?"

"Ten, Chief," Ryan told her in code as he snagged his coffee cup off the table, walked across the fancy slate floor, and stuck the cup into a sparkling chrome coffee machine. "I'm fine. No duress." Then, giving Karla a conspiratorial nod, he pressed the button. "I think we're good. For the moment, Helen's biding her time. My advice is hydrate and eat while you've got the chance. And she wasn't kidding about the hunger kicking in. You'll be ravenous."

"Got burritos," Helen told her. "Fresh made from a little Mexican place down the road. But I'll warn you, they're habanero hot."

Karla gave the woman a nod, watched her pull a foil-wrapped burrito out of the huge Sub-Zero. Before the door could close, Karla reached in and retrieved a bottle of iced tea.

"Skipper, the deal was I pushed the blue button, and you got to go free. I'm here. Now, do you get to go back to the team, or do I practice a little CQB on the *Ennoia* before we both walk out of here."

"Stand down, Chief. I'm told I can go whenever I like. I'm learning. Trying to figure out the best way forward."

Karla inclined her head toward Helen. "You trust her?"

"For the moment."

"What do you mean by 'on the clock'?" Karla asked as Helen put the burrito in the microwave.

The woman leaned her butt against the stove island and crossed her arms. "You know where your prisoner Alpha is? No? Neither does anyone else. Seems Domina Nakeesh took matters into her own hands. She and one of her guards escaped from Stevens' crack commando force. She was last seen in Santa Fe this morning. She and her accomplice—a guy by the name of Hanson Childs—killed a couple of Stevens' men at the Loretto Hotel. Got away with a bag of tactical gear that includes dart guns, an MP-5, smoke grenades, night vision gear, grapples, cable, lockpicks, and the like. At least, that's what's been reported to the Santa Fe police."

"Hanson Childs? Yeah, we've run into him before. I'd like to hammer on his ass for a while. Son of a bitch. So, how do you know all this?"

She tapped her ear. "Police scanner. It's on a satellite relay."

Ryan added, "While you were napping, I called Savage. Gave him an update."

"How's the major doing?" she asked, wary gaze on Helen.

"Let's say he's stressed. The good news is that ET's managed to get a hack on Stevens' Santa Fe team. The detail leader is a guy by the name of Josh Mack. Where it gets interesting is that some tourists were loading their car across the parking lot. Remember Jaime Chenwith?"

"Yeah, he was the Air Force OSI agent who busted us at Buffalo Thunder. He and I need to have a chat sometime, in a dark alley, someplace where I can leave him in a dumpster to be taken out with the rest of the trash."

"He's dead. So's one of Mack's team named Hughes. The tourists say that a woman, tall, ash-blonde, with weird blue eyes shot both men, then pulled Childs over the parking lot wall, and they both disappeared down Cathedral Street."

Helen's gaze cooled. "Too bad your man didn't crack the communications yesterday, Ryan. You and I could have jumped to Santa Fe. I could have killed the sick bitch, and my part would be neatly tied up."

"Your part?" Ryan asked as he retrieved his coffee cup.

The woman turned those frosty green eyes his way. "I can take Nakeesh's navigator with me when I go. You want to give me Fluvium's cerebrum? Hmm? No?"

"General Grazier would object." Ryan sipped his coffee, made a face and spit some back as if it were still too hot.

"And that's going to be a problem for you." Helen stepped over when the microwave dinged. She pulled down a plate and gingerly dragged the steaming burrito onto it.

Karla took it, smelling the odor of beans, cheese, jalapeño, and cilantro. "So, why's that a problem? Cerebrum's no good without a navigator, right?"

"It's missing equipment. Critical equipment." Helen handed her the burrito. "In Fluvium and Nakeesh's timeline, they're both overdue. Powerful people are aware that they, as you say, popped back to a non-essential timeline to conduct an experiment. Given that what you call 'time' essentially doesn't exist, the *Ahau* know something went very wrong. By now they're looking for your timeline."

"Looking how?" Ryan asked, sharing a worried look with Karla.

Helen led the way back to the great room, reseating herself and crossing her legs in something Karla thought might have been the lotus position. Sitting still had never been her thing.

"Without Nakeesh's navigator, they wouldn't have known which timeline Fluvium and Nakeesh chose, just that it was Egypt sometime after your timeline split from theirs. The *Ahau*'s agent would be jumping from timeline to timeline. Searching for any indication the navigator and cerebrum were active. If there were no hits on the suspected timelines, the agent would have returned to the *Ahau*'s timeline and reported."

"Which means what?" Karla asked, shooting Ryan a worried look.

Helen's expression remained placid. "The assumption would be that something happened to Nakeesh and Fluvium. Maybe they were killed the moment they popped into Egypt. Maybe it was a programming mistake, and they popped into someplace in deep space, or underwater. Maybe the error was particularly egregious, and they landed in the wrong timeline. One where no one would ever come searching for them. Or, in the absolute worst case, a timeline that was recohering. That would be any traveler's nightmare. Whatever happened to them was catastrophic enough that the navigator and cerebrum were lost."

"What about Fluvium's cerebrum?" Ryan asked. "It was sitting in that tomb, right?"

"Yeah," Helen agreed. "Fluvium would have turned it off manually to save energy, and it was buried in a mountain. He would have known that placing it in that location would make it almost impossible for any of the *Ahau*'s agents to find. He did that to keep Nakeesh safe. Give her the opportunity to save herself, and perhaps him, if she could."

Karla tested the burrito. Too hot. "So we take out Alpha, you jump back to your wherever with or without her navigator. You're off the hook. Who cares?"

"The *Ahau*," Helen told her in a wooden voice. "You still don't get it."

"Then explain," Ryan prompted.

Helen gestured at the cerebrum and navigator glowing blue on the table. "Those machines, they're the most guarded and dangerous weapons ever produced. In any timeline. Best contemporary analogy for your world? Two of your hydrogen bombs were loaned out. Now they've vanished without a trace along with the people who borrowed them. You going to be concerned about that?"

Again Karla glanced at Ryan, saw the Skipper's slight confusion. She said, "So, a hydrogen bomb can immolate and irradiate an entire city the size of Los Angeles. Kill tens of millions. Not to mention the chaos loosened by the EMP. Millions more will be displaced in the violence and fallout that ensues."

Helen shrugged. "That's crude compared to erasing an entire history. A team with a cerebrum and navigator can go back in time and release a weaponized virus or bacterium that changes the path of all life along that timeline. No immolation or radiation. Tens of billions will simply never exist." She snapped her fingers. "Gone. Erased. In your case— which means your timeline—the *Ahau* will go back a couple thousand years. Everyone who lived after whatever time and place they choose will never be born. Period. They might even choose to extinguish humanity through a genetic plague."

Helen gestured around. "All this. Wilderness. No Egypt. No Rome. No Ming Dynasty. No Tokugawa Shogunate. No England, or France, or Mexico. No Maya or Harrapans." She grimaced. "No Hitler, Stalin,

Pol Pot, or Torquemada. No *Mona Lisa* or Sagrada Familia. No *Star Wars*. Which is a real pity."

"How . . ." Ryan shook his head. "No, never mind. I get it. Time isn't real. It's like the ultimate Sun Tzu. 'Fight the enemy where they are not.' In this case, they're never born."

Karla fixed on the navigator and cerebrum. "Who are these *Ahau?*"

"Means 'the Lords.' Comes from Mayan." Helen's gaze had grown distant. "Lords of time. Lords of creation and death. Lords of science and light. All powerful." Helen's gaze cleared. She shot a hard look at Karla and Ryan. "You people, you have quaint stories about humans who consider themselves to be gods. Among the *Ahau?* Given their technology and science, the power at their fingertips, and their control of time and the timelines, there really isn't much difference between a god and an *Ahau.*"

"Oh, yeah?" Karla asked. "What happens when you shoot one in the head with a high-velocity bullet?"

Helen gave her a deadpan look. "Should you get the unlikely chance, the body will immediately be put on life support while they regrow the head and brain, download the personality, memory, and training to the body, and things go on as they were. The only price is a short-term lack of recollection about whatever happened between the last download and the gunshot."

"You have got to be kidding me," Ryan murmured. "They keep a personality on download? I mean, that's . . . How could they? Impossible. The way the brain is structured . . ." He shook his head in disbelief.

"Maybe in your science," she told him. "When you're a god, you can do these things."

"And this Imperator?" Karla asked.

"He's the right hand, the operative, the enforcer who acts at the direction of the *Ahau.* He attends to the dirty work. Like you, Chief Raven, he carries out the *Ahau's* orders and will. They give him or her the distasteful assignments when action is required in the field."

"So why would Alpha want to contact him?" Ryan asked. "Sounds like he'd take her back to these *Ahau,* and they'd punish her for losing the cerebrum."

Helen's green gaze flashed momentary irritation. Then she sighed.

"You really don't get the time thing, do you? All right, here's the deal: Nakeesh and Fluvium were what you people would call hotshot scientists in *Ti'ahaule*. That's the *Ahau's* name for the Lordship, what they call their civilization. Fluvium and Nakeesh work for one of the *Ahau*. Conduct her research. So does Imperator, who has always lusted after Nakeesh. Wanted her for his own, but she chose Fluvium. And Fluvium and Nakeesh made too good a team, were too valuable to the *Ahau,* for Imperator to take matters into his own hands."

"Wait," Karla raised a hand. "You're telling me she's calling on him anyway?"

The look in Helen's eyes triggered a chill along Karla's spine. "Chief, without Fluvium's cerebrum, Nakeesh can't skip into the past and rescue him. And even if she had it, just like my units on the table, it takes two to jump in time or across timelines."

"Wait a minute," Karla cried. "What about all that business about you can't go back in time because of the grandfather effect. That you can't kill your grandfather because you won't be born? Thought it only went one way."

"The paradox?" Nakeesh asked. "You can't go back. Nor can Dr. Ryan here. Think about the energy that you represent. You're inextricably constrained by decoherence and entanglement. Nakeesh? Fluvium? Me? We're here on loan. Subject to different rules and entanglement."

"So, how does that work?" Ryan asked.

Helen crossed her arms, cocked her head as she studied him through thoughtful green eyes. "If Nakeesh gets her hands on Fluvium's cerebrum, her navigator will give her the exact point in space and time where she left the Nile. She'll reappear an instant after she popped into the future, recalibrate with a slightly mystified Fluvium, and ditch this timeline altogether for home." A pause. "Or, she has to rely on summoning Imperator. He'll ensure they all go together with the added benefit of sterilizing your timeline because you're fiddling with entanglement."

"But what about the tomb?" Ryan asked. "Everything that's happened? You, being here?"

Helen leaned forward, eyes burning into Ryan's. "*It never happens.* Get it?"

"Hard to wrap my head around," Ryan whispered. "The idea that two thousand years can just be reset in the past. That another history, with different people, can just . . ." He shook his head. "How can all that history go away?"

Helen snapped her fingers. "Just like that."

"Let's get back to Nakeesh," Karla said, more than a little unnerved herself.

Helen shot her a glance. "My guess is that she's going to try and send a message to Imperator. Surrender herself to him if he'll pull her and Fluvium out of this mess."

Ryan, refocusing, sipped his coffee. "But, Helen, you told me that he'll make her a slave. Sexually and emotionally abuse her. Why would she agree to that kind of bondage when she could stay here, at least live out her life without degradation?"

"Dr. Ryan, ultimately the *Ahau* will get around to searching your timeline's present. When they do, they'll find Nakeesh's navigator. What they'll do to her when that happens. . . . You seriously can't conceive. It will be long, with unbearable suffering, not to mention creatively painful."

Karla watched the woman unconsciously lay a finger on one of the ever-so-faint scars on her cheek. Helen's hard-as-rock eyes were unfocused, a slight shiver running down her muscular body.

Karla interrupted the woman's reverie, "So, Alpha's going to sell herself to Imperator, who will keep her from this fate worse than death? Earlier, you told the Skipper that Imperator could save Fluvium. Currently, he's a mummy in a lab. How's that work?"

Helen's gaze strengthened. "With Nakeesh's navigator for a guide, Imperator jumps back with his team. They land at the spot where Nakeesh's navigator fixed on your entangled particle signal. They find a surprised—and very much alive Fluvium—standing on the side of the Nile where he's pouring his biological agent into the river. With all the machines linked, they jump back to the *Ti'ahaule* timeline."

Her smile turned grim. "And, for the rest of his days, Fluvium lives knowing that his beloved Nakeesh sacrificed herself to rescue him from what she considers a hideous end. To die alone in ancient Egypt."

Karla asked, "What about Imperator? He's happy just getting away with Alpha as his own personal toy?"

"Of course," Helen answered. "He can use, abuse, and debase her in any way he wants. More so, knowing that Fluvium—whom he's always hated—is powerless to stop whatever degradation Nakeesh is subjected to."

"God, fucking damn!" Karla snapped. "I'm ready to shoot the puss-sucker just thinking about it."

"Don't waste the emotion," Helen told her. "You people still have quaint notions of justice. Imperator might be a twisted bit of work, but Nakeesh is a foul demon in her own right. You might not be so sympathetic if you knew the extent of the woman's cruelty and arrogance."

Ryan had leaned back to cradle his coffee. "Why don't we just let them go?"

"Because of the timeline," Karla told him as the pieces fell in place. "If Alpha and Imperator go back and rescue Fluvium, our timeline dies, vanishes, changes, or whatever. That whole paradox thing, remember? The result is that we vanish. Poof. We're gone."

"Worse, actually," Helen told her. "Imperator will ensure that this entire timeline is left desolate."

"Why? What threat do we pose?" Ryan's brow furrowed as he clutched his coffee cup.

Helen studied them both. "Too late, Dr. Ryan. You sent an entangled signal back into the past. Nakeesh's navigator followed your entangled particles to that lab. You are on the threshold of discovering how to make navigators and cerebrums. And the *Ahau* can't allow that."

ENNOIA

I am growing ever more weary of ancient Egypt. My people are tired, the legionarii in my quinque have been calculating odds, figuring out the number of jumps that we've made, understanding the percentages for success. They know full well that one of these jumps could end up in disaster. I, too, am growing increasingly concerned. All it would take is one slight mistake in the computations, an error as I input the data for a jump. Sak Puh's cerebrum is only as reliable as the navigator that feeds it data.

Tonight we are taking shelter in a squat hut, the walls made of mud. More mud is packed onto the reeds and sticks that compose the roof. Outside, a rare rain is falling, bringing the smells of the desert alive. Water trickles and splashes from the overhanging eaves.

The lowly farmers who live here ran at first sight of us. No doubt, they will be back by dawn, probably accompanied by some local shaman brought to exorcise the demons. For, surely, that is what they will think we are. I will take some limited amusement in cutting them to pieces with my gladius. The legend will endure for centuries. Knowing that warms some deep part of my soul.

I turn back from the door and take in my party. My legionarii are huddled about the fire, oddly quiet. Their eyes are on the tiny flames in the small hearth. Egypt isn't rich with firewood. It's pretty poor doings, but better than nothing.

Sak Puh sits to the right of the door, a listlessness in her eyes. She is seeing things in her head. Imagining, no doubt, the fate of the timelines we've sterilized.

I wonder what she'd think of the ones Ti'ahaule has burned with nuclear fires? Though that isn't common knowledge, even among ah' tzib. Given the complexity of transporting nuclear devices between timelines, that fate is reserved only for the most grievous threats to the Lords.

She surprises me when she says, "Imperator, you told us that the Ennoia might be behind Fluvium and the Domina's disappearance. In each timeline, we scan for her. All we've ever heard is that the Ennoia is the most dangerous criminal ever. That she murdered an entire lineage and stole a navigator and cerebrum. You knew her. If we're to fight her, what do we need to know?"

The eyes of everyone in the hut turn my direction.

I lean my head back. "Domina Nakeesh brought her back as a slave. A curiosity since she was an important woman in several branches of the timeline. She and Fluvium kept her, used her as a slave is used. They thought it amusing to have the Ennoia *genetically augmented. Displayed her as a sort of novelty. Even let her take charge of the* domus. *Nakeesh's household."*

I *shift, drag a sandal-clad foot across the sandy floor.* "What they didn't *understand was how smart the woman was. Or how well she learned our science. She tried to escape, but I caught her. Kept her for almost five years. Used her as a lesson for other* in servus. *An example of the kind of suffering and misery a slave would endure if they ever challenged us. Sought to escape."*

"How did she get away?" Cak be, Publius' *friend, asks.*

"Seduced a friend of mine," I tell him with a shrug. "She has a way with men. I doubt that he understood the lengths to which the Ennoia *would go. Not until it was too late. And by then, there was no going back."*

"As long as she's out there," Publius *says, "others will always think they can do the same."*

"What if we catch her?" Sak Puh *has those irritating doubt lines forming in her forehead.*

"The last time I had her, I tortured her in every excruciating way I could imagine, and for all to see. I cut her, bled her, nailed her to a cross and let her hang, humiliated her in every way I could. Because of her augmentation, she couldn't die. Just had to endure. The next time, I will do the same. The difference will be, that this time, after a couple of years, I will cut off her head." With an anticipatory smile, I add, "For all to see."

42

Childs

Gate security at the Los Alamos lab was going to be a problem. Hanson Childs fully understood that they'd have a description of him and Nakeesh. By now, half the state would have seen his image. Stevens, or so he supposed, would have ensured that Hanson Childs and Nakeesh's photos were displayed on all the local television channels, on social media, and to law enforcement all over the state.

With his white-blond hair, pale blue eyes, and lanky build, he stood out. Not to mention Nakeesh. Just walking into a room, she drew everyone's gaze. And the way she moved? Well, Childs doubted that the woman was capable of acting nondescript even if she tried.

They were sitting in the Escalade on a scenic pull off on New Mexico 501 above Las Alamos. Behind them, the Jemez Mountains blocked the sunset, casting shadows down the slope and across the Rio Grande Valley. A blue haze—smoke from distant forest fires—obscured the distant Sangre de Christo Mountains off to the east.

Childs resealed the Styrofoam container his two chicken enchiladas, refritos, and rice had come in. Then he tossed the container onto the floor in the back. Nakeesh had finished off her two tamales in red sauce, and dropped the box out her window with a nonchalance that made Childs wince. She seemed unaware of the simplest of things.

Or even the most egregious. His stumbling brain kept replaying the way she'd shot Jaime and Hughes down in cold blood. Part of him wanted to believe it hadn't happened. That it was all part of a sick dream.

The knowledge that it was real sent chills down his back. He was an accomplice to two murders, not to mention that of a federal officer. A man he'd considered a friend.

I am past the point of no return.

He glanced sidelong at woman. "Why did you have to shoot them?"

Through thin-lidded eyes, she told him, "They were *stulti. Inutilis.*"

"I don't know those words."

"No. You don't."

He placed his hands on the steering wheel, took a deep breath. Tried to ease the cramp in his stomach. He'd always thought he handled tension well. Considered himself a seasoned professional. But the events of the morning had unnerved him.

The enchiladas—which he'd hoped would help—felt like molten slag in his stomach.

God, how had he come to this?

"Jaime Chenwith was my partner," he said softly. "A man with whom—"

"He will be dead anyway," she told him, voice without inflection. "All of this. It is too late. You cannot save it. I cannot save myself."

"Want to explain that?"

She kept her gaze locked on Los Alamos; the Skientia lab could be seen among the various buildings in the compound. "We don't have much time, Hanson. I am amazed I have made it this far. That I have tells me that we have a chance. That we are still free tells me that I will contact Imperator. I will save Fluvium. The *Ahau* will not punish me."

He placed a hand to his rebellious stomach. "You sound resigned about that."

The snort she made might have been derision. "For everything there is a price, Hanson. I know you are suffering from guilt. That you think your life will be short, and that your people will punish you terribly for the necessary disposal of those two men. But I will ensure that does not happen. Rather, you will save your timeline, *si?* Your people may not know for the moment, but you are the only hope for your world. When the time comes, I need you to help me. Save me, and your world will never be the same. A whole new future. Like nothing you have ever imagined."

He saw the slight smile grow as she talked. As though she knew something he didn't.

"Yeah," he grimaced. "Well, I guess at this point, all the bridges are burned. There's no going back."

"Only forward," she told him. "How soon until we should try to get into the lab?"

He glanced at the dash clock. "Another hour, hour and a half."

She finally shifted her gaze, studying him with an intensity that seemed to burn right through him. "Whatever happens, I may be dead. Perhaps shot getting to the machines I need in the lab. Perhaps captured by the *Ahau*. Or I may contact Imperator." A pause. "There is always a price for failure."

"I don't understand."

"You and I. We may not have much time left together."

"Wow. Thanks for the all the—"

"I want *copulare*. There is room in the back." She continued to fix on him, the abruptness taking him off guard.

"Hey, I'm not in the—"

"Hanson. After this night, I will never know anything but pain. I will never *feel*. Do you understand? Whatever happens, I will not own my body. It will belong to Imperator. This is the last chance to be in control. To be *alive*. Now, get in the back and recline the seats. Do it."

How could she think of sex now? What did it say about her personality?

He blinked, stared off across the slope to where the Skientia lab waited, an ominous white cube among the other laboratories.

"God, you'd think I was a slave," he said as he stepped out and opened the rear door.

Her laughter reeked of bitterness. "What do you know of being *in servus*?"

She met him in the back, kneeling on the seat as she stripped off her blouse. He was still reclining the seat when she attacked his belt and trousers.

43

Ryan

According to my watch it was 1:06, and, yes, I'm old-fashioned. I still wear one. Not everyplace has cell service, and I forget to plug my phone in. I parked the Jeep in my space in the Grantham garage, walked to the double doors, and passed the startled security.

To my surprise, the lights were on, and when I stepped into the outer office, Janeesha sat at her desk, phone to her ear. She glanced up, relief in her dark eyes, and said, "He just walked in the door, General. I'll send him right in."

"Good grief, Janeesha. It's after one in the morning. You should be home. Asleep. Why are you here?"

She laid the phone in its cradle, arched a mocking eyebrow, and told me, "Let's see. Prisoner Alpha is back from the future, missing, probably up to no good, and being hunted by all parties. And worse, she's tied up with that spooky Hanson Childs. Shooting people in parking lots. That man Stevens is chasing after her with a team of commandos. General Grazier is sitting in your office, smoldering like some sort of volcano. Chief Raven was just whisked out of Garden of the Gods Park accompanied by that Helen woman. My boss, who was supposedly held hostage by that same woman, just walked in the door like he was back from the dead. Reports are that the Kaplan woman took Tanner Jackson when he got back from the future and they both seem to have vanished. Oh, and the fate of the world hangs in the balance." She gave me a quizzical look. "So, tell me. Did I miss anything?"

"Um, I suppose not." God, I wished that Falcon wasn't locked away in catatonia. What I would have given for his analysis.

"How'd you get back here, Skipper? Helen pop you back from some other timeline like a ping-pong ball?"

"Sorry, Janeesha. Did it the old-fashioned way. Drove back in my Jeep."

"From where? Alpha Centauri?"

"Oh, no. This time it was an Airbnb in Angel Fire down in New Mexico. Nice big log home with a huge stone fireplace."

"Uh-huh. And how does she afford that?"

"Stock market? Robbing banks? Betting on the World Series? How would I know? But do you really think that a lady with a time machine can't figure out how to make coin?"

Janeesha considered, nodded, and lifted a shoulder in a shrug. "You see Chief Raven? She all right?"

"She is. She's keeping an eye on Helen." I paused at my door. "They're sort of like two wolves pacing around each other. Wary and distrustful, but somehow alike."

"Angel Fire, huh?" Janeesha had arched that eyebrow again. "We gonna call up the team? Get Winny to fly Major Savage down, free Karla, and grab Helen and her machines?"

"Not if I have my way." I grabbed the doorknob. "Karla's the most capable person I know. Whatever Helen's up to, Karla will keep an eye on her."

"Yeah," Janeesha muttered, going back to her computer screen. "Assuming she don't have one of those PTSD episodes at just the wrong moment."

There was that.

I stepped into my office to find Eli Grazier, in uniform, ensconced behind my desk. He had a phone to his ear, listening. At sight of me, his lips flickered in an emotionless smile. With a hand, he waved me over to my visitor's chair, a beat-up old recliner.

"Got it. Do it," Eli ordered whoever was on the other end of the call. He hit the button on his super-secret ultra-encrypted phone. Glancing at me, he said, "Wherever you've been, it better be good. Stevens has a cluster fuck on his hands now that Alpha is gunning people down in fancy hotel parking lots. As far as the president is concerned, we're back in the game. He's a little unhappy with good old Bill Stevens." Without missing a beat, he asked, "So, where did Helen take you this time?"

He took the little pager thing from his pocket, lifted it, and—while pressing the button—said, "Ryan just walked in the door."

"Good. Still monitoring here. As soon as I have something, I'll let you know."

"That thing's a communicator?" I dropped into the recliner.

Replacing it in his pocket, Eli said, "Apparently so. Shocked me when she started speaking to me."

I spread my arms. "So, I'm confused. Do you trust her?"

"Do you?"

I frowned. "Not sure. She may be the toughest woman I've ever met. My impression is that her only goal in all of this is to kill Alpha. Beyond that, she could give a good god damn. Even if she dies in the process. She's monitoring for any hint of Alpha trying to contact Imperator. You've heard of him, right?"

"Something, yes."

I filled Eli in on everything Helen had told me about Imperator, about *Ti'ahaule* and the *Ahau*. In the end, I leaned forward, elbows on my knees, fingers laced. "So, there it is. Normally, I'd call it science fiction. A bunch of godlike Roman-Mayan rulers with an incredible technology running a terrifying empire in an alternate timeline. The uncomfortable fact is that I've been transported by Helen's cerebrum. I've seen the spot where Alpha's time machine vanished."

Eli grunted, nodding to himself before rising to his feet to pace restlessly back and forth. "Tim, tell me. You're a psychiatrist. What do you make of Helen?"

"Driven. Obsessed with stopping Alpha. And I suspect that she'd be more than happy to take out Imperator, as well. She comes across as old, weary, resigned in some ways, as if nothing could surprise her. It's a guess, but given the stories she tells, she's been taken apart and put herself together so many times, she has complete control of her emotions. Says she's two thousand years old."

"Impossible."

"Maybe. She also says she's been bioengineered. Totally regenerative. And that immortality is not all that it's cracked up to be."

"So, if push comes to shove, what's her reaction going to be?"

"Eli, my take is that she'll do whatever she needs to. Her goal is to kill Alpha and keep Fluvium dead. One way or another. I think our only hope is that we can help her do that before Alpha can call Imperator. If we can, Helen says we've got a way out. She can take Alpha's navigator and Fluvium's cerebrum and pop back to the *Ti'ahaule*. Her story is that if she returns the equipment, it will close the door to our timeline. If not, we're going to be wiped out in the end. Considered a threat to the *Ahau* because of our experimentation with entangled particle physics."

"I take it that you believe that?"

"So far." A beat. "You going to let her take Fluvium's cerebrum back?"

"Not a chance."

"I told her you'd say that."

Eli stopped his pacing and squinted. "You did, huh?"

"Yeah. She insists that as long as both machines are missing, eventually agents of the *Ahau* will run them down and destroy us."

"Nice. But no." Eli leaned his head back, that cunning look on his face as he rubbed the bottom of his chin. "I think we're going to figure a way to . . ."

We both jumped when Harvey Rogers flung my office door wide, to announce, "Something's happening?"

"What?" Eli and I both cried as I jumped to my feet.

"I was playing with Fluvium's cerebrum," Harvey blurted, eyes blinking behind his pop-bottle glasses. "Just fooling with it, you know? Running testers over it, seeing if I could detect any kind of energy."

"And?" Eli demanded.

"And it just came to life." Harvey spread his hands wide. "It started emitting that weird blue holographic glow. Projecting symbols over the top of the case."

"Symbols? Saying what?" Eli asked.

"How the hell should I know?" Harvey cried. "Symbols. Some in letters, others in those Mayan pictures."

"Quick," I cried. "Get Murphy and al Amari out of bed. I want them on it."

But the single thought in my head was: Is this good, or very bad?

44

Childs

Hanson Childs wondered if he was the most unhappy person on the planet as he drove to the Los Alamos turnoff. Thoughts of just driving off the road, letting the Escalade tumble and bounce down the side of the mountain to come to rest and explode in a fireball kept resurfacing as he watched the asphalt passing beneath the vehicle's headlights.

But in real life, cars didn't explode like they did in Hollywood movies. And it would be just his luck that the airbags would keep him and Nakeesh from any serious harm. Rather, they'd bounce down the mountainside, crush some trees, smack a couple of rocks, and emerge, only to be picked up by the New Mexico State Police. Handcuffed, they'd be locked away forever.

Or he would.

He suspected that Bill Stevens—being the president's chief of staff—would have Nakeesh spirited away to some high-security facility where she'd never see the light of day again. That would leave Hanson to face the murder raps, thefts, and other high crimes all on his own.

Leavenworth had never looked so bleak.

He glanced at Nakeesh. She sat bolt upright in the passenger seat, her patrician face illuminated by the dash panel. That strange aura still emanated from her. A magnetism that hinted that she indeed came from a different world.

Yeah, one that's oversexed and weird.

He hadn't screwed in the back seat of a car since he was eighteen. Being a football star had its perks. But those fumbling teenage attempts had been nothing like the savaging Nakeesh had put him through. And what did it say about him that he'd responded?

God, am I as fucked up as she is?

Punching the accelerator and shooting the Escalade off into the darkness in a glorious "Thelma and Louise" moment was looking better and better. But he was out of mountain, approaching the speed limit signs telling him to slow down for the Los Alamos town limits.

As he braked to thirty-five, he again studied Nakeesh in the light from the dash. She had her head back, chin forward, looking absolutely regal. Maybe that's how she faced disaster. Because, despite the dart pistol that lay on the console between them and the smoke grenades he'd hung on his belt, he was convinced that these were his last few minutes of freedom.

Sure, they'd try to pass the gate. And if the security so much as hesitated, he'd dart the guy. Then they'd make the break for the Skientia lab. Try the same at the front door.

"All we have to do is make it to the lab with the doohickey," he told himself. "Nakeesh will teleport us out of that fucking building, and they can search all over hell and back trying to find us."

That was it. Just get to the machine.

And Nakeesh would do the rest.

Right.

Why didn't he believe it would work out that seamlessly?

Because I don't fricking trust her, that's why.

But he kept his expression even as she glanced his way. They were passing streets now, hitting the western edge of town. He could see the reflection of the lights in her eyes.

"You are worried?" she asked.

"Guards at the gates, alerted to the fact that we're wanted for murder? And the two of us on the boards as national security risks? Figure we're on the top ten most wanted list. What's to worry about?"

"This I do not understand," she told him in that now half-maddening accent.

Childs took a right, turning onto the avenue that would take him to the Los Alamos gates. Not that the city was that big despite being spread out across four mesas. He couldn't have missed it. The lights were just up ahead.

At this time of night, traffic was dwindling as his anxiety increased. He saw it first. A cardboard sign sitting on the sidewalk. Just a section cut out of a box and scrawled with what looked like three circular designs. Wasn't even artistic. Even as he dismissed the thing, Nakeesh stiffened, pointing. She said something he couldn't understand in a language he thought must be Mayan, given the syllables.

"Turn this road," she told him. "There. Turn right. Onto that *via*. Um, what you call . . . street, *si?*"

Childs hesitated. He'd seen yard sale signs that were better than this.

Nevertheless, he flipped on the signal, cut across a lane of traffic, and took the turn. This led him into the hospital parking lot. A fact that confused him.

"What are you—"

"There." She pointed.

Childs saw the white van, a one-ton Chevy, sitting in the open, bathed by the parking lot lights. It had a single word painted on the van's side: DOMINA.

Childs shot Nakeesh a look as he slowed to a stop. "Who do you know with a white van?"

She had hunched down in the seat, was chewing on her index finger. Eyes squinted in thought, she said, "The words on the sign. 'Turn this road.'"

"That cardboard with the goofy drawings? Those were words?"

"And now they ask for Domina?" she mused thoughtfully.

"Think it's a trap?"

She shrugged her shoulders in a most vulnerable way. "We find out, *si?* If they are *stulti,* I will deal with them."

"Wait. My God, you keep killing people, and we're never going to get to the lab."

"Hanson, they left me a message. Who would know? *Subtilis est.* Um, not for all to see. Careful."

"Trap."

"Then we make trap happen. Drive."

Hanson eased off the brake, let the Escalade roll forward as he settled the dart pistol onto his lap. "If this goes south, let me put them down. Then we'll make a try for the main gate. If you shoot them dead, it will make matters worse. Really, really fast."

"You are too caring."

"You are too bloodthirsty."

"I have a bottle of water. Blood does not *extinguere,* how you say, put out thirst."

"English really is your second language."

"English is seventh language," she retorted.

Childs let the Escalade roll to a stop with two parking spaces between it and the van. Shifting it into park, Hanson left the vehicle running. The dart pistol in hand, thumb on the safety, he opened his door to the ringing of musical chimes and dropped to the pavement.

The van driver's door opened, a woman stepping out.

"Dr. Kaplan," Hanson said, recognizing the woman from the lab. "Is Josh Mack in the van with you?"

Kaplan peered warily at the Escalade, shielding her eyes from the overhead light's glare in an attempt to see through the windshield. "We're on our own. The Domina with you? Tanner and I have a proposition."

At that juncture, an older man, mid-fifties—with thick, black-framed glasses and an oddly shaped bald head that gleamed in the overhead light—stepped out of the passenger door, calling, "Hello. You must be Hanson Childs. I'm Tanner Jackson. Remember me? From the machine in Lab One? I run Skientia. I'm on the Domina's side."

"And how do I know that?"

"Because you're still standing there. Believe me, if I was working with Bill Stevens, you'd already be laid out on the pavement, spread-eagle, while a bunch of his bad boys bundled the Domina up and spirited her away."

At that juncture, Nakeesh opened her door and emerged. She did a slow inspection of the parking lot, paying particular attention to the cluster of cars over in the staff parking by the emergency room entrance. The way she held the HK pistol, she was ready for anything.

"Domina?" Jackson called. "It's all right. We've come to find you."

"How'd you know she'd be coming here?" Hanson asked, his nerves still singing with anxiety. He, too, was letting his gaze rove, trying to keep complete situational awareness.

"Made sense," Maxine Kaplan said, stepping out around the front of the van. "We've been monitoring Stevens. We know about the shooting in Santa Fe. Given what we can monitor of Grazier's people in Washington, they're stymied. Grazier, for the moment, is off the map."

Jackson, hands out to look inoffensive, walked forward, stopping a couple of steps from Nakeesh. "We figured you'd be back. Your only way home is through the lab. Using the machines there. It was a calculated risk that you'd come in this way. So we made the sign out by the road. Wrote it in Maya hieroglyphs. Then parked the van here, at the edge of the parking, out of sight of the security cameras."

Well, that was one worry Hanson hoped he didn't have to keep fretting over.

"I need to get to the doohickey," Nakeesh said flatly. "You can do this, *si*?"

"I can do this." Jackson's grin reeked of assurance. "I've ensured that the proper security personnel will be on duty tomorrow. What's the point of eavesdropping on anyone and everyone if you can't exploit their weaknesses? For example, the good head of security for the labs would lose his job should his collection of child porn come to light. And the sergeant who will pass us at the gate tomorrow has a daughter who is receiving a special and very expensive medical treatment for a genetic disease. Treatment, that after tomorrow, he won't have to pay for. Everything, you see, is a matter of priority."

"If you can get me to doohickey—" Nakeesh fixed him with a challenging glare, "—let us go from here. Now."

"Of course, Domina." The lights shone on Jackson's potato-shaped scalp as the bald man bowed. "After you."

Hanson paused only long enough to grab the black nylon bag from the Escalade's back seat, then he followed Jackson to the van. As Nakeesh climbed up into the passenger seat, Jackson peeled the plastic stick-on "DOMINA" sign from the van's side and rolled it into a tube. Then he opened the sliding side door and gestured for Childs to get in.

"Not much for comfort," he told Hanson. "We'll have to ride on the floor, but it's not far. Got a place where no one will look for us. Just an ordinary house on an ordinary street. We'll have to lay low while I get my people in position. Need to lay a false trail. Direct everyone's attention in another direction." Looking forward, he called, "Don't worry, Domina. I'll have you in that lab no later than tomorrow night. I promise."

"Got all the answers, huh?" Hanson asked as he tossed the tactical bag onto the deck and climbed in.

As Tanner Jackson slammed the door, blocking out the light, he replied, "Not even by half, Agent Hanson. But from here on out, I suspect things are going to get very, very interesting."

45

Ryan

Driven by nervous energy, I retreated to what I always did when I was stressed out. I took a cup of coffee and started walking aimlessly up and down the halls in Ward Six. Maybe because I think better when I'm moving. Or that was bullshit, and what I was really after was a way to burn up nervous energy without screaming, pounding my fists, and appearing like I was a patient rather than a clinician.

As I took in the gleaming floors, the white ceilings, and spotless halls—the featureless doors to the patient's rooms—I wasn't sure what to do next. Ward Six looked too perfect, too polished with its institutional sterility to be on the frontlines of a battle for our world and existence.

For the time being, passing staff, nodding, exchanging smiles, I was grateful to just be alive. Breathing.

That inevitability of the clock counting down was driving me to distraction. I could feel the anxiety rising. With each step, my thoughts went to my son, Eric. Hadn't seen him in a couple of years. Knew if we failed here, he'd never have the chance to become a man, find love, happiness, and heartbreak. Never live. If we . . . If *I* failed here, he'd never know.

I nodded at Janeesha as I headed to my office. Peeked in to see Grazier seated behind my desk. Could see the desperation in his posture. In the strained lines around his mouth. Eli had one ear to his DARPA one-off-supposedly-super-entangled-and-totally-un-decryptable phone to his ear. Un-decryptable? Is that a word?

I backed out, gave Janeesha a reassuring nod I didn't feel.

In Harvey Rogers' lab, both al Amari and Murphy were bent over Fluvium's cerebrum where they struggled to decode the meaning of the symbols, letters, and formulae projected in the holo. The clues had to be in Mayan and Latin. The two men were desperately drawing the various symbols that flickered in the blue screen. Doing their best to record them as they flashed in and out of existence. After my experience on the bridge, they were smart enough not to stick their fingers into the projection. Or to blink suggestively, or to even speak, lest they trigger the device to do something we didn't anticipate.

Like pop them out of this existence and into an *Ahau's* interrogation booth in *Ti'ahaule*. Wherever that timeline might be.

Could Fluvium's cerebrum do that? From everything we'd been told, it couldn't.

But no one wanted to take chances

Just for good measure, I'd placed a couple of armed security sentries in the room under Sergeant Myca Simond's direct command. They had orders to shoot to kill if *anyone* popped into the lab in an attempt to steal Fluvium's cerebrum.

Not that I was sure anyone would be awake to stop the thieves, given that every time the time machines popped someone in or out, everyone in the immediate vicinity seemed to collapse into a comatose pile. Nevertheless, it made me feel better. And maybe added to both al Amari and Murphy's sense of well-being.

Running out of halls to walk, I stuck my head into ET's lair. This was a room that now brimmed wall-to-wall with computer equipment. And, as I had suspected, ET remained at his desk, at least, what you could see of it given the clutter of keyboards, empty coffee cups, and food wrappers.

"What's the news, ET?"

I could see the earbud as he shifted his glance from the wall of monitors. He'd been focused on one in the lower left-hand corner. "Hey, Skip. Um, Stevens is way gone berserk. About an hour ago, he started short-stroking his team in New Mexico. Seems some Cadillac Escalade was found in a hospital lot in Los Alamos. Local law traced the tag to a house in Santa Fe. People that own it are in Mexico. Wouldn't have come up on the radar, but some Los Alamos cop was bored, so he had the crime tech run a print they found on the steering wheel. Seems they've had a bunch of car thefts in Española. Thought they might have a line on the perp. Break the ring. So the NCIC got a hit that put the finger on our old friend, Hanson Childs. And that brings Stevens and the whole NSA roaring down on the house where the Escalade is supposed to be.

Slam, bam, thank you ma'am, and they got Childs' and Alpha's DNA all over the house." ET shoots me his lascivious grin. "Like 'specially the bed, see?"

That surprises me. I consider it for a moment.

"Alpha was always magnetic. A sort of *uber* female." I leaned my shoulder against the doorframe. "A couple of times back in the beginning of her stay here, she signaled her availability. A serious come-on. Seemed irritated when I didn't respond, and she never tried again. I mean, the lady always had a sensual presence in the room, but those times were different. It was all I could do to get out the door and make it to a cold shower."

ET had raised an eyebrow, one eye cocked in curiosity. The question couldn't have been louder if he'd shouted.

"Oh, come on, ET. At the time, she'd barely survived an assassination attempt in the garage. As a psychiatrist, with vulnerable patients who are looking for any kind of reassurance, it happens."

"Wasn't tempted at all, huh, Skipper?"

"Never said that. Helen told us that Alpha can secrete pheromones. And yeah, whatever she was doing, it screwed with my limbic system. But some things, dear Horatio, lie beyond the pale: I don't have sex with my patients."

"So, what's she doing with Hanson Childs? He's the mofo who put Falcon in a coma."

"She's using him. And—partially thanks to you—he was the perfect pigeon in her shooting gallery. You'd taken everything from him. Left him feeling impotent and insecure, his sense of identity shaken to the core. Then Stevens recruits him for a daring rescue mission and, worse, leaves him with the damsel in distress. He's lost everything that has defined him as a man, and he's looking for a purpose. A way to reestablish his sense of self-worth. This is Alpha; she plays him like a finely tuned instrument."

"Screws the daylights out of him, huh?"

"Bonding, ET. Preying on the man's insecurities."

ET pointed at the screen. "Stevens is wondering if they're going for the Skientia lab. Has his guy Josh Mack, as well as the Los Alamos security, checking. So far, they got nothing."

I fingered my chin, felt stubble. How long since I'd shaved? "Grazier doubled his security team after Stevens extracted Alpha. Does he know about Childs and Alpha? About the Escalade?"

"Yeah, I keep him in the loop." ET rolled his eyes. "Gotta be double careful when they's a general in the house. Makes me nervous. 'Specially since he knows all my secrets."

I studied the wall of monitors above ET's desk. In one I could see the main hallway in the Skientia lab. Another flipped between images, as if they switched to whichever camera picked up movement. Still others ran progressive lists of emails. Another ran a continuous feed of code that I'd never understand.

"Whoa." ET tapped his earbud. "Stevens just called this guy Mack. Said that Skientia's lab in Pasadena just made a definite ID on Alpha and Childs. Said their facial recognition program tagged them outside the Lawrence Livermore National Laboratory fifteen minutes ago."

"What about the Escalade in Los Alamos?"

"Lay a false trail? Diversion?" ET shrugged. "Used to be the Brothers'd do that to keep the DEA and Narc Squad sniffin' 'round the wrong drop point while the deal go down in another part of town."

"Why Lawrence Livermore?" I wondered. "Why all of it? Doesn't make sense. Alpha needs Fluvium's cerebrum and someone to operate it. She knows Helen's on the hunt and waiting for an opportunity to kill her. Stevens may or may not know that we have Fluvium's cerebrum. But Alpha's no longer privy to any information from Stevens' quarter. Outside of making a clean escape, her only other hope is contacting this Imperator. But Helen says that she can't do that with just a navigator. So, what's at LLNL?"

ET gave me his "how should I know" look, both eyebrows raised, his mouth pinched into a flat line. "Skipper, I got no idea."

"And that doesn't explain why, after all this time, Fluvium's cerebrum just turned on and started shooting blue holographs out of its top."

"Don't ask me, man. Ask Falcon."

"Yeah," I muttered. "His mind is the only one smart enough to see the pattern."

If he just wasn't locked away in catatonia.

46

Falcon

James Falcon sat on his bed, back pressed into the corner where the walls came together. As he rocked his head back and forth, he kept his pillow scrunched between his chest and drawn-up knees. With each dip, Falcon's chin would just touch the pillow's softness. And each time he pulled his head back, the angles of the wall came hard against his shoulder blades.

In the back of his mind, he could hear Aunt Celia's voice. Couldn't make out the exact words, but the cadence was there. Repeating over and over, like an echo.

Falcon tried to empty his mind. Desperate to keep from hearing Aunt Celia's voice break into his thoughts. If it did, she'd come barreling into his conscious; her words—uttered in that piercing tone—would cut through his head like a chainsaw.

Calm. Stay calm.

The battle was to keep from recognizing any of Celia's words. Once that happened, he was lost.

The room was quiet, which told him it was the middle of the night. It was always quiet during the night. That was when Nurse Seymore was off duty. He couldn't remember the names of the night staff. He just knew that orderlies and nurses came through to check on him.

He could hear them outside the door. The sound of their clothes, the soft hiss of their shoes on the polished vinyl floor. Sometimes they'd talk, their voices low, almost incorporeal.

Falcon wondered how they could do their jobs when those eyes were out there.

On the other side of the door.

Pupils so incredibly black that they ate the light while they floated in washed-out blue irises. How did eyes get that pale? Become that evil?

The eyes of the monster.

The monster that had humiliated him. That had crushed his happiness.

Falcon hated those eyes.

He rocked harder, fragments of voices, harsh, sounding in the air around him. *"Hey, you're gonna show these officers a little respect, or I'm gonna teach it to you, shit bag!"*

Voices. Sound. Simple physics. Vibrations in air. Which was a gas. What process could put hate—let alone so much hate—into simple vibrations? But there it was, each word, like a hammer beating into his head. Striking with an impact that bruised his skin, ruptured blood vessels, and splintered his skull to puncture his brain.

Shit bag. Shit bag. Shit bag.

Non sequitur. Didn't make sense.

Falcon waited for the spike in fear. Cringed in anticipation, tucked tighter around his pillow.

The slap should be coming just like that day at the Buffalo Thunder.

The fear should have been visceral. Should have made his throat go tight. Twisted his stomach sideways. That electric runny tingle in his intestines should have turned liquid by now.

But the slap didn't come.

Falcon blinked, hearing the MP's voice, duller this time, as it repeated, *"I don't know what kind of shit you're pulling, asshole, but you can stop it right now, or you'll wish you were dead . . . wish you were . . . dead . . . wish you . . ."*

And another voice. *"Are you or are you not Captain James Hancock Falcon?"*

Am I?

Falcon looked around his room. The shattered mirror hung in fragments, angular shards of silver that reflected his splintered image. An eye in this one, part of his nose in another, a bit of cheek there, a nostril, lower lip and partial chin there.

Who am I?

"You don't have a fucking clue, pussy," Rudy Noyes' acid voice declared.

Falcon glanced toward his bathroom but saw no one. Further inspection showed the room to be empty, but the door was still there. In the wall. Where it was supposed to be.

The door.

That opened to the hall.

And the monstrous black pupils that terrified him as they floated in that washed-out field of lightless blue.

"I remember that day. I was being charged with a crime," Falcon whispered softly.

Captain James Hancock Falcon was being charged.

"... *Wish you were dead ... wish you were dead ...*"

And he'd died.

Then why am I still afraid?

The dead didn't fear. Didn't hate.

"But I hate," Falcon whispered. He shot a glance at the door, the inevitable colossus. That fucking door. With the shining brass knob. The one everyone wanted him to walk over and open.

But the eyes . . .

"Asshole eyes," Rudy's voice told him.

"Asshole eyes," Falcon agreed.

He laid the pillow to the side, ready to grab it back when the fear came. But it didn't.

"Hanson Childs," Falcon whispered. "That's who those eyes belong to."

God, it felt so good to give the terrible eyes a name. Make them human instead of horrifyingly supernatural and invincible.

"Hanson Childs." Repeating the name, made the eyes smaller in his imagination.

If a monster can be named, it can be killed.

"Hanson Childs." Falcon swallowed hard. "He's the monster."

47

Grazier

On the central monitor in Colonel Ryan's confiscated office, Colonel Brad Becknell gave Eli a salute, saying, "We're on it, sir. I'll have our team ensuring that nothing so much as squeaks its way into that Lawrence Livermore lab."

Eli watched the monitor go dark.

In Ryan's chair, he leaned his head forward, braced his elbows on the desk, and rubbed his tired eyes. The office echoed Tim Ryan's personality. The "Me" wall behind him, was covered with Ryan's diplomas, photos of old spec ops teammates, Ryan shaking hands with various officers as he was presented with medals, a smattering of award plaques from psychiatric organizations. And then there were the floor-to-ceiling bookcases filled with psychology and psychiatric texts, the DSM-5-TR, books on classic racing motorcycles, and, of course, the little model of a red Ducati 916 that sat on the corner of the desk. The motorcycle Eli had been forced to cough up in the flesh—or at least in the plastic, aluminum, steel, and rubber—after losing a bet.

Eli glanced at the clock, seeing it was just a little after eight in the morning.

He had been up most of the night. Damn, he was tired. Hadn't been out of Ryan's office in almost two days except to hit the men's room. Janeesha had brought his meals. He'd taken to catching naps in the ratty old recliner that Ryan had sitting off to the side. Sure, it looked like hell, but Eli had to admit, the thing was comfortable. And he'd bet that was the reason Ryan kept it—and that Eli Grazier wasn't the first person to catch some z's in the thing.

He stood, feeling the muscles in his neck and back pulling and stiff. His coat, with its campaign ribbons was on the hook by the door, and

Eli shrugged it over his wrinkled shirt. Looked down to see the creases on his pants were no longer knife sharp, though his shoes maintained their black-mirror luster.

He hated not looking his absolute best. It wasn't like he was presenting to the Joint Chiefs of Staff or the president. "It's only a mental hospital," he reminded himself as he opened the door.

Janeesha, to his surprise, sat at her desk, face lined as she studied something on the monitor. She glanced up as if in expectation. "Can I get you something, General?"

"Don't you ever go home?"

"Not much to go home to, sir. Not when Alpha's on the loose, and all hell's about to break loose." A shoulder lifted in a shrug. "I caught a couple of winks in one of the empty patient rooms. You need something?"

He considered. "Yes, breakfast." He headed for the door. "And no, you needn't trouble yourself. I'm headed to the cafeteria. If anyone needs me, put them through to my cell."

"I'd go for the breakfast tamales, myself," she suggested, returning her attention to the screen. "Turns out that Doctor Ryan has a thing for them. And after coming back from Santa Fe, they got placed on the menu somehow. But steer clear if you don't have a tongue for spicy. Wouldn't want you breaking into a sweat and gulping water. Might be bad for the general's image, if you know what I mean."

Eli chuckled to himself.

In the hall, it felt good to walk, stretch his muscles, breathe. For the briefest of instants, he shoved the chaos of thoughts out of his head. Tried to clear his mind.

It didn't last beyond the corner and through the doors into the cafeteria. The room was maybe a third full. The long tables were in perfect lines. People were seated in small groups of patients and staff. Patients? This was his Team Psi. By whatever quirk of luck and skill, these people had almost stopped Alpha the first time. And without anything but logistical help from him.

Winny Swink noticed him first, bounced to her feet, and saluted. That triggered a chain of people standing and banging off salutes. At least the ones who were military. The rest of the staff just paused, then went on about their business.

"As you were, people," Grazier called, motioning them back to their seats.

He was aware of the gazes following him across the room, through the buffet line—where he chose the tamales—and as he took his plate, coffee, and silverware to one of the open tables.

Wasn't until he'd taken his first bite that he realized Janeesha had been right. Mistake. This wasn't a fast-food burrito from a drive-through. The jalapeños were real, green. What the little sign on the tamales had called "*arbol*" chili, was unlike anything he'd ever experienced.

"You're a general," he muttered under his breath, sucking down too-hot coffee in an attempt to douse the flames. Made it worse.

But he toughed it out, sweating like he'd been warned he would, nose running, and every sinus burned open. With all those eyes surreptitiously watching, there was no way Elijiah Grazier was going to wuss out. He tried—as covertly as possible—to mop the sweat from his brow and cheeks with his napkin.

To his amusement, two tables down, Dr. Catalina Talavera was forking mouthful after mouthful, heedless of the scorching capsaicin, as she studied something on her tablet. Periodically, she'd reach out a slim finger and scroll the screen up, two delicate lines forming in her brow.

Which got Eli to thinking.

Taking his tray over to the conveyor, he made his way to Talavera's table, asking, "Excuse me. Dr. Talavera? Could you spare me a moment?"

She looked up, blinked, and started as she recognized who had interrupted her study. With a jolt, she said, "Oh, I, uh . . . Sure. What can I help you with, General?"

Eli pulled out the next chair, seating himself. He laced his fingers together and glanced at the report displayed on the tablet. "Looks too complicated for my comprehension. Chemistry?"

"Immunogenetics," she told him.

"Speaking of which, how's Captain Falcon doing?"

She gave him a self-conscious smile, clearly unnerved by his attention. "The brain imaging scans show a marked improvement. Falcon's catatonia was caused by the trauma of his arrest. Being both dissociative and schizophrenic, Falcon is by nature, particularly fragile, and significantly paranoid. As brilliant as he is, you might think of his brain as being almost like delicate crystal lattice. When those agents arrested him, physically assaulted him, it shattered his personality. Sent him into a self-reinforcing loop of anxiety-releasing chemicals that essentially shut down his higher brain function. Like a self-perpetuating chemical roller coaster. It allowed him to lock himself into what you'd call a safe place. Somewhere deep in his consciousness. But it's self-reinforcing. If he tries to come out, it triggers the anxiety, and the whole cycle starts again."

"But he's in there, right? What I know about catatonia is that the patient is fully conscious. He just fails to respond."

"The reason for failing to respond, in Falcon's case, is that when he begins to find stability, that very feeling makes him vulnerable. Vulnerability frightens him, which triggers the amygdala, which then floods his brain with adrenaline and cortisol, which drives him back into catatonia. His brain has been in a constant bootstrapping chemical storm."

Grazier sighed, the *arbol* burn barely fading from his lips and tongue. "Seriously, Dr. Talavera, what are the chances of getting Falcon back?"

"My latest therapy has blocked some of the neural ganglia that cause the anxiety. I guess you could say that I've been able to put a damper on the first stage of the bootstrapping." She studied him thoughtfully. "That's as far as I can go with pharmacology. The rest? Actually making the choice to reengage with the world? That's up to Falcon."

"But he could choose to come back if he wanted to?"

Cat nodded. "Yes, sir. I'm not a psychiatrist, but my suspicion is that you'd have to offer him a really good reason to make that choice." She shrugged. "ET and I, Nurse Seymore, Colonel Ryan, we've all repeatedly told Falcon how important he is. Given him constant reinforcement, assured him that he's safe, and that people care for him. He knows we want him back."

Grazier stroked his chin as he thought. "Maybe you're using the wrong bait."

"Sir?"

"I'm third generation military, Doctor. But my uncle, Albert, he's still living in Mississippi. He's spent his life working for a waste management company in Greenville down in the Delta. When I was a kid—my father being on deployment—rather than hang around base housing, Mother'd take that time to spend with her family in Newark. Me? I *hated* Newark. You ever had to spend time in a rowhouse? No? Call it an acquired taste. So I'd lobby to go live at Uncle Albert's. His passion was fishing. Cane pole and all. Talk about a stereotype of a black man in the South. He was the one who taught me that if you really wanted to lure a big catfish out of his hole, and worms weren't working, you might want to change your bait."

"And you think Falcon's a catfish?"

He gave her a conspiratorial wink. "Dr. Talavera, Uncle Albert would tell you that Captain Falcon is the biggest catfish of them all."

She studied him through those thoughtful dark eyes. "General? Would you like to come with me to the infirmary?"

"Why?"

"Maybe to do a little fishing."

48

Falcon

Pagliacci was playing in the background. Falcon, sitting on his bed, knees up, rocked his body in time to the tenor singing "Vesti la Giubba" in Leoncavallo's masterpiece. Once, he would have thrown his head back and belted out the words, "Laugh, clown, about your broken love. Laugh at the grief that poisons your heart!"

But now, alone on his bed, locked away in the safety of his room, Falcon let the lyrics roll through his head like a wave.

Doing so was better than the voices, so much better than Aunt Celia's rising and shrill castigations of his every action.

"How did I ever disappoint you so?" he wondered as the aria concluded.

Along with Pagliaccio, he laughed in bitter amusement.

What was he, other than a tragic clown himself?

Opera—like the silver-backed glass that now reflected his repaired image—functioned like a mirror.

He felt a prickle as the music faded, replaced by the sounds of someone bending over him, asking, "Falcon? Mind if I talk to you?"

The voice was unfamiliar.

A stranger. Strangers were scary.

A slight shiver ran through him.

"Falcon?" the voice asked most reasonably. "I'm General Elijiah Grazier. I work with Dr. Ryan."

Falcon tucked his knees tighter against his chest. Reached out, drawing his pillow to his side. Grazier! He'd done projects for Grazier many times in the past. And, yes, Falcon had met the general several times back when he still worked out of that basement office in the Pentagon. Back when he'd been called "the Oracle" and been left alone. Grazier had been a one-star general back then. A compact and active African American with a broad and strong jaw, and, of course, those quick and intelligent dark eyes. Generals always dressed well in the Pentagon, but Grazier had always looked sharp, perfect, pins and ribbons, and creases, and shoes immaculate.

Falcon nodded. *Yes, I know you.*

Grazier was one of the good guys. He did things with science. Unlike so many, Grazier was smart. One of the smartest men Falcon had ever met in the military. And now he was here. Like in the old days, when Grazier had come to see him in the basement. When he'd offered his hand, a genuine smile on his lips, and said, "I just came down to thank you, Captain. Because of your work, a lot of my people are alive today."

Then Cat's voice said, "General, from the readings, he hears you."

"Good." Then Grazier said, "Falcon, you were always there for me in the past. I've got a problem, and I need your insight. I don't have to remind you of the threat Alpha poses. You were the first one to recognize her for what she was."

Falcon remembered.

"Well, she's back. Bill Stevens' people were in Lab One when she popped back into existence. Maxine Kaplan was working for Stevens the entire time and ensured that his people would be there when Alpha returned. Both Kaplan and her boss and one-time lover, Tanner Jackson, have vanished. Being that Jackson was the chief operations officer for Skientia, he has considerable resources at his disposal, not to mention some pretty fancy entanglement tech."

Falcon started creating pieces in his head, like tokens, and closed his eyes so he could see them on the backs of his eyelids.

"Meanwhile, Stevens took Alpha, and was in the process of renditioning her and her navigator out of Santa Fe. That's when she and your old friend, agent Hanson Childs, slipped away. She's on the run, Falcon. In the process, she shot two of Stevens' people in Santa Fe, including Jaime Chenwith. Remember him? With Childs' help, Alpha has avoided capture, but a car they were driving was found abandoned in Los Alamos."

Childs? An image of black pupils in a sea of washed-out blue. White-blond hair. That look of hatred, of anger, filled Falcon's memory. Hanson Childs. The terrible eyes had a name.

As Grazier talked, Falcon began moving the pieces around, placing them here and there, trying to form the pattern. Stevens, Kaplan, Jackson, Alpha, Childs, and the navigator. How did they fit? What did they want? How would they get it?

Grazier's soft voice continued. "Now we've intercepted a report that she has been seen outside the Skientia lab building on the grounds at the Lawrence Livermore National Labs. What I can't figure out is what she wants from that lab. Or why she'd be in California at all. Even with Childs helping, she can't get back to her timeline without the cerebrum we have here. We have learned that she can call for help from her timeline if she can build a transmitter for her navigator."

That added an entirely new set of variables to Falcon's data.

Grazier's voice sounded tense when he added, "Meanwhile, our cerebrum turned on by itself. And we don't know what that means."

Alpha can call for help. But needs the cerebrum. Falcon created more pieces, tried to fit them into the pattern. Changed the arrangement. And then the key. *Build a transmitter for her navigator? Build?*

"I assume you've been informed of Helen, the assassin who tried to kill Alpha that day in the garage. Helen and Chief Raven are waiting to target Alpha, using Helen's navigator and cerebrum. She says Alpha will try to contact someone named Imperator to come rescue her and Fluvium before destroying our timeline."

Falcon listened as Grazier continued talking. He kept moving the pieces of data on the backs of his eyes, letting them fall into place like puzzle pieces.

49

Grazier

Seated on the side of the infirmary bed, Eli had taken Falcon's hand, figuring that maybe that bit of human warmth would build the bridge. Touch gave a conversation an intimate quality after all. He'd used it on rare occasions when he absolutely needed to create a connection. What surprised him—given that he didn't really like it when people touched him—was that it worked so often. Especially among the emotionally distraught.

With a sigh, he carefully replaced Falcon's hand on the blanket. Took one look at the man's slack features, brown eyes closed, jaws locked. Most of the top of Falcon's head was covered by the gleaming white casing that circled his skull with monitoring equipment.

As Grazier had talked, Cat Talavera and Nurse Seymore had stood in the back, gazes fixed on the monitor as the activity in Falcon's brain had flickered and shifted, illuminating different parts of the frontal and parietal lobes.

"His brain is working," Cat told him as she scanned the readouts from the monitors tied to the imaging helmet on Falcon's head.

"And the amygdala?"

"Remarkably quiet," Seymore said thoughtfully where she fingered her chin, eyes fixed on the displayed data.

Cat stepped closer, asking, "Falcon? Can you hear me?"

"Nothing," Seymore said where she monitored the image. "Since Grazier started talking, the activity is increasing. Especially the frontal cortex."

"It's a start," Cat admitted. Then her gaze shifted to Grazier's. "Your catfish may not have taken the bait, but it had an effect on him. He's using areas of the prefrontal and parietal cortex in a way that indicates an entirely different pattern."

"Catfish?" Seymore asked.

"Long story," Grazier told her as he stood and straightened his jacket. "It's almost a trope, isn't it? When all of our most sophisticated science stops working, we fall back on folk wisdom. Roll out the aphorisms. 'Why, my grandpa always told me . . .'"

Cat gestured at the screen. "We've made progress, General. I think my latest cocktail worked. Outside of your story, it's the only variable that's changed. This time, that part of his limbic system didn't light up. Maybe, as Falcon realizes that he's not feeling terror every time we ask him to come back to us, he'll feel safe enough to do so."

"And even then," Seymore told him, "there's a lot of therapy ahead. I don't think Falcon will ever leave Grantham again."

"He shouldn't have last time," Cat added, a narrowing of her dark eyes as she turned them on Grazier. "Are we really safe here, General?"

Grazier gave the woman his wolf smile, the one that was part predator. "Dr. Talavera, that entirely depends on whether we can keep Alpha from contacting this Imperator. She gets a line through to him? All bets are off."

"Off how, sir?" Seymore asked.

"Like, end of the timeline off." He gestured around the room. "All of this, gone. You and Dr. Talavera here? Never existed. Along with the country, the world, and well, about two thousand years of history. Poof. Vanished. Wiped clean."

"Wonder what it feels like?" Cat wondered. "To just vanish. I mean, how can I be real, alive, and know all that I've experienced and seen . . ." She knocked on the wall. "All of this can't just disappear. What? Is there a pop, bang, or boom? How does vanishing-and-never-having-been work? Everyone's been a little hazy on that."

Grazier spread his hands impotently as her hot gaze met his. "From what I can tell, we just aren't. No bang or boom. Just . . . nothing."

As he headed for the door, he added, "So, let's hope that we can outsmart Stevens, Alpha, and Childs, and figure out what how to end this because, Dr. Talavera, we're running out of time."

The voice from the bed caught Grazier by complete surprise when Falcon said hoarsely, "Time doesn't exist. But a series of complex actions have to occur as rapidly as possible, and they start here, in this room, right now."

50

Harvey Rogers

"**G**et up!" Staff Sergeant Myca Simond shouted as he leaned in the door and flipped the light switch.

Harvey Rogers blinked, sat up in bed. Took him a second to orient himself. Grantham Barracks. His room. He squinted in the light. "What?"

"Got a phone call," Simond snapped. "Came to Colonel Ryan's office. On a fricking land line, for God's sake. It's that Helen woman. Wants to hold a Zoom meeting. Says you've got to turn off the navigator. That if you don't, all hell's gonna come raining down on our heads."

"Turn off the navigator?" Rogers wondered. "Hell, we don't even know how it turned on."

Harvey stumbled out of bed, grabbed his pants, and almost fell over as he tugged them on while trying to walk.

"My orders, direct from the Skipper, are to motivate your ass down to the vault and give you the link. ET's already setting up the Zoom meeting. Doing his best to cover the tracks. Damn lunatic's grinning like he just got laid. Never seen him so happy. Now, move your butt."

"But wait! I need—"

"Gotta get Murphy and Skylar," Simond called over his shoulder, and then he was gone.

After pulling a T-shirt over his head, a glance at his bedside clock told him it was 11:33.

Four minutes later, Rogers was in his lab. ET was perched over an Apple laptop. The skinny computer wizard muttered to himself and peered at the screen from beneath a pinched brow. Behind him, Colonel Ryan was stretching a bedsheet to mask Rogers' shelves and computer bank.

"What are you doing?" Rogers cried.

Ryan shot a glance over his shoulder. "No sense in letting Helen pick up any more information than she already has. Last thing we want her to know is where Fluvium's cerebrum is stashed."

Rogers lifted a skeptical eyebrow. "Um, didn't she call your land line?"

Ryan narrowed an eye. "Doesn't mean that she knows for sure that the cerebrum's here. Just that we're the only players who might have it. I need you to retrieve it from the vault. You're to be offscreen as she gives instructions. I'll be onscreen with a cell phone to my ear. When she gives instructions, I'll repeat them into the phone. Meanwhile, you, Murphy, and Haines follow my instructions."

Rogers shook his head, stepped back to the imposing vault door and input the combination. "Um, Skipper, why are we shutting the cerebrum off?"

At that point, Sam Savage burst into the room, some evil-looking submachine gun hanging from a strap on his shoulder. "What have we got?"

Ryan told him, "Helen called. Says our cerebrum is broadcasting, and if Alpha turns hers on, she'll know exactly where to find it. Says it's a miracle we're not already compromised. But as soon as ET can establish a link, she'll give us the instructions on how to turn it off."

Oh, so that was why Ryan was so upset. Rogers turned the handle and heard the locking lugs click open. Reaching in, he withdrew the device, all the while being careful to keep his fingers clear of the screen. He placed the machine on a work surface out of view of the laptop.

"Meanwhile," Ryan told Savage, "if anyone pops into the room, or comes charging down the hallway, you're our last line of defense. I want you outside the door, down the hallway, just out of the knockout zone if anyone does a Houdini into the lab. Maybe twenty yards?"

"Yeah, that ought to put me out of the zone," Savage told him. "Meanwhile, Sergeant Simond will keep an eye on our six."

Savage vanished out the door as Rogers took a deep breath. Murphy could be heard running down the hall, the sound of his worn hiking boots unmistakable. He ducked in, panting, his hair sticking out in all directions. "What's up?"

"Got to turn the cerebrum off," Ryan told him as he slipped into the seat ET vacated.

"You all set, Skipper." ET pointed. "Hit that button, you be connected to Helen."

"Roger that," Ryan muttered, squinting, and clicking.

"Dr. Ryan? Do you have the cerebrum?"

From his angle, Rogers couldn't see the infamous Helen. He waved Murphy's question away before the Mayanist could ask. Placed a finger to his lips for silence.

Ryan lifted the cell phone to his ear. "I have a line to where it's kept. That's a secure location that—"

"Stow it," Helen's voice had a sharp tone. *"There should be a* yax *glyph in the middle of your cerebrum's display."*

Rogers saw the symbol glow to life in the center of the screen. A flat oval with two dents in the top.

Murphy nodded, mouthing the word *"Yax."*

"Touch it with your finger," Helen told him.

Ryan started to repeat the command, only to have Helen say, *"It would save us all a great deal of time if you'd let me see the person inputting the commands. I assume that's your Mayanist. He doesn't know the idioms. Your understanding of Mayan has been pieced together from a prehistoric nontechnical culture. The fact that Nakeesh isn't standing in your lab means her navigator is off. That you still have a lab means Imperator hasn't arrived. But we don't have a lot of time. I know you've got the damned machine at Grantham. Let me see the tech so we can turn it off."*

Ryan's expression was strained, his jaws clamped.

Rogers could imagine what he was considering. Weighing his options. Taking a deep breath, he turned the laptop so that it pointed at Rogers, Murphy, and the cerebrum.

Rogers got his first look at Helen, found himself appraising an auburn-haired woman with hard green eyes. Maybe thirty? Seriously? And this woman claimed to be immortal?

"Thank God," she said. *"Now, follow my commands. Touch the glyph."*

Rogers shot a worried glance at Murphy, and with an index finger, extended it to the glowing oval. Immediately, the screen displayed a new series of glyphs. Some, Rogers had learned to recognize.

One by one, Helen spoke words in Mayan. Rogers told Murphy, "You do it. You know what she's saying."

"Not as well as Skylar." With a reluctant finger, Murphy touched glyph after glyph, the display constantly changing. On occasion, he'd say, "That's not in my vocabulary." Helen would then guide him to the right glyph.

Finally, the woman called, *"Homo."*

"End," Murphy said, fingering the glyph, and the holographic display went dark. He looked up. "Did we do it?"

On the monitor, Helen had leaned back, rubbing her eyes. *"You're still there. You haven't vanished into a ball of fire. But the damage is done. Nakeesh's navigator will have recorded the activity. As soon as she turns it on, she's going to know that Fluvium's cerebrum has been activated. And that it's close."*

"What does that mean?" Ryan asked.

In the monitor, Helen studied him. *"We just did what you'd call a hard shutdown. She can't turn the cerebrum on remotely. She has to physically touch the start glyph and input the commands."*

"So, how did we turn it on?" Rogers demanded.

On the screen, Helen gave him a weary shrug. *"One of you monkeys touched the start glyph."*

"Skylar." Rogers and Murphy said in unison.

"What did I do?" Skylar Haines demanded as he ambled through the door wearing a mustard-stained T-shirt and baggy sweatpants; his flip-flops slapped loudly against the soles of his feet. The man's dreadlocks hung in dirty strands.

"Hung from a tree at birth," Murphy told him, wincing as he caught a whiff of body odor. "Now, go take a shower. We got this."

"Yeah, right," Skylar told them, flashing yellow teeth. Then he glanced at the cerebrum. "Hey, what the hell? All that work to turn it on, and now the gizmo's gone off?"

"Yeah, a tragedy, huh?" At the desk, Ryan was pinching the bridge of his nose looking weary.

51

Karla

Karla Raven paced the great room, staring out the windows at the darkness. Only the brightest of stars could be seen, the bulk of the Sangre de Christo Mountains like an opaque curtain beneath them. One hand in her pocket, she fingered the little Zuni bear fetish she'd stolen off the fireplace mantel. It had been carved from some black stone, small enough to fit in the palm of her hand. She had flicked it out of sight with sleight of hand even as Helen watched. The woman hadn't a clue.

On the couch, Helen sat cross-legged, which seemed her preferred style. Instead of her navigator, however, she had her laptop open, was staring into the screen where she'd just cut connection with Colonel Ryan. A Zoom meeting might not have been even close to a secure link.

She kept glancing at the holo projections above the cerebrum and navigator where they sat on the coffee table.

"What are you looking for?" Karla asked, wishing she could exhaust her bundled energy.

"Any kind of activity," Helen said as she snapped the laptop closed. She looked up, grinning. "For whatever reason, Nakeesh wasn't monitoring her navigator. Probably to keep me from tracking her down. However, I can tell you that Fluvium's cerebrum is still functional. How's that for thousand years in a sarcophagus? The atomic core is only depleted by thirty percent."

"Which means?"

"If your Alpha gets her hands on it, she can still make the jump back to *Ti'ahaule*."

Helen made a series of gestures with her fingers, eyes flicking back and forth and blinking. "There, I shut them down again. No sense waving a blazing flag to draw Nakeesh's attention. It's bad enough that she'll know Fluvium's unit was activated. She may even be able to trace it to Grantham."

"It's not at Grantham," Karla told her. "It's buried in Cheyenne Mountain at the NORAD headquarters in a special vault under lock and key. Just because you were talking to the colonel, doesn't mean he and the others were at Grantham. That was a forwarded link to Cheyenne Mountain where—"

"Right." Helen gave her a hooded look. "Keep up that farce if you want to, Chief, but only use it on people you can actually fool. If I can find it, so can anyone else with the right equipment. Nakeesh is going to need something to use as a transmitter that the navigator can link to. With that, she can triangulate."

After a pause, Helen asked, "Who was dumb enough to pluck her out of Grantham in the first place? Stevens? Was he the idiot who gave her access to the Skientia labs and allowed her to build that time displacement generator?"

Karla spun on her heel. "No. She did it on her own. With the doohickey."

"Excuse me?" Helen was giving her a puzzled look

"The doohickey. Some machine she built out of electrical parts in her room at Grantham. Didn't the Skipper tell you?" Even as she said it, Karla could feel a crushing sense of dread. "Holy fuck, if she can get back to the lab . . . Tie her navigator to the doohickey . . ."

"*Ka'uxa k'uli Xibalba!*" Helen cried, setting the navigator to one side and bounding to her feet. She stomped up to Karla, demanding, "'Bout time you told me this? Yes? Like, maybe it might be important when it comes to saving your shitty little world?"

Karla instinctively dropped into a combat crouch, her CQB instincts as sharp as always. "Hey, bitch, we don't know for certain whose side you're on. Get it?"

Helen, almost trembling, raised her hands. "All right. Fair. Water under the bridge and all that. What's this doohickey? How does it work?"

"How the hell should I know? It was made of coils of copper wire. Used an electrical source. Falcon figured it was some sort of transmitter, that it was sending entangled signals. I do know that it was directional. I saw that much the night she disappeared. She'd turn it and tap a wire on the copper coil. Then, everything went apeshit. There was a hollow pop, and the field, or whatever the hell it was, knocked me out."

Helen closed her eyes, her fists knotted. "By the *Ahau*'s bloody balls! What part of 'she's a technical engineer' don't you get? And what fool gave her access to the materials necessary to build a transmitter?"

Karla snapped, "She was a fucking mental patient. Entangled particles? That's the first thing that should have jumped to mind in a psychiatric ward? We'd never even *heard* the term until all this shit came down."

The crow's-feet at the corners of Helen's eyes tightened. "Tell me the whole story. From the beginning."

Karla did. Right down to the night she was knocked flat in the hall outside Alpha's door.

"Nakeesh and the doohickey vanished because she used it to contact her navigator. If the thing's still there, she's going for Los Alamos. She needs that doohickey to contact Imperator. If what you tell me is true, it will take time. That's assuming the machine is really that crude."

Karla flexed her muscles. "Then maybe we better get to the doohickey before Alpha does."

Helen fingered her chin. Glanced at the navigator. "She's not there yet. If she were attempting to hook up the doohickey, I'd be getting readings on my navigator."

Karla pulled her phone from her pocket. "I'm calling the Skipper. I think we need Winny and her helicopter, and *ricky tick* damned quick."

While she listened to the ring tone, she asked, "What did you say in Mayan?"

"*Ka'uxa k'uli Xibalba.* It's Yucatec. Sort of means, 'broke-dick hell.' Sometimes I slip into old habits when I realize just how fucked I really am."

52

Childs

They were back in the van. This time, however, Hanson Childs rode in a large cardboard box labeled CONTAINMENT VESSEL and FRAGILE and HANDLE WITH CARE and THIS END UP. But the most notable marking was WARNING: RADIOACTIVE MATERIAL.

Nakeesh—to her absolute displeasure—had been stuffed into the accompanying box. The quarters, especially for tall persons such as themselves, were anything but comfortable.

"And you think this will pass any kind of inspection?" Childs had asked. "This is as dumb as labeling it 'agricultural equipment.'"

Tanner Jackson had given him a dismissive glance. "Do you think the smartest people in the world apply for security jobs at Los Alamos? In the current labor market, they're just delighted to no longer be waiting tables at the Beer N Burger in Española. That's why we put the boxes on wooden pallets. Makes them look heavy, like you'd need a forklift to unload them."

"Besides," Maxine Kaplan assured, "we've got the bases covered. We know that Grazier is monitoring our communications. We've sent him on a wild-goose chase to our Livermore lab. Our people are in place here. We know exactly which gate to pass. I'll be driving. Sure, they're used to me being in my Volvo, but after fifteen years, I should be visually familiar to a lot of people in the restricted area. No one should look twice."

Childs had watched as a fuming Nakeesh—muttering epithets in Latin and what he assumed was Mayan—had lowered her lithe frame into the big box before being taped in. Then—his black tactical bag beside the box—he'd allowed himself to be closed into the carton's narrow confines. First, he wondered if a human being could suffocate in a cardboard box. Then his legs began to ache and finally go numb from lack of circulation.

The van jolted through a dip, cramming Childs into a painful ball, confined as he was by the thick cardboard.

He heard a muffled curse from the accompanying box.

"Sorry," Kaplan called back.

Childs wondered if he'd be able to walk by the time they finally unpacked him.

"All right, people. Not a sound," Jackson called back. "Domina? *Silentium.*"

"*Certe,*" came her muffled reply. Then she added something in Mayan that Childs was certain had to be profanity.

The van slowed, came to a stop, and through the cardboard, Childs could hear the window rolling down. "Hello, Sam," Kaplan called. "Had to make a pickup for the lab. Given the security, we didn't want to entrust this to the usual trucking company."

"Ms. Kaplan. Good to see you again. You, too, Mr. Jackson." The voice was male. But even through the box, Childs could hear the man's anxiety. "Um, ma'am, with the heightened security, would you mind if I took a look?"

"Of course not, Sam. Let's step around to the back."

The driver's door clicked open as Kaplan got out; a couple of seconds later, he heard the van's rear double doors open as they were swung wide.

Okay, this is it. Childs clutched his pistol to his chest, felt his heart begin to hammer.

He just knew the guard was going to yell, "Freeze! Hands up! You're under arrest for smuggling murderers!" Jammed up in a contorted ball like he was, there was no way he could bunch his legs and push up with enough force to break the tape and pop out like a perverted Playboy Bunny from a big cake.

He did have a folding knife in his pocket, but cramped as he was, no way could he wiggle his fingers past the tight crease to retrieve it. Not that it would do much good if he had it. Cardboard this thick? It would take him five minutes just to cut a long enough slit in the side to make a hole big enough for him to crawl out of. Wishful thinking since the security guard would hear the cut, be watching as the blade carved its way down the side of the box.

So much for the element of surprise.

The next crazy impulse was to shoot through the cardboard.

And do what? Kill Nakeesh or Kaplan?

If he didn't tag each of the security officers, anyone left standing would simply riddle his box with bullets in return fire.

What the hell am I thinking?

He clamped his eyes closed, swallowed hard, hands gripping the pistol so hard it shook.

"Looks good to me," the male voice said.

A moment later, the doors slammed shut.

Gasping for air, his heart battering at his ribs, Childs heard Kaplan open the driver's door. Then she slipped the van in gear with a clunk.

Childs leaned his head against the cardboard and tried to exhale his relief. Then they were moving.

53

Ryan

I sat in the conference room with its pastel-colored walls, cute bunnies, deer, and pretty flowers. ET—computer in his lap—had retreated to the pile of beanbag chairs as was his wont. If there was a way to act like he wasn't in conformity with social norms, ET adopted it. Flopping into the beanbag chairs—especially with Eli Grazier in the room—filled the computer guru with delight. In addition, ET had taken to wearing expensive blaze-orange athletic shoes, baggy pants, and an oversized hoodie. I had no clue where he'd obtained them. Probably didn't want to know.

He called his new sartorial splendor his "woke to the nines" politically correct uniform.

Sam Savage had just rolled his eyes. Grazier's response was to grind his teeth so hard I thought he'd snap the crowns off the roots.

Me? I didn't care as long as ET kept us up to date on what Stevens and his teams in New Mexico, California, and DC were doing.

Glancing his way, I could see the lines deepening in his tall brow, that scrunching of his eyes, and tightening of the lips. That was ET's "something's not right look."

I was about to ask when Sam Savage strode in, gave Grazier a salute, and settled into a chair when Grazier indicated one.

"What's the word?" Sam asked, turning his attention to me. He'd spent the morning in the live-fire training center working with a couple of instructors he'd known in the Rangers. Trying, as he said, to keep his edge and familiarize himself with the 6.8x51 millimeter service cartridge and the advanced rifle that fired it.

Coming straight from the training center, he was wearing his ACU, complete with scuffs of dirt and bits of grass.

Eli laced his thick fingers together on the table, stared thoughtfully at those present. "Chief Raven is flying in with this Helen. She called last night. Asked that Major Swink fly down and collect her and the woman first thing. She wants to grab her kit before hitting the Los Alamos lab. It's her thought—I guess seconded by Helen—that Alpha is going to make a play for the doohickey. That she needs it to contact her timeline."

Savage asked, "What about the intel that said Alpha and Childs were seen outside Skientia's lab on the Lawrence Livermore grounds?"

Eli pursed his lips, hunched his shoulders in a shrug. "I've got a team in place. Some of my best people. We're ready to take them if they make a try for the Skientia lab, though we're not sure what assets it has outside of the entangled particle generator there."

"Doesn't make sense," Savage noted, leaning back in his chair. "The particle generator in Lab Two at Los Alamos is a more powerful device."

"Maybe my security team, after having their asses handed to them, are too formidable?" Grazier asked. "Maybe Alpha figures she's got a better chance of breaking into Pasadena?"

I'd watched the interplay and now asked. "What about Kaplan and Jackson? After Alpha's extraction, they just up and vanished."

"Gone to California with Alpha and Childs?" Grazier wondered, that look of annoyance clouding his brow. "How did they just drop off the face of the earth?"

"This is Tanner Jackson," I reminded. "The mastermind behind the assassination attempts against you in Washington. The man behind Talon Security."

"The guy that snatched my anthropologists out from under my nose on Pennsylvania Avenue." Savage pointed a finger. "And we damn well better not forget that Skientia's entangled physics cyber cryptography allows them to crack just about any communications. How many times were they ahead of us? Playing us?"

I nodded my head at Eli's phone. "I still don't trust that supposed super-secure phone of yours."

"And you dared to hold a Zoom meeting with Helen, shutting down the cerebrum?" Eli rubbed his forehead. Indicated the phone. "Harvey Rogers says it's the best he can come up with. Uses three separate chips, each only sending a third of the conversation. Encrypted. To monitor it,

Skientia would have to be listening to all three at the same time, fitting the bits of code together, and then decrypting them."

"Assuming they don't have ears on the other end," Savage noted. "Maybe that voodoo phone of Harvey's is secure from entangled recovery. Lot of good that does if someone, say Brad Becknell, on the other end, turns to his lieutenant and says, 'Just got an order from Grazier. We're picking Alpha up in the morning outside the Los Alamos lab.'"

"That's a chance we have to take," Grazier told him. "Besides, if that was the case, we should be picking up clues from Stevens' communications. He's been reporting directly to Ben Masters, telling the president everything he's doing. If he had any hint that Jackson was listening in, he should have tipped his hand."

"Not to mention that ET has had access to the Skientia secure systems since we hacked them back at the beginning." I took a deep breath, feeling the building tension. "We're privy to their email, phone logs, you name it."

Savage crossed his muscular arms, biceps swelling the camo sleeves of his shirt. "Like we were to that data Kaplan was collecting on Alpha's time machine? When we interrogated Wixom, the guy was as stunned as we were. He was the one who finally figured out how Kaplan was falsifying the data. That she lied like that really pissed him off. Since then, he's been most helpful when it comes to working out how she tracked Alpha's return."

I turned to Savage. "I need all of our people on their toes. Karla's on the way in with Helen. They'll be here as soon as Winny can set down."

Sam gave me a look of disbelief. "Excuse me, sir? You're letting Karla bring *that woman* into the center of our operations? May I remind you that the most important piece of equipment on the planet is just down the hall in Harvey Rogers' lab? If Helen gets her hands on Fluvium's cerebrum?" He made a face. "Well, sir, God help us."

Eli was giving him his predatory wolf look. The one that always made my stomach start to twitch.

I said, "She already knows it's somewhere close. Karla briefed the general and me. Remember when Skylar turned it on?" I raised a hand. "And no. Don't ask. I don't have a clue as to what it means. Only that we're still here, so we're still in the game. But if Alpha can access the doohickey, Helen says she can triangulate on the cerebrum."

At that point, the faint sound of an approaching helicopter was barely audible.

I glanced around the table. "I want eyes on Helen at all times. Sam, be sure that Myca Simond and Hatcher have her on camera. When she uses the women's room, I want someone with her. Karla preferably."

"Yes, sir." Sam glanced at Grazier. "Anything else?"

"No, Sam. Thank you." Eli took his salute as the major headed for the door.

"So, now what?" Eli asked, looking worn and tired.

I took a deep breath. "Falcon says we had better be ready to move on Los Alamos. Helen says we need to be ready to move on Los Alamos. Your intel says that Alpha's going to try to access the Skientia's Livermore lab, and they've got an ID on Childs to prove it. Which one do we believe?"

"Uh," ET interrupted. "Don't want to bust no bubbles, but I think we got a problem."

I turned in my chair, glancing to where ET was half buried in bean-bag chairs. "Such as?"

ET, those frown lines deeper than ever, was still fixed on his laptop screen. "General Grazier heard from his security team in Los Alamos lately?"

Only ET would talk about Eli in the third person while the general was sitting right there in the room.

"They check in on the hour," Grazier replied. "Standard code."

"Bet the next code word's gonna be 'fractal' and the one after that gonna be 'toothbrush.'"

"How'd you know that?" Grazier snapped.

ET, still not looking up, kept tapping at the keys on his laptop. "'Cause I gotta funny feeling. I mean, I been slippin' through Skientia like a cockroach in the wall. Hear what I'm saying? Ain't nobody been slapping me down for what? Maybe a week? So, I write me a new program, hijack part of Skientia's cryptography. Sort of like layers in an onion."

"And?" Grazier had his full attention on ET.

For the first time, Edwin looked up, meeting the general's dark gaze. "They know I been slipping through their system, and they been letting me. I think they've been trying to keep me from doing what I just did."

"And that is?" I asked.

"Lookin' deeper, Skipper. They figured me for lazy. Shit like that? Pisses me off."

"Get to the point, soldier," Eli insisted.

"They been playing us, General. Feeding us whatever we wanted to hear. My guess, they been doing it to us ever since that Tanner Jackson got back in touch with his people at Skientia. Those code words I told you? They in something called 'Operation Snuggy.' You know what that means?"

Grazier's expression had gone pained. "Yes, soldier, I do. It's when someone reaches down your pants and pulls your skivvies up tight and painful."

54

Kaplan

Maxine Kaplan backed into a space beside the Skientia lab side door, then shifted the van into park. She killed the ignition, laced her fingers over the wheel, and glanced at Jackson. To her surprise, she could see the sheen of perspiration on his bald head. The lenses of his thick glasses reflected smudges, and his suit was rumpled.

That surprised her. Tanner Jackson had always been a master of sartorial perfection. She had always figured it was his way of compensating for his physical features. With his potato-shaped head, triangular nose, and thin lips, the guy looked like a dork. It didn't matter that he was one of the most ruthless and powerful men alive, that he ran a company worth billions, or that he could make or break a corporation, a president, or topple a country through the use of the proprietary information. Skientia, through their entangled surveillance technology and control of information, literally had the power of life and death.

Jackson's public presentation of self was that of a perfectly dressed man in control of all situations. He never quite caught on to the fact that he was an ultimate alpha male. Couldn't quite grasp that, for the most part, women didn't care about his features or physical attraction. Instead, Jackson's underlying insecurity caused him to hire female escorts when he needed arm candy or sex. Knowing that had made it easier for Kaplan to seduce him back in the beginning. And over the years she'd used their casual sex to her own benefit. But she had done so most carefully. Never blatantly. And it had landed her in charge of the Los Alamos lab. Which was where she should have been; because, quite candidly, she was the best person for the job.

Were that not the case, they wouldn't be in this mess. It wasn't her fault that Domina Nakeesh had been standing on the banks of the Nile more than three thousand years ago running a calibration test on her time machine.

In the passenger seat, Jackson had been carefully scanning the area for anything out of place. Now he lifted the cuff that contained his communicator and said, "Blank the cameras. Override and loop the security system. We're headed for the door."

In Skientia's far-off Livermore lab, techs would be using their sophisticated computers and cryptography programs to hijack the Los Alamos lab's security software. Grazier's people wouldn't have a clue.

Kaplan couldn't hear the response in Jackson's earbud, but he gave her a curt smile, and said, "Let's go."

She climbed out as Jackson slid the van's side door open. With a penknife, he slit the tape before folding the box top back. Leaning over, he physically pulled Nakeesh from the confines. The woman kept the navigator tucked tightly to her side as she blinked in the light.

After slitting the tape on Hanson Childs' box, Kaplan, too, had to help the CID agent to his feet. Childs braced himself on the box top, panting, a black pistol gripped in his right hand. His sweaty face a mask of agony, he muttered, "Dear God, the tingles are starting."

"Come on," she told him. "We don't have a lot of time. Suffer on the way. We've got less than ten minutes to get you into the lab and out of sight."

She took his weight as he half fell out of the box. Made a mess out of untangling his long legs, but she got him to the pavement. He snatched up the black tactical bag from the van floor, and like two drunks they staggered toward the door.

"Non auxilium facere necessito," Nakeesh spat as Jackson reached to steady her when she stepped down from the van. Then, in English, "Do not help me!"

Through iron will, she kept her feet and strode—though somewhat uncertainly—for the door.

Jackson hurried forward, pulling a key ring from one pocket. Still scanning for danger, he unlocked the lab door.

Then they were in the cinderblock corridor that led to the main hallway. A stair to the upper floors lay behind the fire door to her left. "Can you climb? We need to get to the third floor."

Childs dropped the tactical bag on the concrete, unzipped it, and pulled out a futuristic-looking gun. The pistol, he jammed into the back of his pants. Standing and slinging the bag over his other shoulder, he said, "All right. Let's go."

"Take me to doohickey," Nakeesh ordered, her desperate eyes flicking this way and that.

"And then what happens?" Jackson asked, looking more than a little nervous himself. He had to be thinking of the last time he'd been in the building, when McCoy had been shot down before his eyes, when Reid Farmer had almost killed him, and how the archaeologist had died when Nakeesh engaged the time machine.

Nakeesh told him, "You will see. After I contact Imperator, nothing will be the same."

Something about the way the woman said it sent a shiver down Kaplan's spine. She gave Domina a sidelong inspection. This wasn't the same imperious Domina Nakeesh she and Wixom had worked with during the building of the time machine. A desperation lay behind the woman's cerulean eyes. Whatever Nakeesh expected, it wasn't going to be good.

"All right," Kaplan told them, opening the fire door to the staircase. "Doohickey's in an electronics lab on the third floor. Quiet, now. The building should be ours, but there's no sense in announcing our presence."

"Why's that?" Childs asked.

Jackson hurried to the stairs, starting up. "Because General Grazier just thinks he's in charge. That son of a bitch is about to have his shorts pulled up over his ears."

Grazier thought he held all the cards, Nakeesh thought she was about to pull a fast one. And good old Tanner Jackson thought he had the world by the short hairs. God, she loved playing the players for fools! Kaplan stifled a smile as she started up the stairs.

55

Childs

By the time he made the second-floor landing, most of the tingle had gone from Hanson Childs' leg muscles, and he would have loved to sprint to the top. Instead, he followed, last in line. He was amazed that Nakeesh had recovered so quickly. He'd half expected to catch her as she struggled with the stairs, but apparently she'd had less discomfort than he from riding in the box. Her long legs attacked the ascent like a mountain climber's. As he watched her muscular body, it struck him again as a sort of miracle that she'd chosen him for a companion.

Watching her climb, how her hips moved, the sway of her back, conjured memories of her. Of the remarkable sex. How her expression had reflected a momentary transcendence in the moment of climax.

Am I in love with her?

The question hit him like a thrown stone.

No. Not love. Something else.

He understood that she was using him for her own purposes. Wondered why he accepted that. He'd never been the subordinate in a sexual relationship. Ever. The very notion should have had him running for the door. This time—for whatever sick and twisted reason—it didn't matter. She'd led him into perdition. With nothing left but her, he didn't care.

He couldn't. Wouldn't.

He would help her get back to her home.

Life didn't exist past that point.

He chuckled as they reached the third-floor landing.

Tanner Jackson stopped at the fire door, glanced through the wire-impregnated glass, and then opened it to the corridor beyond. As he did, he asked, "Which way?"

"Right. Down four doors. It's room three seventeen. The electronics lab. Your security key will open it," Kaplan told him as she followed him into the corridor. She shot a nervous glance up at the security cameras.

Childs followed her gaze, feeling as if eyes were following his every move. Assuming everything was going according to plan, however, Skientia was feeding Grazier's people false images of empty hallways.

That Jackson and Kaplan seemed so sure of themselves was worrisome in its own right. He and Jaime had gained some understanding of the company's clout when they were chasing down Grazier's spec ops team. Now it was hitting home.

"You'd think they were the right hand of God," Jaime had remarked in the aftermath of the attack on the Skientia mansion in Aspen when directives were coming down from on high to return evidence and essentially ignore Skientia's role in the firefight.

Childs was starting to believe it. Kaplan and Jackson didn't even seem to be afraid of Bill Stevens, and that led right to the Oval Office.

Jackson led the way to the security door numbered three seventeen, glanced quickly up and down the hallway, and inserted his key.

Childs caught the expression on Alpha's face: taut, bitter, a glitter of desperation behind her eyes. Once inside, she'd have the means to contact Imperator. And she'd be headed home.

So, why did she look like nothing remained but anguish? She had folded the navigator to her chest as if it were a lifeline.

"You really want to do this?" Childs asked, taking her free hand. That electric thrill was still there.

That she didn't jerk it away was reassuring. Her crystalline blue gaze fixed on his. A faint smile hinting of inevitability on her broad lips. "It . . . must be."

Childs indicated Jackson. "You don't have to do this. Skientia can keep you out of the government's hands. Isn't that right?"

Jackson opened the thick door to the lab, glancing over his shoulder to peer at Nakeesh as the massive portal swung open. "We could indeed."

Kaplan, an amused curl to her lips, strode into the room, flicking on the lights.

"I've seen their capabilities," Childs continued as he followed

Nakeesh into the lab. "You could consult, design whatever you needed. Live out your life in comfort."

"Perhaps with you, Hanson? Among *stulti*?" Her accented voice dropped. "You are a good man. But in some ways, as innocent as a child."

She strode into the room, gaze fixing on the contraption that sat on a dolly in an open space in the center. Stepping over to it, she ran her fingers down the meter-long device with its thick coils of copper wire, the curious electrical doodads, and multicolored 12-gauge wiring.

As she did, Childs glanced around. The room was bigger than he would have thought; he could see down past rows of floor-to-ceiling shelving in either direction. The heavy metal shelves were piled up with equipment the likes of which he'd never seen, and at the same time, there were stacks of conduit, electrical boxes and sockets, rolls of insulated wiring, junction boxes, and lines of stacked trays filled with all manner of odds and ends.

Childs took Nakeesh's arm and turned her to face him. "I'm serious. You don't have to do this. We can make a place for you. Here. If you contact—"

"Too late," she told him, reaching out to place a finger on his lips.

"Yes," Jackson agreed. "I'm afraid it is."

Childs shot him a glance, seeing the man's eyes—almost dreamy behind the too-thick glasses—his smile reeking of satisfaction.

"Why? My God, man. Don't you understand what this woman could do for you? For Skientia?"

"Of course he does," a familiar voice called. Josh Mack stepped out from behind the closest of the packed shelves.

Childs whirled. Started to bring up the dart pistol, and froze.

"Good to see you again, bro," Ted Meyer called as he and the rest of Mack's team appeared from all sides where they'd been hidden by the shelving. Each of them held one of the dart pistols; all were trained on him and Nakeesh. "But we've got some unfinished business."

"More than a little," Mack added, stepping forward to twist the dart pistol out of Childs' grip. Then he efficiently plucked the pistol from his hip before relieving the glaring Nakeesh of her HK where it was stuffed in her waistband.

Childs raised his hands, heart bumping in his chest. "You don't know who you're dealing with. Tanner Jackson—"

"Actually, I do." Mack smiled, stepping back. "You can come out now, sir."

Bill Stevens emerged from behind the packed shelving, looking dapper in a gray silk suit. "Hello, Tanner."

"Hey, Bill," Jackson replied, removing his glasses and pulling a handkerchief from his pocket; he began wiping the smudged lenses. "Like I told you. We didn't need the drama. Maxine and I delivered the Domina right to the lab, and she never suspected a thing."

Stevens, still standing back, crossed his arms, studying Nakeesh. The only clue she gave of her frustration was the frozen chill behind her blue eyes.

"Why?" Childs asked.

Kaplan told him, "Because there's traps inside of traps, Agent Childs. And, it turns out that we need Domina Nakeesh. You see, in order to control time, we need a cerebrum to function with the Domina's navigator. Now, Grazier's people might have Fluvium's cerebrum. We've had hints, but no clue as to where it might be. Since we're not sure if it exists, the next best thing is to have someone bring us another cerebrum and navigator." Her smile held no humor. "It all came together when you told us she could call this Imperator."

"You want to use me as bait?" Nakeesh asked, breaking into panicked laughter. "To call Imperator? You are *socors! Morons!*"

Bill Stevens, arms still crossed, an amused look on his face, said, "I don't think you get it, Domina. I'm President Masters' chief of staff. The entire weight of the United States is behind me, and—as Skientia's work here proves—we're on the verge of controlling the technology on our own. Ready to join the club, so to speak. Now, as you've described it, Imperator works for these *Ahau*. We're interested in establishing diplomatic relations with your timeline."

Childs watched as Nakeesh's disbelief faded into humor. Her sputtering laughter caught him off guard.

"You find that funny?" Jackson asked.

Nakeesh lifted a hand, the gesture that of surrender. She stepped forward with a slight shake of the head. *"Kiimehn ma'ak che'eh ya'ab tzu'u'uy."* And so saying, she laid her navigator on the counter across from the doohickey, and studied the machine.

Turning to Kaplan, she asked, "Do you have electricity for cord?"

"Sure." Kaplan walked to a bench, procuring an extension cord.

"No. Need more of, what you call amperage."

"Of course," Kaplan replied. To Jackson, she said, "I don't care who you get, but I need an electrician."

"On it." Jackson lifted his cuff com, speaking softly.

Childs—under the watchful eyes of Mack's team—eased up beside Nakeesh. In a low voice, he asked, "What was it you just said in Mayan?"

She gave him a sliding glance. "Dead men laugh the hardest."

56

Karla

You'd never know that Winny Swink was flying the Sikorski Defiant X on her first operational mission. She handled it like she'd been born in the beast's right seat. The coaxial helicopter settled onto the grass in the confines of the glassed-in central courtyard in Grantham Barracks' Ward Six. A line of people could be seen behind the windows, watching as the advanced helicopter spooled down.

"What do you think?" Winny called from the pilot's seat.

Beside her, a Sikorski copilot was recording data from the instrumentation. The bird was still new, little more than a prototype. And what better place to test it than where lots of eyes weren't watching it on the flight line?

"Smooth," Karla told her as she unbuckled from the seat and stepped over to help Helen. The way the cabin was laid out, the new Defiant reminded her of a Blackhawk. Same seating arrangement.

"And fast," she added as she checked her gear. "We're here in half the time it would have taken with the Blackhawk."

"Roger that!" Winny pulled her helmet off, running fingers through her flame-red hair.

Karla could see the woman's grin reflected in the glass canopy.

Helen—looking nonchalant after her first helicopter ride—immediately retrieved her pack and slipped it over her shoulder.

Karla opened the door and watched it fold upward. Wasn't sure but that she liked the old sliding door better.

She would have helped Helen down, but the woman dropped spryly to the grass as the support crew came trotting forward, all set to perform post-flight checks on their new favorite toy.

Karla shot Helen a measuring look. "Welcome to Grantham. But don't get too comfortable. We debrief, load up on the gear we're going to need, and we're right back on that bird and headed to Los Alamos." A beat. "Assuming you're right."

"I'm right," Helen told her, stepping aside so that Karla could open the glass door to the Ward Six hallway.

Inside, the vinyl flooring was polished to a military precision, fluorescent lights glowing overhead. Through the windows, she could see the crew swarming over the Defiant.

Karla indicated the way, glancing up at the security cameras they passed beneath. She was acutely aware of Helen's leonine walk, balanced, almost tigerish. The woman just had a charisma that drew the eyes. Call it damned attractive, though Karla couldn't put her finger on why. But how well could the woman handle herself when the shit came down?

Myca Simond and two of his security officers were waiting, the latter standing at ease, their curious gazes fixing on Helen. As they did, all three males seemed to swell, standing more at attention. Karla could see the rise in interest, could almost detect the increased pulse rate.

"Down, boys," she murmured. "She's hands off—and likely to break your necks if you sniff too closely."

"Yes, Chief." Simond gave her a curt nod, gaze straying back to Helen as if she were some exotic moth. The woman's expression was mocking if anything.

"Take Helen to the cafeteria," Karla ordered. "Get her something to eat. We're only here for a half hour at most. Soon as I can grab my shit and Winny can get the bird refueled, we're beating . . ."

Helen stiffened, swinging her pack from her back. Her expression had tightened as she pulled the flap back, glancing inside. "Looks like we're too late, Chief. I've got activity reading on the navigator. Somehow, Nakeesh has access to a transmitter. She's searching, sending out entangled particles. And this time, with her navigator to analyze the signal, she's going to find Fluvium's cerebrum sooner rather than later."

"Can we get to Los Alamos in time to shut her down?"

"From here? Even on that fast helicopter? I doubt it. And if she's in the lab, that means Grazier's people have lost control of the building."

Karla shot Simond a hard glance. "Get on your com. We need everyone in the conference room. Now!"

"You got it, Chief." Simond lifted his cuff, saying, "Emergency meeting. Conference room. Move it, people."

Karla turned on her heel, leading the way. Helen had paused long enough to slip her navigator out of her backpack; she was cradling it with one hand, waving her other through the hazy blue display as she tagged along behind.

"Can she reach Imperator?" Karla asked.

"Not with the signal that I'm reading," Helen told her. Then the woman cursed in some unknown language. "But she's got that damned time machine down in the basement, doesn't she? If she could use that as an amplifier, she could boost her signal. Any way she can power that up?"

Karla shrugged, one hand in her pocket as she fingered the Zuni fetish she'd stolen. "Hell, I don't know. Last time it took most of the electrical output of the entire Southwest to shoot her into the future."

"But does the machine have inter-timeline capabilities? Can it project entangled particles outside of this timeline's amplitude and decoherence?"

"How the hell would I know?" Karla cried.

"Damn it, woman, if you don't, who does?"

"Kaplan, maybe. Or that Virgil Wixom. My job is to kick down doors and break heads, not tinker with time machines."

"Laudable," Helen snapped in outright irritation. "Wish you knew something germane to the problem before we're all dead."

Karla led the way around the corner and straight-armed the conference room door. She noticed that when Myca and his security officers followed Helen into the room, they were rather pale. As if—even as attracted to the alien woman as they might have been—they nevertheless expected Karla to kick her in the head. No one used that tone around Karla Raven.

If things hadn't been so damned dire, Karla would have found it amusing.

Helen—glancing at the walls with their flowers, bunnies, and deer fawns—stopped short. "You have got to be kidding."

"Welcome to the war room," Karla told her. "From here we decide the fate of the world on a regular basis."

Sam Savage burst in next, asking, "What's up? And what the hell is this *woman* doing in here? Chief, you're supposed to be grabbing your first-line gear and heading off to secure—"

"Too late," Karla told him. "Alpha's in the lab. Helen's reading her signals, probably from the doohickey. Somehow, Nakeesh got back inside."

"It's that son of a bitch Stevens!" Eli Grazier barked as he barged in behind Savage. "ET just cracked their communications. Had to hijack Skientia's system to do it. Seems that Tanner Jackson was feeding Stevens information the entire time. Used Skientia's resources to blind and take out my team. I still can't reach them." He shot a hard look at Helen. "So, I see you're here, too? On whose side? Or just your own?"

Helen laid her navigator on the table, pausing to pull out her cerebrum. Not meeting Grazier's eyes, she said, "How about we see if we can stop Nakeesh? Assuming we can, we'll work out the pesky little details later. Deal?"

Ryan was the next one in, asking, "What's gone wrong now?"

Karla told him, "We need someone who can tell us about Alpha's time machine. Can she use it to send a signal—"

"Augment a signal," Helen interrupted. "Your damned doohickey is already sending. She just needs to boost it past timeline decoherence."

Karla wondered what the hell that meant.

"Wixom," Grazier said. "Ryan, I need a signal. Get Wixom on the line. He's under house arrest in Los Alamos." A beat. "At least, I hope he is."

Helen had seated herself behind the navigator and cerebrum, both of which projected blue holographs with their glowing Mayan glyphs and Latin text. With careful fingers, Helen manipulated the display.

"What are you looking for?" Ryan asked, seating himself beside her.

Helen absently replied, "Trying to determine if she has enough energy in her signal to punch through the decoherence barrier. After all, it's holding your timeline together. The problem is, she doesn't need to use a sledgehammer to send a message, just a little pinprick."

The wall monitor flashed on, a serious Harvey Rogers peering through his thick-lensed glasses, blurting, "Skipper? Fluvium's cerebrum just turned on! I swear, we weren't even close to it."

Helen slapped a hand on the table. To Harvey, she said, "Right now. Show me the screen. Get that man Murphy."

"Here," Murphy called, edging his face into the camera's field beside Rogers'.

"Use the *Jom* glyph," she told him. "One finger. Leave it in the glyph while you use another finger to touch the sequence that reads *Och ta chaan-na.*"

"End the sky-entered?" Murphy wondered.

Helen told him, "That translates to 'Terminate the transmitted signal.' We'll worry about idiom later."

"Got it!" Murphy wheeled around, and in the background, Karla could see the Mayan expert stick his left index finger into the blue haze. With his right, he accessed several of the other glowing glyphs. And the holograph vanished.

Helen rubbed her forehead, staring at her navigator in worried irritation. "How the hell did she do that? Turn it on remotely?"

"No clue," Rogers said through the monitor. "How badly are we hurt?"

"Don't know. That's what you call a stopgap, people. But the damage has been done. Nakeesh knows Fluvium's cerebrum is both functional and somewhere close. I think we stopped the transmission before she could get a fix on the cerebrum's location. It will take her a while to figure out where it is."

"How long?" Ryan asked.

Helen shrugged. "That depends. She must have a backdoor into Fluvium's cerebrum. As close as they were, they shared a lot of things. Maybe he gave her a code? Or he might even have reprogrammed his cerebrum as the years passed and he realized that Nakeesh wasn't coming back to rescue him. He was always a devious piece of work. I wouldn't put it past him to have programmed a 'screw you' into the system. Something that Nakeesh could probably figure out, but that would condemn anyone else trying to use his cerebrum."

"Like, what kind of 'screw you'?" Karla asked.

Helen's green eyes cooled. "Maybe a corrupted command that would bias the computational data. Something that would send a linking navigator into a recohering timeline."

"Why would that be bad?" Grazier asked.

Helen spared him a glance. "No one's ever described what it is like to be sucked backward through reality in a collapsing timeline. Some theorize it's like a compression of being. An implosion of consciousness. To the hapless victim, the effect of multidimensional vertigo, falling, spinning, and turning inside out, would seem to last for eternity. Granted, it's only for as many millennia as it takes for the timeline to snap back, but living that hell backward would be unbearable." She winced. "And then there's the eventual instant when the wave function merges with the energy that drives a new wave function. We can't even hypothetically describe what that would feel like."

"I don't get it," the Skipper said. "What makes landing in a recohering timeline any worse than, say, Nakeesh going back in time and stopping this one?"

"Because you *don't belong*." Helen gave him a pained look. "If you land in a recohering timeline, you're like a drop of oil in a barrel of water. Your energy and mass are from *another* timeline. Like that drop of oil, they don't mix. You are not part of the physics, not entangled. Not included in the recoherence. Foreign matter. Get it?"

"So it doesn't follow the same laws?" Grazier asked.

Helen lifted a hand. Let it fall onto the table with a thump. "See? Gravity still works. I'm from a different timeline, but my arm—along with the rest of me—is made of atoms. Physics is still physics. But at the atomic level I'm a drop of oil in your reality. So is Nakeesh." She jerked a thumb at Simond. "Which is one of the reasons why your boy there is panting with a hard on."

Simond gulped, blushed a bright red.

Karla crossed her arms, glanced at the screen where Harvey Rogers was nodding. He said, "Oil in water. That makes sense. But, hey, you've been here. Eating our food, drinking our water. Shedding skin cells and hair."

"Contamination between the timelines," Helen agreed. "The theorists consider the effects to be negligible in the long run." A pause. "As long as the timeline isn't recohering."

Karla saw the holo change on Helen's navigator as it flashed different symbols. "What's that?"

Helen made a command gesture. Flicked her eyes from glyph to glyph and blinked as she did; the navigator's holo shifted images in response. "Nakeesh is searching for Fluvium's cerebrum. Right now, I imagine she's both excited and frustrated as all hell. She had a hit. Escape and survival were at her fingertips, and now Fluvium's cerebrum is turned off. It vanished. She's trying to figure out what happened."

"Will she?" Grazier asked, leaning over the back of Helen's chair to stare at the holo.

"Eventually," Helen told him. "When she does, she's going to be coming for Fluvium's cerebrum. If she can get a fix, she can transport here using the doohickey and navigator. Pop in, as you say."

"That's not so bad," Savage said. "When she does, we've got her and her navigator."

Karla leaned down, bracing her elbows on the table to intercept Helen's gaze. "What do you think, *Ennoia*? You know her better than the rest of us do. Would she just pop in?"

Helen narrowed her gaze as she avoided Karla's stare and studied the wavering images in her holo. "When her navigator pinged on Fluvium's cerebrum, it changed her entire game. Added a whole new dimension. If she can get to it—and has an accomplice to help her—she has a chance to rescue Fluvium. But when we turned the cerebrum off, it told her that I'm using it for bait. No one else would have known which commands to use."

"How does that change her game?" Grazier asked.

Helen leaned forward to prop her chin, still concentrating on the holos. "She knows that if she tries for the cerebrum, I'm waiting to kill her. Meanwhile, how long can she rely on Tanner Jackson and your Mr. Stevens?"

"Not long," Grazier grunted. "They have their own agendas."

"And let's not forget this Imperator," the Skipper added from where he'd backed against the wall and crossed his arms.

"I *never* forget he's out there," Helen told him shortly. "The one thing I can assure you, is that he has a *quinque* searching the potential timelines. A team of five jumping from line to line, popping in, checking readings on their navigators, and popping out. All searching for some signal from Nakeesh or Fluvium."

"And Nakeesh is now broadcasting." Karla pointed at the fluctuating images on the holographic screen. "Is that flashing image her?"

In the wall monitor behind, Murphy and Rogers were leaning forward. They seemed to be studying the changing images in Helen's holo. That's when Karla noted that the little red record light was on at the screen bottom. Figured. Science nerds. The end of the world was coming, and they wanted to know how a gizmo worked.

Helen pursed her lips. Nodded. "That's Nakeesh. Searching. And she's aware, just as I am, that if one of Imperator's teams is in this timeline, they will detect her signal."

"And then what happens?" Grazier asked.

Helen looked up, met the general's eyes. "Then we all die."

57

Childs

When Josh Mack pointed at Childs and made a hand signal, Steth Callaway and Billy Stump started forward, the latter pulling out zip ties. Both men had mean smiles on their faces, that predatory look in their eyes.

"We owe you, bro," Callaway told him. "For Jaime and Hughes."

"You're not gonna make this difficult, are you?" Stump followed up, pointing his dart pistol at Childs' belly. "Please, you piece of shit. Make it difficult."

"Wait a minute, guys." Childs lifted his hands, knowing any retreat to the lab door was blocked by Mack. "I didn't pull the trigger on Jaime or Lonnie. I'm not the enemy."

"I say you're a scum-sucking motherfucker," Calloway told him. "Now, we can do this easy or—"

"*Desistate!* Stop! Now!" Nakeesh snapped, looking up from the doohickey as Maxine Kaplan supervised the electrician hooking the machine to the power. Nakeesh stalked up to Stevens, pointed a finger at Childs. "He is mine. *Servus est.* Mine! Do you understand?"

Stevens cocked a skeptical eyebrow. Glanced at Mack. "You heard the lady. Let him go."

Callaway, leaning close into Childs' space, whispered, "This ain't over, chickenshit."

"It's over," Childs told him, stepping past to join Nakeesh. "Thanks," he told her. "Now, what do you need from me?"

"Help." She gestured him over to the doohickey. A series of lights now glowed on an ad hoc panel on the side of the thing. "Take wire. Tap like so."

She showed Childs how to lightly touch the wire, moving from coil to coil on the device's wrapped surface. Simple duty, actually. And it kept him far from the clutches of Josh Mack and his team.

He did his best not to look in the direction where his one-time teammates milled in a knot by one of the shelves full of electrical parts. They fingered their dart guns and shot him baleful glares. Sure, tapping the wire from one coil to the next was boring, but better than being handcuffed, beaten, and either strangled or shot before being left in a ditch.

He was about a third of the way up the copper wires when Nakeesh caught him by surprise. She'd been peering intently at the blue haze of the navigator's holograph when she shouted, *"Gloriae victorae!"*

Stevens and Kaplan hurried forward, crowding close to squint at the blue images. "What? What is it?"

Nakeesh gestured to Childs. "Do not move. Hold wire there."

"You got it." Childs couldn't see any difference. The coil he was touching was just like any of the others.

Meanwhile, Nakeesh was muttering something he couldn't understand, obviously overjoyed. He thought he heard the words, "Fluvium" and *"Certe est"* that he'd learned meant "Yes, it is."

And then, just as unexpectedly, the glowing symbol in the navigator's holograph blinked out.

Nakeesh flicked her fingers through the display, uttered a couple of incomprehensible commands, and waited. Nothing but the uniform blue glow was visible above the machine.

She glanced sidelong at Childs, ensuring he hadn't moved the wire. Then—lines forming in her brow—she input commands, fingers flying, uttering what sounded like Latin mixed with Yucatec.

"Nihil." She straightened, cried angrily, *"Sacra sputem!"*

"What does this mean?" Stevens asked. "Was that Imperator? Is that who you called?"

She shot Stevens that look that Childs knew so well. The one she used when she called someone a *vermiculus*, which meant worm. "A signal," she told him. "But not Imperator. I need to try some things. Childs, do not move your wire."

For a good five minutes, she used her fingers, eye commands, and blinks, to manipulate the symbols on the navigator, gave the machine commands in Yucatec, and mixed various combinations of symbols. All, apparently, without achieving whatever effect she wanted.

"What just happened?" Kaplan asked as Nakeesh—with a flip of her fingers—shut the navigator down.

Childs recognized the look. The lined brow, the narrowing of the woman's laser-blue eyes. She was thinking through every eventuality. Mindless of the growing anxiety in Bill Stevens' posture, or the skeptical squint in Kaplan's eyes, Nakeesh slowly nodded.

"What is it?" Childs asked softly.

"*Laqueus. Ennoia est.*" Nakeesh glanced at Childs. "Is a trap set by the *Ennoia*. But what does it mean?"

"Excuse me?" Stevens asked, stepping forward. "What kind of trap? Who's the Ennoia? I don't understand."

Nakeesh chuckled, the sound of it bitter. "You would not. My question: Does the *Ennoia* have Fluvium's cerebrum? Or does she send me a signal to make me *think* she does? Just a hint."

"How would she get Fluvium's cerebrum?" Kaplan asked, crossing her arms. "Last we heard, it was lost. Buried somewhere in Egypt."

"Yes." Nakeesh turned, running her fingers along the doohickey's metal housing as she met Childs' gaze. "Or did that *stultus*, Reid Farmer, find it? Hmm? Was it brought back with the other things from the *sepulchrum*?" She shot a questioning glance at Tanner Jackson, who'd stood back, missing nothing. "The cerebrum? Did you have it? Tell me. This is important."

"No, Domina." Jackson stuck his hands into his back pockets, rumpling his suitcoat. "And believe me, we tried turning heaven and earth upside down looking. We still have covert teams searching in Egypt."

She seemed to take his word for it. Glanced again at Stevens. "Could Grazier have taken it?"

Stevens shrugged. "If he did, no one ever let slip that he ever had it. And, if he did—"

"Harvey Rogers," Kaplan said, as if in revelation.

"Who?" Stevens asked.

"Computer engineer and materials scientist from the Aberdeen Proving Ground. Has a lab there where he conducts advanced materials research. He was into trying to figure out how to make a better quantum qubit computer. Does a lot of cutting-edge work for DARPA and the NSA. Or did. Grazier had him transferred to the nuthouse up in Colorado. Or that was the cover story, anyway."

Stevens turned to Josh Mack. "Get on the horn to my office. Have them check out Harvey Rogers. See if they can find him."

"Yes, sir," Mack told him, pulling a phone from his pocket and stepping away between the high shelves.

Meanwhile, Childs watched Nakeesh. The slight flicker of her lips told him that she'd come to some sort of a conclusion. "What?"

She gave him a knowing look. "If it is not Fluvium's cerebrum, but only made to act like it is, then the *Ennoia* is using it as a trap. If it is Fluvium's cerebrum, only the *Ennoia*, in a world filled with *stulti*, would know how to turn it off. Either way, at the other end of that signal, the *Ennoia* is waiting."

"What does she want?"

Nakeesh reached out, ran her caressing finger down the curve of his cheek. "Why, to kill me, *pulcher homo*."

"So, what do we do?" Childs asked, aware that the whole room was fixed on the way Nakeesh was touching him.

"We do the only thing we can." She glanced at Stevens, then at Jackson and Kaplan.

Nakeesh gave Childs an intimate smile. "After our last *copulatio* you said the walls were closing in. A very good description, *amore*. We are running out of options, so the only thing left is to set a trap within a trap."

"And how do we do that?" Childs asked as a weary inevitability grew behind Nakeesh's expression.

"The *Ennoia* leaves me no choice. I will not allow her to win." She stepped over to where the navigator rested on the table. With a flick of her fingers, she did something to the machine's setting.

"What was that?" Stevens demanded, indicting the pulsing images in the holo.

"What you would call a beacon," Nakeesh told him. "Next, I need access to time machine." She raised a hand in a stalling motion. "Not for travel, but to augment signal. You want to establish diplomatic relations with Imperator? With the *Ti'ahaule*? Very well. Give me five minutes with doohickey linked to time machine. Imperator will hear. Then all we have to do is wait."

"For what?" Kaplan asked.

But Childs figured he knew. "For dead men to laugh." Even as he said it, he could see the mixture of resolve and defeat behind Nakeesh's laser-blue eyes.

58

Ryan

"*Hare mezayyane!*" Helen cried as she jolted upright in the chair. Before her, the holographic images were flashing and flickering into and out of existence as her navigator and cerebrum did whatever they did to interface.

"What's that?" I asked.

"Means 'fucking shits' in Aramaic,'" Helen muttered. "It's an old, old curse. What you'd call profanity."

I'd been leaning against the wall in the conference room. From the moment Karla had called the emergency conference, it had seemed like things were spinning out of control. I mean, Helen—who was anything but a trusted ally—was now sitting in our war room. Who knew what she was planning? Like Alpha, she was another alien, with an agenda all her own. What I knew for sure was that in her eyes, we were expendable. And now we were depending on her for intelligence?

Helen slumped back down in the chair as everyone crowded close. "Nakeesh just called our bluff."

"How'd she do that?" Grazier asked from where he'd settled into a chair, his eyes on the fluffy bunnies, deer, and colorful flowers painted on the walls.

"Call this the next best thing to an SOS," Helen told him as she gestured at the images on her holo.

I noticed that from their lab, Rogers and Murphy were both recording everything that transpired on the holographic display. Periodically, they'd seem to catch something that flashed, as if someone, at least, was delighted by it all.

"An SOS?" Grazier asked. "For whom?"

Helen leaned back, studied the general. "The only person in the universe who'd cue on this: she's signaling Imperator. She's got her pinprick. Shooting directed entangled particles outside of decoherence in hopes that he'll pick them up."

"So, what do we do?" I asked.

Helen gave me a measuring look. "Can you blow up the Skientia lab in Los Alamos? Like fast? Level it to rubble?"

I, in turn, asked Eli. "Can we?"

He grunted, rubbed his jaw. "That kind of strike? It would have to go to the president, then through the chain of command, and then the answer would be a resounding 'No!' Seriously, Tim, we're the only people on earth who understand the depth of this thing. And Ben Masters is playing for himself. He's still figuring that there's a way to exploit Alpha and her technology for his personal gain. The last thing he'd sign off on is Stevens' and Alpha's destruction."

"We have the helo," Karla reminded, her gray eyes thinned, expression strained.

"But no ordinance for it," Sam Savage reminded. "Not that we'd use it to make an airstrike on a private facility on American soil. You know what kind of shit that we'd unleash on ourselves?"

"Out of the question," Grazier agreed. He turned to Helen, cocked his head. "How long do we have to shut Alpha's signal down before this Imperator can arrive?"

She gave him a measuring green-eyed stare. "It's sent. He can arrive at any moment. That he hasn't tells me that we still have hope."

"How do you know that?" Savage asked.

She narrowed an eye, gave him a wistful smile. "They're not standing in the room with us."

A moment later the screen where Harvey Rogers and Murphy were watching, recording, split. To my surprise, Falcon, his body hunched on his bed, was looking up at the ceiling camera. He was wearing baggy gray sweatpants and an oversized white shirt on his bony and too-thin frame. He looked up, brown eyes flickering as his lips twitched.

Falcon wearily said, "I got Nurse Seymore to patch me through."

"Who is this?" Helen asked, looking at the nervous Falcon with disdainful eyes.

"Falcon?" I asked stepping forward. "What is it?"

"I've been listening," he said. "The way the pieces are falling together is starting to make sense."

"What pieces, Captain?" Eli had risen to his feet, a flicker of anxiety in his expression.

"The end of the world," Falcon muttered, his gaze shifting. "And how Imperator will kill us all."

"How will he do that?" Savage asked.

"By using our concept of time against us," Falcon replied. "It's how he has always fought. And how he has always won."

I felt the cold screaming willies run down my spine.

"Can we beat him?" I asked.

Falcon slowly shook his head. "We can't stop his arrival. In the end, our timeline will be at his mercy."

"Then, you don't understand Imperator," Helen chided. "He *has* no mercy." She turned her attention on Karla. "I can still save you. If you will operate the cerebrum, I can take you to another timeline. I think you would be an asset."

"I'm not going anywhere," Karla growled as if it were a threat.

"Oh, yes, you are," Falcon told her absently. "But first I need you to bring Helen to my room. I need to talk to her."

Karla stiffened. "Falcon? You out of your mind?"

He blinked. Seemed startled by the question. "No. I'm DID schizophrenic, and it's all inside my mind. But that shouldn't have any impact on the situation."

59

Falcon

Falcon—curled around his pulled-up knees—lay on his side on his bed. He considered all the things Helen had told him. The words she'd used to answer his questions about Imperator, the empire called *Ti'ahaule,* and their rules about jumping between timelines.

He could still smell the woman's scent. Curiously, it lingered in the air.

Falcon wondered what it would be like to spend time with Helen. Not that he'd ever been comfortable with females, but talking to her, listening to her, had excited him.

She knew so much! Had seen so much.

Fascinating. An alternate timeline. One where Rome and the Maya had interacted. Roman practicality and engineering mixed with Mayan science and mathematics. Two empires, separated by an ocean that had precluded them from trying to conquer each other, but allowed the transmission of ideas, philosophy, and knowledge. A cross-fertilization of cosmology, world view, and inquiry based on competitive authoritarian rule. Not that either the Mayans or Romans were ever known for empathy, compassion, or benevolence.

And now one of *Ti'ahaule'*s generals was coming here to recover Alpha and the missing navigator and cerebrum.

And they would take Helen as well. Punish her in terrible ways.

We have to stop that.

Behind his eyes, Falcon watched the fragments of data as he moved them. Bit by bit, the pieces began to fit into place. The pattern slowly emerged.

Time was the key. To think about using it as a gaming piece.

To step outside of time. Look at events as a four-dimensional puzzle.

That was how the mysterious Imperator would see it.

How Alpha and Helen would see it.

Only his people would be locked into the old paradigm. Unable to work except within a perceptive linear prison.

"Very good," Theresa told him.

Falcon opened his eyes as she stepped out of his bathroom, fiddling with her curly black hair as she did. Her knowing gaze fixed on his. "They see the gameboard as you do. What you can't count on is that your people—blinded as they are by what they consider reality—will be able to play the parts they need to play."

From where he sat leaned back in Falcon's chair, Major Marks ran a hand over his close-cropped steel-silver hair. The major's hard gaze fixed on Falcon, measuring and challenging at the same time. "You know, don't you, that you're in a fight for more than just your life. Your entire existence is at stake. You willing to make the sacrifice that's going to entail?"

Falcon swallowed hard. "Chief Raven, Major Savage, even Dr. Ryan. They're all at risk."

"So's the world, Captain." Major Marks took a deep breath, swelling his uniform coat, causing his campaign ribbons, gleaming buttons, and lapel pins to shimmer in the light. "You lose, you just get snuffed. Wonder what that's like? Just to vanish."

"It would be a phase transition," Theresa Applegate told him. "From somethingness to nothingness. The hard part is knowing—assuming Helen's word can be trusted—that these *Ahau* will continue to exist. Continue to erase timelines to maintain their control over entanglement technology."

She smiled. "Fascinating question, isn't it? Historically, we have always based moral arguments on what was good for a person, or a people, or maybe a nation. Over the last century, have we had to expand discussions to include a morality that serves the good of the planet."

She stepped around the major's outstretched feet, his spit-polished shoes gleaming with their mirror shine. Fixing her dark eyes on Falcon's, she said, "How does it feel to be the first person in our history to fight for a moral cause that affects an entire timeline: past, present, and future?"

Falcon—a quivering in his gut—nodded.

In his memory, Aunt Celia's hard glare, her mouth tight with disdain, lurked in the haze.

Falcon made himself forget. Made himself focus on the *Ahau*. Gave them faces. Faces with washed-out blue eyes. Pupils like burning black holes. They were thin, pale-complexioned, with white-blond hair. When they turned their attention on him, they wore the same arrogant expressions that Agent Hanson Childs had worn.

Yes, this was worth fighting for.

"Is this worth your people dying over?" Major Marks asked. "Maybe there's another way? Sometimes, on the battlefield, the best way to win is not to engage."

"But we're already engaged," Falcon told him. "Helen is here. Alpha has raised the stakes."

"Maybe you can find a way to let them go back where they came from," Marks told him. "That, or take out Alpha and the *Ennoia*. Eliminate them. What's Imperator's best tactical move?"

"You're going to say retreat," Theresa told Marks with a huff. "But you heard Helen. She told us that Imperator will sterilize the timeline. That he has to as a means of exterminating any threat to the *Ahau* from our developing entanglement physics technology."

"Really?" Major Marks asked, his cold blue stare shifting from Falcon to Theresa. "What have we got for intel, you skinny little witch? Helen's word? Fact is, we don't have a clue. And remember, the first time any of us ever saw Helen, she was shooting at Dr. Ryan and Alpha. I guess I have to remind you that it was her bullet that blew Captain Stanwick's brains all over the garage."

Theresa snorted her derision. "Now I've heard everything. The warmonger speaking for peace? Do my ears deceive me?"

As they launched into each other, Falcon closed his eyes, letting their argument rage in the background.

What do we know for sure?

That Alpha and Helen are aliens.

That they control a remarkable technology.

And that, ultimately—until Imperator actually showed up on the scene—they both might be deadly threats.

"So," he whispered under his breath. "We know that Alpha and Fluvium were bad. We found the proof of that in that tomb in Egypt."

But what do I do about Helen?

Not to mention that even as he considered, she was just down the hall, helping Karla Raven prepare his operation.

"We need a contingency," Falcon whispered. "Where are the vulnerabilities? What would they least expect? How do we turn their greatest strength against them?"

And, as Theresa Applegate and Major Marks insulted each other in the background, he closed his eyes, moving pieces around on the backs of his eyelids.

We got lucky. That thought fills my head as the world and timeline form around us. This isn't Egypt. Not by a long shot. The grassy plains stretching out in all directions are blanketed by a sea of hip-tall grass that ripples and runs like ocean waves in the wind. I have never seen so much grass. Nothing but grass; it extends in a golden-green to every horizon.

Around me, the quinque are muttering among themselves. They finger their gas guns, shift uneasily as they crush the tall grass beneath their anxious feet. In addition to the exhaustion, I can see the incipient panic in their eyes. It reflects in the set of their lips, the tension in their muscles.

Sak Puh, again, is on the verge of tears. She holds her cerebrum up, alternately glancing from the glowing blue display to the endless horizons of waving grass.

Overhead, a blinding sun boils down from a cloudless blue sky. Only a distant bird, some large thing, can be seen riding the high thermals.

"Imperator?" Publius asks. "Can this be right?"

I curse under my breath, check the readouts in my helmet. "At least, we're still on Earth."

"But where?" Sak Puh asks. "When?"

"Hard to tell."

"If we missed this one," Publius wonders, "what about the next jump?"

That very question is rolling around in the back of my mind. I squint up at the sun, as if the helmet didn't filter the light.

Again I take in the expressions of my team.

I have lost track of time. An almost humorless irony accompanies that thought. Nevertheless, it is true. So many timelines. A universe of them, in fact. We have been jumping almost continuously. From the well-charted ones to the fringe. The terrifying edge of probability where, but for blind luck, I might have just condemned us to eternal disaster. I don't let them see how frightened I am by our close call.

So, what do I do? We are running out of supplies. Each jump takes something out of us. My people are on the verge of collapse from exhaustion, and my scribe recorder is a simpering coward forever teetering on tears.

I toss my cloak back and prop my hand on my gladius where it hangs on my hip. I hope it's a striking pose. Something to hearten the quinque. For Sak Puh, nothing I can do will give her the pluck she needs. At least the data—*of inesti-mable value*—is recorded in her helmet. A record of all we have seen and done.

Returning to Ti'ahaule *isn't an unmitigated disaster.* We've mapped the jump data for six new timelines and sterilized five. Eliminated those possible threats to the safety and security of the Lords. All of it, laudable work. Just not within the scope of the mission. We have not accomplished our goals.

Fluvium and Nakeesh, their machines, and the inexorable Ennoia remain to be located. There is nothing for it but to return, rest for a week or so, and resume the chase with a new quinque *and a competent ah tz'ib.*

I turn back, giving them what I hope is a reassuring smile. "I can see no more prudent move than to return home."

The reaction is immediate. Smiles. Several of the legionarii start slapping each other on the back. I see huge relief flash across Sak Puh's face. It fades as quickly. She knows full well how disappointed and disgusted I am with her sim-pering weakness.

Though I doubt she knows just how much I despise her.

Or what it will cost her.

"Imperator?" Publius asks. "I know we haven't found Fluvium and the Domina. Or the missing navigators and cerebrums, but, well, do you think . . ."

"That you will qualify for Duo Gladii? I do. My recommendation to your consul will be for immediate promotion. You service has been exemplary."

The smiles are even broader.

I experience an odd churning in my stomach as I lift my navigator and acti-vate the holo. I begin entering the data, seeing that no. . . . I pause, getting a reading.

"Ah Tz'ib? Is your cerebrum reading this? Can you analyze it?"

With pinched lips, she studies her cerebrum's display. Nods. "It's a beacon, Imperator. And it's calibrated to your navigator."

"From this timeline?"

Sak Puh's head shakes as she reads the displayed data. "No. But, wherever it's coming from, I think we've just found Domina Nakeesh."

Victoria et tza'a. *Victory and success!*

60

Karla

Karla slapped the cocking lever with her left hand, hearing the bolt snap closed and into battery. She slung the HK MP-5 over her shoulder before grabbing up her first-line gear. There were newer sub guns, lighter, more modern, but she liked the MP-5. Could stake her life on it. Reliable as the tide, with just the right heft and controllability. Besides, this one was special. She'd liberated it during the infiltration of the Skientia compound in Aspen.

Beside her, Helen stood with hands on hips, inspecting the weapons locker with wary eyes. The woman had tied her auburn hair back in a ponytail, was wearing tactical pants, shirt, and vest. Clothing Karla had outfitted her in. Meant for Cat Talavera, the size was just about right for Helen.

"Good thing Cat's small," Karla told her.

"Actually, for my time, I was big." Helen cocked an eyebrow. "One of the few advantages of being in demand at the most prestigious brothel in Tyre was the food. While half the city suffered from malnutrition, I ate a balanced diet, sharing the finest of delicacies, meats, fish, nuts, and greens. Nutrition meant I was able to grow tall and strong."

Karla gave her a sidelong glance. "Hell of a price to pay, if you ask me."

Helen's lips twitched. "It was the only way of life I knew, Chief. At least until Simon came along."

"How'd that work?" Karla asked as she slipped spare magazines into her pack. "You said he bought you?"

Helen shrugged, taking down an M4; she cycled the bolt. "Can I take this one? Mine's back in Angel Fire. Didn't think you'd want me bringing it along."

"You know how it works?"

Helen pressed the release, the upper swinging free of the receiver. With quick fingers, she stripped the bolt, checked it, and slid it back into battery before snapping the M4 back together with an audible click. "Yeah, I can handle it."

"Where'd you pick up on the manual of arms?"

"In Martin's timeline." Helen began dropping loaded magazines into a pack she pulled down.

"That's a timeline parallel to ours, right? What were you doing there?"

"Looking for Alpha. She and Fluvium had to have gone somewhere, right? They didn't make it back to *Ti'ahaule*. Best bet was that they'd skipped to another timeline. Somewhere they thought was safe from Imperator. Martin and I had been searching. Tricky business, that. Jumping from timeline to timeline."

Helen rapped one of the magazines against the shelf to ensure the cartridges weren't bound before slapping it home and cycling the bolt. "Then, landing in yours, we got a hit on entangled particle generation. My navigator picked up on Nakeesh's jump when her navigator fixed on Los Alamos. By eavesdropping on Skientia's monitoring of Grazier's communications, we figured out the best place to take out Nakeesh would be your parking garage."

"And we know how that worked out. But get back to Simon Magus."

Helen pulled a ballistic vest from the stores, scowled as she held it to her chest to check size. The thing was way too big, and she discarded it. "You'd have to understand Hellenistic culture. Who the *hetaira* were. Best comparison? High-class call girls. A paid sexual companion who is educated, cultured, and socially skilled. Simon knew my reputation, that I'd read philosophy, history, and could recite poetry. That afternoon, when he and his friends arrived, he specifically asked for me. We spent the evening talking, bantering the nature of the soul, discussing the mystical origins of the universe, why Greek gods couldn't exist, arguing about history."

Helen smiled, having forgotten her pack. Her eyes had softened, a smile on her lips. "That was the first magical moment in my life. He and I, two halves that had been lost and searching. Halves that instantly fit together to make a whole. It hit us at the same moment. That this was a revelation. An understanding of God's creation: That male and female elements of the soul had to come together in unity before they could transcend the flesh and be resurrected into perfection."

She glanced at Karla. "You can imagine how a philosophy based on *that* went over with a bunch of conceited male-bastard Greeks and hyper-paternalistic arrogant Romans."

"About as well as it would with the Taliban?"

"You're getting there." Helen slipped her arms through a smaller ballistic vest, tightened the straps, and assessed it for fit. "That's one of the reasons I really despise your timeline. Simonian philosophy depends on the ability to think critically. That requires education, deliberation, the ability to compare differences and baseline assumptions rationally. Critical thinking. Concepts totally beyond your Christian founders like Hippolytus, Eusebius, that idiot Justin Martyr, or—corruption take him—that foul monster Constantine and his malignant line of narcissistic popes."

"And your timeline is filled with all these great—"

"My timeline is *dead*! Get it?" Helen wheeled to face her, green eyes hot. "Fluvium and Nakeesh destroyed it. Took me to see what it was becoming, right up to the moment Cedric Harmonium conducted his first entangled particle physics experiments. Then they handed me over to a *quinque* team, while the two of them went back and seeded an engineered Ebola on every continent. It's one of Fluvium's bio-warfare triumphs. You think the gain-of-function engineered into COVID was masterful? He designed his Ebola to be endemic in dogs, but lethal in humans. Took less than twenty years and every human in my timeline was dead."

Karla zipped her pack closed. "Jesus. What kind of sick—"

"Yeshua wasn't sick. A bit of a radical and a firebrand, perhaps, and way too political. Which is why the Romans had to take him out."

Karla shook her head. "You *met* him?"

"No. Simon studied with him, but that was before my time. They were both students of the man you call John the Baptist. The two of them studied Therapeutae magic at the same time in Alexandria. Yeshua was into action. Simon was more cerebral."

"Damn, you could rewrite the history books."

"Nope." Helen added a water bottle and IFAK—or "blow out"

medical kit—to her pack. "People don't want truth or facts. Makes them too uncomfortable. They'd rather believe the impossible stories and myths they've been fed for centuries by the ruling elite. Things like the virgin birth? That's a whole lot better than the fact that Yeshua was illegitimate. That Jesus' body vanished from the tomb? Better a miracle than the fact that his family removed it to keep it from being desecrated."

"That could get you mobbed in the streets."

Helen hesitated. "You got any gas masks in here?"

"Yeah, M53A1s are over there." Karla pointed. "Gas masks? Seriously?"

Helen ripped the carton open, pulling two of the packaged masks and tossing one to Karla. "Depends on which *quinque* Imperator brings."

Karla clipped on her holster, double-checked her HK .45, and snapped the restraining strap.

"You good to go?"

Helen slipped a Surefire flashlight into a loop on the outside of her pack. Checked to see that her navigator would fit the outside pocket. "That should do it." She studied Karla, eyes quizzical. "You really going to stake everything on Falcon? I mean, the guy's weird."

"Can you think of any way we can win this thing after Imperator meets up with Alpha?"

Helen pursed her lips, gaze thinning. She gave a slight shake of her head. "Win? No. But after I kill Nakeesh, you and I can still get out. I have a refuge. A timeline no one from *Ti'ahaule* has found yet. You'll have to learn another language, but the—"

"My team's here, *Ennoia*. SEALs don't run just 'cause the shit gets deep."

Helen nodded, muttered, "Figures. An infinite number of timelines to choose from, and I get stuck in one with a fucking hero."

"There's worse things."

Helen fixed her green gaze on Karla. "Falcon's . . . unique. Even after two thousand years. Any other time and place, they'd have stoned him to death as a witch. That, or he'd be locked away in some temple as an oracle making a bunch of fat priests a huge fortune in offerings."

"Just be happy the major, Theresa, and that piece of shit, Rudy Noyes, weren't there."

"Who are they?"

"Falcon's hallucinated alter egos. Different parts of his dissociated personality. Figments of his imagination that he believes are real." Karla hesitated. Grunted. "Hell, maybe, when you get to talking about Hilbert space, alternate realities, other worlds existing at angles to ours, maybe he's the sane one and the rest of us are nuts."

Helen's expression tightened. "You think this crazy plan of Falcon's is going to work?"

"No clue," Karla replied. "But it's the best we've got."

Helen headed for the door. "Like I told Ryan, immortality sucks. All right. But before I die, I *will* see Nakeesh's body lying dead on the floor. Beyond that, Imperator and his navigator are your responsibility."

"You tag Alpha, I'll take down this Imperator guy." Karla shouldered her pack and followed Helen out into the hallway.

"Right. Whatever," Helen told her. "Just be sure you don't forget what Falcon told you is the first priority."

Yeah, double-roger that, Karla thought. But Falcon had laid out the rules of engagement. What had to be done first. And, once that was taken care of, only then could she leave Imperator smoke-checked on the floor.

61

Childs

Lab One gave Hanson Childs the willies. Especially being this close to the time machine. At least someone had cleaned up the gore and removed the remains of Reid Farmer's body. But every time Childs stepped over the line where the divot had been, he felt a shiver run through him. A curious and unsettling queasiness in his muscles, bones, and nerves caused a tickle in the pit of his stomach.

Just so long as it isn't me who's cut in half by this thing next time.

Seeing the remains of Farmer's body had been spooky enough the first time. And he'd had Jaime to buck him up. But the second time, it had almost weirded him out to the point that, had Nakeesh not been his primary focus—someone to play off of—he'd have puked his guts out the way Tanner Jackson had.

Nakeesh led the way, Kaplan and Tanner Jackson following. Josh Mack's Talon guys, Cal Spicer and Al Allison, muscled the heavy doo-hickey down the stairs to the concrete, then set it on a dolly. Several technicians, dressed in overalls, were reattaching thumb-thick electrical cables to the time machine. They glanced up, wary eyes on Nakeesh as she strode imperiously past. But when Tanner walked by, they averted their eyes entirely.

What do they know that I don't?

But then, spending a night at Tanner Jackson's safe house in a Los Alamos suburb had given Hanson Childs a pretty good notion of the sort of man Jackson was. The thought of "human scorpion" had crossed Childs' mind a time or two.

Nakeesh, however, had seemed nonplussed. Even comfortable in the man's presence. As if she were almost dismissive of Tanner Jackson's creepy personality, or the fact that when he looked at Childs, it was as if he were an object. Disposable.

Childs followed at Nakeesh's back, casting worried glances at the time machine's curving arches; his image contorted in the concave mirrors. Made him wonder if that's who he was anymore. Just a monstrous and distorted reflection of the man he'd been before being detailed to this insanity.

Nakeesh's declaration of "He's mine!" still echoed in the back of Hanson Childs' mind. The way she'd said it, like he was property. *"Servus est."* What did that mean?

The feeling of drowning—that there was no way out—just kept spiraling him downward into the darkness. Ever down. And what happened to him when he finally found the depths? Hit rock bottom?

A glance at Chief of Staff Stevens, where he followed in the rear, was sufficient for Childs' cop sense. The guy was playing a deeper game. That look on his face reeked of victory. Sure, he'd told Nakeesh that she could hook up the machine to augment the doohickey's signal—and with Kaplan present to ensure that the machine didn't snap Nakeesh somewhere into the future, Stevens' expression was almost giddy with anticipation. The guy really thought that he was about to win it all.

Yeah, sure. Childs could almost believe it. Right up to the moment he caught a glimpse of Nakeesh's face. Call it implacable. Heartless. As if she, too, were about to commit an unforgivable act.

"What's the matter?" Childs asked as she laid her navigator on the elevated workstation. The others were just out of hearing.

"It is time," she told him. "Nothing left. Only one way to save Fluvium." With that, she waved her hand above the navigator, activating the blue holograph. Then, with a series of quick flicks of her fingers, she rearranged the icons.

Nakeesh glanced at Stevens and Jackson, who'd stopped a couple of steps up from the floor, well out of range of the time radius. Josh Mack and the rest of his Talon mercs blocked the stairs. Kaplan and the techs had finished connecting the electrical cables to the time machine. The doohickey had been plugged in, the lights on the control panel gleaming.

"You know we don't have the power to do a time run," Kaplan said as she stepped back and crossed her arms. "Domina, if you try and roll that much power, you'll trip the breakers."

Nakeesh spoke in a wooden tone. "There is enough for our purposes."

Childs saw her take a final glance at Stevens, before she asked, "You wish to meet Imperator?"

"I most certainly do," Stevens called from the steps. "I'm ready, willing, and able to do business."

"Yes," she said, resignation in her tone. "I'm sure you are."

Childs, keeping a close eye on the rest, watched her turn to the navigator. With a flick of her fingers, the holograph changed. A low whine sounded. The hairs on Childs' neck stood on end, as if he were in the corona of a high-voltage line. An eerie prickle shot along his nerves.

And faded.

"What just happened?" Tanner Jackson called.

"Felt like being on a ridge in a lightning storm," Stevens remarked. "Maxine? What do you get on the readings?"

"I'm not sure," she replied, frowning down at one of the computer screens. She tapped keys. "We definitely drew on the grid. Pulled some serious amperage. But it was only for a millisecond."

Childs stepped around, seeing the look in Nakeesh's cold blue eyes. How her jaw was set. "You all right?"

"No." She sighed. "It is done."

"What?"

"Tragoedia. Calamitas. Teehn Sahtik." Again the bitter smile. "I lose."

"Lose how?" Childs asked, taking her hand. Trying to comfort her obvious upset.

"Because Imperator wins," she told him softly, gaze fixed on some distance in her mind. "But Fluvium will live. It is a price worth paying."

"How soon will Imperator be here?" Stevens asked anxiously. He was tapping away at his phone, obviously texting.

Nakeesh glanced at her navigator where the Mayan glyphs and occasional Latin words were shifting. "He is already here."

"How's that possible?" Tanner shifted where he stood on the stairs, arms crossed. "You just sent the signal. Surely you can't expect the man to just appear in an instant."

Nakeesh breathed the word, *"stulti"* and shot a futile sidelong glance at Childs. "Perhaps terminating this timeline is a mercy. No one will weep for its loss."

"What do you mean, terminate?" Childs demanded, a sudden chill running through him. "You said Imperator was coming to rescue you. At the price of your freedom, sure. But terminate this timeline? How can anyone do that?"

"More ways than you know, *amore.*" That half-mocking smile was back.

"Hey," Stevens called, stepping down to the floor. "How will we know Imperator has arrived? Where will he appear? The president wants to be sure that he's appropriately greeted. We need to make the right impression. In fact, we'd like to hold a reception for him in the White House. For that, we'll need a complete—"

"I told you, he's here." Nakeesh snapped. She indicated the navigator with a slight cant of her head. "I will tell you as if you are a child: He and his *quinque* arrived the moment we sent the signal. Understand? Coming from another timeline, he can arrive at any moment he desires. Past, present, or future. What you call time . . ." She laughed bitterly, ". . . is a weapon we mastered long ago."

Unfazed, Stevens looked around, hands spread. "Then, where is he?"

As if on cue, the door at the top of the stairs swung open; two re-markably clad individuals—images of white and silver—each bearing curiously designed tube devices, stepped onto the upper landing. Like a well-rehearsed team, they cleared the area, including the row of chairs and upper workstations. Then, as they started down, two more entered and stepped to the side, as if taking stations.

Childs tried to place the garb. Like tunics, but with metallic shoulder pads, and each had a feather splay that stuck up from the upper arms. Instead of boots, they wore silver knee-high laced sandals. Their heads were contained in shiny gray helmets, each decorated by colorful de-signs on the side. Some sort of insignia. Reminded him of the sorts of designs that had been painted on shields in the Middle Ages.

And then came a single figure. Tall, wearing a white tunic that ex-tended to the knees. A riot of rainbow-colored feathers, arranged in splays, rose behind each shoulder. A gleaming gem-encrusted breastplate covered his chest. Even more elaborate sandals clad the man's feet. What looked like a thick sheet or robe was wrapped around the man's shoulders to hang in graceful folds. The arms were bare, tattooed in intricate designs, gleaming gold-and-silver armbands on the biceps. The wrists bore some sort of cuffs or guards, each glinting with what looked like gemstones. What had to be a navigator was cradled in his ring-jeweled hands.

In a wooden, almost listless tone, Nakeesh said, "Imperator. The final stone is cast."

Childs couldn't make out the great man's helmet-shadowed features. Took him a moment to identify the helmet's design. He'd studied Ancient Greeks when he was boy. It hit him that this thing had the look of an old Corinthian-style helmet. The kind with the noseguard, flared cheekpieces, and football-shaped eyeholes. And the shell seemed to glow. As if it radiated an aura all its own.

What appeared to be an aide followed immediately behind him. Not so stunningly dressed, the woman's tunic wasn't as glistening white. Her feather splays looked to be made from some hawk, falcon, or maybe even eagle feathers. Her helmet—also with a silver-bronze sheen—was studded with electronics. A thick chrome tube, maybe a meter in length, like a map case, was slung across her back. The holograph played in translucent blue haze above the cerebrum she carried. Like Nakeesh, the woman had piercing eyes, black as midnight, a pinched expression on what could be seen of her triangular brown face.

The first escorts had stopped, raising their tube devices as they studied Eugene Chalmers and Cal Spicer who blocked the stairs.

"Stevens! Call your men down," Nakeesh ordered. "Do it now. They are not to interfere."

"You heard the lady," Stevens ordered. "Josh, get your people down here to the floor."

"Do it," Mack called. "Let them come."

Off to the side, Kaplan asked Tanner Jackson, "Why didn't we feel that weird prickle? Like when Nakeesh popped in the first time, or when she used the time machine?"

Mack's security guys slowly backed down the stairs, filing in behind Stevens and Jackson. They kept a wary distance from the time machine, all the while fingering their pistols, sending withering glances at the bizarrely dressed newcomers.

"What the hell are they wearing?" Jackson asked.

"Vestimenta urbana," Nakeesh replied. *"B'uk kokonob.* Civilized clo-thing."

"Looks like they're missing from the wardrobe department in a bad Hollywood movie," "Dirty Harry" Logan muttered.

"Enough," Stevens barked. Then he stepped forward, starting up the stairs. Hands outstretched, he called. "Imperator, welcome. I am Chief of Staff Bill Stevens. On behalf of the United States of—"

He'd only made it up three steps before a hollow pop sounded from one of the tubes the escorts carried. What looked like a puff of powder exploded in a ring around Stevens' face. The man jerked, went limp, and toppled backward like he'd been poleaxed. But for Josh Mack catching him, easing him down, he'd have smashed the back of his head on the concrete.

"Oh, shit!" Childs muttered as Josh Mack's team clawed for their pistols.

62

Karla

"**G**ot it!" Helen cried as her navigator's holo projected glowing blue icons. "Major incursion at the lab in Los Alamos. My guess? Imperator's here."

Karla leaped to her feet, knocking her chair back. So much for finishing supper. And tonight's meal had been filet of sole with cornbread and spinach. She hadn't had a chance to catch much of a lunch.

"Go," ET told her. The computer super geek sat at the table to her right. "And, hey, Chief. You come back, huh? Need you to keep my skinny ass out of trouble."

Around them, the cafeteria had frozen, forks halfway to mouths, the clatter of plates and conversation silent as people stared.

Helen was in the process of slipping her arms through the straps in her pack. Her gaze remained fixed on her navigator's holo display even as she slung the M4 to hang muzzle-down from its sling.

Ryan and Savage leaped to their feet where they'd been eating at the next table.

Karla swung her pack into place, clicked her MP-5 to its sling. She gave Savage a nod, knocked off a quick salute to Grazier, calling, "See you on the other side, sir."

"Hey!" Ryan had a half-panicked look. "You be careful, Chief. Whatever you run into, don't—"

"Roger that, sir!" Karla—heart doing flips and twists—glanced at Helen. "Got your shit wired?"

The woman blinked green eyes. "Got my . . . what?"

"Just say yes." Karla slapped the woman on the shoulder. To the others, she called, "Hey! Give us some room! Anyone in the zone is going to find themselves flat, fucked, and stupid on the floor! Now, clear out."

She watched the mass exodus as people ran for the doors. Word about the effects of teleporting had apparently made the rounds.

Karla fixed her gaze on the glowing blue symbols above the cerebrum as she picked it up. "Tell me when to put my finger on the blue button."

Taking a deep breath, Helen placed her finger on a glowing orb in her navigator's display. "Any time, Chief."

Karla—heart hammering at the bottom of her throat—reached out. Damn, for a woman who'd jumped out of aircraft, swam miles underwater in pitch-black conditions, been blown up by an IED, shot, shit at, and hit, why was she so jumpy?

She felt the eerie tingle and touched the blue glow that looked sort of like a button. Not that her finger felt anything but . . .

Falling . . .

Being torn apart . . . turned inside out . . .

Agony . . .

Cold . . .

And then lights.

Gravity.

Karla staggered, got her feet under her as her balance returned. The weight of the cerebrum—the only constant—reassured her where it was supported by her left hand. Helen was right beside her. Still holding her navigator and totally solid.

The world began to weave itself out of nothingness around them. Fading into being like stringers of mist spun of a gray haze. Call it batshit strange, like reality solidified around her out of nothingness. And the weirdest part? That sensation that she was the middle of it. That existence was establishing itself around her, and somehow, she was the epicenter.

Karla's heart still hammered, her throat gone dry, a trembling in her muscles. And—wow. After the chaos of the transport, she had the oddest sensation of jubilance, almost a giddy adrenal high.

As the last of the solidification took place, she found herself in the Skientia building. Third Floor. Right over there—next to the stairs—was the maintenance closet where she and Savage had cut through the roof. And yonder was the door behind which Reid Farmer and Yusif had been tortured and held.

Helen dropped to a knee, slipping her pack off and sliding her navigator into the side pocket. "Don't have much time, Chief. Gawk later."

Karla shivered, shook it off, and snapped her cerebrum into the side pocket on her own pack. "What now?"

"My bet? They'll be using gas guns rather than flechettes. Imperator won't want to use lethal force until he knows who's on whose side."

"Roger that." Karla stripped the mask out of its container, checked the filters, and slipped the straps over her head. As she did, she wondered what else Helen might know but hadn't bothered to tell her.

Still making it up as we go.

And that worried her.

"All right, *Ennoia*," Karla told the woman. "It's about to get real hairy. So, no bullshit, what are the rules of engagement? My call is to smoke-check each invader, right up to Imperator. So, what's the word on 'shoot no-shoot?'"

"Follow my lead." Helen's voice was muffled by the mask. "And remember what Falcon told you is the priority."

"Yeah. We're clear on that." Karla reshouldered her pack, bringing the MP-5 up. She started for the stairs, remembering the cameras, wondering if they were already being followed by whoever's security now controlled Skientia.

Damn, woman, she told herself. *You just teleported across a couple hundred miles. And you were awake to remember it!*

Talk about a game changer.

If she lived.

If Imperator and his goons hadn't been warned that their security had been breached.

A lot could still go sideways and south with this whole operation.

And she had to trust Helen, which was going to be really hard to do.

But they made it down the stairs without issue. No one had bothered to fix the bullet scars from the last time she'd passed this way. When she slipped the first-floor door open and used her mirror to scan the hallway, it was to find no waiting assailants.

Helen following, Karla humped it to the Lab One door. Last time she did this, Bill Minor had burst out and damned near killed her. This time—as she sidled up to the door—no one came barging out. Karla gave Helen the wait signal. Reached into her pack, she pulled out one of the small canisters—the latest version of Cat Talavera's knockout gas. She reached for the door, pushed it open the slightest bit, and dropped the canister inside.

"Five, four, three, two, one," she counted. "And the good news is that with masks, we don't even have to hold our breath."

To her surprise, Helen stepped around, and—muttering something in Greek Karla couldn't understand—pushed the door open wide. Karla followed, her establishing glance taking in the two bizarrely dressed people lying inert at the head of the stairs. Cat's gas had worked like a charm. She'd catalog the robes, helmets, silver sandals, and metallic breastplates later.

Her next concern was the corners. "Clear," she called from habit as she searched the line of empty chairs and the neighboring workstation. Then she focused her attention on the stairs.

People were still turning, looking up in surprise. More silver-dressed aliens—might as well call them that—were in formation around a central figure in flowing white. Looked like a tall man with a gaudy silver-bronze helmet covering most of his head. Weirdest of all were the colorful splays of feathers pinned to stand up in sunbursts behind his shoulders. And the long flowing robe around his shoulders might have come off the Hollywood set from *Ben Hur.*

At the foot of the stairs, a muscular man was on one knee, cradling Chief of Staff Stevens' limp body. Tanner Jackson was to the left. Alpha, that shit-bag Hanson Childs, and Kaplan were off to the right side by the elevated control panel. A bunch of security types—Talon mercs, had to be—in tac dress, hands on pistols, were crowded around what had to be the time machine.

And that was a fricking shock. Last time Karla had been here, it was a hole in the concrete.

Helen charged down the steps, bellowing something that sounded Mayan, the words slightly muffled by the M51 mask.

The uppermost aliens spun on their heels, lifting some kind of tube weapons. The things—stolen from a sci-fi film's prop department—snapped off shots, puffs of gas exploding in a ring before Karla's face.

Helen's M4 banged out a three-round burst. Then another, the reports and bullets' supersonic crack reverberating and deafening in the room.

Both aliens crumpled, weapons clattering; their comrades retreated from the limp bodies that tumbled down a couple of steps before sprawling limbs stopped them.

The remaining aliens stared in horror.

"Desisterte!" Helen bellowed from behind the shouldered M4.

"Sacra sputi!" Alpha cried. *"Ennoia est! Morite!"*

Karla glimpsed Alpha's movement as she pulled a black semiautomatic from behind her waist. Then the aliens—six of them—came rushing up the stairs. As they charged, their tube guns were spitting pellets that exploded into rings of iridescent gas.

Helen's M4 opened with a full burst.

Falcon's words echoed in Karla's mind. *"Don't forget the objective!"*

She lifted the MP-5, waited, and as the guards stumbled, jerked, and fell under the assault of Helen's concentrated fire, saw her opening.

The guy in the ancient-looking Greek helmet was gaping in disbelief. Had to be Imperator. Even as the guy lifted the device he held, and a blue holo gleamed to life above it, Karla got her sight picture. Stopped to settle her aim and dropped her finger to the trigger.

The MP-5 chattered, a string of golden brass rising high as the cases ejected. She'd placed her shots perfectly, seeing Imperator's white toga flutter from the impact. The shot string rose in recoil, nine-millimeter slugs hammering into the navigator the man held, smashing it from his hands. The impact rolled him backward, sent him falling. He hit on his back, bounced, and tumbled down the stairs in a jumble of white robes, banging helmet, and flying silver calf-high sandals.

A black-haired woman, helmeted, with terrified, wide eyes, had dropped to a hunched ball, cradling a cerebrum to her breast. The gleaming chrome tube on her back clattered and caught awkwardly on the stairs.

Karla took a breath, tripped the mag release, and slammed a new mag into the well. With a deft left hand, she slapped the cocking piece down. Turning her attention to the security guys—had to have been Tanner Jackson's Talon goons—she settled the front sight post on Stevens, shouting, "First one of you who moves, Stevens gets smoked!"

Helen was advancing down the stairs. The M4 trained on the writhing and dying aliens. So this was the notorious *quinque*? The implications hadn't sunk in, but Karla had that uneasy feeling that shit had come down too fast. That Helen better be fucking goddamned right about shooting first, talking later.

A pistol shot popped.

The bullet hit with a slapping sound. Helen staggered, almost dropped the M4. Karla caught sight of Alpha as the tall woman bent, turned. A black HK kept popping covering shots from her right hand, Alpha used her left to poke a finger into the blue haze on the elevated workstation beside her.

In that instant, Alpha stuffed the pistol into her waist and reached for Hanson Childs' hand.

Karla felt the prickle.

Instinctively, she dropped to a knee. Swung her HK in Alpha's direction and triggered the gun. The MP-5s deafening racket vanished as Karla jerked, euphoria burning electric through her body. Then a sinking feeling in her gut as she went weightless.

And fell into a stygian blackness that . . .

She blinked. Coming to. Experienced the electric tingling of every nerve in her body. Why had she ever called this orgasmic?

Oh, yeah. She knew this. Had felt it the first time when Alpha had transported out of her high-security room in Grantham Barracks.

Karla groaned, forced herself to remember where she was.

A glance told her: Skientia Lab One. But this time, the Alpha's fantastic time gizmo was still dominating the floor. A bunch of guys were passed out around the doohickey, guns scattered from limp fingers. Kaplan, Tanner Jackson, and Stevens were sprawled at the landing. All down the stairs, a bunch of shiny, silver-clad, helmeted aliens were bleeding a very familiar crimson that spread on their clothes and leaked onto the steps.

"*Kopros kai uros!*" Helen—piled in disarray at Karla's side—gasped as she sat up. Her face a mask of pain. The woman reached over, pulled at her shirt where it was tucked in. Tensed with pain.

"Alpha shot you," Karla told her. "Pull your shirt open. I need to see where you're hit."

When Helen did, it was to show the impact low and left. But for the vest it would have taken out the woman's colon and kidney.

Karla collected her MP-5 where it hung from its sling. Fought her way to her feet, and started to pick her way down the stairs. As she stepped around the bodies, she took stock of the dead and dying aliens. Any question of Helen's proficiency with an automatic rifle was moot. She'd taken them out with center-of-mass bursts.

The white-dressed woman with the tube had tumbled down a couple of steps, was coming to, gasping, fingers spasming where she'd dropped the cerebrum. Karla fought the impulse to snatch it up, stuff it into her pack.

Falcon's voice echoed from within. *"Don't forget the mission."*

Karla pulled her HK .45; the USP's bang echoed around the room as she shot the thing dead center. The 185-grain slug knocked the device off the step to clatter down onto the concrete below, bits of qubit lattice spilling like powder out of the hole she'd blown in the cerebrum's top.

The woman in white cried out, clapping her hands to her helmeted head, wincing, no doubt at the ringing in her ears.

The people on the floor below began moaning and shifted, some reaching for their heads. Blinking.

"Son of a bitch," Karla muttered.

Alpha and Hanson were gone.

Imperator's smashed navigator still lay two steps up from the bottom, but of Imperator?

There was no trace.

63

Childs

After surviving the sensation of his body falling through eternity while his limbs were disintegrating and being jerked from their sockets, Hanson Childs somehow landed upright. The first thing he knew was that his feet were on a floor. Second was Nakeesh clutching his hand. Glancing down, he was reassured to see her fingers interlaced with his. Raising his gaze, it was to see her, brow furrowed as she stared at the holo projected by her navigator.

Around him, the haze—that eerie nacre that had appalled him the first time he'd seen it—began to fade, weirdly replaced by bits, wisps, and streamers of . . . Well, okay, reality. Like the world was assembling itself around him.

And the image that was piecing itself together? Somehow familiar. As reality formed of combining atoms, it merged into the Pojoaque house. The living room—complete with the copper breakfast bar—leading into the kitchen where he'd made breakfast for Nakeesh.

"What are we doing here?" Childs demanded.

"Only place to go," Nakeesh told him.

Childs started to turn, leaped back. A body lay on the Saltillo tiles at his feet. A man in silver armor, a swirl of milky white cape beneath him. Remarkable iridescent feathers in rainbow colors stood up like fans from his shoulders. A colorful—but bullet-damaged—breastplate, sort of like a Hebrew hoshen but with gems cut in the shape of Mayan glyphs, lay on his chest. The man was tall, his head covered by a Corinthian-style helmet that seemed to glow either golden or silver, depending on the light.

The man let out a shuddering gasp, tried to draw up one leg, and moaned.

The action caused his robe to fall to one side, exposing an ornate short sword in a bejeweled scabbard that was clipped to the right side of his thick equipment belt with its assorted pouches and cases.

Nakeesh let loose of Childs' hand, bending down and calling, "Imperator?" She followed that with a string of what Childs had come to understand was Yucatec mixed with Latin.

"*Inferni et Xibalba*," the man told her through a pained exhale, invoking both the Mayan and Roman hells.

Nakeesh looked to Childs. "Hanson, help me. We need to get him to the bed. Get his armor off. See how badly Imperator is hurt."

Childs bent down, got a grip under the man's armpit, feeling some tough fabric beneath. Trying to keep from fouling the gaudy feather splays, he helped Nakeesh pull the guy up, heard the man's choked cry.

Getting an arm over the man's shoulder, Childs, with Nakeesh's help, walked the staggering Imperator down the hall to the master bedroom. Setting him on the bed, he helped Nakeesh unclip the feather splays and remove the silky white cape that had draped so artistically from the man's shoulders. With deft fingers, Nakeesh unclasped the sword belt. Childs lifted him as she pulled it out from beneath.

All the while, Nakeesh kept up a running dialog, her voice matter-of-fact. Not for the first time did Childs wish he knew was she was saying. Whatever it was, it sounded tense. Had to be after the disastrous attack in Lab One. The scope of the calamity was just hitting home.

With careful fingers, Nakeesh eased the massive helmet from the man's head. Childs got a glimpse of what looked like a thick web of electronics and interfaces where padding didn't obscure the interior.

The man revealed had close-cropped hair with a clean-shaven jaw. His wide-set eyes were a light brown, nose and chin knobby. Complexion was what Childs would have called Mediterranean. Despite the expression of pain, the man was studying him with a look of total disdain, and asked, "*Germania?*"

"*Non.*" Nakeesh told him. "American. *Novus populus.*" Then she rattled off some more before adding, "*Nomen* Hanson Childs *est. Meus servus.*"

Imperator's lips flickered with an attempt to hide his pain. "*Fidelus est?*"

"*Certe,*" she told him with a wry smile. "*Et similis cum tauri quando copluatamus.*"

Childs winced. Could feel his ears burning red. She'd used the phrase when they'd been screwing. Had told him in essence, that he fucked like a bull. It barely got a chuckle out of Imperator, but it made Hanson Childs damned uncomfortable.

Following Nakeesh's instructions, he helped her peel the man's underlying silver suit from his arms and torso. The center of it, over the lower chest and abdomen, was hard as steel. And, damn, it covered an ugly bruise that was red and blue-black. No wonder the guy was hurting. Which made sense since Childs had seen Karla Raven unload most of a magazine into Imperator's midriff.

"Nice armor," he admitted, running the light fabric over his fingers. How did the stuff react, being that thin, to protect from repeated impacts from close-range nine-millimeter slugs? Whatever it was, the fabric had saved Imperator's life.

Then, stripping the man's legs down to his silky undershorts, Childs helped Nakeesh settle him on the oversized bed. He was propping the man's head on the pillows when he noticed that the spread was different.

He looked around. "Um, Nakeesh? Someone's been here."

She nodded. "I know. Maybe the people come back? Someone bought the house?"

"We can't stay here."

Nakeesh sighed, rubbed her temples. One of the few times he'd seen her looking overwhelmed. "What can we do? Imperator needs time to fix. Couple of days for medicines to work, *si*?"

And with that, she retrieved the man's belt, pulled it around until she could open one of the ornate cases. From a collection, she removed one of the small syrettes. This she jabbed into the center of the wicked bruise.

Imperator gave a grunt, followed a couple of seconds later by a relaxed sigh. Then his expression softened, his breathing coming easier.

Childs made sure to remember which pouch that was.

"Come," Nakeesh told him, rising and leading the way into the living room.

"How'd he get here?" Childs asked. "You had my hand. I get that. And your navigator used the doohickey and time machine to augment its capability. But Imperator was lying on the floor."

"His, *Kohaw*. Um, *galea* in Latin." She made a gesture of encircling her head. "What is word?"

"Helmet." And suddenly the electronics he'd seen made sense. "He can link to your navigator?"

"*Certe.* And more. Has sensors, translator, optics, communications. Does many things."

"I don't get the style. Seriously. The best your Imperator can do is that garish antique Corinthian design? Makes him look like he's from the fifth century BC. And what's with the stubby little sword?"

Nakeesh picked up her navigator where she'd left it on the couch. "First thing: Imperator *is* Corinthian. Though from my time." She shrugged. "He is Imperator. He can be as, what did you say? Garish? *Si.* He can be that. Who will tell him otherwise?

"Second thing? His helmet has lots of room for what you call qubit computer space. He has more data processing than your entire planet. Almost as much as cerebrum and navigator together."

"And the sword?"

"It is . . ." She frowned. "Um, like rank of office. A symbol, yes? Is styled to be exact replica of Lucas Magna Nauta's *gladius.* The one he carried on his first crossing of ocean to what you call South America. The one Magna Nauta wore when he met the first *Ahau.* It signifies that Imperator can travel to any place, across any distance, to do the bidding of the *Ultima Ahau,* and that he is a warrior of *Ti'ahaule.*"

Yeah, Childs thought. Lot of good that did him.

Now, looking around, Childs could sure as hell see that someone was living here. Coffee cups were out, magazines on the breakfast bar. Dishes in the sink. Not good.

"We've got to get out of here." He stalked through the kitchen, opened the door to the garage, and nodded. "Well, at least they brought the Escalade back." He fished in his pocket, finding the key fob and pushed the button to hear the door locks cycle. They were good to go.

"They come, we shoot," Nakeesh told him as she tapped the pistol shoved in her waist.

Childs took a deep breath. Turned and faced her. "Listen to me. Think. We kill these people, we're going to be in the center of an erupting fountain of shit. You get it? Law enforcement is already looking for us for murdering Jaime and Meyer. Any more bodies, and we'll become a media sensation. If that happens, you know what? We're not making it back to *Ti'ahaule*. We're not making it out of this house, unless it's in body bags or handcuffs."

"So, what?" she asked bitterly. "Hanson, we are cut off. Do you understand? The *Ennoia* destroyed Imperator's navigator. They have taken his *ah tz'ib* prisoner along with her cerebrum. Killed or captured the *quinque*. Maybe I killed *Ennoia*. Maybe she lived. What was bad is now worse."

"Hey, we got wheels," he told her. "And the seats in the Escalade lean back so we can make a bed for Imperator. But first I need a hammer and screwdriver. Once I disable the vehicle's GPS and tracker, all we need are different license plates. A bunch of rattle cans of spray paint, and someplace out of the way where I can work on the car."

"And then what?" she demanded.

"Then we go after the people who attacked us."

"The *Ennoia*? You know where she is?"

"Got an idea," Childs told her. "I wouldn't have known the *Ennoia* from Eve's second sister. But that woman who was with her? The tall one with black hair? The one that tried to kill Imperator? That was Chief Petty Officer Karla Raven."

He smiled. "And, *amore*, I think I know just where to find her."

Nakeesh studied him thoughtfully.

Childs heard it first. The sound of a vehicle in the driveway. Headlights flashed on the curtains. Childs leaped to the window, peered past the shade to see an Acura MDX pulling in. The garage's overhead door could be heard as it ground slowly open.

Nakeesh pulled the pistol from her waistband and headed for the garage.

64

Ryan

"**S**o, just how bad is it?" I asked as I stepped down from Winny's new coaxial Sikorsky helicopter. She'd set the Defiant down on the Skientia Lab helipad just out from the lab's front doors. Didn't matter that it was new and state of the art. My stomach was still fluttering and jumping. And that was with less than half the airtime the Blackhawk would have necessitated.

Karla Raven waited by the door, dressed in tactical gear, her HK sub gun hanging from its sling; she stood with a cocked hip in the glow of the big Sikorsky's landing lights, her black hair back in a severe ponytail. A fire burned behind her gray eyes.

Behind me, Eli Grazier hopped down, took a moment to straighten his uniform jacket. As if there was anyone to see. It was the middle of the night.

Karla banged off a salute to Grazier, turned her attention to me. "We're in the middle of a shitstorm, sir. Got three dead aliens, and three alive and bound. One's Imperator's scribe, or administrative second. Two are part of a *quinque* team. Helen's shot, but her vest took the impact. Got Chief of Staff Stevens and a bunch of Talon security personnel in zip ties, and just for pissing me off, I've got Maxine Kaplan and Tanner Jackson bound to desk chairs with duct tape. Ran out of zip ties."

A pause. "But, as per Falcon's instructions, we've got Imperator's navigator and cerebrum." She grinned. "Turns out the things aren't bulletproof."

"No sign of Alpha, Imperator, or Childs?" Grazier asked.

"Sir. No, sir," Karla told him crisply. "Wherever they teleported to, it wasn't in the Lab One building."

Eli asked, "Chief, how is this anything but an unmitigated cluster fuck?"

"We're still here, sir." Karla's lips quirked. "Weirdest sit-rep I've ever given, but as long as we're standing here, and I'm bitchin' to the head shed, means we're still in the game, sir. Alpha and Imperator haven't won. Falcon's plan is working."

"She has a point, Eli," I told him.

He resettled his hat, pulling it down tight, and pointed a finger at the lab. "Ben Masters' chief of staff is in there. Tied up with zip ties you say?"

Karla, standing at attention, said, "Sir. Yes, sir. Seemed the thing to do, sir."

Eli stroked his thick jaw. "I'm in a goddamned shooting war with the president's chief of staff. And you've just yanked the son of a bitch's shorts up over his head."

Figured that Eli would be more focused on the political ramifications. I asked, "What about Alpha and Imperator? Any clue where they might have gotten off to?"

"No, sir. But Helen insists that with Imperator's navigator shot to hell, they can't have skipped the timeline. Somehow, the doohickey, or maybe the time machine, or some combination of both, allowed them transport. But Helen insists that they're still here. That Falcon was right. Take out the navigator and cerebrum, and they're stranded." She took a deep breath. "Sir, I center-punched Imperator while I was taking out his navigator. Thought I'd killed him. But Helen tells me the guy wears armor. Must be tough stuff because I found the bullets scattered on the stairs. Still should have bruised the hell out of him. And he's got most of his *quinque* either captured or lying dead in Lab One. Wherever he is, he's really pissed off, sir."

"At least we have prisoners," Eli mused. "That's a start. I want to see them. Now."

"Yes, sir," Karla told him. "Most of the Talon mercs are locked in a basement storeroom. The aliens, Stevens, Kaplan, and Jackson are under Helen's watchful eye in the main conference room."

Lowering her window, Winny called down from the pilot's seat, "Orders, sir?"

"Be ready to dust off at a moment's notice, Major," Eli called. "Consider the situation superfluid."

"Roger that." Winny was grinning as she actually managed a semblance of a salute.

"Where the hell is my security team?" Eli stormed as we entered the lab's front door.

"According to Stevens," Karla told him, "they were sent orders to evacuate the premises this morning. Their orders were to report to DC, and that transport was awaiting them at Kirtland Air Force Base." She checked her watch. "They should just about be wheels down at Andrews by now."

"Stevens!" Eli almost spit the name.

I gave him a wary sidelong glance. Psychopaths like Eli may not feel remorse or empathy, but they are cunning, keep score, and definitely bear a grudge. "Think this through," I told him.

His dark eyes flashed my way. "I'm never an idiot, Ryan."

Karla led the way past reception, down the hall, to the plush corporate boardroom with its exotic-wood table. Entering, I found Helen propped on the coffee table in the room's corner, the pistol grip of her M4 clutched tightly in her right hand, left supporting the forearm. Her cold green gaze was fixed on the people seated at the long table. From her expression I could tell Helen was in pain. Had to be after her ballistic vest had stopped a slug.

Sitting prominently in the middle of the table were the bullet-smashed remains of a navigator and cerebrum. Harvey Rogers would be so delighted to have a look inside.

"Grazier!" Stevens barked, his arms straining where thick silver tape bound them behind him. "When I'm done with you, you're going to be rotting in a cell so far underground, you'll be hearing Chinese through the floor. Do you know what kind of—"

"*Shut up!*" Helen snapped, raising her M4, lips grimacing from pain. "I don't give a shit who you think you are. I said no talking."

Stevens paled when the muzzle settled in line with his face.

"Stand down," Eli told her, raising a calming hand.

Helen gave him a bitter smile. "The moron thought he was going to open diplomatic relations with *Ti'ahaule*. Honestly, do you people live in the golden age of stupid, or what?"

I think her reply actually amused Eli. Maybe because no one *ever* used that tone of voice with him, or because anything derogatory about Stevens tickled him.

I took the opportunity to catalog the other people seated at the long table. Maxine Kaplan might have been chewing tenpenny nails as she sat, her entire body encased in silver duct tape. She'd barely glanced up and was now glaring at the table's woodgrain. I had no clue who the muscular guy was in the seat next to hers, but whoever had tied him into the chair had taken no chances. Talon merc, had to be. Then came Tanner Jackson. The lights were shining on his bald potato head; the guy looked pale, half sick behind his thick-lensed glasses. Unnerved. Given the bloodbath in Lab One that Karla had described, maybe that wasn't so far off.

To his left a woman, maybe late twenties, in a white outfit with silver shoulder pads backed by gaudy feather splays that looked like spreading wings, seemed really out of place. Thick black hair tumbled down her back. She had a triangular face, and from her complexion and features, she looked Mayan. Not only that, but she had a powerful presence behind those glowing black eyes and shared that haunting charisma common to Helen and Alpha. Her gaze kept going longingly to the helmets that were stacked in the corner of the room. What looked like weapons were piled beside them.

To her left were two young men, both glowing with health, looking fit, and wearing silver outfits They, too, had feather splays at the shoulders. One of the guys looked Central American, the other might have been another Mayan. If I knew anything about expressions, they were both traumatized, angry, shocked, and more than a little stunned.

But then, a bunch of what Alpha would call *stulti* had just murdered most of their fellows, shot up their Imperator, and taken them prisoner.

"So, these are the aliens?" Eli asked, walking down the length of the table.

Helen said, "The woman's name is Resplendent Reed, or *Sak Puh* in her language. She's also Imperator's aide, or second. The official term is *ah tz'ib*. Her job is to record everything that transpires on a jump. Most of the com gear is contained in her helmet. Additionally, she serves as Imperator's personal attendant, sees to his needs, ensures his orders are carried out. You name it."

On hearing her name, the woman shot a scathing glare Helen's way. The look she gave the rest of us was truly baleful.

Eli studied her. "Do you understand English?"

"They do not," Helen said. "Remember. In their timeline, Rome didn't fall. Britain remained a province. No Saxons, Danegeld, or Norman conquest. English is a term from a language they've never heard."

"How do we communicate?" Eli asked.

"Through me," Helen told him. "The computer in her helmet has a language program, but it needs time to analyze vocabulary, syntax, grammar, structure, as well as body language and facial expressions. My advice however is that you don't let her put it back on."

"Grazier," Stevens cried. "For God's sake, man, let's be reasonable. Do you realize what just happened here? What these women have gotten us into? They've *murdered* foreign emissaries who have come to us from—"

"I told you to shut the fuck up!" Helen snapped, shifting her M4 to cover Stevens. To Karla, she said, "Can I just shoot him for being an idiot?"

"He's the president's chief of staff," Eli told her sympathetically. "It wouldn't be wise."

Stevens rolled his eyes. In a calm voice, he said, "Eli, I'm telling you, we can work together. Come on, man. You've been DOD's liaison with DARPA. You, better than anyone, understand the implications of Imperator's technology. With it, we can change the world. Reestablish—"

"They're here to kill you," Helen told him. "Get it? This entire lab, it's a threat to them. Like your nuclear technology was to the Russians in 1945. Think—supposed Chief of Staff Stevens—what would the world be like today if only the US had nuclear weapons? Hmm? You'd be the big dog, able to dictate to all the other nations. But in comparison to entangled particle technology, a hydrogen bomb is just piddling. With time travel and entanglement, you control everything. You don't like Grazier? Send someone from another timeline back to slip a birth control pill into his grandmother's iced tea ten months before his mother is born. You get it?"

I saw the glint of understanding in Stevens' eyes.

"Yes, you're catching on," I told Stevens as I took a position across the table from him. "That kind of ultimate power. Currently, *Ti'ahaule* controls it. They'll do anything to stop its spread or discovery in other timelines."

"Better believe him," Helen told the man. "You're playing out of your league."

Eli was pinching the bridge of his nose. Under the room lights, I could see the fatigue, the swelling under his eyes. "All right, people. Let's think. We stopped the *quinque*. Imperator is now just as stuck as Alpha is."

"Alpha has a navigator, but no way to get a cerebrum unless she can get to Helen's." I shot a warning look at Eli and Helen. No sense in letting out that another cerebrum was no farther away than Grantham.

Helen—an eye narrowed—said, "I'll blow it up before either of those slime lays a finger on it."

I turned to Kaplan, who was still obviously mad enough to spit staples. "Maxine, as you understand it, can Alpha and Imperator jump back to the *Ti'ahaule* timeline just by using the doohickey and the time machine as amplifiers?"

She considered, probably thinking of what kind of profanity she wanted to throw my way, then said, "I don't think so. If she could, she would have used those devices to go home last time. My guess is that she's got to have the cerebrum's computational abilities to make a safe time jump. Nothing in our timeline can handle the kind of data necessary."

"She's right," Helen agreed. "A cerebrum is their ticket back to *Ti'ahaule*. And Imperator knows it."

Turning my attention to Helen, it was to see a cold calculation behind her eyes. As if she was thinking three steps ahead of the rest of us.

"Thoughts?" I asked her.

"You really going to bet everything on crazy old Falcon?"

I glanced at Eli, nodded. "It's endgame, Helen. And the bodies are just starting to pile up."

65

Childs

Being well trained as an observer had its benefits: On the trip up from Albuquerque with Chenwith, Hanson Childs had seen both the auto parts place and the sporting goods megastore. Leaving Nakeesh in the Escalade to care for Imperator, he'd stopped at both, checking out with his purchases as the lights were being shut off.

He just prayed that his luck would continue to hold.

Turned out that, back in Pojoaque, Phyllis and Stew Steingarten had been most accommodating people. Though he suspected that Nakeesh holding her .45 had something to do with it. They'd parked the Acura, collected sacks of groceries from the back seat, and walked into the kitchen, checking the security system by the door on the way in. Reassured that no one had broken into their house while they'd been shopping, they had no clue.

Turns out that transporting into a residence from another location via navigator wasn't covered by the security company's technology. Who would have guessed?

After dropping their purchases on the table, Stew and Phyllis had turned, both horrified to find Nakeesh pointing her HK .45 at them.

When Childs had explained that either they could allow him to tie them up and restrain them, or he could let Nakeesh shoot them both on the spot, the Steingartens had been most cooperative. Though Stew had explained that—being a partner in a large Pittsburgh law firm—the consequences would ultimately be severe. Fine, he could file suit once Childs and Nakeesh were back in *Ti'ahaule.*

Childs had seen that they were both fed, had plenty to drink, and were thoroughly bound—but comfortable—on the couch. Meanwhile Nakeesh had gone about packing Imperator's gear into the Escalade.

What the hell, by the time the Steingartens were finally free, telling their story to the police, and initiating a search for the Escalade, Hanson Childs, Nakeesh, and Imperator might already be hours dead. That, or the New Mexico authorities would have to serve a warrant on the *Ultima Ahau* petitioning for extradition.

The drive north on US 285 had taken him into the piñon-juniper breaks on the way to Tres Piedras. Pulling off on a ranch access, he banged over a cattle guard and followed a two-track around behind a rise where no one could see him from the highway. Then, in the Escalade's lights, he went to work with the brown, green, and buff spray paints. Some part of him—a twisted and long-sublimated bit of his personality—had always wanted to do this; he spray-painted the body in a winding, splotched camo pattern. In the glowing vehicle lights, it looked like shit. But then, that was the point.

The back window and rear bumper, he plastered with hunting stickers that he'd found at the sporting goods checkout. His favorites, were "BOWHUNTERS DO IT IN THE BLIND" and "PETA = PEOPLE EATING TASTY ANIMALS." But he had an entire collection promoting public lands, elk, mule deer, and turkey foundations, along with a bunch of gun rights stickers. Took him almost an hour to assemble and figure out how to attach the roof rack from the auto parts store, but only fifteen minutes to put the bumper rack together and slide it into the hitch receiver. The license plates—stolen from a big Dodge Ram 3500—were a five-minute job.

By the time he rolled back out onto the highway, the only things missing were a lift kit and big gnarly tires.

Nakeesh stepped out periodically to observe, only lifting a skeptical eyebrow before going back to check on Imperator where he was laid out in the back seat.

"You think this will keep us safe?" she asked as the Escalade's headlights illuminated the strip of asphalt.

"I'm just bummed that I couldn't get a brush guard for it. Hundred-thousand-dollar vehicle, and the guy at the counter tells me I can't put a winch on the front?"

"This, I do not understand," she told him with a sidelong glance.

"I don't either," he muttered. "Whatever happened to America?"

She retrieved her navigator, powering it up with a flick of her fingers.

In the glow of the dash lights, the eerie blue holograph seemed unusually bright. Nakeesh flipped back and forth among the icons, then shut it down.

"What did you find?" Childs asked.

"Only the signal from Imperator's *Kohaw*. There is nothing from the *ah tz'ib*'s cerebrum. Either she has turned it off for some reason, or the *stulti* have destroyed it." She frowned. "So . . . was the woman you call Raven trying to kill Imperator? Or was she trying to destroy his navigator? But why? Stevens tells me his president wants the machines, *si*? The more machines he has, the better. Why would that woman destroy the machines?"

Childs slowed for a deer that ran across the road, then accelerated. From the corner of his eye, he watched Nakeesh's brow line with worry.

In the back, Imperator grunted as he resettled himself in the reclined seat. He asked a question, to which Nakeesh replied. It all sounded like gobbles and mishmash.

In the mirror, Childs watched Imperator gasp as he resettled himself and pulled his arms up. They'd dressed the guy in a bathrobe, walked him past the wide-eyed Steingartens, and made him as comfortable as they could in the back of the Escalade. Fortunately, good forward-looking lawyer that Stew was, they'd bought the big ESV.

But Imperator was weird. Spooky in his own way. For instance, the guy had insisted on wearing his helmet and sword belt. A peculiar image of an ancient Greek with a gleaming Corinthian helmet in a bathrobe, wearing a gaudy Roman sword.

"This is *Ennoia*'s work," Nakeesh finally said. "I think I understand. The *stulti* wouldn't be smart enough to know the risk they were taking. Even though they are greedy, desperate to get their hands on the technology. But how did *Ennoia* convince them of the danger? Especially when she could care less if these silly beasts were terminated or not?"

"Terminated?" Childs shifted uneasily behind the wheel.

Nakeesh turned unyielding eyes on his. Then her smile widened. "No matter what, *amore*, you are safe. But you must understand: The *Ennoia* is what you would call a criminal in any timeline. She murdered hundreds to steal her machines. Incinerated entire timelines to cover her tracks. She has no honor, no loyalty. The only master she serves is hate."

Nakeesh laughed. "Your people put me in Grantham because they thought I was crazy." She tapped her head. "And now, it seems that they have taken one of the most diabolically insane and psychotic monsters ever to have lived into their lair. She will burn them all in the fires of her hate."

"Maybe you better elaborate on this *Ennoia*." Childs shifted his hand on the wheel.

"Detestablis et odiis," Imperator growled from the back seat before rattling on if a series of what had to be curses.

"What did he say?" Childs asked.

"Detestable and foul. He damns the *Ennoia* to *Xibalba*'s depths after the White Bone Snake consumes her soul and defecates it out as a gift to the Lord of Pus and Pestilence for eternal torture."

"Huh?"

"The Mayan hell is a lot more colorful and entertaining than the Roman one," she added.

"Why does this *Ennoia* hate you so much?"

A thin smile, one without humor, curled Nakeesh's lips. "She was *servus* once. A long time ago. Fluvium and I, we considered her a prize. Special. Taken for her knowledge, training, beauty, and sharp mind."

So, what was this *servus*? What did it really mean? But he asked, "What went wrong?"

Nakeesh gave him a probing look. "She grew insolent and resentful. Forgot her place. Began to consider herself above her betters."

The tone sent a shiver down Childs' back.

And . . . what does Nakeesh think is my place? he wondered.

"She was clever," Nakeesh continued. "She learned. Used people. Almost like she was able to enchant them. Men thought they loved her. Women considered her an intimate. Before Fluvium and I understood what she was, we shared her with others. Considered ourselves lucky to have found such a remarkable talent, one that brought us wealth and acclaim. Right up until the end."

"What happened?"

Nakeesh grunted. "We barely escaped with our lives. The *Ennoia* disappeared with Consul Rudius' cerebrum and navigator, accompanied by his son, Callimachus. The boy thought he loved her."

She paused. "I wonder if poor Callimachus ever learned that she'd cut his father's throat the night she tempted the lad to help her escape *Ti'ahaule?*"

"So, what happened to Callimachus?" Childs asked.

"No clue. Left behind in whatever *stulti*-filled timeline she fled to. The miracle is that she didn't end up in a recohering timeline. We should all have been so lucky." A beat. "Served the young idiot right for thinking with his penis instead of his head."

"So, you've never seen her since? Not until now, here, in our timeline?"

"Caught her once. After we had finished wreaking our displeasure upon her, as was our duty, we turned her over to Imperator and the *Ultima Ahau.* Considered her fate finished. Complete. With a certain poetry of justice for her crimes."

Childs wondered what "wreaking our displeasure upon her" meant.

"Canis muliebris!" Imperator almost spat the words from the back seat.

"Your term," Nakeesh told Childs. "Bitch, *si?*"

"But she got away again?" Childs shifted his grip on the wheel as a semi roared past headed the other way.

"She, how you say? Exploded? Yes? Bang! With a fission reactor. Many dead. And when the pieces are cleaned up, there is no Helen. And a navigator and cerebrum are missing."

"And now she is here," Childs mused. "Somewhere. Probably just up the road."

"Waiting," Nakeesh agreed. "But she has a cerebrum. We will find it and take it. And there will be death."

66

ET

Bleary-eyed, ET sat back in his chair, one long leg drawn up, skinny knee under his left hand as he scowled at the monitor. How long had he been staring at these same glyphs? They were about to drive him mad. This was all nonsense. Fucking idiocy. None of this weird Maya shit made sense. Like, who could program with pictures? Right?

On the screen, the little icons, collections of bars, dots, and little football-shaped ovals might have been someone's artwork, maybe a wall-paper design, or a pattern to print on bolts of cheap Taiwanese cloth. The fact that it was programming for the most sophisticated computer anyone had ever seen left him frustrated and irritable.

"I oughtta be able to crack this, you know?" With his right hand, he rubbed his eyes, wondering when he'd ever felt so tired. Glancing at the clock just reinforced the fact that he'd been up all night. And still, after all that, none of this made sense.

But then, Falcon had asked him to tackle the program. Had actually called ET to his room, where, sitting propped in his bed, a pillow clutched defensively to his chest, Falcon had said, "I know how we have to do this. What our only chance is."

"And what's that, Falcon, my man?" ET had kept his cheery smile on his face, hoping it hid the deep-seated worry in his gut.

Falcon hadn't looked good. And it wasn't just being sallow and skinny. Too pale even for a white dude. It was the sunken flesh around those normally thoughtful brown eyes. The mussed brown hair and dark stubble on the man's cheeks. Falcon always shaved. Now he just sat, his back crammed into the corner where his bed was against the back wall. Reminded ET of a broken child.

"It's a code, ET," Falcon had whispered, his eyes vacant. "I can see the patterns, but I can't . . . I can't . . ."

"Hey, can't what?" ET had glanced suspiciously around the room. "What kind of code, my man?"

"Computer," Falcon's hoarse whisper could barely be heard. "You're smart enough. Maybe the only one smart enough. If you can't learn it, no one can."

"Yeah, sure. You know me. But what code we talking about?"

"The programming." Falcon had blinked, as if trying to keep his thoughts centered. "Theresa figured it out. She's a very bright lady, you know? She sees things I don't."

Yeah, sure. Didn't matter that she was a hallucination. ET figured he didn't need to remind Falcon that he talked to imaginary people. "Yo, Falcon. Come back to me, bro. What kind of programming? Tell me what Theresa said."

Falcon had frowned, the corners of his mouth quivering. "It's been right there in front of us the entire time. The solution to all of our problems."

"Explain," ET had prompted when Falcon went silent, his gaze rising to the overhead camera, the one that monitored his room day and night.

"Falcon? You with me here?"

"It's the last part of the plan. I worked it out with the major."

"Yo, right. You and Major Marks? That who you're talking about?"

Falcon nodded. "It's the final piece. All we need is for you to reprogram Fluvium's cerebrum."

"Say what?" ET had made a face. "That's crazy, man. I don't speak no Mayan."

Falcon's gaze had cleared as he tucked the pillow tight against his chest. "No. But you have people who do. All you need to figure out is how to reprogram it."

"To do what?"

"Let them escape." Falcon had met his eyes. "Do you understand? As long as they're here, we're in danger. That we're still here? Haven't vanished? That means there's a chance, ET. You can save us. Save Cat. Everything. But you have to understand, time is a weapon."

"Hey, I don't know how I can—"

"We have to use time, and the timelines, against them. It's all in the wave function."

"I don't know about no wave function, man."

"No." Falcon smiled wistfully. "But I do. Assuming you can figure out how to reprogram the cerebrum. Once again, Edward, it all falls on your shoulders. You're our only hope."

You're our only hope. Those words had been echoing in ET's mind for hours.

He had been amazed when he'd sent a message to Grazier, asked for access to the cerebrum, and was granted it. Now—the image piped from Harvey Rogers' lab—he studied the various Mayan glyphs and the few Latin words.

"Try that little glyph. The one what looks like a mad dude with a Band-Aid on his cheek. The one that be scowling at the beaded necklace."

In the screen, he could see Skylar Haines' finger as it indicated the glyph. The Mayanist told him, *"That's Ch'ul Ixik Ki and translates to 'Divine Woman.'"*

After Skylar touched it, a whole series of glyphs, interspersed with packed Mayan mathematical equations, appeared on the screen.

Skylar's voice asked. *"That's the noun form. Or do you need the adjective? The one before a proper name? Like 'divine woman Mary, mother of God'?"*

"How the hell do I know? Just push the fucking button."

In the monitor, Skylar's finger stabbed through the glowing glyph. *"That help you?"*

Shit, no! But ET said, "Give me a minute. Gotta be a clue in here."

Through the speakers, he could hear Skylar Haines talking to Dan Murphy about all the meanings, how affixes could change the interpretation of the noun. Stuff that made no sense in ET's world.

"Come on," he whispered to himself. "It's code, man. Someone had to write it. Got to be a logic to it here somewhere."

He barely heard the door open behind him, Cat Talavera calling, "Where you been? You didn't show up last night. I was worried."

"Hey, girl!" He reached a hand over his shoulder as she walked up and took it. "Been working. Falcon, can you believe? Wants me to figure out how to run a Maya program. But, like, look at this. It's all pictures.

Little cartoons and lots of fricking Mayan math. I mean, this be alien shit, babe. How am I 'spposed know alien programming?"

"How are you supposed to think on an empty stomach?" she asked, reaching around with her other hand to set a Styrofoam box on the corner of his desk.

"Wish I had someone beautiful to bring me food," Murphy's voice came through the speakers.

"He said I'm beautiful," Cat bent down to whisper into ET's ear.

"You more than that," ET told her, reaching for the box as his stomach growled to remind him of how empty it was.

He opened the box, found scrambled eggs with cheddar and ham covered with a smothering of pinto beans and jalapeños in pork gravy. With the fork Cat handed him, ET attacked the meal. Finished, he tossed the box in the trash and beamed up at Cat.

"You're more than beautiful. You're a *Ch'ul Ixik Ki.* A divine woman. Sent from above as a gift. A special . . ." And it hit him: "Not another one like you," he murmured, letting loose of her hand and leaning forward. "Code always start the same. I'm thinking it's alien, huh?"

"What are you talking about?"

He looked up at her, gave her a conspiratorial wink. "It don't matter where code's written, girl. Computers work the same way. You got to start in the RAM, follow the same steps. Sure, this be quantum qubit technology, but there's got to be a beginning. Can't go about changing the order the commands come in. First is first, then second is second. Third is third. And so on."

"What are you saying, ET?" Murphy's voice came through the speakers.

He grinned, looked up at Cat, at her sparking eyes, and let his soul dance. "I'm saying, bro, that I been staring at the fucking forest, and I ain't been seeing the trees. What we're looking for? It be the first tree. Find that, and the rest of the forest gonna make sense, dude. You with me?"

"Hell, no," came Skylar's snorted reply.

ET kissed the back of Cat's hand. "Gonna be a while, babe. You wanna pull up a chair?"

"While you ignore me and write code?" Cat asked. "I'd rather watch railroad tracks rust." Then she smiled. "But if it helps you to make magic, hey, I'm in."

ET extended his hands, cracked his knuckles, and leaned forward. As if seeing the image on the monitor through new eyes, he studied the order of the symbols.

Got to look for repeats. It's not the glyphs, it's the repeats.

He could do this.

Assuming there wasn't something really weird and tricky in the way the *Ahau* wrote their code.

He shot a furtive glance at Cat, fully aware that if he couldn't figure this out, he wouldn't just be letting himself down, but all of the rest of them, too.

67

Childs

The way Hanson Childs saw it, if he hadn't been a cop, they'd have never managed to stay free for as long as they had. Nakeesh would have been fine pulling into the first motel they passed coming into Colorado Springs. She'd figured that—like the Loretto in Santa Fe—all motels were the same.

Hanson had carefully explained that motels—especially the ones off interstate highways—were regularly cruised by the local police. That the Escalade, being an upscale-that-year's-model-hundred-grand SUV wasn't the sort of thing to show up in at a cheap motel. Not with a tacky camo-spray-paint job. Any passing cop would note the anomaly, and, curiosity piqued, would call it in.

No, they needed a better hideout. And—once again—the Internet real estate sites took him to a delightful five-thousand-square-foot, five-acre, custom home not more than two miles up the canyon from Grantham Barracks. Unlike the Steingartens' house outside of Santa Fe, this one was empty, leaving them to sleep on the floor. A plushly carpeted floor on a very cushy pad. The good news? Electricity and water both worked.

The security system—being an older version—proved easy for Childs to neutralize. Breaking a window in the rear allowed him entry, and it took him only moments to clear the house, ensuring it was vacant. The openers worked on the three-car garage bay. Within moments, he had the Escalade inside and hidden from view.

However, being after dark, and the house supposedly being vacant, Childs was careful to turn on the lights only in the living room when the thick shades had been completely drawn. Didn't matter that it was on a forested lot. He didn't want any passerby to raise the alarm. How fricking pathetic would that be? Arrested for breaking and entering, not to mention trespass, when he was a wanted fugitive in the company of desperate alien time travelers? Even Cap would have found that unconscionable.

After clearing the house, he was taking stock of the place, wondering what it must be like to have the kind of money necessary to buy a property like this; it listed for 1.8 million. The living room itself had to be almost four hundred square feet. Even empty, the house was palatial. Fancy cabinets, gourmet kitchen, high-beamed ceilings, full bar and movie room, giant hot tub, luxurious master bedroom with fireplace and walk-out deck.

He was admiring the layout when Imperator entered from the garage. The man appeared to be on the mend. He walked straight now, with a lordly bearing. The aqua bathrobe came off as ludicrous given the dangling short sword on its chrome-pouched belt.

Imperator stopped short, helmeted head making a slow inspection of the living room. *"Otot b'atz,"* he said dryly.

Nakeesh—entering behind him and bearing the man's clothes and armor—translated. "He says it's a monkey house."

"Sounds derogatory."

"It is," she told Childs, pausing to lay Imperator's clothing and armor to the side. "But Imperator understands and appreciates the efforts you are making on his behalf. Because of his rank, it would be beneath him to demonstrate it to an inferior."

"Excuse me? What part of inferior—"

"You do not know our ways, Hanson. But you will learn." She straightened, looking around.

"Nakeesh," Imperator said, turning to face the woman. *"In verba inuarete."*

Childs saw her stiffen, expression gone masklike. She nodded, whispering "My oath of fealty." Nakeesh stepped forward and dropped to her knees before Imperator. As she extended her hands, the man took them both, tilting his helmet as he waited.

Childs heard her say, "For Fluvium."

His first impulse was to step forward. Interfere. But some fragment of good sense held him back as he listened to Nakeesh rattle off a long string of Latin mixed with Mayan. He didn't need to know the language;

the anguish in her voice was enough to communicate what this was costing her.

"Finis est." Imperator's grim smile was visible behind the opening in his oversized Corinthian helmet.

"It is done," Childs said, figuring out the words.

She'd gone through with it. Bonded herself to Imperator. Childs guessed that from here on out, she was his to order around. Like some kind of employee or special agent.

Nakeesh had kept her gaze locked with Imperator's. Now, he pulled her to her feet. Letting loose of her hands, he reached up, winced as he removed his mirrorlike helmet.

Childs could read the building desire in the man's expression as he looked Nakeesh up and down. Then, as if inspecting a cow at an auction, he walked around her, gaze going from the top of her ash-blonde hair to her toes. She stood, head back, looking proud under his scrutiny.

"Servus meum," he told her. And then uttered a short command ending in *"copulare."*

"Hey, wait a minute," Childs cried, starting forward.

Both Nakeesh and Imperator shot startled gazes his way.

"No, Hanson," she told him. "I am his now. As you are mine. What is your word? Stand down?"

"But . . ."

"This is not your business," she told him. "I am honored to serve my master in any way that pleases him. As you are honored to serve me."

He gaped, felt his heart as it began to hammer in his chest.

You do not know our ways.

But . . . damn it. She was his . . . His what? Girlfriend?

Hardly.

I am his as you are mine?

What the fuck?

Grinding his teeth, Childs watched as Imperator led Nakeesh to the corner of the room. He extended his helmet. Let her take it and place it on the thick carpet. Holding his arms out to the sides, he raised his chin, a victorious smile on his lips. Nakeesh, with supple fingers, unsnapped and removed his sword belt. Then she slipped the bathrobe from his shoulders. The way she did it was with ritual precision. A servant removing her master's garments until he stood naked before her. The mostly healed bruise on his muscular stomach didn't seem to inhibit his erection in the least.

She began removing her own clothes when Childs—unable to stand it—retreated to the kitchen and wished he had a bottle of whiskey.

68

Ryan

I pondered where, in the scale of "deep in the shit," I and my people were. I had President Masters' chief of staff confined in a padded cell down in solitary. Eight Talon mercenaries and their detail leader were locked literally "where the daylight didn't shine." Maxine Kaplan and Tanner Jackson—both "most powerful people"—were more comfortably housed, if just as securely constrained, in controlled-access rooms on Ward Six's main floor. In individual rooms were the scribe Sak Puh, Publius Atole, and Chak Be, or "Red Road" in Mayan. The latter two, Skylar Haines assured me, were *"tres gladii"* A ranking used by *Ti'ahaule's* legionnaires. Or "three-sword" soldiers. Whatever that meant.

So—as I sipped my coffee that morning—I tried to get my head around all the laws we'd broken, the rules we'd violated, the regulations we'd flaunted. Whether, in the end we'd just be taken out and summarily shot. If we'd be quietly locked away forever. Or simply murdered in our sleep, wrapped up in canvas, and have our bodies sunk at sea so that no one ever knew we'd existed, let alone the extent of our malfeasance.

God himself knew where our actions ranked under the rubric of "Threats to National Security."

As I stepped out of my office, Janeesha arched her "did-you-really-do-that" disapproving eyebrow. Said, "Seriously? You just sent three alien bodies from another timeline off to Kilgore France's forensic lab back east?" She waved the shipping order as if it were a little flag. "And we rented a U-Haul to do it?"

"Sergeant Daniels says if he and Kalkovich drive straight through, he can have them on Kilgore's loading dock in forty-six hours. Which will be plenty of time since we bought all the dry ice that Costco and

Safeway had." I shrugged. "The invoice for that should be somewhere in the file."

"Dry ice?" Janeesha shook her head. "In a U-Haul?"

"Hey, the weather forecast for the East predicts a cold front. Temperature's going to be twenty degrees colder than normal." I paused. "Oh, and I told them they could fly back first class."

"You worry me."

She went back to her invoices, and I decided I'd best not share my earlier thoughts about firing squads. I've overheard Chief Raven telling Winny Swink that I spent too much time preoccupying over trivia. No sense foisting that burden off on Janeesha.

Treason, kidnapping a federal cabinet officer, gunfights, and transporting corpses being the petty sorts of offenses that they were, I figured we were in the clear when it came to shooting and detaining aliens and confiscating their equipment. I assumed that people from other timelines who had come to do us harm weren't covered by the Geneva Convention.

And then there was colluding with Helen. A self-proclaimed alien, a woman from a destroyed timeline, and one who most definitely might be a high-security risk to ours.

So, how did I defend that when we were finally called on the carpet?

Assuming we were around to be called on the carpet. If we were, that meant that Alpha and the missing Imperator didn't win. Because, if they did, we'd just vanish. A circumstance that would make any sort of punishment for our transgressions a sort of moot point.

My steps took me straight to Harvey Rogers' lab. In one corner, a space had been cleared. There, hunched shoulder-to-shoulder before a large computer monitor, both Dan Murphy and Skylar Haines were studying an image of one of the holographic displays they'd recorded from Helen's cerebrum. More worrying, Fluvium's cerebrum sat on a cleared space just to the left, its holo display glowing in eerie blue.

In the bottom right corner of the computer monitor Murphy and Haines studied, I could see Falcon's image. I could tell from the background that he was in his bed, wedged in the corner of his room. As he rocked, the tip of his pillow could be seen. Falcon had it scrunched between his knees and chest. Defensive behavior.

Through the speaker, Falcon's voice said, *"Theresa and I agree. The Chanal K'u glyph is the 'initiate action' command. It must come before the predictive statistic."*

From the speaker, ET's voice said, *"Okay, I got this. Simple code, right?"*

"It should be," Falcon replied. *"Language may vary in infinite ways, various pronunciations, syntax, grammar, and structure. Mathematics, be it base five, base ten, or base twenty, is a constant in any timeline in our universe."*

"Same with programming, my man," ET's voice said through the monitor. *"Gotta follow the rules. Same here as Teehowlay."*

"Ti'ahaule," Skylar corrected.

"Whatever, man." ET's voice sounded annoyed. *"It don't change nothing. Computers got to follow the rules. Change the order, even the slightest, ain't no program gonna work."*

I could hear keys clicking, at which time the display on the lab computer changed, several of the icons shifting.

"Try that," ET's voice carried a hint of challenge.

"Reads right to me," Skylar muttered. "What about the math?"

"Give me a second," Murphy told him absently, leaning forward. Using a finger on the interactive screen, he pointed, asking Skylar, "That's the *pis* icon?"

"Yeah. *Pis*." He pronounced it peece. "Means numerical classifier. Touch it, and it should give you the equation."

With that assurance, Murphy reached over, found the *pis* glyph, and touched it. As he did, the larger computer monitor reflected the cerebrum's display, the screen packed with clusters of those dots, bars, and ovals that composed Mayan base twenty mathematics.

Murphy took a deep breath, asking, "Falcon? You seeing this?"

"On my screen," Falcon told him.

"Holy shit," Murphy muttered under his breath.

"Yeah," Skylar told him. "Now it's all up to you and Falcon." The guy stood, scratched under his dreadlocks, and seeing me, grinned to expose yellow teeth. "Hey, Colonel. Been a hell of a day, huh?"

"Got that right." I didn't like Skylar. Could catch his odor from where I stood. "Nothing like raiding, shooting, and kidnapping until dawn's early light. Just glad our people made it back from Los Alamos in one piece."

Skylar looked puzzled, frown bunching under his thick-lensed glasses. "Los Alamos? Oh, yeah. Wait. That's where Helen's program took her and Raven, right? How'd that come out?"

Like I hadn't just told him. "Um, yeah. We stopped Imperator, Alpha, and their invasion."

"Awesome," Skylar grinned wider, exposing more yellow. He blinked behind his thick-lensed glasses. "So, like, I'm hungry. Think I'll go see if supper's ready."

"Breakfast," I told him. "It's a little before eight."

"Wow," Skylar rubbed the small of his back. "When'd that happen?"

"A little less than an hour after it was seven."

From where he hunched over the computer, Murphy called, "Since Raven and Helen transported out. Guess time got away from us."

"Yeah," Harvey Rogers called from his lab door. "They've been at it all night. Come on in, Skipper. I've got something to show you."

I followed the guy through the door and into his secure lab. "Grazier know that you've got the cerebrum out? That you're fooling with the programming?"

"Yeah. Told him that Falcon wanted it, and Eli said, 'Do it. Whatever he wants.'"

I rubbed the back of my neck. "Not that I'm against any kind of therapy, but Falcon just came out of a catatonic state. I'm not sure that giving him free rein while he's still in such a fragile condition—"

"Take it up with Grazier. For myself, knowing that Skylar and Murphy are out there poking buttons sends shivers up my backbone. From second to second, I keep expecting to vanish in a searing white explosion that sends up the kind of mushroom cloud that can be seen all the way from Kansas." Rogers gave me a knowing glance. "But who wants to live forever, right?"

"From time to time, I've toyed with the notion that it might have more appeal than the alternatives." A beat. "What have you got?"

Rogers led me over to his workbench where Sak Puh's helmet rested. Off to the right, side-by-side, the bullet-smashed navigator and cerebrum had been placed on the scarred wood. A series of electrical probes hooked to monitors showed that Harvey had already been playing with the things.

I was staring thoughtfully at them, wondering if Falcon's insistence that we destroy them had been the right decision.

Instead, Rogers led me to the gleaming helmet. The mirrorlike silver-gold surface was now studded with stick-on sensors attached to wires that led to one of Harvey Rogers' electrical devices. Said device was about the size of a small microwave, and the analog gauges that covered the front of the thing had their needles wiggling. Beside it was a monitor on which oscillating waves were being recorded. It all looked very scientific, even if I didn't have a clue about what I was seeing.

"That helmet?" Harvey pointed to it. "It's another quantum computer. I suspect it interfaces with the cerebrum, not that we'll ever know for sure. Up under the rim are small lenses, lots of sensors that I've barely begun to understand, microphones, micro antennae, and a host of micro circuitry I can only guess at. Power, like in the cerebrum and navigators, is by radioactive decay in a small, very-well-shielded power pack. Hard to call it a battery. A nuclear generator is a lot better term. That technology alone has the potential to revolutionize our power production."

"Any idea of the range it can broadcast?"

"No clue. I'm not that far into it yet. What I suspect is that it interfaces directly to Sak Puh's brain. Maybe she's got an implant in her head, maybe the technology is so developed she doesn't need it. You, of all people, know where we're at with brain imaging and mapping. What we're doing is like stone ax technology compared to where *Ti'ahaule* must be." He nodded at the helmet. "Where that helmet suggests they are."

"So, we'd need Sak Puh to put it on? Use her to run tests?"

Rogers shrugged, expression severe. "I don't think that's a good idea. Not until we know a whole lot more about what we're dealing with. There's a lot of quantum circuitry in that thing I don't have a clue about. And I'm not going to stake my life and future happiness on the assumption that some of it isn't weaponized."

I crossed my arms, staring at the thing. "Karla tells me that Sak Puh offered no resistance. She just cowered down, terrified, and then collapsed under the electrical pulse when Alpha and Imperator teleported out. If it were a weapon? Well, she sure didn't use it."

"Terrified?" Rogers shrugged. "Maybe there's your answer. She's young, right?"

"How do I know? If what Helen tells me is true, Sak Puh could be a thousand years old. These people seem to have overcome the barriers to immortality."

"And maybe, Skipper, she's never been in the middle of a gunfight before."

"So, what happens in the meantime?"

"I assume that if she doesn't have the helmet on, she can't contact anyone. Assuming it's a communications device. Which I suspect it is." He pointed at a wavering needle on one of his gauges. "That's detecting entangled particles. For all I know, they're coming from somewhere in our future, from another timeline, or even from Imperator. He got away wearing a helmet, right? Want to bet he's broadcasting, seeking any response from his missing *ah tz'ib*?"

"No bets." Even as I watched, the needle rose, seemed to quiver, and dropped back. "That didn't look random."

"No, it didn't," Rogers agreed. "The needle is essentially a one-dimensional binary reading. Present or absent. Now, if I take and graph that two-dimensionally, let's see what we get."

He used an app on his phone and tapped in a series of commands. On the monitor, a line formed at the bottom, then began vibrating. If that wasn't speech, it was something damn close. Looked like the track from a voice recording.

"Any way to decipher that?"

"Might be." Rogers was stroking his chin. "Might take a while."

"Yeah, well, meantime, I've got to have a talk with Helen."

As I strode for the door, I glanced at where Murphy was squinting at the complicated Mayan mathematics on the computer screen. He was saying, "Falcon? I just don't get it."

"*It's a fifty-fifty proposition,*" Falcon said through the monitor. "*As many timelines as are in decoherence, the same number must be in recoherence. By their very nature, wave functions cannot exist in any other permutation.*"

As I stepped out into the hallway, I wondered what the hell that meant. It felt to me like everything was out of control. Fact was, this new Falcon, unlike the old one I'd known, stayed locked in his room. And now, Grazier had given him control of the entire operation? Supposedly, Falcon had a plan. But what?

What I did know was that Murphy was fiddling with the cerebrum, which could be detected by Alpha's navigator. That Imperator was out there in Alpha's company, and that he was wearing a helmet similar to Sak Puh's. A helmet whose capabilities we barely understood.

Worse, someone was sending messages via entangled particles.

Messages asking . . . what?

I made a face as that cold runny feeling of impending doom tickled in my gut.

69

Childs

As morning light shone through gaps in the curtains, Childs lay on the thick carpet in the empty living room. He was sprawled on his stomach beside Nakeesh, watching as she studied her navigator. The woman had her hair pulled back, was reclining in her tactical wear. They'd been in the same clothes for days. A change definitely was in order. And worse, he could detect the faint sexual musk that remained from her night of servicing Imperator.

He couldn't miss the difference in Nakeesh. The hard pinch in her lips, the glitter of distaste behind her eyes. The way she ground her teeth. The lady had always been hard, implacable, but now her expression hinted at barely hidden rage. The worst kind—the sort that was focused on one's self.

He'd know that she was desperate, that calling Imperator had been a last resort. Only now was the price she'd paid coming clear to him.

In the corner, Imperator—dressed in his armor again, cloak on his feather-splayed shoulders—was reclined on a pack. From behind the man's shining helmet, his hard eyes fixed on them. Childs couldn't read the man's thoughts, but from the periodic statements—and the clipped tone in which he uttered them—Imperator was anything but a happy man.

Yeah, well, that made it unanimous. Childs kept stumbling over the stubborn fact that Nakeesh had fucked the guy. Did for him like a whore did a john. No, that wasn't right. A whore got paid. What Nakeesh had done for Imperator was more like carnal obedience. Not that Childs had been a voyeur, but what he'd gleaned from being in the same house was that she did whatever Imperator told her to, however he wanted her to do it. Used her as a sexual thing, no matter how demeaning. And it had gone on for the entire night.

The more Childs figured out what *servus* meant, the less he liked it. And it didn't matter that he'd serviced her the same way. That was willing sex. Consensual.

Or was it?

God, he was so confused.

Well, but for the fact that he *hated* Imperator. Wanted the son of a bitch dead.

"I am reading Fluvium's cerebrum," Nakeesh declared, her tone ominous and flat. "And no, this time, I do not think it's a fake." She shot a look over her shoulder, adding something in Mayan to Imperator.

The man perked up, gaze sharpening. A flickering of holo light played before the man's helmet, as he and Nakeesh had a rapid exchange of terse sentences. Childs could see a faint blue glow intensify where it was framed in the eyeholes of the Corinthian-style helmet.

"*Certe,*" Imperator announced. "*Fluvii cerebri est.*"

Childs had heard enough Latin now, that he recognized the words: It was Fluvium's cerebrum. He wondered how Imperator's helmet could tell. What sort of signals it was picking up.

"So, what's the plan?" Childs pulled himself into a seated position next to Nakeesh while she studied the holos shifting over her navigator.

"We bring this to an end." The woman fixed hard eyes on him. "You understand, yes? They have killed our people. Attacked Imperator. They are working with the *Ennoia.* What you would call a mass murderer who is willing to burn entire timelines to serve her desires. It is my duty, owed to Imperator and the *Ahau,* to finish this."

"Finish it, how?" Childs had nervous butterflies in his stomach as the woman's hatred laced her words.

He shot a sidelong glance at Imperator, who seemed to be listening to every word.

"We must go and take back what is ours." Nakeesh inclined her head toward Imperator. "Two things must be done: First, we must lay our hands on Fluvium's cerebrum. Once in our control, time is ours. Then all things are undone. Fluvium is rescued. He never dies. We go back to *Ti'ahaule.* The damage is repaired."

"Sounds easy," Childs told her, hoping she couldn't read the growing disquiet within. Like, she wasn't telling him everything. "What about the *Ennoia?*"

No humor lay behind Nakeesh's smile as she told him, "She goes back in, how you say, chains?"

Imperator snapped something harsh; the man was still watching them. Seemed to be catching on to a lot of the conversation. Fricking helmet with its electronics probably had a translation program hidden somewhere in its guts.

"I didn't get that. What did he say?"

Nakeesh turned her attention back to the navigator's shimmering display. "He says this time, she will be banished. Imperator, with the *Ultima Ahau*'s blessing, will send her to a collapsing timeline."

"That's bad?"

She told him, "It doesn't get any worse."

"And if she doesn't want to come along peacefully?"

"Shoot her, Hanson. Try to maim, yes? An upper leg? Through the jaw? Perhaps the lower guts. Maybe a shoulder. The more painful the shot, the better. And then, no matter what, you must remove her pack, make sure the navigator and cerebrum she stole are recovered. As soon as you have them, we transport to *Ti'ahaule*. You will remain there while Imperator and I jump back and rescue Fluvium. Simple, *si*?"

Childs chewed his thumb as he thought it through. "What if they're waiting? You said it yourself: This is most likely a trap. What if they're expecting us to pop into Grantham, right into a free-fire zone? They have to know that we're coming for Fluvium's cerebrum. That it's your only way home."

She nodded. "That is correct. *Ennoia* will have them ready. But she plays her own game, and they are serving as her *stulti*. Her only purpose is to kill me and, now, Imperator. That she was able to surprise us at Los Alamos was due to my inability to warn Imperator of the danger. I had no idea that she would react so quickly, or with such strength. And Imperator, without knowledge of the danger, came protected only by a *quinque* that anticipated minimal resistance. Had I been able to transmit the full extent of the threat, he would have come with a *mille* and blasted this entire hive of insects into rubble." She knotted a fist. "And *Ennoia* along with it."

"So, how are we going to do this?" he asked. "We'll be beaming into their territory. I was in Grantham Barracks, but I didn't get much of a chance to scope the place out. You were held there. You know it better than I do."

She pursed her lips, attention fixed on the navigator's holo. "I have the *locus,* um, the coordinates for the room I was held in. The navigator was in Los Alamos and was able to home in on the doohickey. Returning is different than going, *si*? We do not want to appear in that same room with its locked door." She tapped the device with a slim finger, saying, "Navigator knows where it is going, not how to get there. That is the purpose of the cerebrum. To compute the location."

"But you can get us into the Grantham Barracks, right?"

"*Certe.* And linking through Imperator's helmet, I can get us close. But that is what they will be expecting. It is a hard question. Appear too close to Fluvium's cerebrum, and we are in the jaws of the trap. Too far, down too many corridors, and we have to fight our way to where they have the cerebrum."

"Close," Imperator interrupted, speaking in English.

Childs whirled, blurting, "How'd he do that?"

Imperator ignored him, saying, *"Dirumpo habeo."*

Alpha translated, "He has explosives."

Childs shot a calculating glance at the man's belt. Considered. "So, like, we pop in, he tosses out the explosives, and we pop out? Use it as a diversion, and transport directly to where they've got the cerebrum?"

She nodded. Eyes like laser-blue slits. "Something like that."

"Get ready," Imperator told them in precise English. Then he stood. The Corinthian helmet allowed only a glimpse of the pained expression as he stretched. Then the man strode from the room on his way to the bathroom down the hall.

Nakeesh took Childs' hand, her seething gaze fixing on his. "Hanson, if this goes, as you say, sideways, these are your orders: You *must* kill the *Ennoia*. You must ensure Imperator has Fluvium's cerebrum so he can return to *Ti'ahaule* and remove the danger posed by this timeline. That is victory. But no matter what, if *Ennoia* wins, kill me. Do you understand?"

"Kill you? Are you nuts? That's—"

"If I cannot save Fluvium, there is nothing to live for."

He wasn't sure why he said it, but he asked, "So, if we get away, you want me to kill Imperator, too? Or would that damn me to exile?"

A flicker of empty smile died on her lips. "You are already damned, *amore*"

70

Cat

atalina Talavera crossed her arms as she watched Sak Puh demol-
ish the last of the plate of tamales covered as they were with red
chili and fresh slices of jalapeño. The woman—who called herself a
Yucateca—sat on the edge of her bed, dressed in a patient's smock. She
wasn't much bigger than Cat, with fine brown skin, thick black hair,
and that broad face and dark eyes common to Central American *Indio*
populations.

Cat had volunteered for this task not only because she was the least
threatening person in Grantham . . . well, except for Falcon, perhaps,
but because it was her tailor-made drug that the woman had just unwit-
tingly ingested along with the thick red chili sauce that drenched the
chicken-stuffed masa. Cat wanted to be here, observing the woman's
pupil dilation, her breathing, and perspiration.

Not that Cat anticipated an adverse reaction. She'd been up all night
tailoring the chemistry to Sak Puh's genetics. Her cocktail should slip
right past the blood-brain barrier and latch onto receptors in the woman's amygdala, hippocampus, and pre-frontal cortex. Funny how much
of her research was leading to those centers of the brain, all building on
what she'd learned from treating Falcon This was just another step.

Sak Puh's brain was being lulled, the fear and inhibition responses
dulled, and at the same time, her pleasure centers were being stimulated.
As the tailored drug cocktail began to reach the targeted areas, the
woman would begin to feel a warm glow. One that, hopefully, she
would equate with having eaten a tasty meal.

Cat asked, *"Beesh a beel?"* How are you? Skylar Haines had supplied
the term.

Sak Puh smiled, a warm twinkle in her dark eyes. She chattered Mayan in a lively response.

In her earbud, Cat heard Skylar translate, *"I'm doing much better. Great food. I'm so glad you speak my language. I was afraid this entire timeline was filled with monkey people."* She called them, *ba'atz.*

"Try the speaker," Cat whispered into her collar mic, seeing the woman's smile turn radiant. She had the same softening of expression that intoxicated people adopted.

Skylar's voice came through the room speaker, a cadence of Yucatec Maya, rising and falling as he asked the first of Grazier's prerecorded questions.

For now, however, Cat's job was to stand there, smile encouragingly, and appear to dwell on every word Sak Puh uttered. Meanwhile, Skylar was translating in her earbud.

And, to Cat's delight, Sak Puh began to answer without the least hesitation. Didn't seem like she even hesitated before gushing on about Imperator, her helmet, or the ultimate goals of the *Ahau* when it came to Cat's timeline and future.

Grim as that might have been, she was struck with the realization, that if Sak Puh had no inhibitions about telling these "monkey people" about how they were going to be destroyed, there was a fortune to be made selling her "truth" serum to women wondering if their men were faithful.

But then—if Sak Puh could be believed—no one would be selling anything to anyone on the sterile and cold rock that had once been called Earth.

71

Ryan

I had my butt planted in a chair across from Eli Grazier at the table in the conference room. Helen sat two chairs down opposite Karla Raven and Sam Savage. On the wall, the bunnies, fawns, and wildflowers looked remarkably unconcerned despite having been in the same room as we were, having heard what we just heard, as the drugged Sak Puh cheerfully laid out the coming apocalypse.

What we now knew: Imperator wasn't dead. As we'd suspected, he wore armor. Worse, his helmet could interact with Alpha's navigator as a limited cerebrum. In short, he and Nakeesh could pop in at any time in a bid to grab Fluvium's cerebrum. Falcon had been right: After the destruction of Imperator and Sak Puh's equipment, it was their only way home.

And, of course, Helen was part of the equation. Sak Puh made it clear that the *Ennoia* was the most feared terrorist in the history of *Ti'ahaule.* That the *Ultima Ahau* would grant any wish to the person who laid Helen's head at the great lord's feet.

When that had been translated, I'd been watching Helen's expression. Her green eyes had taken on a look of frosty satisfaction. Gave me yet another glimpse of her complex personality.

Sak Puh had said, "Domina Nakeesh will have sworn herself *in servus* to Imperator. She is now his. To do with as he wishes."

"Why would she do that?" Skylar had asked on Grazier's prompting.

"To save herself," Sak Puh had explained. "Until this timeline is rendered inoperable, the stolen machines are recovered, and the *Ennoia* is punished, Domina Nakeesh's life is forfeit." She had paused. "You don't know the Domina. What it cost her to call Imperator. Do you understand? She has nothing left. You people have cost her everything.

She has nothing to live for but your destruction and the chance to rescue Fluvium."

"Cheery thought," Grazier muttered.

On the screen, Skylar was fielding questions from Harvey Rogers about Sak Puh's helmet. Skylar, his command of Yucatec stretched to its limits, was trying to translate the Mayan into English.

In my limited understanding of engineering and design, it all sounded like gobbledygook.

Grazier had fixed on Savage and Karla. They'd both arrived in tactical gear. Looked like they were ready for war: armed and with all of their gear strapped on. "What's our defensive situation given that, if Sak Puh's analysis is correct, Alpha and Imperator could drop in at any moment, and at any place?"

Savage replied, "Standard protocol, sir. There's at least the two of them. Maybe with Hanson Childs as a third, given his escape with Alpha from Lab One. Cat helped us set up the lab. Cerebrum's on Harvey's box. Built just like Falcon said to—"

"They're coming!" Helen cried where she'd been monitoring her navigator.

I wasn't even out of my seat by the time Karla and Savage had leaped to their feet and were through the door.

I'd barely cleared my chair when a concussion shook the building, followed by a sharp bang. My first thought was a grenade. Had that same sound and feel.

My last thought was, *Where the hell did they get explosives?*

72

Karla

Karla led the way, feet slapping on the vinyl floor as she pelted down the gleaming hallway, Savage's boots pounding behind.

A couple of the kitchen staff, wide-eyed, threw themselves out of the way, flattening against the wall. The lights overhead flickered and died as Karla made the right and charged down the hallway toward Harvey Rogers' lab.

Karla pulled up, panting, just outside the door, and whipping out her mirror, eased it past the jamb, searching the interior.

"They're early." Savage huffed and puffed behind her as he covered the hallway with his rifle.

"Time travelers, huh? You'd have thought they would have arrived last week."

"Might have," Savage agreed, watching their six. "I think, Chief, they had to be able to key on Fluvium's cerebrum in real time. Like, for anybody who absorbed an entire magazine from an MP-5, even with body armor, this is a really quick recovery time. And we don't know how he might have been injured falling down those stairs at Lab One."

"I can see the cerebrum," she told him. "Sitting right out in the open. No sign of Harvey. Hope he's back in the lab. Door leading to his secure room is locked."

"I guess we'll just have to . . ." Savage didn't finish.

The tingle started in Karla's spine. Electric, exciting. A thousand prickling ant feet danced across her skin.

"Here we go!" Karla dropped, propping herself on the floor.

She got a glimpse of Savage's face. Realized the guy had never experienced the full effect of teleportation before.

Would have been funny, but the wave hit her, the crackling of her hair vanishing in a feeling of euphoria followed by the sinking in her stomach. Then the world went black, seemed to explode in a thousand . . .

She came to, some part of her brain urging her to action.

Hallway floor. She was crouched, back against the wall, wearing tactical gear. Her mirror on its extendable stalk lay beside her, her MP-5, slung, was on her lap. Beside her, Savage was laid out like a side of beef. Eyes just starting to blink.

"Time jump," she whispered, clawing her senses together.

They were outside Harvey Rogers' lab. They'd practiced this. Like in the drills, she reached for the gas mask, ripped the M51 from her belt, and slipped it over her head. A quick finger sealed it.

Okay, Cat. Let's see how this works for real.

Leaping to her feet, she charged for the door.

7З

Childs

Each time Nakeesh stuck her finger into the glowing blue orb projected by her navigator, Hanson Childs thought his body was
exploding. Like his arms and legs were torn loose from his torso and his
head was being pulled apart. Then the nausea and vertigo as he fell
through an endless black void, only to snap into one piece as the universe
started to assemble itself out of haze. He'd stagger, surprised to find his
feet under him. And there would be Nakeesh and, to his disgust, Imperator. The only things that were "real" as bits and pieces of the world
fitted themselves together from a pastiche of nothingness.

The first jump had him reeling, clutching madly onto Nakeesh's
arm. No sooner had reality formed, than Imperator pulled a silver globe
from one of his belt pouches, thumbed its top, and tossed it. Childs got
the briefest glance of a lit hallway, polished floors, doors, and acoustical
ceiling tiles as the silver globe went arcing toward what looked like a
sprawled janitor who lay on his side by a push broom.

Childs had seen Nakeesh finger the blue orb that projected above her
navigator, and was again dropping into chaos as a hollow bang faded
behind him. Once more, he was being ripped apart.

. . . To reform once again, in yet another hallway. Looked just like
the last one except that it had windows on one side. He caught a glimpse
of an oddly designed helicopter on the other side of the windows
along with a bunch of technicians, the closest of whom were sprawled
on the grass.

Again Imperator tossed one of his little grenades.

Childs tightened his grip on Nakeesh as she pressed her finger into
the glowing blue orb.

"Fuck me!" he heard himself scream over the distant bang of the grenade and shattering glass. He dropped into the sickening vortex again. Wasn't as bad this time, and he had to wonder if maybe he was getting used to having his joints pulled out of their sockets, just to reassemble themselves out of nothingness.

Seemed like he was better balanced as what looked like a laboratory built itself out of wispy fragments of image. Sort of like torn shreds of a jigsaw puzzle appearing out of nacre and gray to fit themselves into a picture.

Nakeesh, firm and solid, had his hand. She was staring at where her navigator glowed. The thing rested on the palm of her right hand. And never had it glowed as brightly as it did now, a strange image dominating the display.

"Finis viae," she stated. *"Venimus in victoriae."*

Something in Childs' head translated, "End of the road. We arrive in triumph."

The lab solidified around them, the last of the haze gone. The overhead light, the electrical equipment on the shelves, were dark, glowing in the holographic light cast by Nakeesh's navigator.

Beside him, Imperator pulled his short sword. Right. As if that was going to stand up against firearms.

Both Nakeesh and Imperator had fixed on the cerebrum where it projected a blue glow. The device sat atop a shelf, a sort of elevated . . . Wait. Even as he watched, the shelf was dropping. Like the whole thing was on an axle of sorts. And as the navigator rotated out of sight, it dropped into the box upon which it had been set. The back slipped up, slid around, and closed with a finality. A loud click could be heard, the apparent lock dogging.

Imperator began barking out curses as he walked over, tried to open the box, and cried out in rage as it defied him. Then, raising his *gladius,* he pointed it at the steel box.

"Non!" Nakeesh cried, rushing forward.

Before she could reach him, a searing white-blue light shot like a thread from the tip of the ornate sword to blaze and burn on the metal. Childs had to raise an arm to shield his eyes. Nakeesh, shouting in a mix of Mayan and Latin dragged at Imperator's arm. In doing so, she pulled the sword to one side, the thread of blue-white light shearing through electronic equipment, severing wiring, setting fire to paper, and melting plastic casing.

Okay, so maybe Imperator's sword was even cooler than Childs had suspected.

The lights flickered back on, revealing even more of the lab.

Childs reached for his pistol, pulling it from the back of his waistband. He turned, trying to get an idea of the place. Figuring that someone . . .

He stopped short, hearing the faint hiss over the fight as Imperator and Nakeesh shouted at each other. The sound reminded him of a puncture in a tire. The sort made when compressed air . . .

"Gas!" he cried, raising his sleeve to his nose. "We gotta get . . ." He lost the words, started to turn, to reach for Nakeesh. Only to topple sideways.

He had slammed into the floor, when, from the corner of his eye, he saw Chief Raven barge in, head covered in a gas mask.

And then there was an image. A fading streak of white-blue light slicing across the room in Raven's direction. He heard the distant staccato of automatic weapons fire . . . fade . . . into . . . .

74

Karla

Karla took in the room at a glance. The navigator—the intricately prepared bait—had just disappeared into Harvey Rogers' trick lockbox. He'd built the mechanism according to Falcon's instructions.

"We need something to lure them close, and then deny them the use of it."

All it took to trigger the mechanism was the corona effect, the one caused by "popping in" when the electricity blacked out. The moment that happened, it opened the electrical circuit that held the box open. Gravity did the rest. Let the drum rotate down into place for the lock to click home.

The same with Cat's knockout gas. As soon as the power kicked back on, the solenoid was activated and started pumping gas into the room.

Karla should have charged in to find the invaders passed out on the floor. And yeah, she pegged Child. Slumped beside him, Alpha. They were still wearing the same outfits they'd had on when they popped out of Lab One.

The problem was Imperator. He was pointing that short sword at the lockbox. Took her half a heartbeat to figure out that it was the source of the laser that was burning a cut across the top of the box.

Karla was raising the MP-5 as Imperator wheeled, the sword cutting an arc across the lab. Heard the popping, hissing, and crackling as the beam sliced through Harvey Rogers' stacked equipment on the shelving.

Training saved her. Karla threw herself under the beam. Hit the floor. Rolled onto her side as the line of blue-white cut along the open door behind her. Imperator adjusted, flicked the sword back her way. Karla triggered the MP-5 From the angle—and given her hold on the gun—the first rounds missed, but she took out his right leg. Saw the man buckle, and somehow recover his balance.

As he did, the laser burned a streak across the concrete within inches of her face.

Savage's M4 was deafening as he unleashed a burst from the doorway; the supersonic cracking of the bullets passing over her head made Karla wince. But she was already scrambling to get behind the worktable on one side of the room.

Making cover, she heard Savage scream. Heard a clatter. Shot a glance his way. Tried to make sense of it: Savage staggering back, ducking behind the door, and part of his arm was missing. The hand and forearm now lay on the floor atop the smoking M4.

Karla bit off a curse, tucked the MP-5 close, and filled her lungs in preparation. Charging her muscles, she prepared to make the son of a bitch hurt before he took her out.

"Prepare to die, *stultia.*" Imperator's voice had a mechanical quality to it.

Even as he stepped around the table, pointing the sword in her direction, Savage appeared in the doorway. With his left hand, he clutched a flash-bang. Using his teeth, he pulled the pin and tossed it into the room. It hit, bounced, and rolled toward Imperator.

The man leaped back, correctly sensing the danger as he flicked the sword down, slicing back and forth with it as he tried to destroy the rolling cylinder.

Karla hunched into a ball, cradling her MP-5 in her lap. Eyes squeezed shut, she pressed both hands to her ears.

The white light and bang still shook her to the bones.

Karla got a grip on her MP-5, leaped to her feet, and caught the reeling Imperator in the sights. She fixed the red dot on his chest and triggered the gun. The short burst took him in the upper chest, two rounds glancing off the helmet's left chin piece. The clang could be heard over the MP-5's report

To her amazement, Imperator just took it. Sure, he jerked under the impact as the 124-grain bullets hit, but the man should have been down.

"What the hell?" Karla wondered as she thumbed the magazine release and ripped one of the spares from her belt.

"*Moritiuus!* Eh? Now die!" the mechanical voice told her.

Karla hadn't even slapped the magazine into the well when Imperator raised his sword, pointing it at her breast.

She was dropping, trying to duck when the hot white-blue light shot out.

75

Karla

Pain seared Karla's left shoulder as she hit the floor, barely kept hold of the MP-5. Flipping to her side, she tried to steady the HK, wiggled around to rest the weapon on its magazine, realized the bolt lock was still open. With her left arm useless, she couldn't slap it closed. Cursing, she let it fall on its side. One-handed, she tried to slap the bolt latch closed. But the gun just spun on the concrete.

Through the table legs, she could see Imperator's limping approach. In moments, he would round the edge of the workbench. Tucking her legs up, Karla got her right hand under her and ripped her .45 from its holster. Thumbing the safety off, she lifted the pistol.

Imperator rounded the edge of the table; she stared up at him. Like some cartoon villain, he stood over her with blue light glowing around the eyeholes in his ancient Greek helmet. Rays of golden silver reflected from its crest. The white cloak hanging around his shoulders swayed as he took another limping step. From above, the fluorescent lights shot iridescent colors through the feathers in the shoulder splays. His silvered armor had irregular gray smudges where it had absorbed bullet strikes.

Each time her HK .45 banged and spit brass, she watched the silver armor puff at the impacts. The 185-grain slugs fell like obscene nuts to bounce on the floor among the litter of spent casings already spewed out by her MP-5.

Think! Where do you shoot the motherfucker?

Karla shifted her aim to the man's left eye, barely visible behind the haze of blue that surrounded the helmet's spheroid eyehole.

As the HK fired, cycled, and spit the brass to one side, Karla saw the helmet buck at the hit; to her amazement the flattened bullet popped back and arced as it fell to the floor.

"What the hell?" she whispered.

"Rusticus mulier!" Again he raised the sword.

She could see the shadow of his smile behind the opening in his helmet.

Karla froze, that moment of realization—that this was death—leaving her numb with inevitability.

She jerked, startled by a deafening eruption of gunfire from the door. Bullets ripped through the air above her. Saw Imperator staggering as slugs shredded his cape, hammered his armor, and sent the man staggering. As he did, the vicious sword discharged, its white-blue laser slicing through Karla's MP-5 where it lay beside her.

Cringing away from the painful muzzle blast and crack that split Karla's skull, she stared up through squinted eyes as Helen darted in, emptying a magazine from Savage's M4 as she reached down, grabbed Karla by the collar, and dragged her bodily across the concrete. Pulling her through the door, Helen let Karla drop, triggered the magazine release, and while the empty clattered on the floor, pulled another from her belt, slapping it into the gun.

Ears aching, Karla tried to get her bearings. Was surprised to see that Savage, and his severed arm, were missing. Grazier was crouched against the wall, one of the new 6.8 mm Sigs at the ready. Karla had never seen his complexion that pale.

She could barely hear Helen through the ringing as the woman bent down. "Hell of a fight. But you're going to need a bigger gun than a 5.56 to get through that armor."

"Yeah?" Karla yelled to hear herself over the damage to her hearing. "What have you got in mind?"

"Distraction," Helen yelled back.

Then the woman leaned out just far enough to reach out one-handed and spray the room with another magazine. The crazy image of it reminded Karla of the old videos of Vietnam where soldiers raised their M16s above the trenches to "spray and pray."

Helen counted, her lips moving, and jerked the smoking M4 back. No sooner had she done so, than the white-blue laser burned on the far wall before carving a piece out of the doorjamb where Helen's arm had extended.

Karla gritted her teeth against the searing pain in her left shoulder, shifted on the concrete flooring, and fumbled around behind her with her right hand. She found the flash-bang, pulled it around. Helen was slapping another magazine into the M4's well, when Karla said, "Gotta get that door closed. He steps out here in the hall, we're all dead."

"Good point." Helen dropped, jutted the M4, and fired a fast, one-handed burst. Jerking the gun back, it was followed an instant later by a burning white-hot beam from the sword.

Karla, her left arm still useless, followed Savage's good example, pulling the pin with her teeth. Flopping around, she tossed the flash-bang into the lab. She counted, one, two, three, then, as the glaring white was accompanied by the deafening bang, shoved to her feet.

Helen was spraying the room with the M4. Karla, howling from the pain, stepped around her, ducked in, and grabbed the lab door. She pulled it shut behind her, then sagged to the floor, panting from the pain and exhaustion.

"What's to keep him from opening the door and wasting us?" Grazier asked.

Helen reached down, twining her hand in Karla's collar again. "My bet? He won't. He's hurting. He had Nakeesh pulled out of the way. Don't know about that other guy. But while the armor's bulletproof, all that energy has to go somewhere. That's into his skin, muscle, and bone. Imperators aren't outfitted for long, drawn-out combat. The suit's designed to keep them protected until they can jump out, leaving the hard fighting for the *quinque*. And if they can't handle it, a *mille* is supposed to jump in on their heels and finish it."

"So now what happens?" Grazier asked.

"I take your gun and try to figure out how to keep him from cutting Fluvium's cerebrum free," Helen told the general. "And you get Karla to the infirmary. She needs that laser cut taken care of. Hard to believe she's still on her feet. Tough lady."

You have no fucking idea, Karla thought. The hallway began to spin. Her stomach lurched. She bent, stomach pumping as she spewed her guts all over the brass-littered hallway.

And then the world turned gray and she felt herself . . . felt . . .

76

Childs

The flickering thought in Hanson Childs' mind was that he heard gunfire. Then the bang brought him around. A white flash blinding him despite his closed eyes. It was loud, painful. When his brain cleared a bit more, it was to hear silence, or what he supposed was silence given the ringing in his ears.

But where the hell . . . ? The sensation was like someone had stuffed his head full of the cushy stuff they packed into sleeping bags. That cottony white smooshy insulation. Though why that image lodged in his head was a mystery.

He swallowed hard. Had a funny taste in his mouth. And he smelled gun smoke. Did that mean he was on a range? Was he supposed to be qualifying? Then why was he flat on his back?

Childs flexed his hand. No pistol. Where the hell was his pistol if he was supposed to be qualifying? And what was his score? CID demanded . . . What? How many points?

Damn the fog in his head.

It took him two tries to blink. Get his eyes open. Tried to make sense of where he was. On the floor. What looked like an electronics storage facility. But, by damn, everything was wrecked. And the fricking floor was covered with gleaming brass casings. A lot of spent cases.

Okay, so maybe he was on the range? But when had they ever qualified in an electronics warehouse?

Through the pesky ringing in his ears, he heard a curse. Looked off to the side to see a comic book character dressed in a torn white cloak, shoulders decorated with really awesome feather splays, and a helmet that almost blinded it was so reflective. The weird warrior was cutting some metal box with a laser sword, the cut metal glowing as the white-blue beam sliced along. The guy had almost cut a square out when his short laser sword flickered and died.

"Inferno et Xibalba!" the man cursed, stepping back, swinging the sword to clang on the resisting steel of the metal box. The square he'd been cutting, held by an inch or so of remaining steel, gave slightly under the blow.

When the warrior . . . Imperator. Yes, that was the name. It was coming back. Imperator shifted, stepping closer to the box, which allowed Childs to see Nakeesh. She was propped next to Imperator's leg, her back against the stack of drawers beneath the workbench. Childs saw her head lift, spilling ash-blonde hair. She blinked, clearing laser-blue eyes.

"Cacame!" she exclaimed, winced, and rubbed her ears. Then she glanced around, fixed on Childs, and slowly shook her head, as if remembering just how fucked they were.

Nakeesh painfully dragged herself to her feet, wobbling. She turned, nodded, saying, "Imperator?" And then a string of Latin and Mayan mixed together.

Imperator replied, stepping forward to stick the tip of his sword into the slit he'd cut. Levering it back and forth, he got the blade partway in and leaned; the metal bent outward.

Crying with glee, he slung the sword to the side where it clattered metallically on the bench. Then, calling to Nakeesh, he braced himself. Stepping next to him, she took hold of the resisting metal with both hands, and together they pulled, bending the square out.

Chuckling, Imperator reached in. Childs watched him retrieve a square, boxlike . . . Yes, it was a cerebrum. Fluvium's. Good to know his brain was working.

Smashed lab. He was in Grantham Barracks. They were here to get the cerebrum, and then Nakeesh, he, and Imperator would jump time-lines to *Ti'ahaule.*

Where I will be Nakeesh' slave while she's Imperator's.

"How the hell is that supposed to work?" he wondered, reaching up to rub his aching eyes.

Is that what I want to do?

How in the name of fuck had he gotten into this mess? Thoughts went back to DC, his ruined credit. Stevens. The Talon mercs and Lab

One. And Nakeesh. In Santa Fe. The look in her eyes as they shared great sex. Jaime Chenwith's body next to Lonnie Hughes' bleeding corpse. Being on the run. Feeling hopeless. Watching Nakeesh kneel and swear herself into Imperator's bondage.

"Why am I living this shit?" He let his chin sag on his chest, dull eyes on the brass-littered floor with its occasional flattened bullet. Hell of a fight had come off here. The miracle was that they were all alive. That no stray round had hit him where he lay off to the side.

Nakeesh sounded a victorious cry as the cerebrum's holo flashed to life. She had retrieved her navigator from where it had fallen, flicking her fingers to bring it online. The woman almost sounded giddy as she played her fingers through the display.

And both she and Imperator, their backs turned, completely missed the door swinging open. Childs recognized the woman from Lab One, had seen her striding down the stairs with an M4, shooting down Imperator's men. Now she carried one of the new Sig Sauer Automatic Rifles, the one chambered for the 6.8 mm round.

Before Childs could fill his lungs to shout, the woman leveled it, bellowing, *"Vinco!"* I win. Then the long gun let loose with a string of automatic fire.

Childs gaped, watched as the rounds hammered into Imperator. Saw Nakeesh catch at least two rounds down low.

His reaction was instinctive. He grabbed for the pistol that lay on the floor beside him. Lifted it. Shot the woman with a double tap as he'd been trained. Saw her start, eyes wide, as the slugs tore into her chest. She dropped. The big gun clattered as it hit the concrete. The woman lay crumpled beside it, gasping, green eyes wide.

I just killed the Ennoia.

He'd gotten that part right.

Childs stumbled his way up, stepped wearily over to Imperator where the man—obviously hit hard—was holding Nakeesh. Childs could see the blood, down low. Looked like two rounds had torn through Nakeesh's lower left side. Would have clipped her colon and kidney for sure.

"Help me," Imperator told him, the voice oddly mechanical. Red was welling where the slugs had finally torn through his over-extended armor.

"How?" In the mirrorlike helmet, Childs was staring at his reflection, at the way it curved, bending out of shape, weirdly contorted. *That's me. How I look these days.*

"Hold her hand up," Imperator told him. "You know how." He gave a slight nod. "To press her finger . . . into the display."

Childs did as he was told.

He could hear feet hammering in the hallway. People were coming.

"Are you sure they didn't screw up the setting?" Childs asked.

"These are *stulti*," Imperator told him. "Monkey people. Now, let's go home."

Hanson Childs, helping to support Nakeesh, hesitated. If he did this, there would be no going back. Whatever *Ti'ahaule* was, it would be his future.

The feet were closer. Sounded like a lot of them.

With an image of Jaime Chenwith's stunned face in his memory, he whispered, "Sorry, old friend," and extended Nakeesh's finger into the glowing blue orb on the navigator's display.

In an instant, his body felt like every atom was exploding, and then, with a feeling of bliss, he was aware of Nakeesh, her body still pressed against his as they dropped into . . . into . . .

Insanity.

77

Ryan

I picked myself up off the polished vinyl flooring in the hallway outside of Harvey Rogers' lab. Faint light was shining in from the windows at the end of the corridor. I don't know what I expected, but Karla Raven's description of the ultimate orgasm mixed with the sensation of sticking your finger into a light socket wasn't that far out of line. Figured I didn't need to be close to another time jump. Once was enough.

Behind me, Myca Simond was gathering his wits along with a bunch of the security guys. We'd all dropped like our puppet-strings were cut. Now, like me, they were collecting their guns, shaking their heads. Then the hallway lights came on.

I heard Corporal Hatcher mutter, "Motherfucker" under his breath; I wasn't sure that I disagreed with either the sentiment or choice of words.

Finding I could stand, I cradled the Sig Sauer 6.8 and advanced on the door. The floor here was littered with spent brass. With a quick glance past the melted-looking doorjamb, I took in the carnage. The lab had been blasted to bits. More brass littered the floor.

And there, gasping and bleeding, lay Helen.

Setting the rifle to one side, I leaned in, peering around warily for danger, and dragged her back out into the hall. "Myca, Julian, get her to the infirmary. Now, people!"

Myca Simond and Julian Hatcher, together, slung Helen's body between them and hustled off down the hall.

Retrieving my rifle, I stepped into the lab, glancing around at the wreckage. No Imperator, Nakeesh, or Childs. Just the safe box, its side pried open, a lot of wrecked electrical equipment, and—on the bench to the right—a rather ornate, engraved, and bejeweled Roman *gladius*.

I picked it up, surprised by the thing's weight. Hefted it. Wondered what kind of miracles Harvey Rogers was going to find hidden away in its depth.

Oh, and there was blood, too. Enough of it to demonstrate that when Imperator and Alpha made their escape, both had been critically wounded.

"Holy shit," Eli muttered behind me as he stepped into the room. "We're sure they got away?"

"Yep," I told him, staring warily at the sword as I held it up to the light. "But we can walk away from it knowing it was a tightly run thing."

"Shit." Eli kicked some of the brass out of the way. It tinkled musically as it rolled across the concrete. "Think we're about to disappear? Vanish? Poof?"

I glanced sidelong at him. "I wonder if we'll ever know? Or if we'll just sort of . . . well, never have been in the first place?"

"Got me. But, for the moment, Ryan, I'm headed for the cafeteria. I just got a call. President Masters is on the way. I gather that he just figured out his chief of staff is missing. It's going to take Rogers and the rest some time to get the recordings sorted out. Meanwhile, I'm scorching my tonsils with tamales before I vanish."

And with that, he turned and walked out of the room.

78

Karla

The way the surf rolled in—the lines of curling breakers separating the sparkling turquoise waters from the stark white of the beach—was the same. Didn't matter which timeline. Here the sea was called the *Mare Maya* instead of the Caribbean. To her surprise, the city was still called Tulum—translated as "Rabbit Land" from the original Mayan. In her timeline it was an archaeological ruin. Here it was a colorful seaside city of two and a half million, composed of awesome pyramid-shaped arcologies, broad elevated causeways called *sacbe* and stunning green spaces filled with giant trees and eye-dazzling flower gardens.

She couldn't have picked a more delightful place to recover. She hadn't had the inclination to steal anything since arriving here.

The city was mesmerizing. A mixture of Mayan and Roman influences. Way different. Like a universe away from the tourist mecca of Cancun and Playa del Carmen that she knew from her timeline. Here, the modern Mayan architecture favored towering buildings painted in bright red, vivid blues, and startling whites that contrasted with the cloud-hazy skies. And the layout was distinctly non-Cartesian. The city was laid out along astronomical lines with solar and lunar orientations, radii—all actually refreshingly different from a grid. Not to mention the hanging gardens and sculptural reliefs decorating the buildings.

The balcony where she rested was two stories up. Had a marvelous view of the beach and was placed to take advantage of the cooling breezes coming in from the sea. Karla shifted on the recliner, reached for the iced cup of chili-chocolate with its subtle rum taste. Overhead, two aircars, painted in almost psychedelic colors, whisked by on their way down the coast.

Karla could hear a band playing somewhere in the plaza behind the housing complex where she lounged. The building itself reminded her of a step pyramid topped by an arched portico. Music here was very much what she'd call non-European. A series of hollow flutes, lyres, and xylophone.

On the beach, a group of sun-browned, black-haired children ran naked, screaming in delight, as they sprinted across the pale sand and into the surf. It brought a smile to Karla's lips. At the same time, a flock of macaws and quetzals broke from the trees in the garden to her left. The raucous calls made by the fleeing birds was accented by the howler monkey that reveled in having chased from the prime fruits.

"Still soaking up the sun?" Helen asked as she strode out from the air-conditioned recesses of their apartment. The woman wore a dazzling wrap-around skirt in crimson, black, and yellow and an airy feather-light cape called a *ha'ay*. The scars marking the healing bullet wounds in the left side of her chest had faded from an angry red to a gentle pink. Just two more to add to the others that patterned so much of Helen's body. Karla had asked once, wondering at the origin of the faint white lines that made patterns on the woman's skin.

All she'd received was a faint smile in return and a dismissive: "Some other time."

Karla lifted the brim of her straw hat and took off her sunglasses as Helen seated herself on the next recliner and let the breeze play with her loose auburn hair.

"How's the shoulder?" Helen asked.

"Good as new." Karla replaced her drink. "I should be going back. Skipper's going to have a kitten as it is. I'd better be there to face the shit coming down from the head shed when they learn you're gone."

Helen studied her. "You didn't have to help me."

"I owed you one, *Ennoia*. And you were right. If they'd tried to hold you, it would have ended badly." She gestured. "And your docs did a lot better job patching up those holes."

Helen was still giving her that knowing look. "You could stay, Karla. Your timeline? Given what I saw? The population has already overrun the resource base. Geopolitical forces are about to unleash global conflict. You're on the brink of civil war. The climate is choking on too many emissions, and the world economy is coming apart in your not-too-distant future. When it does, it will be ugly."

Karla turned her attention back to the beach. Fact was, she'd liked it here. Not that people weren't still people, but mixed Simonianism and syncretic native beliefs had been refreshing. As had the gender equality. An entire religion built on the premise that male and female were two halves of creation that needed to be united in order for the soul to find enlightenment.

And what if I did stay?

Karla chewed at her lip, frowning out at the crystalline sea. Her original plan had been to operate Helen's cerebrum to help the woman escape to her timeline.

Lying in the infirmary bed in Grantham, waiting to be transported to Denver for surgery, Helen had pulled the respirator mask from her face, whispered, *"Just get me there. Their medicine is better than yours."*

Half delirious from the pain in her own wounded shoulder, Karla had gasped, sat up. Had almost passed out when the weight of her arm pulled at the slice that partially transected her shoulder and scapula. Maybe she hadn't been thinking clearly, doped as she had been by Nurse Seymore's pain killers. Nevertheless, Karla had bent down, almost passed out, and tugged the navigator from Helen's pack. Laid it on the woman's bed. Then retrieved the cerebrum.

Awkwardly, Helen had stabbed shaking fingers into the holo projection. Seemed on the verge of collapse, and finally shifted her pained gaze to Karla's. "Now."

And with that, Karla had placed her finger on the glowing blue ball of light that appeared in the center of her cerebrum.

That had been four months ago.

Helen hadn't been bragging. The medical services in Tulum were indeed superior. Helen, it seemed, got outstanding care. The damage to Karla's back and shoulder had been repaired with what might have seemed magical ease. What would have taken six months of physical therapy back home had taken three weeks and left her with full mobility, complete function, and a vanishing scar.

The rest of the time had been spent in runs down the beach. Swimming. Keeping her now-tanned body toned and fit. She'd never felt better.

"I know that frown," Helen told her. "That's guilt."

"Thinking of the Skipper. What I owe him. What I owe all of them.

All of my training, all that I ever wanted to be. The team was everything. Being the best. Being known for having your shit wired tight. It's who I am."

"We could bring them here, you know," Helen told her. "Your timeline—"

"I know." Karla glanced sidelong at the woman. "I saw how you looked at the Skipper. That little secret smile."

Helen chuckled dryly. "In another age, in another time. He reminds me of Simon in a lot of ways, though more pragmatic. He's a good man." As she always did when things got personal, Helen changed the subject. "Stay, Karla. You have skills we need. You understand the threat posed by *Ti'ahaule*. You could build another team. Here. With us."

"And become an immortal like you?"

"The treatment takes about a year. Not that it's pleasant, but . . ." Helen ended with an arched and questioning brow.

Paradise and immortality? A new team? One dedicated to taking the fight to *Ti'ahaule*?

Not to mention the remarkable things she'd learn. See. Live.

All those timelines.

All she had to do was say yes.

79

Ryan

God, what a horrible night. I still didn't know what it meant for us. One minute, Helen was laid out in bed, two bullets in her chest and dying from a hemothorax. Karla disabled by two hideous wounds in her shoulder. The next, the lights went out, everything went dark, and when people came to, Helen was gone.

How the hell had she even managed to get her hands on the navigator and cerebrum? I pondered that as I plodded my weary way down the hall toward the conference room. The woman had been critical. Incapacitated. And Karla—who'd been right there in the next bed—insisted that the blackout had taken her entirely by surprise.

I walked into the conference room before the others. Frowned at the warm bunnies and fawns painted on the wall. Considered the oddity of big yellow flowers and puffy white clouds against a sky of robin's-egg blue. There were worse places from which to fight for one's world. Nevertheless, one of these days, the pile of beanbag chairs would really have to go.

I cradled my cup of coffee, delighted that Janeesha had used the fancy Capresso machine and had it ready when she awakened me. After it had become apparent that no amount of self-castigation was going to bring Helen back, I'd spent the night in the old, battered recliner in my office. Figured today was about as big a day as Grantham Barracks—not to mention a reactivated colonel in the Marines—could have.

And it couldn't have come at a worse time. When it came to Helen's vanishing act, there would be hell to pay. Nurse Seymore had checked on her and Karla just before the flight-for-life chopper had been scheduled to arrive out front. Found both women to be incapacitated, Helen barely hanging on. Seymore assumed Helen's navigator and cerebrum were in the pack beside her bed.

Just after that, the electricity had blacked out in the infirmary. People down the hall had reported a prickling sensation.

When the medevac team arrived, Helen and her pack were gone. Karla insisted she'd been asleep and declined to be airlifted to Denver for surgery. Insisted that her wound had only looked gruesome. That it was just a scratch. Then demonstrated it by moving her arm around and threatening to snap anyone's neck if they messed with her. The bloody compresses in the trash suggested otherwise, but how did you argue with an inspection of Karla's shoulder, and what seemed a well-healed scar?

This was going to be a fun thing to explain to the powers that be.

All that said, a part of me was delighted that Helen had removed herself from any chance of detainment by the president, Stevens, or who knew what agency and security concerns. Another part of me was saddened, as if something wonderful had gone from my life.

I heard the faint roar of Winny's SB-1 Defiant as it settled in the courtyard. I checked my watch. "Early," I noted.

Karla Raven was next into the room, a cup of cafeteria coffee in her left hand where it stuck out of the sling. She looked too healthy, too bouncy. Like she was putting up with the sling, but it wasn't all that necessary. And it might have been the lights, but I'd swear the woman looked remarkably tan and fit. And she didn't have that delicate movement like someone recovering from a wound.

Savage was a different story. He was having his arm reattached at a clinic in Salt Lake City. They were reputed to be the best in the business when it came to such mutilations. Poor Savage. Seemed he always got the worst of these things.

Karla stopped just inside the door, shifted her coffee, and knocked off a salute. "Sir," she greeted. "We really doing this?"

"Have a seat, Chief," I told her, actually feeling butterflies now that she mentioned it. "Just another day at the funny farm."

She smiled at that, and the way she dropped into the chair—heedless of the sling—should have had her wincing.

ET and Cat were next in. Both looking a little owly, but before I could reassure them, Eli Grazier came hustling through the door, the exotic chrome tube that Sak Puh had carried that day at Lab One in his hands. "You know what this is?" he asked, face lit with excitement.

"Yusif told me on the way here," I replied. "Another layer of peculiar added to an already weird situation." I wish I could have been the one to tell Helen. I suspect it would have been the best thing that had happened to her in two thousand years.

I turned to the com system, asking, "Corporal Hatcher? Could you bring the monitors online?"

"Aye, Skipper." And as he said it, the screen that covered one wall came alive with images of my team: Harvey Rogers, Murphy, Yusif al Amari, and, finally, Falcon's nervous-looking visage where he clutched his pillow and rocked on his bed.

Eli, instead of his usual seat at the head of the table, took the chair to the right. I settled at the far end, wanting to be as far from the fireworks as I could get.

In the hall, the sound of feet could be heard. Two Secret Service guys entered first, scanning the room's occupants. Checked us all against their lists and matched photos to faces. ET, his dark complexion looking almost white-guy-pale, kept his eyes averted as he pulled out his laptop, flipped it open, and attempted to look busy while his long fingers tapped at the keyboard.

After the all clear by the Secret Service agents, another agent announced, "The President of the United States."

We stood as Ben Masters walked into the room. Eli, Karla, and I saluted.

"At ease," Masters snapped, walking to the head of the table. "Be seated."

As we all settled into chairs, more Secret Service agents took positions in the doorway and around the room. Karla looked like she was sizing them up the way a lion did a bunch of rabbits. President Masters straightened his cuffs. He shot a hard look around the table, taking in the attendees, then fixed on Eli. "Okay, so you've got Tanner Jackson and that Kaplan woman locked up like the criminally insane. I want them turned loose. Now, what the hell happened here?"

Eli—fingers tapping a cadence on the chrome tube—shot a sidelong glance at Masters. "We won, Mr. President."

"Won, how?" Masters asked, leaning forward, a look of smoldering anger barely hidden behind his blue eyes. "If what Bill Stevens tells me is true, it sounds like you screwed the pooch! Destroyed invaluable equipment. Allowed the escape of—"

"We're still here, sir," Eli said easily. "For the time being, the timeline is secure."

"What about this Helen?" Masters demanded. "I get a cryptic message that she's gone? Escaped?"

Eli glanced at me, Masters' eyes following. The butterflies were turning my stomach inside out. "Our best guess is that she's transported herself to another timeline," I told him. "One where, if *Ti'ahaule* comes looking, she can hide. We didn't want her here."

"Christ, Ryan. Why not? She was privy to information that could rewrite our science. In my book, that's what I call a high-value asset. If you don't, I guess I'd like to know what the hell you're thinking."

I nerved myself, took a deep breath. "Sir, she possessed both a navigator and cerebrum. Either one of which—had it remained in our timeline—eventually would have been traced to us. If the *ahau* send investigators here, they *will* find the entangled particle trail. They *will* know that Helen, Fluvium, Alpha, and Imperator were here. But most of all, they will know that they left."

"But not where they went," Eli added. "The fact that we're still here? It means that no one has gone back into our timeline and changed it. For now, barely, we've dodged the bullet, sir."

"But we still have three aliens? Aren't they a threat?"

Eli caressed the chrome tube. "We have the Imperator's scribe, Sak Puh, and the two *quinque* warriors. Sak Puh has a better understanding of what's happened than the warriors. They still think someone's going to come rescue them. But the scribe? She knows she's marooned. Blames Imperator for betraying her and has been most forthcoming. So, sir, we still have a most high-value asset. She's been a font of information on *Ti'ahaule*. Has been advising us about the technology Imperator left behind. It'll be years before we can completely debrief her."

Masters grunted. Then asked, "What about Helen? She still poses a threat, doesn't she? I read that she was called *Ennoia*. That she's from our past? I'm supposed to believe that she's two thousand years old?"

"Sak Puh says she is," Eli told him. "And, while Helen was being treated, Nurse Seymore took some blood and tissue samples. Dr. Kilgore

France will run them in her lab. She'll also be able to run tests on the dead *quinque* warriors. We'll have a much better understanding of the kind of world they live in when Kilgore is finished. A fingerprint of their genetics, environment, energy production, and subsistence from trace-element studies."

"So," Masters asked, indicating the tube, "What's that?"

Eli smiled, opened the end, and lifting the tube, shook out a roll of what looked like thick paper. "Dr. al Amari confirms that the writing is Aramaic. Sak Puh tells us that Imperator insisted she bring these documents along. Imperator suspected that if Alpha and Fluvium were in trouble, Helen was probably at the bottom of it. His hope was to use what's in the tube as leverage in one circumstance, bait in another. And in the final act of punishment, he was going to burn the contents before Helen's eyes and as the ashes settled, cut off her head. Which is apparently one of the few ways she can be killed."

"So?" Masters gestured at the tube. "What's in there that's so important?"

Grazier had a satisfied cat's grin. "These are the books written by Helen when she was the *Ennoia*. Books she wrote two thousand years ago in Alexandria, Jerusalem, and Rome. They were in her possession when Fluvium and Nakeesh first abducted her from Simon Magus' side back in Helen's timeline. You see, he was the messiah, their version of Jesus, and Helen and Simon were the founders of a remarkable religion that treated the male-female duality as reconciliation of the soul. That without the mystical and physical joining of male and female, salvation could not be achieved."

"Why don't those books exist in our timeline?" Masters was staring at the ancient-looking parchments.

I said, "Because in our timeline St. Peter assassinated Simon, thereby eliminating his greatest rival and going on to establish the Roman Catholic church. It's another reason that Helen wanted to leave. Being here reminds her of St. Peter, of a different past. One where her husband was callously murdered."

"But you could have stopped her." Masters extended a finger my way. "You could have separated her from her equipment."

Eli intervened. "Sir, we've told you why that was a bad idea. You've got to understand. Get it through your head. Helen stole that equipment from the *Ti'ahaule*. The *ahau* want it back. If that navigator and cerebrum were here, even if they so much as discover we're experimenting with entangled particles, they will destroy us."

Masters was staring at the sheaf of parchment laid out across the table. Big thick pages all covered with script. "That really comes from another timeline? From two thousand years ago?"

"It does."

"So, what about Alpha and this Imperator?" Masters glanced around the table.

"It was Falcon's doing." Eli leaned back. "He was the one who put it all together. Fit the pieces of disparate data into a plan that would allow us to survive. I then oversaw the operation to ensure a successful outcome."

In the monitor, Falcon's gaze had gone distant, his lips moving. He cuddled the pillow tighter.

"Took all of us," Rogers said from the wall monitor. "Murphy, Skylar, and ET. Falcon laid out the key aspects of the operation. It was up to us to make it just difficult enough to force Alpha and Imperator to take the bait."

"And that was?"

"Fluvium's cerebrum," I said. "The thing they wanted most. On Falcon's orders, Rogers rearranged his lab, built the lockbox, figuring it would delay them. We also employed Cat's knockout gas, used it as insurance to give us a little extra time. Turns out that Imperator's helmet filters air. Sak Puh confirmed that. So Karla, um, Chief Petty Officer Raven, and Major Savage, they walked right into a fight that almost took them out. We had no clue about that laser sword. But for Helen pulling Karla out of the line of fire, we'd have lost the advantage. Might have given them enough time to check the settings."

"What do you mean, check the settings?" Masters still looked unhappy.

"Why, it be a computer, right?" ET glanced up for the first time. "So, Skylar and Murphy, they translate the commands, and I figure out what the code is. Then, with help from Falcon, Major Marks, and Theresa Applegate, we figure out the commands."

"Major Marks? Theresa Applegate?" Masters interrupted. "I don't remember them from my briefing."

"They just hallucinations," ET rambled on. "Invisible to you and me, but we managed. Got the code in. Then, with all the shooting and chaos, Imperator and Alpha cut the cerebrum out of the lockbox."

"Helen almost blew the whole operation," Eli muttered. "I could have shot her myself when I saw her charge into that room."

"She wanted Alpha dead," I reminded. "Was willing to die to do it."

Masters was looking confused, but Eli plowed ahead. "Didn't matter. Hanson Childs turned out to be the wild card. We had written him out of the equation. He took out Helen at the last moment. Alpha and Imperator were wounded. They were in a hurry. With Childs' help, they activated the cerebrum and navigator. Pop. They were gone."

"It was the only way." Falcon's voice sounded remote through the speakers. "We'd destroyed Imperator's navigator and cerebrum. Had we failed, we would have had to rely on Helen's. But the odds for success would have fallen to less than a two percent probability."

"Right," Harvey Rogers chimed in from the monitor. "We've watched the video record taken from a camera I left in the lab. Right there at the end, when Childs asks him to check the settings, Imperator says, 'They're just *stulti*.' Means fools. Calls us monkey people, which, Sak Puh tells us is a terrible insult in Mayan. The guy didn't think we were smart enough to have sabotaged Fluvium's cerebrum."

"I still don't see how we're any safer," Masters declared, almost hot under the collar. "They're still out there, right? They could be sitting in *Ti'ahaule* as we speak. Sending agents to destroy our past."

"That's the beauty of it," Falcon said from the screen. A slight smile illuminated his wistful face. "If they'd made it to *Ti'ahaule*, they'd have sent agents back into our history. It would have already happened. But we're still here. It was a fifty–fifty probability. We had to choose randomly. Guess."

"Guess what?" the president asked shortly.

"Where to send them," Rogers answered. "But we got lucky."

Eli was grinning when he said, "Not bothering to check the settings? They jumped from our timeline right into one that was recohering."

"What does that mean?" Masters was glaring daggers.

I tried to keep my voice dispassionate. "It means that, wounded, maybe dying, the three of them are going to spend a perceptual eternity falling backward in time. The way Helen described it, you don't die. You can't. It's a sort of never-ending plunge. Forever backward and down. With no escape. No hope. An infinity of suffering that will end in oblivion."

Grazier gave Masters a knowing look. "Ben, when I asked you for permission to create Team Psi, I told you we'd be our timeline's first line of defense. We've passed our baptismal test. Learned some hard lessons in the process. But we'll be better next time."

"Next time?"

"Mr. President," Grazier asked, "Whatever makes you think they can't find us again?"

Ben Masters, wordless, just stared in return.

EPILOG

Eli—always adept at advancing his status and position—left with President Masters and his Secret Service security detail. Standing just inside the glass door, I watched them climb into the big Sikorsky that sat in the courtyard. The counter-rotating rotor blades sent a shiver through me as Winny spun them up. Looked like a disaster waiting to happen. I should have been awed, humbled that I was watching the President of the United States leaving my little corner of the world. That he'd been here on the heels of a battle fought with people from a different world, an alien timeline. A battle we'd won.

Instead, the thought kept rolling through my head: *God, please tell me I don't have to fly in that thing!*

But I would. Eventually. The universe is a perverse place to live.

Beside me, Karla watched the SB-1 lift and clear the roof. The plywood where Imperator and Alpha had blown out the windows facing the courtyard rattled horribly in the down draft. As Winny Swink wheeled the bird and accelerated off to the east and Peterson Air Base where Air Force One waited, it reminded me of a dark predator darting off in search of prey.

I glanced sidelong at Karla. "Seems we made it."

She gave me a knowing, gray-eyed glance. "You missing Helen? Not that I'm any judge, but you seemed taken with her. Like, with the right signals, you two might have hooked up."

"I'm knocking on sixty, Karla. Helen is still in her—"

"Yeah," Karla interrupted. "That two-thousand-year age difference is a bitch, isn't it?"

I turned, heading back down the hall toward my office. Karla kept step as I told her, "It was just pheromones. Bioengineering. They made her look that way. Besides, you saw how it worked out with Hanson Childs and Alpha. Nothing good ever comes of a relationship with a woman who's a couple of millennia older than you are."

Before she could respond with something that was going to make me even more uncomfortable, I added, "So, what's with you and Grazier? I saw that chummy hug you gave him just before he climbed into the Sikorsky."

Karla gave an off-balance shrug, given her sling. "Had a talk with Helen while we were in the infirmary together. Tough lady. I owed her for pulling me out before Imperator could slice me into cube steaks. With two bullets in her chest, she got downright chatty." A beat. "And she liked you, Skipper. Said you were a good man."

"Uh-huh. Listen, even if there wasn't an age barrier, she's still gone. Hiding in a distant timeline. Not exactly the sort of situation conducive to a long-distance relationship. We can't even send emails."

Passing the cafeteria doors, I nodded to Myca Simond as he stepped out. Inside, I could see Cat, ET, and Murphy sharing lunch at one of the tables. Saviors of humanity should have dressed better.

"Helen doesn't know you've got her books," Karla said thoughtfully. "Seems like that would get you more traction with the lady than even red roses."

"Like I said, she's in another timeline where . . ."

Karla held up the little pager-like device. The one with the button that I'd seen Grazier use as a communicator.

"Where the hell did you get . . . ?" But I knew. That chummy hug she'd shared with Grazier? Karla was one of the best pickpockets I'd ever seen.

"Like I said, Helen got pretty chatty. Bet even Grazier didn't know this thing can send a signal across timelines."

I stopped, frowned. "Wait a minute. Something doesn't make sense. It takes two people, one with the navigator, the other with the cerebrum, to jump timelines. How did Helen, from her bed in the infirmary, make the jump all by herself?" And it came together, the bloody bandages, the neatly healed scar. In the light, I got a better look at Karla's brown tan. "Oh, for the love of Pete."

Karla, standing with her hip cocked, studied me. "Skipper, the lady saved my life. Savage's, too. I owed her. Turns out that jumping timelines is pretty fucking awesome. And, on the other side. Where we went. Well, I could go back without thinking twice."

At a loss for words, trying to synthesize this new data, I blinked, saw that satisfied tilt of her lips.

I shook my head. "Holy shit. So, you and Helen both jumped. How'd you get back?"

"She has confederates in her timeline. People she's helped over the centuries. When she brought me back, she and a colleague returned to her timeline with the machines."

I took another look at her: tanned, healthy, that sparkle in her gray eyes. "How long were you there?"

"A little over four months."

"But that was just last night."

"You really don't get this time thing, Skipper. I had her jump me back within seconds after we left." The smile turned wistful. "I could have stayed. Really easily. You'd like it there, Skipper. Whole different culture. The food and people are fascinating. Let me repeat: pretty fucking awesome. And the lady would like to see you again."

"If it's so great, why'd you come back?"

"SEALs don't leave their team behind, sir. And there's no telling what kind of trouble might be in our future." Karla handed me the pager. "She said to keep this. That if we ever needed her, to just push the button."

I stared down at the device, still warm from Karla's pocket.

Helen was just a press of the button away.

But then, she wouldn't have made the offer if she didn't think we might need it.

Karla was giving me that knowing hard-eyed appraisal as I tried to balance my desire to see Helen again against the knowledge that it would come at the peril of my world.

"Nothing comes free, Chief," I told her as I dropped the pager in my pocket and headed for my office.